Man in Control
by Diana Palmer

'Don't stop,' she whispered, moving her hips again.

He was tempted. It showed. But that iron control wouldn't let him slip into carelessness. She'd been drinking. In fact, she was drunk. He had his own suspicions about her innocence, and they wouldn't shut up. His body was begging him to forget her lack of experience and give it relief. But his will was too strong. He was the man in control. It was his responsibility to protect her, even from himself.

Thorn's Challenge
by Brenda Jackson

ꕎ ✵ꗞ

'There is no us, Thorn.

As a matter of fact, I had the distinct impression that you don't even like me.'

Man, was she wrong, Thorn thought. There were several emotions he'd always felt towards Tara Matthews, but *dislike* had never been one of them.

He took a couple of steps forward, which brought his body to within inches of hers. 'I've never disliked you, Tara. Actually, I think of you as my challenge,' he said. 'I'm not sure whether or not I can handle you.'

'Handle me?'

His gaze ran provocatively down the full length of her body. 'Handle you as a woman,' he said.

Too late Tara realised he had taken another step forward, bringing them thigh-to-thigh and chest-to-chest.

'Thorn, I'm not anyone's challenge.'

'Tara, you are definitely *mine*,' he said and began lowering his head towards hers…

Available in October 2004 from Silhouette Desire

Man in Control
by Diana Palmer
(Texan Lovers)
and
Thorn's Challenge
by Brenda Jackson

Shameless
by Ann Major
(The Country Club)
and
Desperado Dad
by Linda Conrad

Billionaire Boss
by Meagan McKinney
(Matched in Montana)
and
In Bed with Beauty
by Katherine Garbera
(King of Hearts)

Man in Control
DIANA PALMER

Thorn's Challenge
BRENDA JACKSON

SILHOUETTE®
Desire™

*Silhouette, Silhouette Desire and Colophon
are registered trademarks of Harlequin Books S.A.,
used under licence.*

*First published in Great Britain 2004
Silhouette Books, Eton House, 18-24 Paradise Road,
Richmond, Surrey TW9 1SR*

The publisher acknowledges the copyright holders of the
individual works as follows:

Man in Control © Diana Palmer 2003
Thorn's Challenge © Brenda Streater Jackson 2003

ISBN 0 373 04998 6

51-1004

*Printed and bound in Spain
by Litografía Rosés S.A., Barcelona*

MAN IN CONTROL
by
Diana Palmer

Dear Reader,

I can hardly believe that *Man in Control* is my 100th book. In 1979, when I sold my first romance, I had very modest ambitions of being able to sell even one novel to a publisher. Beyond that, I assumed I would go on working as a newspaper reporter for the rest of my life.

There are a lot of people I have to thank for my success, besides God, my family and friends. First, my readers, who buy my books and make me feel as if I have talent. Second, my wonderful editors, most especially my friend Tara Gavin, whose idea it was to create my own town in Texas and populate it with my characters. Third, the unsung heroes behind the scenes, which includes the associate editors and copy editors and artists and publicists who make me look so good. Fourth, Frank Yerby, one of the greatest historical novelists of the twentieth century, a fellow Georgian who encouraged me to follow my ambitions to publication. Last, but not least, bookshop owners and employees all over the world who stocked and recommended my books, and the sales reps who sell them to the bookshops and the distributors who send them out.

As I mark this great milestone in my career, I do it humbly and with great delight that I have found so many friends and fans in the world. As always, I am your greatest fan.

Love,

Diana Palmer

In loving memory of Diana Galloway

Prologue

Alexander Tyrell Cobb glared at his desk in the Houston Drug Enforcement Administration office with barely contained frustration. There was a photograph of a lovely woman in a ball gown in an expensive frame, the only visible sign of any emotional connections. Like the conservative clothes he wore to work, the photograph gave away little of the private man.

The photograph was misleading. The woman in it wasn't a close friend. She was a casual date, when he was between assignments. The frame had been given to him with the photo in it. He'd never put a woman's photo in a frame. Well, except for Jodie Clayburn. She and his sister, Margie, were best friends from years past. Most of the family photos he had included Jodie. She wasn't really family, of course. But there was no other Cobb family left, just as there was no other Clayburn family left. The three survivors of the two families were a forced mixture of different lifestyles.

Jodie was in love with Alexander. He knew it, and tried

not to acknowledge it. She was totally wrong for him. He had no desire to marry and have a family. On the other hand, if he'd been seriously interested in children and a home life, Jodie would have been at the top of his list of potential mates. She had wonderful qualities. He wasn't about to tell her so. She'd been hung up on him in the past to a disturbing degree. He'd managed to keep her at arm's length, and he had no plans to lessen the space between them. He was married to his job.

Jodie, on the other hand, was an employee at a local oil corporation which was being used in an international drug smuggling operation. Alexander was almost certain of it. But he couldn't prove it. He was going to have to find some way to investigate one of Jodie's acquaintances without letting anyone realize they were being watched.

In the meantime, there was a party planned at the Cobb ranch in Jacobsville, Texas, on Saturday. He dreaded it already. He hated parties. Margie had already invited Jodie, probably because their housekeeper, Jessie, refused to work that weekend. Jodie cooked with a masterful hand, and she could make canapés. Kirry had been invited, too, because Margie was a budding dress designer who needed a friend in the business. Kirry was senior buyer for the department store where she worked. She was pretty and capable, but Alexander found her good company and not much more. Their relationship had always been lukewarm and even now, it was slowly fizzling out. She was demanding. He had enough demands on the job.

He put the picture facedown on his desk and pulled a file folder closer, opening it to the photograph of a suspected drug smuggler who was working out of Houston. He had his work cut out for him. He wished he could avoid going home for the party, but Margie would never forgive him. If he didn't show up, neither would Kirry, and Alexander would never hear the end of it. He put the weekend to the back of his mind and concentrated on the job at hand.

One

There was no way out of it. Margie Cobb had invited her to a party on the family ranch in Jacobsville, Texas. Jodie Clayburn had gone through her entire repertoire of excuses. Her favorite was that, given the right incentive, Margie's big brother, Alexander Tyrell Cobb, would feed her to his cattle. Not even that one had worked.

"He hates me, Margie," she groaned over the phone from her apartment in Houston, Texas. "You know he does. He'd be perfectly happy if I stayed away from him for the rest of my natural life and he never had to see me again."

"That's not true," Margie defended. "Lex really likes you, I know he does," she added with forced conviction, using the nickname that only a handful of people on earth were allowed to use. Jodie wasn't one of them.

"Right. He just hides his affection for me in bouts of bad temper laced with sarcasm," came the dry reply.

"Sure," Margie replied with failing humor.

Jodie lay back on her sofa with the freedom phone at her

ear and pushed back her long blond hair. It was getting too long. She really needed to have it cut, but she liked the feel of it. Her gray eyes smiled as she remembered how much Brody Vance liked long hair. He worked at the Ritter Oil Corporation branch office in Houston with her, and was on the management fast track. As Jody was. She was administrative assistant to Brody, and if Brody had his way, she'd take his job as Human Resources generalist when he moved up to Human Resources manager. He liked her. She liked him, too. Of course he had a knockout girlfriend who was a Marketing Division manager in Houston, but she was always on the road somewhere. He was lonely. So he had lunch frequently with Jodie. She was trying very hard to develop a crush on him. He was beginning to notice her. Alexander had accused her of trying to sleep her way to the executive washroom…

"I was not!" she exclaimed, remembering his unexpected visit to her office with an executive of the company who was a personal friend. It had played havoc with her nerves and her heart. Seeing Alexander unexpectedly melted her from the neck down, despite her best efforts not to let him affect her.

"Excuse me?" Margie replied, aghast.

Jodie sat up quickly. "Nothing!" she said. "Sorry. I was just thinking. Did you know that Alexander has a friend who works for my company?"

There was a long pause. "He does?"

"Jasper Duncan, the Human Resources manager for our division."

"Oh. Yes. Jasper!" There was another pause. "How do you know about that?"

"Because Mr. Duncan brought him right to my desk while I was talking to a…well, to a good friend of mine, my boss."

"Right, the one he thinks you're sleeping with."

"Margie!" she exploded.

There was an embarrassed laugh. "Sorry. I know there's

nothing going on. Alexander always thinks the worst of people. You know about Rachel.''

"Everybody knows about Rachel," she muttered. "It was six years ago and he still throws her up to us."

"We did introduce him," Margie said defensively.

"Well, how were we to know she was a female gigolo who was only interested in marrying a rich man? She should have had better sense than to think Alexander would play that sort of game, anyway!"

"You do know him pretty well, don't you?" Margie murmured.

"We all grew up together in Jacobsville, Texas," Jodie reminded her. "Sort of," she added pensively. "Alexander was eight years ahead of us in school, and then he moved to Houston to work for the DEA when he got out of college."

"He's still eight years ahead of us," Margie chuckled. "Come on. You know you'll hate yourself if you miss this party. We're having a houseful of people. Derek will be there," she added sweetly, trying to inject a lure.

Derek was Margie's distant cousin, a dream of a man with some peculiar habits and a really weird sense of humor.

"You know what happened the last time Derek and I were together," Jodie said with a sense of foreboding.

"Oh, I'm sure Alexander has forgotten about *that* by now," she was assured.

"He has a long memory. And Derek can talk me into anything," Jodie added worriedly.

"I'll hang out with both of you and protect you from dangerous impulses. Come on. Say yes. I've got an opportunity to show my designs. It depends on this party going smoothly. And I've made up this marvelous dress pattern I want to try out on you. For someone with the body of a clotheshorse, you have no sense of style at all!"

"You have enough for both of us. You're a budding fashion designer. I'm a lady executive. I have to dress the part."

"Baloney. When was the last time your boss wore a black dress to a party?"

Jodie was remembering a commercial she'd seen on television with men in black dresses. She howled, thinking of Alexander's hairy legs in a short skirt. Then she tried to imagine where he'd keep his sidearm in a short skirt, and she really howled.

She told Margie what she was thinking, and they both collapsed into laughter.

"Okay," she capitulated at last. "I'll come. But if I break a tree limb over your brother's thick skull, you can't say you weren't forewarned."

"I swear, I won't say a word."

"Then I'll see you Friday afternoon about four," Jodie said with resignation. "I'll rent a car and drive over."

"Uh, Jodie…"

She groaned. "All right, Margie, all right, I'll fly to the Jacobsville airport and you can pick me up there."

"Great!"

"Just because I had two little bitty fender benders," she muttered.

"You totaled two cars, Josie, and Alexander had to bail you out of jail after the last one…"

"Well, that stupid thickheaded barbarian deserved to be hit! He called me a…well, never mind, but he asked for a punch in the mouth!" Josie fumed.

Margie was trying not to laugh. Again.

"Anyway, it was only a small fine and the judge took my side when he heard the whole story," she said, ignoring Margie's quick reminder that Alexander had talked to the judge first. "Not that your brother ever let me forget it! Just because he works for the Justice Department is no reason for him to lecture me on law!"

"We just want you to arrive alive, darling," Margie drawled. "Now throw a few things into a suitcase, tell your boss you have a sick cousin you have to take care of before rush hour, and we'll…*I'll*…meet you at the airport Friday afternoon. You phone and tell me your flight number, okay?"

"Okay," Josie replied, missing the slip.

"See you then! We're going to have a ball."

"Sure we are," Josie told her. But when she hung up, she was calling herself all sorts of names for being such a weakling. Alexander was going to cut her up, she just knew it. He didn't like her. He never had. He'd gotten more antagonistic since she moved to Houston, where he worked, too. Further, it would probably mean a lot of work for Jodie, because she usually had to prepare meals if she showed up. The family cook, Jessie, hated being around Alexander when he was home, so she ran for the hills. Margie couldn't cook at all, so Jodie usually ended up with KP. Not that she minded. It was just that she felt used from time to time.

And despite Margie's assurances, she knew she was in for the fight of her life once she set foot on the Cobb ranch. At least Margie hadn't said anything about inviting Alexander's sometimes-girlfriend, Kirry Dane. A weekend with the elegant buyer for an exclusive Houston department store would be too much.

The thing was, she had to go when Margie asked her. She owed the Cobbs so much. When her parents, small Jacobsville ranchers, had been drowned in a riptide during a modest Florida vacation at the beach, it had been Alexander who flew down to take care of all the arrangements and comfort a devastated seventeen-year-old Jodie. When she entered business college, Alexander had gone with her to register and paid the fees himself. She spent every holiday with Margie. Since the death of the Cobbs' father, and their inheritance of the Jacobsville ranch property, she'd spent her vacation every summer there with Margie. Her life was so intertwined with that of the Cobbs that she couldn't even imagine life without them.

But Alexander had a very ambiguous relationship with Jodie. From time to time he was affectionate, in his gruff way. But he also seemed to resent her presence and he picked at her constantly. He had for the past year.

She got up and went to pack, putting the antagonism to the back of her mind. It did no good to dwell on her confrontations with Alexander. He was like a force of nature which had to be accepted, since it couldn't be controlled.

The Jacobsville Airport was crowded for a Friday afternoon. It was a tiny airport compared to those in larger cities, but a lot of people in south Texas used it for commuter flights to San Antonio and Houston. There was a restaurant and two concourses, and the halls were lined with beautiful paintings of traditional Texas scenery.

Jodie almost bowed under the weight of her oversized handbag and the unruly carry-on bag whose wheels didn't quite work. She looked around for Margie. The brunette wouldn't be hard to spot because she was tall for a woman, and always wore something striking—usually one of her own flamboyant designs.

But she didn't see any tall brunettes. What she did see, and what stopped her dead in her tracks, was a tall and striking dark-haired man in a gray vested business suit. A man with broad shoulders and narrow hips and big feet in handtooled leather boots. He turned, looking around, and spotted her. Even at the distance, those deep-set, cold green eyes were formidable. So was he. He looked absolutely furious.

She stood very still, like a woman confronted with a spitting cobra, and waited while he approached her with the long, quick stride she remembered from years of painful confrontations. Her chin lifted and her eyes narrowed. She drew in a quick breath, and geared up for combat.

Alexander Tyrell Cobb was thirty-three. He was a senior agent for the Drug Enforcement Administration. Usually, he worked out of Houston, but he was on vacation for a week. That meant he was at the family ranch in Jacobsville. He'd grown up there, with Margie, but their mother had taken them from their father after the divorce and had them live with her in Houston. It hadn't been until her death that they'd finally been allowed to return home to their father's ranch. The old man had loved them dearly. It had broken his heart when he'd lost them to their mother.

Alexander lived on the ranch sporadically even now, when he wasn't away on business. He also had an apartment in Houston. Margie lived at the ranch all the time, and kept things running smoothly while her big brother was out shutting down drug smugglers.

He looked like a man who could do that single-handed. He had big fists, like his big feet, and Jodie had seen him use them once on a man who slapped Margie. He rarely smiled. He had a temper like a scalded snake, and he was all business when he tucked that big .45 automatic into its hand-tooled leather holster and went out looking for trouble.

In the past two years, he'd been helping to shut down an international drug lord, Manuel Lopez, who'd died mysteriously in an explosion in the Bahamas. Now he was after the dead drug lord's latest successor, a Central American national who was reputed to have business connections in the port city of Houston.

She'd developed a feverish crush on him when she was in her teens. She'd written him a love poem. Alexander, with typical efficiency, had circled the grammatical and spelling errors and bought her a supplemental English book to help her correct the mistakes. Her self-esteem had taken a serious nosedive, and after that, she kept her deepest feelings carefully hidden.

She'd seen him only a few times since her move to Houston when she began attending business college. When she visited Margie these days, Alexander never seemed to be around except at Christmas. It was as if he'd been avoiding her. Then, just a couple of weeks ago, he'd dropped by her office to see Jasper. It had been a shock to see him unexpectedly, and her hands had trembled on her file folders, despite her best efforts to play it cool. She wanted to think she'd outgrown her flaming crush on him. Sadly, it had only gotten worse. It was easier on her nerves when she didn't have to see him. Fortunately it was a big city and they didn't travel in the same circles. But she didn't know where Alexander's office or apartment were, and she didn't ask.

In fact, her nerves were already on edge right now, just from the level, intent stare of those green eyes across a crowded concourse. She clutched the handle of her wheeled suitcase with a taut grip. Alexander made her knees weak.

He strode toward her. He never looked right or left. His gaze was right on her the whole way. She wondered if he was like that on the job, so intent on what he was doing that he seemed relentless.

He was a sexy beast, too. There was a tightly controlled sensuality in every movement of those long, powerful legs, in the way he carried himself. He was elegant, arrogant. Jodie couldn't remember a time in her life when she hadn't been fascinated by him. She hoped it didn't show. She worked hard at pretending to be his enemy.

He stopped in front of her and looked down his nose into her wide eyes. His were green, clear as water, with dark rims that made them seem even more piercing. He had thick black eyelashes and black eyebrows that were as black as his neatly cut, thick, straight hair.

"You're late," he said in his deep, gravelly voice, throwing down the gauntlet at once. He looked annoyed, half out of humor and wanting someone to bite.

"I can't fly the plane," she replied sarcastically. "I had to depend on *men* for that."

He gave her a speaking glance and turned. "The car's in the parking lot. Let's go."

"Margie was supposed to meet me," she muttered, dragging her case behind her.

"Margie knew I had to be here anyway, so she had me wait for you," he said enigmatically. "I never knew a woman who could keep an appointment, anyway."

The carry-on bag fell over for the tenth time. She muttered and finally just picked the heavy thing up. "You might offer to help me," she said, glowering at her companion.

His eyebrows arched. "Help a woman carry a heavy load? My God, I'd be stripped, lashed to a rail and carried through Houston by torchlight!"

She gave him a seething glance. "Manners don't go out of style!"

"Pity I never had any to begin with." He watched her struggle with the luggage, green eyes dancing with pure venom.

She was sweating already. "I hate you," she said through her teeth as she followed along with him.

"That's a change," he said with a shrug, pushing back his jacket as he dug into his slacks pocket for his car keys.

A security guard spotted the pistol on his belt and came forward menacingly. With meticulous patience, and very carefully, Alexander reached into the inside pocket of his suit coat and produced his badge and ID. He had it out before the guard reached them.

The man took it. "Wait a minute," he said, and moved aside to check it out over the radio.

"Maybe you're on a wanted list somewhere," Jodie said enthusiastically. "Maybe they'll put you in jail while they check out your ID!"

"If they do," he replied nonchalantly, "rent-a-cop over there will be looking for another job by morning."

He didn't smile as he said it, and Jodie knew he meant what he was saying. Alexander had a vindictive streak a mile wide. There was a saying among law enforcement people that Cobb would follow you all the way to hell to get you if you crossed him. From their years of uneasy acquaintance, she knew it was more than myth.

The security guard came back and handed Alexander his ID. "Sorry, sir, but it's my job to check out suspicious people."

Alexander glared at him. "Then why haven't you checked out the gentleman in the silk suit over there with the bulge in his hatband? He's terrified that you're going to notice him."

The security guard frowned and glanced toward the elegant man, who tugged at his collar. "Thanks for the tip," he murmured, and started toward the man.

"You might have offered to lend him your gun," she told Alexander.

"He's got one. Of a sort," he added with disgust at the pearl-handled sidearm the security guard was carrying.

"Men have to have their weapons, don't they?" she chided.

He gave her a quick glance. "With a mouth like yours, you don't need a weapon. Careful you don't cut your chin with that tongue."

She aimed a kick at his shin and missed, almost losing her balance.

"Assault on a law enforcement officer is a felony," he pointed out without even breaking stride.

She recovered her balance and went out the door after him without another word. If they ever suspended the rules for one day, she knew who she was going after!

Once they reached his car, an elegant white Jaguar S-type, he did put her bags in the trunk—but he left her to open her own door and get in. It wasn't surprising to find him driving such a car, on a federal agent's salary, because he and Margie were independently wealthy. Their late mother had left them both well-off, but unlike Margie, who loved the social life, Alexander refused to live on an inheritance. He enjoyed working for his living. It was one of many things Jodie admired about him.

The admiration didn't last long. He threw down the gauntlet again without hesitation. "How's your boyfriend?" he asked as he pulled out into traffic.

"I don't have a boyfriend!" she snapped, still wiping away sweat. It was hot for August, even in south Texas.

"No? You'd like to have one, though, wouldn't you?" He adjusted the rearview mirror as he stopped at a traffic light.

"He's my boss. That's all."

"Pity. You could hardly take your eyes off him, that day I stopped by your office."

"*He's* handsome," she said with deliberate emphasis.

His eyebrow jerked. "Looks don't get you promoted in the Drug Enforcement Administration," he told her.

"You'd know. You've worked for it half your life."

"Not quite half. I'm only thirty-three."

"One foot in the grave…"

He glanced at her. "You're twenty-five, I believe? And never been engaged?"

He knew that would hurt. She averted her gaze to the window. Until a few months ago, she'd been about fifty pounds overweight and not very careful about her clothing or makeup. She was still clueless about how to dress. She dressed like an overweight woman, with loose clothing that showed nothing of her pretty figure. She folded her arms over her breasts defensively.

"I can't go through with this," she said through her teeth. "Three days of you will put me in therapy!"

He actually smiled. "That would be worth putting up with three days of you to see."

She crossed her legs under her full skirt and concentrated on the road. Her eyes caressed the silky brown bird's-eye maple that graced the car's dash and steering wheel.

"Margie promised she'd meet me," she muttered, repeating herself.

"She told me you'd be thrilled if I did," he replied with a searing glance. "You're still hung up on me, aren't you?" he asked with faint sarcasm.

Her jaw fell. "She lied! I did not say I'd be thrilled for you to meet me!" she raged. "I only came because she promised that she'd be here when I landed. I wanted to rent a car and drive!"

His green eyes narrowed on her flushed face. "That would have been suicide," he murmured. "Or homicide, depending on your point of view."

"I can drive!"

"You and the demolition derby guys," he agreed. He accelerated around a slow-moving car and the powerful Jaguar growled like the big cat it was named for. She glanced at him and saw the pure joy of the car's performance in his face as he slid effortlessly back into the lane ahead of the slow car. He enjoyed fast cars and, gossip said, faster women. But that side of his life had always been concealed from Jodie. It was as if he'd placed her permanently off-limits and planned to keep her there.

"At least I don't humiliate other drivers by streaking past them at jet fighter speed!" she raged. She was all but babbling, and after only ten minutes of his company. Seething inwardly, she turned toward the window so that she wouldn't have to look at him.

"I wasn't streaking. I'm doing the speed limit," he said. He glanced at the speedometer, smiled faintly and eased up on the accelerator. His eyes slid over Jodie curiously. "You've lost so much weight, I hardly recognized you when I stopped by to talk to Jasper."

"Right. I looked different when I was fat."

"You were never fat," he shot back angrily. "You were voluptuous. There's a difference."

She glanced at him. "I was terribly overweight."

"And you think men like to run their hands over bones, do you?"

She shifted in her seat. "I wouldn't know."

"You had a low self-image. You still have it. There's nothing wrong with you. Except for that sharp tongue," he added.

"Look who's complaining!"

"If I don't yell, nobody listens."

"You never yell," she corrected. "You can look at people and make them run for cover."

He smiled without malice. "I practice in my bathroom mirror."

She couldn't believe she'd heard that.

"You need to start thinking about a Halloween costume," he murmured as he made a turn.

"For what? Are you going to hire me out for parties?" she muttered.

"For our annual Halloween party next month," he said with muted disgust. "Margie's invited half of Jacobsville to come over in silly clothes and masks to eat candy apples."

"What are you coming as?"

He gave her a careless glance. "A Drug Enforcement Agency field agent."

She rolled her eyes toward the ceiling of the car.

"I make a convincing DEA field agent," he persisted.

"I wouldn't argue with that," she had to agree. "I hear that Manuel Lopez mysteriously blew up in the Bahamas the year before last, and nobody's replaced him yet," she added. "Did you have anything to do with his sudden demise?"

"DEA agents don't blow up drug lords. Not even one as bad as Lopez."

"Somebody did."

He glanced at her with a faint smile. "In a manner of speaking."

"One of the former mercs from Jacobsville, I heard."

"Micah Steele was somewhere around when it happened. He's never been actually connected with Lopez's death."

"He moved back here and married Callie Kirby, didn't he?. They have a little girl now."

He nodded. "He's practicing medicine at Jacobsville General as a resident, hoping to go into private practice when he finishes his last semester of study."

"Lucky Callie," she murmured absently, staring out the window. "She always wanted to get married and have kids, and she was crazy about Micah most of her life."

He watched her curiously. "Didn't you want to get married, too?"

She didn't answer. "So now that Lopez is out of the way, and nobody's replaced him, you don't have a lot to do, do you?"

He laughed shortly. "Lopez has a new successor, a Peruvian national living in Mexico on an open-ended visa. He's got colleagues in Houston helping him smuggle his product into the United States."

"Do you know who they are?" she asked excitedly.

He gave her a cold glare. "Oh, sure, I'm going to tell you their names right now."

"You don't have to be sarcastic, Cobb," she said icily.

One thick eyebrow jerked. "You're the only person I know, outside work, who uses my last name as if it were my first name."

"You don't use my real name, either."

"Don't I?" He seemed surprised. He glanced at her. "You don't look like a Jordana."

"I never thought I looked like a Jordana, either," she said with a sigh. "My mother loved odd names. She even gave them to the cats."

Remembering her mother made her sad. She'd lost both parents in a freak accident during a modest vacation in Florida after her high school graduation. Her parents had gone swimming in the ocean, having no idea that the pretty red flags on the beach warned of treacherous riptides that could drown even experienced swimmers. Which her mother and father were not. She could still remember the horror of it. Alexander had come to take care of the details, and to get her back home. Odd how many tragedies and crises he'd seen her through over the years.

"Your mother was a sweet woman," he recalled. "I'm sorry you lost her. And your father."

"He was a sweet man, too," she recalled. It had been eight years ago, and she could remember happy times now, but it still made her sad to think of them.

"Strange, isn't it, that you don't take after either of them?" he asked caustically. "No man in his right mind could call you 'sweet.'"

"Stop right there, Cobb," she threatened, using his last name again. It was much more comfortable than getting personal with the nickname Margie used for him. "I could say things about you, too."

"What? That I'm dashing and intelligent and the answer to a maiden's prayer?" He pursed his lips and glanced her way as he pulled into the road that led to the ranch. "Which brings up another question. Are you sleeping with that airheaded boss of yours at work yet?"

"He is not airheaded!" she exclaimed, offended.

"He eats tofu and quiche, he drives a red convertible of uncertain age, he plays tennis and he doesn't know how to program a computer without crashing the system."

That was far too knowledgeable to have come from a dossier. Her eyes narrowed. "You've had him checked out!" she accused with certainty.

He only smiled. It wasn't a nice smile.

Two

"You can't go around snooping into people's private lives like that," Jodie exclaimed heatedly. "It's not right!"

"I'm looking for a high-level divisional manager who works for the new drug lord in his Houston territory," he replied calmly. "I check out everybody who might have an inkling of what's going on." He turned his head slightly. "I even checked you out."

"Me?" she exclaimed.

He gave her a speaking look. "I should have known better. If I had a social life like yours, I'd join a convent."

"I can see you now, in long skirts…"

"It was a figure of speech," he said curtly. He pulled into the road that led up to the ranch house. "You haven't been on a date in two years. Amazing, considering how many eligible bachelors there are in your building alone, much less the whole of Houston." He gave her a penetrating stare. "Are you sure you aren't still stuck on me?"

She drew in a short breath. "Oh, sure, I am," she muttered. "I only come down here so that I can sit and moon over you and think of ways to poison all your girlfriends."

He chuckled in spite of himself. "Okay. I get the idea."

"Who in my building do you suspect, exactly?" she persisted.

He hesitated. His dark brows drew together in a frown as the ranch house came into view down the long, dusty road. "I can't tell you that," he said. "Right now it's only a suspicion."

"I could help you trap him," she volunteered. "If I get a gun, that is. I won't help you if I have to be unarmed."

He chuckled again. "You shoot like you drive, Jodie."

She made an angry sound in her throat. "I could shoot just fine if I got enough practice. Is it my fault that my landlord doesn't like us busting targets in my apartment building?"

"Have Margie invite you down just to shoot. She can teach you as well as I can."

It was an unpleasant reminder that he wasn't keen on being with her.

"I don't remember asking you to teach me anything," she returned.

He pulled up in front of the house. "Well, not lately, at least," he had to agree.

Margie heard the car drive up and came barreling out onto the porch. She was tall, like Alexander, and she had green eyes, too, but her dark hair had faint undertones of auburn. She was pretty, unlike poor Jodie, and she wore anything with flair. She designed and made her own clothes, and they were beautiful.

She ran to Jodie and hugged her, laughing. "I'm so glad you came!"

"I thought you were going to pick me up at the airport, Margie," came the droll reply.

Margie looked blank for an instant. "Oh, gosh, I was, wasn't I? I got busy with a design and just lost all track of time. Besides, Lex had already gone to the airport to pick up

Kirry, but she couldn't get his cell phone, so she phoned me and said she was delayed until tomorrow afternoon. He was right there already, so I just phoned him and had him bring you home.''

Kirry was Alexander's current girlfriend. The fashion buyer had just returned home recently from a buying trip to Paris. It didn't occur to Margie that it would have been pure torture to have to ride to the ranch with Alexander and his girlfriend. But, then, Margie didn't think things through. And to give her credit, she didn't realize that Jodie was still crazy about Alexander Cobb.

"She's coming down tomorrow to look at some of my new designs," Margie continued, unabashed, "and, of course, for the party in her honor that we're giving here. She leads a very busy life.''

Jodie felt her heart crashing at her feet, and she didn't dare show it. A weekend with Kirry Dane drooling over Alexander, and vice versa. Why hadn't she argued harder and stayed home?

Alexander checked his watch. "I've got to make a few phone calls, then I'm going to drive into town and see about that fencing I ordered.''

"That's what we have a foreman for," Margie informed him.

"Chayce went home to Georgia for the weekend. His father's in the hospital.''

"You didn't tell me that!''

"Did you need to know?'' he shot right back.

Margie shook her head, exasperated, as he just walked away without a backward glance. "I do live here, too," she muttered, but it was too late. He'd already gone into the house.

"I'm going to be in the way if the party's for Kirry," Jodie said worriedly. "Honestly, Margie, you shouldn't have invited me. No wonder Alexander's so angry!''

"It's my house, too, and I can invite who I like," Margie replied curtly, intimating that she and Alexander had argued about Jodie's inclusion at the party. That hurt even more. "You're my best friend, Jodie, and I need an ego boost," Margie continued unabashed. "Kirry is so worldly and sophisticated. She hates it here and she makes me feel insecure. But I need her help to get my designs shown at the store where she works. So, you're my security blanket." She linked her arm with Jodie's. "Besides, Kirry and Lex together get on my nerves."

What about my nerves? Jodie was wondering. And my heart, having to see Alexander with Kirry all weekend? But she only smiled and pretended that it didn't matter. She was Margie's friend, and she owed her a lot. Even if it was going to mean eating her heart out watching the man she loved hang on to that beautiful woman, Kirry Dane.

Margie stopped just before they went into the house. She looked worried. "You have gotten over that crush you had on my brother...?" she asked quickly.

"You and your brother!" Jodie gasped. "Honestly, I'm too old for schoolgirl crushes," she lied through her teeth, "and besides, there's this wonderful guy at the office that I like a lot. It's just that he's going with someone."

Margie grimaced. "You poor kid. It's always like that with you, isn't it?"

"Go right ahead and step on my ego, don't mind me," Jodie retorted.

Margie flushed. "I'm a pig," she said. "Sorry, Jodie. I don't know what's the matter with me. Yes, I do," she added at once. "Cousin Derek arrived unexpectedly this morning. Jessie's already threatened to cook him up with a pan of eggs, and one of the cowboys ran a tractor through a fence trying to get away from him. In fact, Jessie remembered that she could have a weekend off whenever she wanted, so she's gone to Dallas for the weekend to see her brother. And here I am with no cook and a party tomorrow night!"

"Except me?" Jodie ventured, and her heart sank again when she saw Margie's face. No wonder she'd been insistent.

There wouldn't be any food without someone to cook it, and Margie couldn't cook.

"You don't mind, do you, dear?" Margie asked quickly. "After all, you do make the most scrumptious little canapés, and you're a great cook. Even Jessie asks you for recipes."

"No," Jodie lied. "I don't mind."

"And you can help me keep Derek out of Alexander's way."

"Derek." Jodie's eyes lit up. She loved the Cobbs' renegade cousin from Oklahoma. He was a rodeo cowboy who won belts at every competition, six foot two of pure lithe muscle, with a handsome face and a modest demeanor—when he wasn't up to some horrible devilment. He drove housekeepers and cowboys crazy with his antics, and Alexander barely tolerated him. He was Margie's favorite of their few cousins. Not that he was really a cousin. He was only related by marriage. Of course, Margie didn't know that. Derek had told Jodie once, but asked her not to tell. She wondered why.

"Don't even think about helping him do anything crazy while you're here," Margie cautioned. "Lex doesn't know he's here yet. I, uh, haven't told him."

"Margie!" came a thunderous roar from the general direction of Alexander's office.

Margie groaned. "Oh, dear, Lex does seem to know about Derek."

"My suitcase," Jodie said, halting, hoping to get out of the line of fire in time.

"Lex will bring it in, dear, come along." She almost dragged her best friend into the house.

Derek was leaning against the staircase banister, handsome as a devil, with dancing brown eyes and a lean, good-looking face under jet-black hair. In front of him, Alexander was holding up a rubber chicken by the neck.

"I thought you liked chicken," Derek drawled.

"Cooked," Alexander replied tersely. "Not in my desk chair pretending to be a cushion!"

"You could cook that, but the fumes would clear out the kitchen for sure," Derek chuckled.

Cobb threw it at the man, turned, went back into his office and slammed the door. Muttered curses came right through two inches of solid mahogany.

"Derek, how could you?" Margie wailed.

He tossed her the chicken and came forward to lift her up and kiss her saucily on the nose. "Now, now, you can't expect me to be dignified. It isn't in my nature. Hi, sprout!" he added, putting Margie down only to pick up Jodie and swing her around in a bear hug. "How's my best girl?"

"I'm just fine, Derek," she replied, kissing his cheek. "You look great."

"So do you." He let her dangle from his hands and his keen dark eyes scanned her flushed face. "Has Cobb been picking on you all the way home?" he asked lazily.

"Why can't you two call him Lex, like I do?" Margie wanted to know.

"He doesn't look like a Lex," Derek replied.

"He always picks on me," Jodie said heavily as Derek let her slide back onto her feet. "If he had a list of people he doesn't like, I'd lead it."

"We'd tie for that spot, I reckon," Derek replied. He gave Margie a slow, steady appraisal. "New duds? I like that skirt."

Margie grinned up at him. "I made it."

"Good for you. When are you going to have a show of all those pretty things you make?"

"That's what I'm working on. Lex's girlfriend Kirry is trying to get her store to let me do a parade of my designs."

"Kirry." Derek wrinkled his straight nose. "Talk about slow poison. And he thought Rachel was bad!"

"Don't mention Rachel!" Margie cautioned quickly.

"Kirry makes her look like a church mouse," Derek said flatly. "She's a social climber with dollar signs for eyes. Mark my words, it isn't his body she's after."

"He likes her," Margie replied.

"He likes liver and onions, too," Derek said, and made a horrible face.

Jodie laughed at the byplay.

Derek glanced at her. "Why doesn't he ever look at you, sprout? You'd be perfect for him."

"Don't be silly," Jodie said with a forced smile. "I'm not his type at all."

"You're not mercenary. You're a sucker for anyone in trouble. You like cats and dogs and children, and you don't like night life. You're perfect."

"He likes opera and theater," she returned.

"And you don't?" Derek asked.

Margie grabbed him by the arm. "Come on and let's have coffee while you tell us about your latest rodeo triumph."

"How do you know it was?" he teased.

"When have you ever lost a belt?" she replied with a grin.

Jodie followed along behind them, already uneasy about the weekend. She had a feeling that it wasn't going to be the best one of her life.

Later, Jodie escaped from the banter between Margie and her cousin and went out to the corral near the barn to look at the new calves. One of the older ranch hands, Johnny, came out to join her. He was missing a tooth in front from a bull's hooves and a finger from a too-tight rope that slipped. His chaps and hat and boots were worn and dirty from hard work. But he had a heart of pure gold, and Jodie loved him. He reminded her of her late father.

"Hey, Johnny!" she greeted, standing on the top rung of the wooden fence in old jeans, boots, and a long-sleeved blue checked shirt. Her hair was up in a ponytail. She looked about twelve.

He grinned back. "Hey, Jodie! Come to see my babies?"

"Sure have!"

"Ain't they purty?" he drawled, joining her at the fence, where she was feeding her eyes on the pretty little white-faced, red-coated calves.

"Yes, they are," she agreed with a sigh. "I miss this up in Houston. The closest I get to cattle is the rodeo when it comes to town."

He winced. "You poor kid," he said. "You lost everything at once, all them years ago."

That was true. She'd lost her parents and her home, all at once. If Alexander hadn't gotten her into business college, where she could live on campus, she'd have been homeless.

She smiled down at him. "Time heals even the worst wounds, Johnny. Besides, I still get to come down here and visit once in a while."

He looked irritated. "Wish you came more than that Dane woman," he said under his breath. "Can't stand cattle and dust, don't like cowboys, looks at us like we'd get her dirty just by speaking to her."

She reached over and patted him gently on the shoulder. "We all have our burdens to bear."

He sighed. "I reckon so. Why don't you move back down here?" he added. "Plenty of jobs going in Jacobsville right now. I hear tell the police chief needs a new secretary."

She chuckled. "I'm not going to work for Cash Grier," she assured him. "They said his last secretary emptied the trash can over his head, and it was full of half-empty coffee cups and coffee grounds."

"Well, some folks don't take to police work," he said, but he chuckled.

"Nothing to do, Johnny?" came a deep, terse voice from behind Jodie.

Johnny straightened immediately. "Just started mucking out the stable, boss. I only came over to say howdy to Miss Jodie."

"Good to see you again, Johnny," she said.

"Same here, miss."

He tipped his hat and went slowly back into the barn.

"Don't divert the hired help," Alexander said curtly.

She got down from the fence. It was a long way up to his

eyes in her flat shoes. "He was a friend of my father's," she reminded him. "I was being polite."

She turned and started back into the house.

"Running away?"

She stopped and faced him. "I'm not going to be your whipping boy," she said.

His eyebrows arched. "Wrong gender."

"You know what I mean. You're furious that Derek's here, and Kirry's not, and you want somebody to take it out on."

He moved restlessly at the accusation. His scowl was suddenly darker. "Don't do that."

She knew what he meant. She could always see through his bad temper to the reason for it, something his own sister had never been able to do.

"Derek will leave in the morning and Kirry will be here by afternoon," she said. "Derek can't do that much damage in a night. Besides, you know how close he and Margie are."

"He's too flighty for her, distant relation or not," he muttered.

She sighed, looking up at him with quiet, soft eyes full of memories. "Like me," she said under her breath.

He frowned. "What?"

"That's always been your main argument against me—that I'm too flighty. That's why you didn't like it when Derek was trying to get me to go out with him three years ago," she reminded him.

He stared at her for a few seconds, still scowling. "Did I say that?"

She nodded then turned away. "I've got to go help Margie organize the food and drinks," she added. "Left to her own devices, we'll be eating turkey and bacon roll-ups and drinking spring water."

"What did you have in mind?" he asked amusedly.

"A nice baked chicken with garlic-and-chives mashed potatoes, fruit salad, homemade rolls and biscuits, gravy, fresh asparagus, and a chocolate pound cake for dessert,'' she said absently.

"You can cook?" he asked, astonished.

She glared at him over one shoulder. "You didn't notice? Margie hasn't cooked a meal any time I've been down here for the weekend, except for one barbecue that the cowboys roasted a side of beef for."

He didn't say another word, but he looked unusually thoughtful.

The meal came out beautifully. By the time she had it on the table, Jodie was flushed from the heat of the kitchen and her hair was disheveled, but she'd produced a perfect meal.

Margie enthused over the results with every dish she tasted, and so did Derek. Alexander was unusually quiet. He finished his chocolate pound cake and a second cup of coffee before he gave his sister a dark look.

"You told me you'd been doing all the cooking when Jessie wasn't here and Jodie was," he said flatly.

Margie actually flushed. She dropped her fork and couldn't meet Jodie's surprised glance.

"You always made such a fuss of extra company when Jessie was gone," she protested without realizing she was only making things worse.

Alexander's teeth ground together when he saw the look on Jodie's face. He threw down his napkin and got noisily to his feet. "You're as insensitive as a cactus plant, Margie," he said angrily.

"You're better?" she retorted, with her eyebrows reaching for her hairline. "You're the one who always complains when I invite Jodie, even though she hasn't got any family except us…oh, dear."

Jodie had already gotten to her own feet and was collecting dirty dishes. She didn't respond to the bickering. She felt it, though. It hurt to know that Alexander barely tolerated her; almost as much as it hurt to know Margie had taken credit for her cooking all these years.

"I'll help you clear, darlin'," Derek offered with a meaningful look at the Cobbs. "Both of you could use some sensitivity training. You just step all over Jodie's feelings without the least notice. Some 'second family' you turned out to be!"

He propelled Jodie ahead of him into the kitchen and closed the door. For once, he looked angry.

She smiled at him. "Don't take it so personally, Derek," she said. "Insults just bounce off me. I'm so used to Alexander by now that I hardly listen."

He tilted her chin up and read the pain in her soft eyes. "He walks on your heart every time he speaks to you," he said bluntly. "He doesn't even know how you feel, when a blind man could see it."

She patted his cheek. "You're a nice man, Derek."

He shrugged. "I've always been a nice man, for all the good it does me. Women flock to hang all over Cobb while he glowers and insults them."

"Someday a nice, sweet woman will come along and take you in hand, and thank God every day for you," she told him.

He chuckled. "Want to take me on?"

She wrinkled her nose at him. "You're very sweet, but I've got my eye on a rather nice man at my office. He's sweet, too, and his girlfriend treats him like dirt. He deserves someone better."

"He'd be lucky to get you," Derek said.

She smiled.

They were frozen in that affectionate tableau when the door opened and Alexander exploded into the room. He stopped short, obviously unsettled by what he thought he was seeing. Especially when Jodie jerked her hand down from Derek's cheek, and he let go of her chin.

"Something you forgot to say about Jodie's unwanted presence in your life?" Derek drawled, and for an instant, the smiling, gentle man Jodie knew became a threatening presence.

Alexander scowled. "Margie didn't mean that the way it sounded," he returned.

"Margie never means things the way they sound," Derek said coldly, "but she never stops to think how much words can hurt, either. She walks around in a perpetual Margie-haze of self-absorption. Even now, Jodie's only here because she can make canapés for the party tomorrow night—or didn't you know?" he added with absolute venom.

Margie came into the room behind her brother, downcast and quiet. She winced as she met Derek's accusing eyes.

"I'm a pig," she confessed. "I really don't mean to hurt people. I love Jodie. She knows it, even if you don't."

"You have a great way of showing it, honey," Derek replied, a little less antagonistic to her than to her brother. "Inviting Jodie down just to cook for a party is pretty thoughtless."

Margie's eyes fell. "You can go home if you want to, Jodie, and I'm really sorry," she offered.

"Oh, for heaven's sake, I don't mind cooking!" Jodie went to Margie and hugged her hard. "I could always say no if I didn't want to do it! Derek's just being kind, that's all."

Margie glared at her cousin. "Kind."

Derek glared back. "Sure I am. It runs in the family. Glad you could come, Jodie, want to wash and wax my car when you finish doing the dishes?" he added sarcastically.

"You stop that!" Margie raged at him.

"Then get in here and help her do the dishes," Derek drawled. "Or do your hands melt in hot water?"

"We do have a dishwasher," Alexander said tersely.

"Gosh! You've actually seen it, then?" Derek exclaimed.

Alexander said a nasty word and stormed out of the kitchen.

"One down," Derek said with twinkling eyes and looking at Margie. "One to go."

"Quit that, or she'll toss you out and I'll be stuck here with them and Kirry all weekend," Jodie said softly.

"Kirry?" He gaped at Margie. "You invited Kirry?"

Margie ground her teeth together and clenched her small hands. "She's the guest of honor!"

"Lord, give me a bus ticket!" He moved toward the door. "Sorry, honey, I'm not into masochism, and a night of un-adulterated Kirry would put me in a mental ward. I'm leaving."

"But you just got here!" Margie wailed.

He turned at the door. "You should have told me who was coming to the party. I'd still be in San Antonio. Want to come with me, Jodie?" he offered. "I'll take you to a fiesta!"

Margie looked murderous. "She's my friend."

"She's not, or you wouldn't have forced her down here to suffer Kirry all weekend," he added.

"Give me a minute to get out of the line of fire, will you?" Jodie held up her hands and went back to the dining room to scoop up dirty dishes, forcibly smiling.

Derek glanced at the closed door, and moved closer to Margie. "Don't try to convince me that you don't know how Jodie feels about your brother."

"She got over that old crush years ago, she said so!" Margie returned.

"She lied," he said shortly. "She's as much in love with him as she ever was, not that either of you ever notice! It's killing her just to be around him, and you stick her with Kirry. How do you think she's going to feel, watching Kirry slither all over Cobb for a whole night?"

Margie bit her lower lip and looked hunted. "She said…"

"Oh, sure, she's going to tell you that she's in love with Cobb." He nodded. "Great instincts, Marge."

"Don't call me Marge!"

He bent and brushed an insolent kiss across her parted lips, making her gasp. His dark eyes narrowed as he assayed the unwilling response. "Never thought of me like that, either, huh?" he drawled.

"You're…my…cousin," she choked.

"I'm no close relation to you at all, despite Cobb's antagonism. One day I'm going to walk out the door with you over my shoulder, and Cobb can do his worst." He winked at her. "See you, sweetheart."

He turned and ambled out the door. Margie was still staring after him helplessly and holding her hand to her lips when Jodie came in with another stack of dishes.

"What's wrong with you?" Jodie asked.

"Derek kissed me," she said in a husky tone.

"He's always kissing you."

Margie swallowed hard. "Not like this."

Jodie's eyebrows went up and she grinned. "I thought it was about time."

"What?"

"Nothing," Jodie said at once. "Here, can you open the dishwasher for me? My hands are full."

Margie broke out of her trance and went to help, shell-shocked and quiet.

"Don't let Derek upset you," Jodie said gently. "He thinks he's doing me a favor, but he's not. I don't mind helping out, in any way I can. I owe you and Cobb so much…"

"You don't owe us a thing," Margie said at once. "Oh, Jodie, you shouldn't let me make use of you like this. You should speak up for yourself. You don't do that enough."

"I know. It's why I haven't advanced in the company," she had to admit. "I just don't like confrontations."

"You had enough of them as a kid, didn't you?" Margie asked.

Jodie flushed. "I loved my parents. I really did."

"But they fought, too. Just like ours. Our mother hated our father, even after he was dead. She drank and drank, trying to forget him, just the same. She soured my brother on women, you know. She picked on him from the time he was six, and every year it got worse. He had a roaring inferiority complex when he was in high school."

"Yes? Well, he's obviously got over it now," Jodie said waspishly.

Margie shook her head. "Not really. If he had, he'd know he could do better than Kirry."

"I thought you liked her!"

Margie looked shamefaced. "I do, sort of. Well, she's got an important job and she could really help me get my foot in the door at Weston's, the exclusive department store where she works."

"Oh, Margie," Jodie said wearily, shaking her head.

"I use people," Margie admitted. "But," she added brightly, "I try to do it in a nice way, and I always send flowers or presents or something afterward, don't I?"

Jodie laughed helplessly. "Yes, you do," she admitted. "Here, help me load up the dishes, and then you can tell me what sort of canapés you want me to make for tomorrow."

She didn't add that she knew she'd spend the whole day tomorrow making them, because the party was for almost forty people, and lunch had to be provided as well. It was a logistical nightmare. But she could cope. She'd done it before. And Margie was her best friend.

Three

Jodie was up at dawn making biscuits and dough for the canapés. She'd only just taken up breakfast when Alexander came into the kitchen, wearing jeans and boots and a long-sleeved chambray shirt. He looked freshly showered and clean-shaven, his dark hair still damp.

"I've got breakfast," Jodie offered without looking too closely at him. He was overpowering in tight jeans and a shirt unbuttoned to his collarbone, where thick curling black hair peeked out. She had to fight not to throw herself at him.

"Coffee?" he murmured.

"In the pot."

He poured himself a cup, watching the deft motions of her hands as she buttered biscuits and scooped eggs onto a platter already brimming over with bacon and sausages.

"Aren't you eating?" he asked as he seated himself at the table.

"Haven't time," she said, arranging a layer of canapés on

a baking sheet. "Most of your guests are coming in time for lunch, so these have to be done now, before I get too busy."

His sensuous lips made a thin line. "I can't stand him, but Derek is right about one thing. You do let Margie use you."

"You and Margie were there when I had nobody else," she said without seeing the flinch of his eyelids. "I consider that she's entitled to anything I can ever do for her."

"You sell yourself short."

"I appreciate it when people do things for me without being asked," she replied. She put the canapés in the oven and set the timer, pushing back sweaty hair that had escaped from her bun.

His eyes went over her figure in baggy pants and an over-size T-shirt. "You dress like a bag lady," he muttered.

She glanced at him, surprised. "I dress very nicely at work."

"Like a dowager bag lady," he corrected. "You wear the same sort of clothes you favored when you were overweight. You're not anymore. Why don't you wear things that fit?"

It was surprising that he noticed her enough to even know what she was wearing. "Margie's the fashion model, not me," she reminded him. "Besides, I'm not the type for trendy stuff. I'm just ordinary."

He frowned. She had a real ego problem. He and Margie hadn't done much for it, either. She accepted anything that was thrown at her, as if she deserved it. He was surprised how much it bothered him, to see her so undervalued even by herself. Not that he was interested in her, he added silently. She wasn't his type at all.

"Kirry's coming this morning," he added. "I have to pick her up at the airport at noon."

Jodie only smiled. "Margie's hoping she'll help her with a market for her designs."

"I think she'll try," he said conservatively. "Eat breakfast," he said. "You can't go all day without food."

"I don't have time," she repeated, starting on another

batch of canapés. "Unless you want to sacrifice yourself in a bowl of dough?" she offered, extending the bowl with a mischievous smile.

His green eyes twinkled affectionately in spite of himself. "No, thanks."

"I didn't think so."

He watched her work while he ate, nebulous thoughts racing through his mind. Jodie was so much a part of his life that he never felt discomfort when they were together. He had a hard time with strangers. He appeared to be stoic and aloof, but in fact he was an introvert who didn't quite know how to mix with people who weren't in law enforcement. Like Jodie herself, he considered. She was almost painfully shy around people she didn't know—and tonight, she was going to be thrown in headfirst with a crowd she probably wouldn't even like.

Kirry's friends were social climbers, high society. Alexander himself wasn't comfortable with them, and Jodie certainly wouldn't be. They were into expensive cars, European vacations, diamonds, investments, and they traveled in circles that included some of the most famous people alive, from movie stars to Formula 1 race car drivers, to financial geniuses, playwrights and authors. They classified their friends by wealth and status, not by character. In their world, right and wrong didn't even exist.

"You're not going to like this crowd," he said aloud.

She glanced at him. "I'll be in the kitchen most of the time," she said easily, "or helping serve."

He looked outraged. "You're a guest, not the kitchen help!"

"Don't be absurd," she murmured absently, "I haven't even got the right clothes to wear to Kirry's sort of party. I'd be an embarrassment."

He set his coffee cup down with muted force. "Then why the hell did you come in the first place?" he asked.

"Margie asked me to," she said simply.

He got up and went out without another word. Jodie was going to regret this visit. He was sorry Margie had insisted that she come.

The party was in full swing. Alexander had picked up Kirry at the airport and lugged her suitcases up to the second guest room, down the hall from Jodie's. Kirry, blond and svelte and from a wealthy background was like the Cobbs, old money and family ties. She looked at Jodie without seeing her, and talked only to Margie and Alexander during lunch. Fortunately there were plenty of other people there who didn't mind talking to Jodie, especially an elderly couple apparently rolling in wealth to judge by the diamonds the matron was decked out in.

After lunch, Kirry had Alexander drive her into town and Jodie silently excused herself and escaped to the kitchen.

She had a nice little black dress, off the rack at a local department store, and high heels to match, which she wore to the party. But it was hidden under the big apron she wore most of the evening, heating and arranging canapés and washing dishes and crystal glasses in between uses.

It was almost ten o'clock before she was able to join Margie and her friends. But by then, Margie was hanging on to Kirry like a bat, with Alexander nearby, and Jodie couldn't get near her.

She stood in a corner by herself, wishing that Derek hadn't run from this weekend, so that she'd at least have someone to talk to. But that wasn't happening. She started talking to the elderly matron she'd sat beside at lunch, but another couple joined them and mentioned their week in Paris, and a mutual friend, and Jodie was out of her depth. She moved to another circle, but they were discussing annuities and investments, and she knew nothing to contribute to that discussion, either.

Alexander noticed, seething, that she was alone most of the evening. He started to get up, but Kirry moved closer and clung to his sleeve while Margie talked about her latest collection and offered to show it to Kirry in the morning. Kirry was very possessive. They weren't involved, as he'd been with other women. Perhaps that was why she was reluctant to let him move away. She hated the very thought of any other woman looking at him. That possessiveness was wearing thin. She was beautiful and she carried herself well, but she had an attitude he didn't like, and she was positively rude to any of his colleagues that spoke to him when they were together. Not that she had any idea what Alexander actually did for a living. He was independently wealthy and people in his and Margie's circle of friends assumed that the ranch was his full-time occupation. He'd taught Jodie and Margie never to mention that he worked in Drug Enforcement. They could say that he dabbled in security work, if they liked, but nothing more. When he'd started out with the DEA, he'd done a lot of undercover work. It wasn't politic to let people know that.

Jodie, meanwhile, had discovered champagne. She'd never let herself drink at any of the Cobb parties in the past, but she was feeling particularly isolated tonight, and it was painful. She liked the bubbles, the fragrance of flowers that clung to the exquisite beverage and the delicious taste. So she had three glasses, one after the other, and pretty soon she didn't mind at all that Margie and Alexander's guests were treating her like a barmaid who'd tried to insert herself into their exalted circles.

She noticed that she'd had too much to drink when she walked toward a doorway and ran headfirst into the door facing. She began to giggle softly. Her hair was coming down from its high coiffure, but she didn't care. She took out the circular comb that had held it in place and shook her head, letting the thick, waving wealth of hair fall to her shoulders.

The action caught the eye of a man nearby, a bored race car driver who'd been dragged to this hick party by his wife. He sized up Jodie, and despite the dress that did absolutely nothing for her, he was intrigued.

He moved close, leaning against the door facing she'd hit so unexpectedly.

"Hurt yourself?" he asked in a pleasant deep drawl, faintly accented.

Jodie looked up at the newcomer curiously and managed a lopsided grin. He was a dish, with curly black hair and dancing black eyes, an olive complexion and the body of an athlete.

"Only my hard head," she replied with a chuckle. "Who are you?"

"Francisco," he replied lazily. He lifted his glass to her in a toast. "You're the first person tonight who even asked." He leaned down so that he was eye to eye with her. "I'm a foreigner, you see."

"Are you, really?"

He was enchanted. He laughed, and it wasn't a polite social laugh at all. "I'm from Madrid," he said. "Didn't you notice my accent?"

"I don't speak any foreign languages," she confessed sadly, sipping what was left of her champagne. "I don't understand high finance or read popular novels or know any movie stars, and I've never been on a holiday abroad. So I thought I'd go sit in the kitchen."

He laughed again. "May I join you, then?" he asked.

She looked pointedly at his left hand. There was no ring.

He took a ring out of his slacks pocket and dangled it in front of her. "We don't advertise our commitment at parties. My wife likes it that way. That's my wife," he added with pure disdain, nodding toward a blond woman in a skintight red dress that looked sprayed on. She was leaning against a very handsome blond man.

"She's beautiful," she remarked.

"She's anybody's," he returned coldly. "The man she's stalking is a rising motion picture star. He's poor. She's rich. She's financing his career in return for the occasional loan of his body."

Her eyes almost popped out of her eyelids.

He shook his head. "You're not worldly, are you?" he

mused. "I have an open marriage. She does what she pleases. So do I."

"Don't you love her?" she asked curiously.

"One marries for love, you think." He sighed. "What a child you are. I married her because her father owned the company. As his son-in-law, I get to drive the car in competition."

"You're the race car driver!" she exclaimed softly. "Kirry mentioned you were coming."

"Kirry." His lips curled distastefully and he glanced across the room into a pair of cold, angry green eyes above the head of Kirry Dane. "She was last year's diversion," he murmured. "She wanted to be seen at Monaco."

Jodie was surprised by his lack of inhibition. She wondered if Alexander knew about this relationship, or if he cared. She'd never thought whether he bothered asking about his date's previous entanglements.

"Her boyfriend doesn't like me," he murmured absently, and smiled icily, lifting his glass.

Jodie looked behind her. Kirry had turned away, but Alexander was suddenly making a beeline across the room toward them.

Francisco made a face. "There's one man you don't want to make an enemy of," he confided. "Are you a relation of his, by any chance?"

Jodie laughed a little too loudly. "Good Lord, no." She chuckled. "I'm the cook!"

"I beg your pardon?" he asked.

By that time, Alexander was facing her. He took the crystal champagne flute from her hands and put it gingerly on a nearby table.

"I wasn't going to break it, Alexander," she muttered. "I do know it's Waterford crystal!"

"How many glasses have you had?" he demanded.

"I don't like your tone," she retorted, moving clumsily, so that Francisco had to grab her arm to keep her upright. "I had three glasses. It's not that strong, and I'm not drunk!"

"And ducks don't have feathers," Alexander replied tersely. He caught her other arm and pulled her none too gently from Francisco's grasp. "I'll take care of Jodie. Hadn't you better reacquire your wife?" he added pointedly to the younger man.

Francisco sighed, with a long, wistful appraisal of Jodie. "It seems so," he replied. "Nice to have met you—Jodie, is it?"

Jodie grinned woozily. "It's Jordana, actually, but most people call me Jodie. And I was glad to meet you, too, Francisco! I never met a real race car driver before!"

He started to speak, but it was too late, because Alexander was already marching her out of the room and down the hall.

"Will you stop dragging me around?!" she demanded, stumbling on her high heels.

He pulled her into the dark-paneled library and closed the door with a muted thud. He let go of her arm and glared down at her. "Will you stop trying to seduce married men?" he shot back. "Gomez and his wife are on the cover of half the tabloids in Texas right now," he added bluntly.

"Why?"

"Her father just died and she inherited the car company. She's trying to sell it and her husband is fighting her in court, tooth and nail."

"And they're still married?"

"Apparently, in name, at least. She's pregnant, I hear, with another man's child."

She looked up at him coldly. "Some circles you and Margie travel in," she said with contempt.

"Circles you'd never fit into," he agreed.

"Not hardly," she drawled ungrammatically. "And I wouldn't want to. In my world, people get married and have kids and build a home together." She nodded her head toward the closed door. "Those people in there wouldn't know what a home was if you drew it for them!"

His green eyes narrowed on her face. "You're smashed. Why don't you go to bed?"

She lifted her chin and smiled mistily. "Why don't you come with me?" she purred.

The look on his face would have amused her, if she'd been sober. He just stared, shocked.

She arched her shoulders and made a husky little sound in her throat. She parted her lips and ran her tongue slowly around them, the way she'd read in a magazine article that said men were turned on by it.

Apparently they were. Alexander was staring at her mouth with an odd expression. His chest was rising and falling very quickly. She could see the motion of it through his white shirt and dinner jacket.

She moved closer, draping herself against him as she'd seen that slinky blond woman in the red dress do it. She moved her leg against his and felt his whole body stiffen abruptly.

Her hands went to the front of his shirt under the jacket. She drew her fingers down it, feeling the ripple of muscle. His big hands caught her shoulders, but he wasn't pushing.

"You look at me, but you never see me," she murmured. Her lips brushed against his throat. He smelled of expensive cologne and soap. "I'm not pretty. I'm not sexy. But I would die for you...!"

His hard mouth cut off the words. He curled her into his body with a rigid arm at her back, and his mouth opened against her moist, full, parted lips with the fury of a summer storm.

It wasn't premeditated. The feel of her against him had triggered a raging arousal in his muscular body. He went in headfirst, without thinking of the consequences.

If he was helpless, so was she. As he enveloped her against him, her arms slid around his warm body under the jacket and her mouth answered the hunger of his. She made a husky little moan that apparently made matters worse. His mouth became suddenly insistent, as if he heard the need in her soft cry and was doing his best to satisfy the hunger it betrayed.

Her hands lifted to the back of his head and her fingers

dug into his scalp as she arched her body upward in a hope-
less plea.

He whispered something that she couldn't understand before he bent and lifted her, with her mouth still trapped under
his demanding lips, and carried her to the sofa.

He spread her body onto the cold leather and slid over it,
one powerful leg inserting itself between both of hers in a
frantic, furious exchange of passion. He'd never known such
raging need, not only in himself, but in Jodie. She was liquid
in his embrace, yielding to everything he asked without a
word being spoken.

He moved slightly, just enough to get his hand in between
them. It smoothed over her collarbone and down into the soft
dip of her dress, over the lacy bra she was wearing underneath. He felt the hard little nipple in his palm as he increased
the insistent pressure of the caress and heard her cry of
delight go into his open mouth.

Her hands were on the buttons of his shirt. It was dangerous. It was reckless. She'd incited him to madness, and he
couldn't stop. When he felt the buttons give, and her hands
speared into the thick hair over his chest, he groaned harshly.
His body shivered with desire.

His mouth ground into hers as his leg moved between hers.
One lean hand went under her hips and gathered her up
against the fierce arousal of his body, moving her against
him in a blatant physical statement of intent.

Jodie's head was spinning. All her dreams of love were
coming true. Alexander wanted her! She could feel the insistent pressure of his body over hers. He was kissing her as
if he'd die to have her, and she gloried in the fury of his
hunger. She relaxed with a husky little laugh and kissed him
back languidly, feeling her body melt under him, melt into
him. She was on fire, burning with unfamiliar needs, drown-
ing in unfamiliar sensations that made her whole body tingle
with pleasure. She lifted her hips against his and gasped at
the blatant contact.

Alexander lifted his head and looked at her. His face was

a rigid mask. Only his green eyes were alive in it, glittering down at her in a rasping, unsteady silence of merged breathing.

"Don't stop," she whispered, moving her hips again.

He was tempted. It showed. But that iron control wouldn't let him slip into carelessness. She'd been drinking. In fact, she was smashed. He had his own suspicions about her innocence, and they wouldn't shut up. His body was begging him to forget her lack of experience and give it relief. But his will was too strong. He was the man in control. It was his responsibility to protect her, even from himself.

"You're drunk, Jodie," he said. His voice was faintly unsteady, but it was terse and firm.

"Does it matter?" she asked lazily.

"Don't be ridiculous."

He moved away, getting to his feet. He looked down at her sprawled body in its disheveled dress and he ached all the way to his toes. But he couldn't do this. Not when she was so vulnerable.

She sighed and closed her eyes. It had been so sweet, lying in his arms. She smiled dreamily. Was she dreaming?

"Get up, for God's sake!" he snapped.

When her eyes opened, he was standing her firmly on her feet. "You're going to bed, right now, before you make an utter fool of yourself!"

She blinked, staring up at him. "I can't go to bed. Who'll do the dishes?"

"Jodie!"

She giggled, trying to lean against him. He thrust her away and took her arm, moving her toward the door. "I told Francisco I was the cook. That's me," she drawled cheerfully. "Cook, bottle-washer, best friend and household slave." She laughed louder.

He propelled her out the door, back down the hall toward the staircase, and urged her up it. She was still giggling a little too loudly for comfort, but the noise of the music from the living room covered it nicely.

He got her to the guest room she was occupying and put her inside. "Go to bed," he said through his teeth.

She leaned against the door facing, totally at sea. "You could come inside," she murmured wickedly. "There's a bed."

"You need one," he agreed tersely. "Go get in it."

"Always bossing me around," she sighed. "Don't you like kissing me, Alexander?"

"You're going to hate yourself in the morning," he assured her.

She yawned, her mind going around in circles, like the room. "I think I'll go to bed now."

"Great idea."

He started to walk out.

"Could you send Francisco up, please?" she taunted. "I'd like to lie down and discuss race cars with him."

"In your dreams!" he said coldly.

He actually slammed the door, totally out of patience, self-control and tact. He waited a minute, to make sure she didn't try to come back out. But there was only the sound of slow progress toward the bed and a sudden loud whoosh. When he opened the door again and peeked in, she was lying face-down in her dress on the covers, sound asleep. He closed the door again, determined not to get close to her a second time. He went back to the party, feeling as if he'd had his stomach punched. He couldn't imagine what had possessed him to let Jodie tempt him into indiscretion. His lack of control worried him so much that he was twice as attentive to Kirry as he usually was.

When he saw her up to her room, after the party was over, he kissed her with intent. She was perfectly willing, but his body let him down. He couldn't manage any interest at all.

"You're just tired," she assured him with a worldly smile. "We have all the time in the world. Sleep tight."

"Sure. You, too."

He left her and went back downstairs. He was restless, angry at his attack of impotence with the one woman who was capable of curing it. Or, at least, he imagined she was. He and Kirry had never been lovers, although they'd come close at one time. Now, she was a pleasant companion from time to time, a bauble to show off, to take around town. It infuriated him that he could be whole with Jodie, who was almost certainly a virgin, and he couldn't even function with a sophisticated woman like Kirry. Maybe it was his age.

The rattle of plates caught his attention. He moved toward the sound and found a distressed Margie in the kitchen trying to put dishes in the dishwasher.

"That doesn't look right," he commented with a frown when he noticed the lack of conformity in the way she was tossing plates and bowls and cups and crystal all together. "You'll break the crystal."

She glared at him. "Well, what do I know about washing dishes?" she exclaimed. "That's why we have Jessie!"

He cocked his head. "You're out of sorts."

She pushed back her red-tinged dark hair angrily. "Yes, I'm out of sorts! Kirry said she doesn't think I'm ready to show my collection yet. She said her store had shows booked for the rest of the year, and she couldn't help me!"

"All that buttering up and dragging Jodie down here to work, for nothing," he said sarcastically.

"Where is Jodie?" she demanded. "I haven't seen her for two hours, and here's all this work that isn't getting done except by me!"

He leaned back against the half open door and stared at his sister. "She's passed out on her bed, dead drunk," he said distastefully. "After trying to seduce the world's number one race car driver, and then me."

Margie stood up and stared back. "You?"

"I wish I could impress on you how tired I am of finding Jodie underfoot every time I walk into my own house," he said coldly. "We can't have a party without her, we can't have a holiday without her. My own birthday means an invitation! Why can't you just hire a cook when you need one instead of landing me with your erstwhile best friend?"

"I thought you liked Jodie, a little," Margie stammered.

"She's blue collar, Margie," he persisted, still smarting under his loss of control and furious that Jodie was responsible for it. "She'll never fit in our circles, no matter how much you try to force her into them. She was telling people tonight that she was the cook, and it's not far wrong. She's a social disaster with legs. She knows nothing about our sort of lifestyle, she can't carry on a decent conversation and she dresses like a homeless person. It's an embarrassment to have her here!"

Margie sighed miserably. "I hope you haven't said things like that to her, Lex," she worried. "She may not be an upper class sort of person, but she's sweet and kind, and she doesn't gossip. She's the only real friend I've ever had. Not that I've behaved much like one," she added sadly.

"You should have friends in your own class," he said coldly. "I don't want Jodie invited down here again," he added firmly, holding up a hand when Margie tried to speak. "I mean it. You find some excuse, but you keep her away from here. I'm not going to be stalked by your bag lady of a friend. I don't want her underfoot at any more holidays, and God forbid, at my birthday party! If you want to see her, drive to Houston, fly to Houston, stay in Houston! But don't bring her here anymore."

"Did she really try to seduce you?" Margie wondered aloud.

"I don't want to talk about it," he said flatly. "It was embarrassing."

"She'll probably be horrified when she wakes up and remembers what happened. Whatever did," Margie added, fishing.

"I'll be horrified for months myself. Kirry is my steady girl," he added deliberately. "I'm not hitting on some other woman behind her back, and Jodie should have known it. Not that it seemed to matter to her, about me or the married racer."

"She's never had a drink, as far as I know," Margie ventured gently. "She's not like our mother, Lex."

His face closed up. Jodie's behavior had aroused painful memories of his mother, who drank often, and to excess. She was a constant embarrassment anytime people came to the house, and she delighted in embarrassing her son any way possible. Jodie's unmanageable silliness brought back nightmares.

"There's nothing in the world more disgusting than a drunk woman," he said aloud. "Nothing that makes me sicker to my stomach."

Margie closed the dishwasher and started it. There was a terrible cracking sound. The crystal! She winced. "I don't care what's broken. I'm not a cook. I can't wash dishes. I'm a dress designer!"

"Hire help for Jessie," he said.

"Okay," she said, giving in. "I won't invite Jodie back again. But how do I tell her, Lex? She's never going to understand. And it will hurt her."

He knew that. He couldn't bear to know it. His face hardened. "Just keep her away from me. I don't care how."

"I'll think of something," Margie said weakly.

Outside in the hall, a white-faced Jodie was stealthily making her way back to the staircase. She'd come down belatedly to do the dishes, still tingling hours after Alexander's feverish lovemaking. She'd been floating, delirious with hope that he might have started to see her in a different light. And then she'd heard what he said. She'd heard every single word. She disgusted him. She was such a social disaster, in fact, that he never wanted her to come to the house again. She'd embarrassed him and made a fool of herself.

He was right. She'd behaved stupidly, and now she was going to pay for it by being an outcast. The only family she had no longer wanted her.

She went back to her room, closed the door quietly, and picked up the telephone. She changed her airplane ticket for an early-morning flight.

* * *

The next morning, she went to Margie's room at daybreak. She hadn't slept a wink. She'd packed and changed her clothes, and now she was ready to go.

"Will you drive me to the airport?" she asked her sleepy friend. "Or do you want me to ask Johnny?"

Margie sat up, blinking. Then she remembered Lex's odd comments and her own shame at how she'd treated her best friend. She flushed.

"I'll drive you," Margie said at once. "But don't you want to wait until after breakfast?" She flushed again, remembering that Jodie would have had to cook it.

"I'm not hungry. There's leftover sausage and bacon in the fridge, along with some biscuits. You can just heat them up. Alexander can cook eggs to go with them," she added, almost choking on his name.

Margie felt guilty. "You're upset," she ventured.

Keeping quiet was the hardest thing Jodie had ever done. "I got drunk last night and did some…really stupid things," she summarized. "I'd just like to go home, Margie. Okay?"

Margie tried not to let her relief show. Jodie was leaving without a fuss. Lex would be pleased, and she'd be off the hook. She smiled. "Okay. I'll just get dressed, and then we'll go!"

Four

If running away seemed the right thing to do, actually doing it became complicated the minute Jodie went down the staircase with her suitcase.

The last thing she'd expected was to find the cause of her flight standing in the hall watching her. She ground her teeth together to keep from speaking.

Alexander was leaning against the banister, and he looked both uncomfortable and concerned when he saw Jodie's pale complexion and swollen eyelids.

He stood upright, scowling. "I'm driving Kirry back to Houston this afternoon," he said at once, noting Jodie's suitcase. "You can ride with us."

Jodie forced a quiet smile. Her eyes didn't quite meet his. "Thanks for the offer, Alexander, but I have an airplane ticket."

"Then I'll drive you to the airport," he added quietly.

Her face tightened. She swallowed down her hurt. "Thanks, but Margie's already dressed and ready to go. And we have some things to talk about on the way," she added before he could offer again.

He watched her uneasily. Jodie was acting like a fugitive evading the police. She wouldn't meet his eyes, or let him near her. He'd had all night to regret his behavior, and he was still blaming her for it. He'd overreacted. He knew she'd had a crush on him at one time. He'd hurt her with his cold rejection. She'd been drinking. It hadn't been her fault, but he'd blamed her for the whole fiasco. He felt guilty because of the way she looked.

Before he could say anything else, Margie came bouncing down the steps. "Okay, I'm ready! Let's go," she told Jodie.

"I'm right behind you. So long, Alexander," she told him without looking up past his top shirt button.

He didn't reply. He stood watching until the front door closed behind her. He still didn't understand his own conflicting emotions. He'd hoped to have some time alone with Jodie while he explored this suddenly changed relationship between them. But she was clearly embarrassed about her behavior the night before, and she was running scared. Probably letting her go was the best way to handle it. After a few days, he'd go to see her at the office and smooth things over. He couldn't bear having her look that way and knowing he was responsible for it. Regardless of his burst of bad temper, he cared about Jodie. He didn't want her to be hurt.

"You look very pale, Jodie," Margie commented when she walked her best friend to the security checkpoint. "Are you sure you're all right?"

"I'm embarrassed about how I acted last night, that's all," she assured her best friend. "How did you luck out with Kirry, by the way?"

"Not too well," she replied with a sigh. "And I think I broke all the crystal by putting it in the dishwasher."

"I'm sorry I wasn't able to do that for you," Jodie apologized.

"It's not your fault. Nothing is your fault." Margie looked

tormented. "I was going to ask you down to Lex's birthday party next month…"

"Margie, I can't really face Alexander right now, okay?" she interrupted gently, and saw the relief plain on the taller woman's face. "So I'm going to make myself scarce for a little while."

"That might be best," Margie had to admit.

Jodie smiled. "Thanks for asking me to the party," she managed. "I had a good time."

That was a lie, and they both knew it.

"I'll make all this up to you one day, I promise I will," Margie said unexpectedly, and hugged Jodie, hard. "I'm not much of a friend, Jodie, but I'm going to change. I am. You'll see."

"I wouldn't be much of a friend if I wanted to remake you," Jodie replied, smiling. "I'll see you around, Margie," she added enigmatically, and left before Margie could ask what she meant.

It was a short trip back to Houston. Jodie fought tears all the way. She couldn't remember anything hurting so much in all her life. Alexander couldn't bear the sight of her. He didn't want her around. She made him sick. She…disgusted him.

Most of her memories of love swirled around Alexander Cobb. She'd daydreamed about him even before she realized her feelings had deepened into love. She treasured unexpected meetings with him, she tingled just from having him smile at her. But all that had been a lie. She was a responsibility he took seriously, like his job. She meant nothing more than that to him. It was a painful realization, and it was going to take time for the hurt to lessen.

But for the moment it was too painful to bear. She drew the air carrier's magazine out of its pocket in the back of the seat ahead of her and settled back to read it. By the time she finished, the plane was landing. She walked through the

Houston concourse with a new resolution. She was going to forget Alexander. It was time to put away the past and start fresh.

Alexander was alone in the library when his sister came back from the airport.

He went out into the hall to meet her. "Did she say anything to you?" he asked at once.

Surprised by the question, and his faint anxiety, she hesitated. "About what?"

He glowered down at her. "About why she was leaving abruptly. I know her ticket was for late this afternoon. She must have changed it."

"She said she was too embarrassed to face you," Margie replied.

"Anything else?" he persisted.

"Not really." She felt uneasy herself. "You know Jodie. She's painfully shy, Lex. She doesn't drink, ever. I guess whatever happened made her ashamed of herself and uncomfortable around you. She'll get over it in time."

"Do you think so?" he wondered aloud.

"What are you both doing down here?" Kirry asked petulantly with a yawn. She came down the staircase in a red silk gown and black silk robe and slippers, her long blond hair sweeping around her shoulders. "I feel as if I haven't even slept. Is breakfast ready?"

Margie started. "Well, Jessie isn't here," she began.

"Where's that little cook who was at the party last night?" she asked carelessly. "Why can't she make breakfast?"

"Jodie's not a cook," Alexander said tersely. "She's Margie's best friend."

Kirry's eyebrows arched. "She looked like a lush to me," Kirry said unkindly. "People like that should never drink. Is she too hung over to cook, then?"

"She's gone home," Margie said, resenting Kirry's remarks.

"Then who's going to make toast and coffee for me?" Kirry demanded. "I have to have breakfast."

"I can make toast," Margie said, turning. She wanted Kirry's help with her collection, but she disliked the woman intensely.

"Then I'll get dressed. Want to come up and do my zip, Lex?" Kirry drawled.

"No," he said flatly. "I'll make coffee." He went into the kitchen behind Margie.

Kirry stared after him blankly. He'd never spoken to her in such a way before, and Margie had been positively rude. They shouldn't drink, either, she was thinking as she went back upstairs to dress. Obviously it was hangovers and bad tempers all around this morning.

Two weeks later, Jodie sat in on a meeting between Brody and an employee of their information systems section who had been rude and insulting to a fellow worker. It was Brody's job as Human Resources Generalist to oversee personnel matters, and he was a diplomat. It gave Jodie the chance to see what sort of duties she would be expected to perform if she moved up from Human Resources Generalist to manager.

"Mr. Koswalski, this is Ms. Clayburn, my administrative assistant. She's here to take notes," he added.

Jodie was surprised, because she thought she was there to learn the job. But she smiled and pulled out her small pad and pen, perching it on her knee.

"You've had a complaint about me, haven't you?" Koswalski asked with a sigh.

Brody's eyebrows arched. "Well, yes…"

"One of our executives hired a systems specialist with no practical experience in oil exploration," Koswalski told him. "I was preparing an article for inclusion in our quarterly magazine and the system went down. She was sent to repair it. She saw my article and made some comments about the terms I used, and how unprofessional they sounded. Obviously she didn't understand the difference between a rigger and a roughneck. When I tried to explain, she accused me of talking down to her and walked out." He threw up his hands. "Sir, I wasn't rude, and I wasn't uncooperative. I was trying to teach her the language of the industry."

Brody looked as if he meant to say something, but he glanced at Jodie and cleared his throat instead. "You didn't call her names, Mr. Koswalski?"

"No, sir, I did not," the young man replied courteously. "But she did call me several. Besides that, quite frankly, she had a glazed look in her eyes and a red nose." His face tautened. "Mr. Vance, I've seen too many people who use drugs to mistake signs of drug use. She didn't repair the system, she made matters worse. I had to call in another specialist to undo her damage. I have his name, and his assignment," he added, producing a slip of paper, which he handed to Brody. "I'm sorry to make a countercharge of incompetence against another employee, but my integrity is at stake."

Brody took the slip of paper and read the name. He looked at the younger man again. "I know this technician. He's the best we have. He'll confirm what you just told me?"

"He will, Mr. Vance."

Brody nodded. "I'll check with him and make some investigation of your charges. You'll be notified when we have a resolution. Thank you, Mr. Koswalski."

"Thank you, Mr. Vance," the young man replied, standing. "I enjoy my job very much. If I lose it, it should be on merit, not lies."

"I quite agree," Brody replied. "Good day."

"Good day." Koswalski left, very dignified.

Brody turned to Jodie. "How would you characterize our Mr. Koswalski?"

"He seems sincere, honest, and hardworking."

He nodded. "He's here on time every morning, never takes longer than he has for lunch, does any task he's given willingly and without protest, even if it means working late hours."

He picked up a file folder. "On the other hand, the systems specialist, a Ms. Burgen, has been late four out of five mornings she's worked here. She misses work on Mondays every other week. She complains if she's asked to do overtime, and her work is unsatisfactory.'' He looked up. ''Your course of action, in my place?''

''I would fire her,'' she said.

He smiled slowly. ''She has an invalid mother and a two-year-old son,'' he said surprisingly. ''She was fired from her last job. If she loses this one, she faces an uncertain future.''

She bit her lower lip. It was one thing to condone firing an incompetent employee, but given the woman's home life the decision was uncomfortable.

''If you take my place, you'll be required to make such recommendations. In fact, you'll be required to make them to me,'' he added. ''You can't wear your heart on your sleeve. You work for a business that depends on its income. Incompetent employees will cost us time, money, and possibly even clients. No business can exist that way for long.''

She looked up at him with sad eyes. ''It's not a nice job, Brody.''

He nodded. ''It's like gardening. You have to separate the weeds from the vegetables. Too many weeds, no more vegetables.''

''I understand.'' She looked at her pad. ''So what will you recommend?'' she added.

''That our security section make a thorough investigation of her job performance,'' he said. ''If she has a drug problem that relates to it, she'll be given the choice of counseling and treatment or separation. Unless she's caught using drugs on the job, of course,'' he added coolly. ''In that case, she'll be arrested.''

She knew she was growing cold inside. What had sounded like a wonderful position was weighing on her like a rock.

''Jodie, is this really what you want to do?'' he asked gently, smiling. ''Forgive me, but you're not a hardhearted person, and you're forever making excuses for people. It isn't the mark of a manager.''

''I'm beginning to realize that,'' she said quietly. She

searched his eyes. "Doesn't it bother you, recommending that people lose their jobs?"

"No," he said simply. "I'm sorry for them, but not sorry enough to risk my paycheck and yours keeping them on a job they're not qualified to perform. That's business, Jodie."

"I suppose so." She toyed with her pad. "I was a whiz with computers in business college," she mused. "I didn't want to be a systems specialist because I'm not mechanically-minded, but I could do anything with software." She glanced at him. "Maybe I'm in the wrong job to begin with. Maybe I should have been a software specialist."

He grinned. "If you decide, eventually, that you'd like to do that, write a job description, give it to your Human Resources manager, and apply for the job," he counseled.

"You're kidding!"

"I'm not. It's how I got my job," he confided.

"Well!"

"You don't have to fire software," he reminded her. "And if it doesn't work, it won't worry your conscience to toss it out. But all this is premature. You don't have to decide right now what you want to do. Besides," he added with a sigh, "I may not even get that promotion I'm hoping for."

"You'll get it," she assured him. "You're terrific at what you do, Brody."

"Do you really think so?" he asked, and seemed to care about her reply.

"I certainly do."

He smiled. "Thanks. Cara doesn't think much of my abilities, I'm afraid. I suppose it's because she's so good at marketing. She gets promotions all the time. And the travel…! She's out of town more than she's in, but she loves it. She was in Mexico last week and in Peru the week before that. Imagine! I'd love to go to Mexico and see Chichen Itza." He sighed.

"So would I. You like archaeology?" she fished.

He grinned. "Love it. You?"

"Oh, yes!"

"There's a museum exhibit of Mayan pottery at the art museum," he said enthusiastically. "Cara hates that sort of thing. I don't suppose you'd like to go with me to see it next Saturday?"

Next Saturday. Alexander's birthday. She'd mourned for the past two weeks since she'd come back from the Cobbs' party, miserable and hurting. But she wouldn't be invited to his birthday party, and she wouldn't go even if she was.

"I'd love to," she said with a beaming smile. "But... won't your girlfriend mind?"

He frowned. "I don't know." He looked down at her. "We, uh, don't have to advertise it, do we?"

She understood. It was a little uncomfortable going out with a committed man, but it wasn't as if he were married or anything. Besides, his girlfriend treated him like dirt. She wouldn't.

"No, we don't," she agreed. "I'll look forward to it."

"Great!" He beamed, too. "I'll phone you Friday night and we'll decide where and when to meet, okay?"

"Okay!"

She was on a new track, a new life, and she felt like a new person. She'd started going to a retro coffeehouse in the evenings, where they served good coffee and people read poetry on stage or played folk music with guitars. Jodie fit right in with the artsy crowd. She'd even gotten up for the first time and read one of her poems, a sad one about rejected love that Alexander had inspired. Everyone applauded, even the owner, a man named Johnny. The boost of confidence she felt made her less inhibited, and the next time she read her poetry, she wasn't afraid of the crowd. She was reborn. She was the new, improved Jodie, who could conquer the world. And now Brody wanted to date her. She was delighted.

That feeling lasted precisely two hours. She came back in after lunch to find Alexander Cobb perched on her desk, in her small cubicle, waiting for her.

She hadn't had enough time to get over her disastrous last meeting with him. She wanted to turn and run, but that wasn't going to work. He'd already spotted her.

She walked calmly to her desk—although her heart was doing cartwheels—and put her purse in her lower desk drawer.

"Hello, Alexander," she said somberly. "What can I do for you?"

Her attitude sent him reeling. Jodie had always been unsettled and full of joy when she came upon him unexpectedly. He didn't realize how much he'd enjoyed the headlong reaction until it wasn't there anymore.

He stared at her across the desk, puzzled and disturbed. "What happened wasn't anybody's fault," he said stiffly. "Don't wear yourself out regretting it."

She relaxed a little, but only a little. "I drank too much. I won't do it a second time," she assured him. "How's Margie?"

"Quiet," he said. The one word was alarming. Margie was never quiet.

"Why?" she asked.

Shrugging, he picked up a paper clip from her desk and studied it. "She can't get anywhere with her designs. She expected immediate success, and she can't even get a foot in the door."

"I'm sorry. She's really good."

He nodded and his green eyes met hers narrowly. "I need to talk to you," he said. "Can you meet me downstairs at the coffee bar when you get off from work?"

She didn't want to, and it was obvious. "Couldn't you just phone me at home?" she countered.

He scowled. "No. I can't discuss this over the phone." She was still hesitating. "Do you have other plans?" he asked.

She shook her head. "No. I don't want to miss my bus."

"I can drive you…"

"No! I mean—" she lowered her voice "—no, I won't

put you to any trouble. There are two buses. The second runs an hour after the first one.''

''It won't take an hour,'' he assured her. But he felt as if something was missing from their conversation. She didn't tease him, taunt him, antagonize him. In fact, she looked very much as if she wanted to avoid him altogether.

''All right, then,'' she said, sitting down at her desk. ''I'll see you there about five after five.''

He nodded, pausing at the opening of the cubicle to look back at her. It was a bad time to remember the taste of her full, soft mouth under his. But he couldn't help it. She was wearing a very businesslike dark suit with a pale pink blouse, her long hair up in a bun. She should have looked like a businesswoman, but she was much too vulnerable, too insecure, to give that image. She didn't have the self-confidence to rate a higher job, but he couldn't tell her that. Jodie had a massive inferiority complex. The least thing hurt her. As he'd hurt her.

The muscles in his jaw tautened. ''This doesn't suit you,'' he said abruptly, nodding around the sterile little glass and wood cage they kept her in. ''Won't they even let you have a potted plant?''

She was aghast at the comment. He never made personal remarks. She shifted restlessly in her chair. ''It isn't dignified,'' she stammered.

He moved a step closer. ''Jodie, a job shouldn't mimic jail. If you don't like what you do, where you do it, you're wasting the major part of your life.''

She knew that. She tasted panic when she swallowed. But jobs were thin on the ground and she had the chance for advancement in this one. She put to the back of her mind Brody's comments on her shortcomings as a manager.

''I like my job very much,'' she lied.

His eyes slid over her with something like possession. ''No, you don't. Pity. You have a gift for computer programming. I'll bet you haven't written a single routine since you've been here.''

Her face clenched. "Don't you have something to do? Because I'm busy."

"Suit yourself. As soon after five as you can make it, please," he said, adding deliberately, "I have a dinner date."

With Kirry. Always with Kirry. She knew it. She hated Kirry. She hated him, too. But she smiled. "No problem. See you." She turned on her computer and pulled up her memo file to see what tasks were upcoming. She ignored Alexander, who gave her another long, curious appraisal before he left her alone.

She felt the sting of his presence all the way to her poor heart. He was so much a part of her life that it was like being amputated when she thought of a lifetime without his complicated presence.

For the first time, she thought about moving to another city. Ritter Oil Corporation had a headquarters office in Tulsa, Oklahoma. Perhaps she could get a transfer there...and do what, she asked herself? She was barely qualified for the predominantly clerical job she was doing now, and painfully unqualified for firing people, even if they deserved it. She'd let her pride force her into taking this job, because Alexander kept asking when she was going to start working after her graduation from business college. He probably hadn't meant that he thought she was taking advantage of his financial help—but she took it that way. So she went to work for the first company that offered her a job, just to shut him up.

In retrospect, she should have looked a little harder. She'd been under consideration for a job with the local police department, as a computer specialist. She had the skills to write programs, to restructure software. She was a whiz at opening protected files, finding lost documents, tracking down suspicious e-mails and finding ways to circumvent write-protected software. Her professor had recommended her for a career in law enforcement as a cyber crime specialist, but she'd jumped at the first post-college job that came her way.

Now here she was, stuck in a dead-end job that she didn't

even like, kept in a cubicle like a box of printer paper and only taken out when some higher-up needed her to take a letter or organize a schedule, or compile his notes…

She had a vision of herself as a cardboard box full of supplies and started giggling.

Another administrative assistant stuck her head in the cubicle. "Better keep it down," she advised softly. "They've had a complaint about the noise levels in here."

"I'm only laughing to myself," Jodie protested, shocked.

"They want us quiet while we're working. No personal phone calls, no talking to ourselves—and there's a new memo about the length of time people are taking in the bathroom…"

"Oh, good God!" Jodie burst out furiously.

The other woman put a feverish hand to her lips and looked around nervously. "Shhh!" she cautioned.

Jodie stood up and gave the woman her best military salute.

Sadly the vice president in charge of personnel was walking by her cubicle at the time. He stopped, eyeing both women suspiciously.

Already in trouble, and not giving a damn anymore, Jodie saluted him, too.

Surprisingly he had to suppress a smile. He wiped it off quickly. "Back to work, girls," he cautioned and kept walking.

The other woman moved closer. "Now see what you've done!" she hissed. "We'll both be on report!"

"If he tries to put me on report, I'll put him on report as well," Jodie replied coolly. "Nobody calls me a 'girl' in a working office!"

The other woman threw up her hands and walked out.

Jodie turned her attention back to her chores and put the incident out of her mind. But it was very disturbing to realize how much authority the company had over her working life, and she didn't like it. She wondered if old man Ritter, the head of the corporation, encouraged such office politics.

From what she'd heard about him, he was something of a renegade. He didn't seem to like rules and regulations very much, but, then, he couldn't be everywhere. Maybe he didn't even know the suppressive tactics his executives used to keep employees under control here.

Being cautioned never to speak was bad enough, and personalization of cubicles was strictly forbidden by company policy. But to have executives complain about the time employees spent in the bathroom made Jodie furious. She had a girlfriend who was a diabetic, and made frequent trips to the rest room in school. Some teachers had made it very difficult for her until her parents had requested a teacher conference to explain their daughter's health problem. She had a feeling no sort of conference would help at this job.

She went back to work, but the day had been disturbing in more ways than one.

At exactly five minutes past quitting time, she walked into the little coffee shop downstairs. Alexander had a table, and he was waiting for her. He'd already ordered the French Vanilla cappuccino she liked so much, along with chocolate biscotti.

She was surprised by his memory of her preferences. She draped her old coat over the empty chair at the corner table and sat down. Fortunately the shop wasn't crowded, as it was early in the evening, and there were no customers anywhere near them.

"Right on time," Alexander noted, checking his expensive wristwatch.

"I usually am," she said absently, sipping her cappuccino. "This is wonderful," she added with a tiny smile.

He seemed puzzled. "Don't you come here often?"

"Actually, it's not something I can fit into my budget," she confessed.

Now it was shock that claimed his features. "You make a good salary," he commented.

"If you want to rent someplace with good security, it costs

more," she told him. "I have to dress nicely for work, and that costs, too. By the time I add in utilities and food and bus fare, there isn't a lot left. We aren't all in your income tax bracket, Alexander," she added without rancor.

He let his attention wander to his own cappuccino. He sipped it quietly.

"I never think of you as being in a different economic class," he said.

"Don't you?" She knew better, and her thoughts were bitter. She couldn't forget what she'd overheard him say to his sister, that she was only blue collar and she didn't fit in with them.

He sat up straight. "Something's worrying you," he said flatly. "You're not the same. You haven't been since the party."

Her face felt numb. She couldn't lower her pride enough to tell him what she'd overheard. It was just too much, on top of everything else that had gone haywire lately.

"Why can't you talk to me?" he persisted.

She looked up at him with buried resentments, hurt pride, and outraged sentiment plain in her cold eyes. "It would be like talking to the floor," she said. "If you're here, it's because you want something. So, what is it?"

His expression was eloquent. He sipped cappuccino carefully and then put the delicate cup in its saucer with precision.

"Why do you think I want something?"

She felt ancient. "Margie invites me to parties so that I can cook and clean up the kitchen, if Jessie isn't available," she said in a tone without inflection. "Or if she's sick and needs nursing. You come to see me if you need something typed, or a computer program tweaked, or some clue traced back to an ISP online. Neither of you ever come near me unless I'm useful."

His breath caught. "Jodie, it's not like that!"

She looked at him steadily. "Yes, it is. It always has been. I'm not complaining," she added at once. "I don't know what I would have done if it hadn't been for you and Margie. I owe you more than I can ever repay in my lifetime. It's just that since you're here, there's something you need done, and I know it. No problem. Tell me what you want me to do.''

His eyes closed and opened again, on a pained expression. It was true. He and Margie had used her shamelessly, but without realizing they were so obvious. He hated the thought.

"It's a little late to develop a conscience," she added with a faint smile. "It's out of character, anyway. Come on. What is it?"

He toyed with his biscotti. "I told you that we're tracking a link to the drug cartel."

She nodded.

"In your company," he added.

"You said I couldn't help," she reminded him.

"Well, I was wrong. In fact, you're the only one who can help me with this."

A few weeks ago, she'd have joked about getting a badge or a gun. Now she just waited for answers. The days of friendly teasing were long gone.

He met her searching gaze. "I want you to pretend that we're developing a relationship," he said, "so that I have a reason to hang around your division."

She didn't react. She was proud of herself. It would have been painfully easy to dump the thick, creamy cappuccino all over his immaculate trousers and anoint him with the cream.

His eyebrow jerked. "Yes, you're right, I'm using you. It's the only way I can find to do surveillance. I can't hang around Jasper or people will think I'm keen on him!"

That thought provoked a faint smile. "His wife wouldn't like it."

He shrugged. "Will you do it?"

She hesitated.

He anticipated that. He took out a photograph and slid it across the table to her.

She picked it up. It was of two young boys, about five or six, both smiling broadly. They had thick, straight black hair and black eyes and dark complexions. They looked Latin. She looked back up at Alexander with a question in her eyes.

"Their mother was tired of having drug users in her neighborhood. They met in an abandoned house next door to her. There were frequent disputes, usually followed by running gun battles. The dealer who made the house his headquarters got ambitious. He decided to double-cross the new drug leadership that came in after Manuel Lopez's old territory was finally divided," he said carelessly. "Mama Garcia kept a close eye on what was going on, and kept the police informed. She made the fatal error of telling her infrequent neighbor that his days in her neighborhood were numbered. He told his supplier.

"All this got back to the new dealer network. So when they came to take out the double-crossing dealer, they were quite particular about where they placed the shots. They knew where Mama Garcia lived, and they targeted her along with their rival. Miguel and Juan were hit almost twenty times with automatic weapon fire. They died in the firefight, along with the rebellious dealer. Their mother was wounded and will probably never walk again."

She winced as she looked at the photograph of the two little boys, so happy and smiling. Both dead, over drugs.

He saw her discomfort and nodded. "The local distributor I'm after ordered the hit. He works in this building, in this corporation, in this division." He leaned forward, and she'd never seen him look so menacing. "I'm going to take him out. So, I'll ask you one more time, Jodie. Will you help me?"

Five

Jodie groaned inwardly. She knew as she looked one last time at the photograph that she couldn't let a child-killer walk the streets, no matter what the sacrifice to herself.

She handed him back the photograph. "Yes, I'll do it," she said in a subdued tone. "When do I start?"

"Tomorrow at lunch. We'll go out to eat. You can give me the grand tour on the way."

"Okay."

"You still look reluctant," he said with narrowed eyes.

"Brody just asked me out, for the first time," she confessed, trying to sound more despondent than she actually was. It wouldn't hurt to let Alexander know that she wasn't pining over him.

His expression was not easily read. "I thought he was engaged."

She grimaced. "Well, things are cooling off," she defended herself. "His girlfriend travels all over the world. She just came back from trips to Mexico and Peru, and she

doesn't pay Brody much attention even when she's here!"
she muttered.

"Peru?" He seemed thoughtful. He studied her quietly for
a long moment before he spoke. "They're still engaged, Jodie."

And he thought less of her because she was ignoring another woman's rights. Of course he did. She didn't like the
idea, either, and she knew she wasn't going to go out with
Brody a week from Saturday. Not now. Alexander made her
feel too guilty.

She traced the rim of her china coffee cup. "You're right,"
she had to admit. "It's just that she treats him so badly,"
she added with a wistful smile. "He's a sweet man. He's
always encouraging me in my job, telling me I can do things,
believing in me."

"Which is no damned reason to have an affair with a
man," he said furiously. It made him angry to think that
another man was trying to uplift Jodie's ego when he'd done
nothing but damage to it.

She lowered her voice. "I am not having an affair with
him!"

"But you would, if he asked," he said, his eyes as cold
as green glass.

She started to argue, then stopped. It would do no good to
argue. Besides, it was her life, and he had no business telling
her how to live it.

"How do you want me to act while we're pretending to
get involved?" she countered sourly. "Do you want me to
throw myself at you and start kissing you when you walk
into my cubicle?"

His eyes dilated. "I beg your pardon?"

"Never mind," she said, ruffled. "I'll play it by ear."

He really did seem different, she thought, watching him
hesitate uncharacteristically. He drew a diskette in a plastic
holder out of his inside jacket pocket and handed it to her.

"Another chore," he added, glancing around to make sure
they weren't being observed. "I want you to check out these

Web sites, and the e-mail addresses, without leaving footprints. I want to know if they're legitimate and who owns them. They're password protected and in code.''

"No problem," she said easily. "I can get behind any firewall they put up."

"Don't leave an address they can trace back to you," he emphasized. "These people won't hesitate to kill children. They wouldn't mind wasting you."

"I get the point. I'm not sloppy." She slipped the diskette into her purse and finished her coffee. "Anything else?"

"Yes. Margie said to tell you that she's sorry."

Her eyebrows arched. "For what?"

"For everything." He searched her eyes. "And for the record, you don't owe us endless favors, debt or no debt."

She got to her feet. "I know that. I'll have this information for you tomorrow by the time you get here."

He got up, too, catching the bill before she had time to grab it. "My conference, my treat," he said. He stared down at her with an intensity that was disturbing. "You're still keeping something back," he said in a deep, low tone.

"Nothing of any importance," she replied. It was disconcerting that he could read her expressions that well.

His eyes narrowed. "Do you really like working here, Jodie?"

"You're the one who said I needed to stop loafing and get a job," she accused with more bitterness than she realized. "So I got one."

He actually winced. "I said you needed to get your priorities straight," he countered. "Not that you needed to jump into a job you hate."

"I like Brody."

"Brody isn't the damned job," he replied tersely. "You're not cut out for monotony. It will kill your soul."

She knew that; she didn't want to admit it. "Don't you have a hot date?" she asked sarcastically, out of patience with his meddling.

He sighed heavily. "Yes. Why don't you?"

"Men aren't worth the trouble they cause," she lied, turning.

"Oh, you'd know?" he drawled sarcastically. "With your hectic social life?"

She turned, furious. "When Brody's free, look out," she said.

He didn't reply. But he watched her all the way down the hall.

She fumed all the way home. Alexander had such a nerve, she thought angrily. He could taunt her with his conquests, use her to do his decryption work, force her into becoming his accomplice in an investigation…!

Wait a minute, she thought suddenly, her hand resting on her purse over the diskette he'd entrusted her with. He had some of the best cyber crime experts in the country on his payroll. Why was he farming out work to an amateur who didn't even work for him?

The answer came in slowly, as she recalled bits and pieces of information she'd heard during the Lopez investigation. She knew people in Jacobsville who kept in touch with her after her move to Houston. Someone had mentioned that there were suspicions of a mole in the law enforcement community, a shadowy figure who'd funneled information to Lopez so that he could escape capture.

Then Alexander's unusual request made sense. He suspected somebody in his organization of working with the drug dealers, and he wanted someone he could trust to do this investigation for him.

She felt oddly touched by his confidence, not only in her ability, but also in her character. He'd refused to let her help him before, but now he was trusting her with explosive information. He was letting her into his life, even on a limited basis. He had to care about her, a little.

Sure he did, she told herself glumly. She was a computer whiz, and he knew it. Hadn't he paid for the college education that had honed those skills? He trusted her ability to manipulate software and track criminal activity through cyberspace. That didn't amount to a declaration of love. She had to stop living in dreams. There was no hope of a future with Alexander. She wasn't even his type. He liked highly intelligent, confident women. He liked professionals. Jodie was more like a mouse. She kept in her little corner, avoiding confrontation, hiding her abilities, speaking only when spoken to, never demanding anything.

She traced the outline of the diskette box through the soft leather of her purse, bought almost new at a yard sale. She pursed her lips. Well, maybe it was time she stopped being everybody's lackey and started standing up for herself. She was smart. She was capable. She could do any job she really wanted to do.

She thought about firing a woman with a dependent elderly mother and child and ground her teeth together. It was becoming obvious that she was never going to enjoy that sort of job.

On the other hand, tracking down criminals was exciting. It made her face flush as she considered how valuable she could be to Alexander in this investigation. She thought of the two little Garcia boys and their poor mother, and her eyes narrowed angrily. She was going to help Alexander catch the animal who'd ordered that depraved execution. And she was just the woman with the skills to do it.

Jodie spent most of the evening and the wee hours of the morning tracking down the information Alexander had asked her to find for him. She despaired a time or two, because she ran into one dead end after another. The drug dealers must have cyber experts of their own, and of a high caliber, if they could do this sort of thing.

She finally found a Web site that listed information which was, on the surface, nothing more than advisories about the best sites to find UFO information. But one of the addresses coincided with the material she'd printed out from Alexander's diskette, as a possible link to the drug network. She opened site after site, but she found nothing more than double-talk about possible landing sites and dates. Most covered pages and pages of data, but the last one had only one page of information. It was oddly concise, and the sites were all in a defined area—Texas and Mexico and Peru. Strange, she thought. But, then, Peru was right next door to Colombia. And while drugs and Colombia went together like apples and pie, few people outside law enforcement would connect Peru with drug smuggling.

It was two in the morning, and she was so sleepy that she began to laugh at her own inadequacy. But as she looked at the last site she made sudden sense of the numbers and landing sites. Quickly she printed out the single page of UFO landing sites.

There was a pattern in the listings. It was so obvious that it hit her in the face. She grabbed a pencil and pad and began writing down the numbers. From there, it was a quick move to transpose them with letters. They spelled an e-mail address.

She plugged back into her ISP and changed identities to avoid leaving digital footprints. Then she used a hacker's device to find the source of the e-mail. It originated from a foreign server, and linked directly to a city in Peru. Moreover, a city in Peru near the border with Colombia. She copied down the information without risking leaving it in her hard drive and got out fast.

She folded the sheets of paper covered with her information—because she hadn't wanted to leave anything on her computer that could be accessed if she were online—and placed them in her purse. She smiled sleepily as she climbed into bed with a huge yawn. Alexander, she thought, was going to be impressed.

In fact, he was speechless. He went over the figures in his car in the parking lot on the way to lunch. His eyes met Jodie's and he shook his head.

"This is ingenious," he murmured.

"They did do a good job of hiding information…" she agreed.

"No! Your work," he corrected instantly. "This is quality work, Jodie. Quality work. I can't think of anyone who could have done it better."

"Thanks," she said.

"And you're taking notes for Brody Vance," he said with veiled contempt. "He should be working for you."

She chuckled at the thought of Brody with a pad and pen sitting with his legs crossed under a skirt, in front of her desk. "He wouldn't suit."

"You don't suit the job you're doing," he replied. "When this case is solved, I want you to consider switching vocations. Any law enforcement agency with a cyber crime unit would be proud to have you."

Except his, she was thinking, but she didn't say it. A compliment from Alexander was worth something. "I might do that," she said noncommittally.

"I'll put this to good use," he said, sliding the folded sheets into his inside suit pocket. "Where do you want to eat?" he added.

"I usually eat downstairs in the cafeteria. They have a blue plate special…"

"Where does your boss have lunch?"

"Brody?" She blinked. "When his girlfriend's in town, he usually goes to a Mexican restaurant, La Rancheria. It's three blocks over near the north expressway," she added.

"I know where it is. What's his girlfriend like?"

She shrugged. "Very dark, very beautiful, very chic. She's District Marketing manager for the whole southwest. She oversees our sales force for the gas and propane distribution network. We sell all over the world, of course, not just in Texas."

"But she travels to Mexico and Peru," he murmured as he turned the Jaguar into traffic.

"She has family in both places," she said disinterestedly. "Her mother was moving from a town in Peru near the Colombian border down to Mexico City, and Cara had to help organize it. That's what she told Brody.'' She frowned. ''Odd, I thought Brody said her mother was dead. But, then, I didn't really pay attention. I've only seen her a couple of times. She leads Brody around by the nose. He's not very forceful.''

''Do you like Mexican food?''

''The real thing, yes,'' she said with a sigh. ''I usually get my chili fix from cans or TV dinners. It's not the same.''

''No, it's not.''

''You used to love eggs ranchero for breakfast,'' she commented, and then could have bitten her tongue out for admitting that she remembered his food preferences.

''Yes. You made them for me at four in the morning, the day my father died. Jessie was in tears, so was Margie. Nobody was awake. I'd come from overseas and didn't even have supper. You heard me rattling around in the kitchen trying to make a sandwich,'' he recalled with a strangely tender smile. ''You got up and started cooking. Never said a word, either,'' he added. ''You put the plate in front of me, poured coffee, and went away.'' He shrugged. ''I couldn't have talked to save my life. I was too broken up at losing Dad. You knew that. I never understood how.''

''Neither did I,'' she confessed. She looked out the window. It was a cold day, misting rain. The city looked smoggy. That wasn't surprising. It usually did.

''What is it about Vance that attracts you?'' he asked abruptly.

''Brody? Well, he's kind and encouraging, he always makes people feel good about themselves. I like being with him. He's...I don't know...comfortable.''

''Comfortable.'' He made the word sound insulting. He turned into the parking lot of the Mexican restaurant.

''You asked,'' she pointed out.

He cut off the engine and glanced at her. ''God forbid that a woman should ever find me comfortable!''

"That would take a miracle," she said sweetly, and unfastened her seat belt.

He only laughed.

They had a quiet lunch. Brody wasn't there, but Alexander kept looking around as if he expected the man to materialize right beside the table.

"Are you looking for someone?" she asked finally.

He glanced at her over his dessert, a caramel flan. "I'm always looking for someone," he returned. "It's my job."

She didn't think about what he did for a living most of the time. Of course, the bulge under his jacket where he carried his gun was a dead giveaway, and sometimes he mentioned a case he was working on. Today, their combined efforts on the computer tracking brought it up. But she could go whole days without realizing that he put himself at risk to do the job. In his position, it was inevitable that he would make enemies. Some of them must have been dangerous, but he'd never been wounded.

"Thinking deep thoughts?" he asked her as he registered her expression.

"Not really. This flan is delicious."

"No wonder your boss frequents the place. The food is good, too."

"I really like the way they make coffee…"

"Kennedy!" Alexander called to a man just entering the restaurant, interrupting Jodie's comment.

An older man glanced his way, hesitated, and then smiled broadly as he joined them. "Cobb!" he greeted. "Good to see you!"

"I thought you were in New Orleans," Alexander commented.

"I was. Got through quicker than I thought I would. Who's this?" he added with a curious glance at Jodie.

"Jodie's my girl," Alexander said carelessly. "Jodie, this is Bert Kennedy, one of my senior agents."

They shook hands.

"Glad to meet you, Mr. Kennedy."

"Same here, Miss…?"

Alexander ignored the question. Jodie just smiled at him.

"Uh, any luck on the shipyard tip?" Kennedy asked.

Alexander shook his head. "Didn't pan out." He didn't meet the older man's eyes. "We may put a man at Thorn Oil next week," he said in a quiet tone, glancing around to make sure they weren't subject to eavesdroppers. "I'll tell you about it later."

Kennedy had been nervous, but now he relaxed and began to grin. "Great! I'd love to be in on the surveillance," he added. "Unless you have something bigger?"

"We'll talk about it later. See you."

Kennedy nodded, and walked on to a table by the window.

"Is he one of your best men?" she asked Alexander.

"Kennedy is a renegade," he murmured coolly, watching the man from a distance. "He's the bird who brought mercenaries into my drug bust in Jacobsville the year before last, without warning me first. One of their undercover guys almost got killed because we didn't know who he was."

"Eb Scott's men," she ventured.

He nodded. "I was already upset because Manuel Lopez had killed my undercover officer, Walt Monroe. He was my newest agent. I sent him to infiltrate Lopez's organization." His eyes were bleak. "I wanted Lopez. I wanted him badly. The night of the raid, I had no idea that Scott and his gang were even on the place. They were running a Mexican national undercover. If Kennedy knew, he didn't tell me. We could have killed him, or Scott, or any of his men. They weren't supposed to be there."

"I expect Mr. Kennedy lived to regret that decision."

He gave her a cool look. "Oh, he regretted it, all right."

She wasn't surprised that Mr. Kennedy was intimidated by Alexander. Most people were, herself included.

She finished her coffee. "Thanks for lunch," she said. "I really enjoyed it."

He studied her with real interest. "You have exquisite manners," he commented. "Your mother did, too."

She felt her cheeks go hot. "She was a stickler for courtesy," she replied.

"So was your father. They were good people."

"Like your own father."

"I loved him. My mother never forgave him for leaving her for a younger woman," he commented in a rare lapse. "She drank like a fish. Margie and I were stuck with her, because she put on such a good front in court that nobody believed she was a raging alcoholic. She got custody and made us pay for my father's infidelities until she finally died. By then, we were almost grown. We still loved him, though."

She hadn't known the Cobbs' mother very well. Margie had been reluctant to invite her to their home while the older woman was still alive, although Margie spent a lot of time at Jodie's home. Margie and Alexander were very fond of Mr. and Mrs. Clayburn, and they brought wonderful Christmas presents to them every year. Jodie had often wondered just how much damage his mother had done to Alexander in his younger, formative years. It might explain a lot about his behavior from time to time.

"Did you love your mother?" she asked.

He glared at her. "I hated her."

She swallowed. She thought back to the party, to her uninhibited behavior when she'd had those glasses of champagne. She'd brought back terrible memories for Alexander, of his mother, his childhood. Only now did she understand why he'd reacted so violently. No wonder she'd made him sick. He identified her behavior with his mother's. But he'd said other things as well, things she couldn't forget. Things that hurt.

She dropped her eyes and looked at her watch. "I really have to get back," she began.

His hand went across the table to cover hers. "Don't," he said roughly. "Don't look like that! You don't drink nor-

mally, not ever. That's why the champagne hit you so hard.
I overreacted. Don't let it ruin things between us, Jodie.''

She took a slow breath to calm herself. She couldn't meet
his eyes. She looked at his mouth instead, and that was
worse. It was a chiseled, sensuous mouth and she couldn't
stop remembering how it felt to be kissed by it. He was
expert. He was overwhelming. She wanted him to drag her
into his arms and kiss her blind, and that would never do.

She withdrew her hand with a slow smile. ''I'm not holding grudges, Alexander,'' she reassured him. ''Listen, I really
have to get back. I've got a diskette full of letters to get out
by quitting time.''

''All right,'' he said. ''Let's go.''

Kennedy raised his hand and waved as they went out. Alexander returned the salute, sliding his hand around Jodie's
waist as they left the building. But she noticed that he
dropped it the minute they entered the parking lot. He was
putting on an act, and she'd better remember it. She'd already
been hurt once. There was no sense in inviting more pain
from the same source.

He left her at the front door of her building with a curious,
narrow-eyed gaze that stayed with her the rest of the day.

The phone on her desk rang early the following morning
and she answered it absently while she typed.

''Do you still like symphony concerts?'' came a deep
voice in reply.

Alexander! Her fingers flew across the keys, making errors. ''Uh, yes.''

''There's a special performance of Debussy tomorrow
night.''

''I read about it in the entertainment section of the newspaper,'' she said. ''They're doing 'Afternoon of a Faun' and
'La Mer,' my two favorites.''

He chuckled. ''I know.''

''I'd love to see it,'' she admitted.

''I've got tickets. I'll pick you up at seven. Will you have time to eat supper by then?'' he added, implying that he was asking her to the concert only, not to dinner.

"Of course," she replied.

"I have to work late, or I'd include dinner," he said softly.

"No problem, I have leftovers that have to be eaten," she said.

"Then I'll see you at seven."

"At seven." She hung up. Her hands were ice cold and shaking. She felt her insides shake. Alexander was taking her to a concert. Mentally her thoughts flew to her closet. She only had one good dress, a black one. She could pair it with her winter coat and a small strand of pearls that Margie and Alexander had given her when she graduated from college. She could put her hair up. She wouldn't look too bad.

She felt like a teenager on her first date until she realized why they were going out together. Alexander hadn't just discovered love eternal. He was putting on an act. But why put it on at a concert?

The answer came in an unexpected way. Brody stopped by her office a few minutes after Alexander's call. He came into the cubicle, looking nervous.

"Is something wrong?" she asked.

He drew in a long breath. "About next Saturday…" he began.

"I can't go," she blurted out.

His relief was patent. "I'm so glad you said that," he replied, relief making him limp. "Cara's going to be home and she wants to spend the day with me."

"Alexander's having a birthday party that day," she replied, painfully aware that she wouldn't be invited, although Alexander would surely want her co-workers to think that she was.

"I, uh, couldn't help but notice that he took you out to lunch yesterday," he said. "You've known him for a long time."

"A very long time," she confessed. "He just phoned, in fact, to invite me to a concert of Debussy…"

"Debussy?" he exclaimed.

"Well, yes…?"

"I'll see you there," he said. "Cara and I are going, too. Isn't *that* a coincidence?"

She laughed, as he did. "I can't believe it! I didn't even know you liked Debussy!"

He grimaced. "Actually, I don't," he had to confess. "Cara does."

She smiled wickedly. "I don't think Alexander's very keen on him, either, but he'll pretend to be."

He smiled back. "Forgive me, but he doesn't seem quite your type," he began slowly, flushing a little. "He's a rather tough sort of man, isn't he? And I think he was wearing a gun yesterday, too…Jodie?" he added when she burst out laughing.

"He's sort of in security work, part-time," she told him, without adding where he worked or what he did. Alexander had always made a point of keeping his exact job secret, even among his friends, for reasons Jodie was only beginning to understand.

"Oh. Oh!" He laughed with sheer relief. "And here I thought maybe you were getting involved with a mobster!"

She'd have to remember to tell Alexander that. Not that it would impress him.

"No, he's not quite that bad," she assured him. "About next Saturday, Brody, I would have canceled anyway. It didn't feel right."

"No, it didn't," he seconded. "You and I are too conventional, Jodie. Neither of us is comfortable stepping out of bounds. I'll bet you never had a speeding ticket."

"Never," she agreed. "Not that I drive very much anymore. It's so convenient to take buses," she added, without mentioning that she'd had to sell her car months ago. The repair bills, because it was an older model, were eating her alive.

"I suppose so. Uh, I did notice that your friend drives a new Jaguar."

She smiled sedately. "He and his sister are independently wealthy," she told him. "They own a ranch and breed some of the finest cattle in south Texas. That's how he can afford to run a Jaguar."

"I see." He stuck his hands in his pockets and watched her. "Debussy. Somehow I never thought of you as a classical concert-goer."

"But I am. I love ballet and theater, too. Not that I get the opportunity to see much of them these days."

"Does your friend like them, too?"

"He's the one who taught me about them," she confided. "He was forever taking me and his sister to performances when we were in our teens. He said that we needed to learn culture, because it was important. We weren't keen at the time, but we learned to love it as he did. Except for Debussy," she added on a chuckle. "And I sometimes think I like that composer just to spite him."

"It's a beautiful piece, if you like modern. I'm a Beethoven man myself."

"And I don't like Beethoven, except for the Ninth Symphony."

"That figures. Well, thanks for understanding. I, uh, I guess we'll see you at the concert tonight, then!"

"I guess so."

They exchanged smiles and then he left. She turned her attention back to her computer, curious about the coincidence.

Had Alexander known that Brody and his girlfriend Cara were going to the same performance? Or had it really been one of those inexplicable things?

Then another thought popped into her mind. What if Alexander was staking out her company because he suspected Brody of being in the drug lord's organization?

Six

The suspicion that Alexander was after Brody kept Jodie brooding for the rest of the day. Brody was a gentle, sweet man. Surely he couldn't be involved in anything as unsavory as drug smuggling!

If someone at the corporation was under investigation, she couldn't blow Alexander's cover by mentioning anything to her boss. But, wait, hadn't Alexander told his agent, Kennedy, that they were investigating a case at Thorn Oil Corporation? Then she remembered why Alexander wanted to pretend to be interested in Jodie. Something was crazy here. Why would he lie to Kennedy?

She shook her head and put the questions away. She wasn't going to find any answers on her own.

She'd been dressed and ready for an hour when she buzzed Alexander into her apartment building. By the time he got to her room and knocked at the door, she was a nervous wreck.

She opened the door, and he gave her a not very flattering scrutiny. She thought she looked nice in her sedate black dress and high heels, with her hair in a bun. Obviously he didn't. He was dashing, though, in a dinner jacket and slacks and highly polished black shoes. His black tie was perfectly straight against the expensive white cotton of his shirt.

"You never wear your hair down," Alexander said curtly. "And you've worn that same dress to two out of three parties at our house."

She flushed. "It's the only good dress I have, Alexander," she said tightly.

He sighed angrily. "Margie would love to make you something, if you'd let her."

She turned to lock her door. Her hands were cold and numb. He couldn't let her enjoy one single evening without criticizing something about her. She felt near tears…

She gasped as he suddenly whipped her around and bent to kiss her with grinding, passionate fervor. She didn't have time to respond. It was over as soon as it had begun, despite her rubbery legs and wispy breathing. She stood looking up at him with wide, misty, shocked eyes in a pale face.

His own green eyes glittered into hers as he studied her reaction. "Stop letting me put you down," he said unexpectedly. "I know I don't do much for your ego, but you have to stand up for yourself. You're not a carpet, Jodie, stop letting people walk on you."

She was still trying to breathe and think at the same time.

"And now you look like an accident victim," he murmured. He pulled out a handkerchief, his eyes on her mouth. "I suppose I'm covered with pink lipstick," he added, pressing the handkerchief into her hand. "Clean me up."

"It…doesn't come off," she stammered.

He cocked an eyebrow and waited for an explanation.

"It's that new kind they advertise. You put it on and it lasts all day. It won't come off on coffee cups or even linen." She handed him back the handkerchief.

He put it up, but he didn't move. His hands went to the pert bun on the top of her head and before she could stop him, he loosed her hair from the circular comb that held the wealth of hair in place. It fell softly, in waves, to her shoulders.

Alexander caught his breath. "Beautiful," he whispered, the comb held absently in one hand while he ran the other through the soft strands of hair.

"It took forever…to get it put up," she protested weakly.

"I love long hair," he said gruffly. He bent, tilting her chin up, to kiss her with exquisite tenderness. "Leave it like that."

He put the comb in her hand and waited while she stuck it into her purse. Her hands shook. He saw that, too, and he smiled.

When she finished, he linked her fingers into his and they started off down the hall.

The concert hall was full. Apparently quite a few people in Houston liked Debussy, Jodie thought mischievously as they walked down the aisle to their seats. She knew that Alexander didn't like it at all, but it was nice of him to suffer through it, considering her own affection for the pieces the orchestra was playing.

Of course, he might only be here because he was spying on Brody, she thought, and then worried about that. She couldn't believe Brody would ever deal in anything dishonest. He was too much like Jodie herself. But why would Alexander be spending so much time at her place of work if he didn't suspect Brody?

It was all very puzzling. She sat down in the reserved seat next to Alexander and waited for the curtain to go up. They'd gotten into a traffic jam on the way and had arrived just in the nick of time. The lights went out almost the minute they sat down.

In the darkness, lit comfortably by the lights from the stage where the orchestra was placed, she felt Alexander's big, warm hand curl into hers. She sighed helplessly, loving the exciting, electric contact of his touch.

He heard the soft sound, and his fingers tightened. He didn't let go until intermission.

"Want to stretch your legs?" he invited, standing.

"Yes, I think so," she agreed. She got up, still excited by his proximity, and walked out with him. He didn't hold her hand this time, she noticed, and wondered why.

When they were in the lobby, Brody spotted them and moved quickly toward them, his girlfriend in tow.

She was pretty, Jodie noted, very elegant and dark-haired and long-legged. She wished she was half as pretty. Brody's girlfriend looked Hispanic. She was certainly striking.

"Well, hello!" Brody said with genuine warmth. "Sweetheart, this is my secretary, Jodie Clayburn…excuse me," he added quickly, with an embarrassed smile at Jodie's tight-lipped glance, "I mean, my administrative assistant. And this is Jodie's date, Mr., uh, Mr.…"

"Cobb," Alexander prompted.

"Mr. Cobb," Brody parroted. "This is my girlfriend, Cara Dominguez," he introduced.

"Pleased to meet you," Cara said in a bored tone.

"Same here," Jodie replied.

"Cara's in marketing," Brody said, trying to force the conversation to ignite. "She works for Bradford Marketing Associates, down the street. They're a subsidiary of Ritter Oil Corporation. They sell drilling equipment and machine parts for oil equipment all over the United States. Cara is over the southwestern division."

"And what do you do, Mr. Cobb?" Cara asked Alexander, who was simply watching her, without commenting.

"Oh, he's in security work," Brody volunteered.

Cara's eyebrows arched. "Really!" she asked, but without much real interest.

"I work for the Drug Enforcement Administration," Alexander said with a faint smile, his eyes acknowledging Jodie's shock. "I'm undercover and out of the country a lot of the time," he added with the straightest face Jodie had ever seen. "I don't have to work at all, of course," he added with a cool smile, "but I like the cachet of law enforcement duties."

Jodie was trying not to look at him or react. It was difficult.

"How nice," Cara said after a minute, and she seemed disconcerted by his honesty. "You are working on a case now?" she fished.

One of the first things Jodie and Margie had learned from Alexander when he went with the DEA was not to mention what he did for a living, past the fact that he did "security work." She'd always assumed it had something to do with his infrequent undercover assignments. And here he was spilling all the beans!

"Sort of," Alexander said lazily. "We're investigating a company with Houston connections," he added deliberately.

Cara was all ears. "That would not be Thorn Oil Corporation?"

Alexander gave her a very nice shocked look.

She laughed. "One hears things," she mused. "Don't worry, I never tell what I know."

"Right," Brody chuckled, making a joke of it. He hadn't known what Alexander did for a living until now.

Alexander laughed, too. "I have to have the occasional diversion," he confessed. "My father was wealthy. My sister and I were his only beneficiaries."

Cara was eyeing him with increased interest. "You live in Houston, Mr. Cobb?"

He nodded.

"Are you enjoying the concert?" Brody broke in, uncomfortable at the way his girlfriend was looking at Alexander.

"It's wonderful," Jodie said.

"I understand the Houston ballet is doing *The Nutcracker* starting in November," Cara purred, smiling at Alexander. "If you like ballet, perhaps we will meet again."

"Perhaps we will," Alexander replied. "Do you live in Houston, also, Miss Dominguez?"

"Yes, but I travel a great deal," she said with careless detachment. "My contacts are far reaching."

"She's only just come back from Mexico," Brody said with a nervous laugh.

"Yes, I've been helping my mother move," Cara said tightly. "After my father...died, she lost her home and had nowhere to go."

"I'm very sorry," Jodie told her. "I lost my parents some years ago. I know how it feels."

Cara turned back to Brody. "We need to get back to our seats. Nice to have met you both," she added with a social smile as she took Brody's hand and drew him along with her. He barely had time to say goodbye.

Alexander glanced down at Jodie. "Your boss looked shocked when I told him what I did."

She shook her head. "You told me never to do that, but you told them everything!"

"I told them nothing Cara didn't know already," he said enigmatically. He slid his hand into hers and smiled secretively. "Let's go back."

"It's a very nice concert," she commented.

"Is it? I hate Debussy," he murmured unsurprisingly.

The comment kept her quiet until they were out of the theater and on their way back to her apartment in his car.

"Why did you ask me out if you don't like concerts?" she asked.

He glanced at her. "I had my reasons. What do you think of your boss's girlfriend?"

"She's nice enough. She leads Brody around like a child, though."

"Most women would," he said lazily. "He's not assertive."

"He certainly is," she defended him. "He has to fire people."

"He's not for you, Jodie, girlfriend or not," he said surprisingly. "You'd stagnate in a relationship with him."

"It's my life," she pointed out.

"So it is."

They went the rest of the way in silence. He walked her

to her apartment door and stood staring down at her for a long moment. "Buy a new dress."

"Why?" she asked, surprised.

"I'll take you to see *The Nutcracker* next month. As I recall, it was one of your favorite ballets."

"Yes," she stammered.

"So I'll take you," he said. He checked his watch. "I've got a late call to make, and meetings the first of the week. But I'll take you to lunch next Wednesday."

"Okay," she replied.

He reached out suddenly and drew her against him, hard. He held her there, probing her eyes with his until her lips parted. Then he bent and kissed her hungrily, twisting his mouth against hers until she yielded and gave him what he wanted. A long, breathless moment later, he lifted his head.

"Not bad," he murmured softly. "But you could use a little practice. Sleep well."

He let her go and walked away while she tried to find her voice. He never looked back once. Jodie stood at her door watching until he stepped into the elevator and the doors closed.

She usually left at eleven-thirty to go to lunch, and Alexander knew it. But he was late the following Wednesday. She'd chewed off three of her long fingernails by the time he showed up. She was in the lobby where clients were met, along with several of her colleagues who were just leaving for lunch. Alexander came in, looking windblown and half out of humor.

"I can't make it for lunch," he said at once. "I'm sorry. Something came up."

"That's all right," she said, trying not to let her disappointment show. "Another time."

"I'll be out of town for the next couple of days," he continued, not lowering his voice, "but don't you forget my birthday party on Saturday. Call me from the airport and I'll pick you up. If I'm not back by then, Margie will. All right?"

Amazing how much he sounded as if he really wanted her to come. But she knew he was only putting on an act for the employees who were listening to him.

"All right," she agreed. "Have a safe trip. I'll see you Saturday."

He reached out and touched her cheek tenderly. "So long," he said, smiling. He walked away slowly, as if he hated to leave her, and she watched him go with equal reluctance. There were smiling faces all around. It was working. People believed they were involved, which was just what he wanted.

Later, while Brody was signing the letters he'd dictated earlier, she wondered where Alexander was going that would keep him out of town for so long.

"You look pensive," Brody said curiously. "Something worrying you?"

"Nothing, really," she lied. "I was just thinking about Alexander's birthday party on Saturday."

He sighed as he signed the last letter. "It must be nice to have a party," he murmured. "I stopped having them years ago."

"Cara could throw one for you," she suggested.

He grimaced. "She's not the least bit sentimental. She's all business, most of the time, and she never seems to stop working. She's on a trip to Arizona this week to try to land a new client."

"You'll miss her, I'm sure," Jodie said.

He shrugged. "I'll try to." He flushed. "Sorry, that just popped out."

She smiled. "We all have our problems, Brody."

"Yes, I noticed that your friend, Cobb, hardly touches you, except when he thinks someone is watching. He must be one cold fish," he added with disgust.

Jodie flushed then, remembering Alexander's ardor.

He cleared his throat and changed the subject, and not a minute too soon.

* * *

Jodie was doing housework in her apartment when the phone rang Saturday morning.

"Jodie?" Margie asked gently.

"Yes. How are you, Margie?" she asked, but not with her usual cheerful friendliness.

"You're still angry at me, aren't you?" She sighed. "I'm so sorry for making you do all the cooking…"

"I'm not angry," Jodie replied.

There was a long sigh. "I thought Kirry would help me arrange a showing of my designs at her department store," she confessed miserably. "But that's never going to happen. She only pretended to be my friend so that she could get to Alexander. I guess you know she's furious because he's been seen with you?"

"She has nothing to be jealous about," Jodie said coldly. "You can tell her so, for me. Was that all you wanted?"

"Jodie, that's not why I called!" Margie exclaimed. She hesitated. "Alexander wanted me to phone you and make sure you were coming to his birthday party."

"There's no chance of that," Jodie replied firmly.

"But…but he's expecting you," Margie stammered. "He said you promised to come, but that I had to call you and make sure you showed up."

"Kirry's invited, of course?" Jodie asked.

"Well…well, yes, I assumed he'd want her to come so I invited her, too."

"I'm invited to make her jealous, I suppose."

There was a static pause. "Jodie, what's going on? You won't return my calls, you won't meet me for lunch, you don't answer notes. If you're not mad at me, what's wrong?"

Jodie looked down at the floor. It needed mopping, she thought absently. "Alexander told you that he was sick of tripping over me every time he came back to the ranch, and that you were especially not to ask me to his birthday party."

There was a terrible stillness on the end of the line for

several seconds. "Oh, my God," Margie groaned. "You heard what he said that night!"

"I heard every single word, Margie," Jodie said tightly. "He thinks I'm still crazy about him, and it…disgusts him. He said I'm not in your social set and you should make friends among your own social circle." She took a deep, steadying breath. "Maybe he's right, Margie. The two of you took care of me when I had nobody else, but I've been taking advantage of it all these years, making believe that you were my family. In a way I'm grateful that Alexander opened my eyes. I've been an idiot."

"Jodie, he didn't mean it, I know he didn't! Sometimes he just says things without thinking them through. I know he wouldn't hurt you deliberately."

"He didn't know I could hear him," she said. "I drank too much and behaved like an idiot. We both know how Alexander feels about women who get drunk. But I've come to my senses now. I'm not going to impose on your hospitality…"

"But Alexander wants you to come!" Margie argued. "He said so!"

"No, he doesn't, Margie," Jodie said wistfully. "You don't understand what's going on, but I'm helping Alexander with a case. He's using me as a blind while he's surveilling a suspect, and don't you dare let on that you know it. It's not personal between us. It couldn't be. I'm not his sort of woman and we both know it."

Margie's intake of breath was audible. "What am I going to tell him when you don't show up?"

"You won't need to tell him anything," Jodie said easily. "He isn't expecting me. It was just for show. He'll tell you all about it one day. Now I have to go, Margie. I'm working in the kitchen, and things are going to burn," she added, lying through her teeth.

"We could have lunch next week," the other woman offered.

"No. You need to find friends in your class, Margie. I'm not part of your family, and you don't owe me anything. Now, goodbye!"

She hung up and unplugged the phone in case Margie tried to call back. She felt sick. But severing ties with Margie was the right thing to do. Once Alexander was through with her, once he'd caught his criminal, he'd leave her strictly alone. She was going to get out of his life, and Margie's, right now. It was the only sensible way to get over her feelings for Alexander.

The house was full of people when Alexander went inside, carrying his bag on a shoulder strap.

Margie met him at the door. "I'll bet you're tired, but at least you got here." She chuckled, trying not to show her worry. "Leave your bag by the door and come on in. Everybody's in the dining room with the cake."

He walked beside her toward the spacious dining room, where about twenty people were waiting near a table set with china and crystal, punch and coffee and cake. He searched the crowd and began to scowl.

"I don't see Jodie," he said at once. "Where is she? Didn't you phone her?"

"Yes," she groaned, "but she wouldn't come. Please, Lex, can't we talk about it later? Look, Kirry's here!"

"Damn Kirry," he said through his teeth, glaring down at his sister. "Why didn't she come?"

She drew in a miserable breath. "Because she heard us talking the last time she was here," she replied slowly. "She said you were right about her not being in our social class, and that she heard you say that the last thing you wanted was to trip over her at your birthday party." She winced, because the look on his face was so full of pain.

"She heard me," he said, almost choking on the words. "Good God, no wonder she looked at me the way she did. No wonder she's been acting so strangely!"

"She won't go out to lunch with me, she won't come here, she doesn't even want me to call her anymore," Margie said sadly. "I feel as if I've lost my own sister."

His own loss was much worse. He felt sick to his soul.

He'd never meant for Jodie to hear those harsh, terrible words. He'd been reacting to his own helpless loss of control with her, not her hesitant ardor. It was himself he'd been angry at. Now he understood why Jodie was so reluctant to be around him lately. It was ironic that he found himself thinking about her around the clock, and she was as stand-offish as a woman who found him bad company when they were alone. If only he could turn the clock back, make everything right. Jodie, so sweet and tender and loving, Jodie who had loved him once, hearing him tell Margie that Jodie disgusted him…!

"I should be shot," he ground out. "Shot!"

"Don't. It's your birthday," Margie reminded him. "Please. All these people came just to wish you well."

He didn't say another word. He simply walked into the room and let the congratulations flow over him. But he didn't feel happy. He felt as if his heart had withered and died in his chest.

That night, he slipped into his office while Kirry was talking to Margie, and he phoned Jodie. He'd had two straight malt whiskeys with no water, and he wasn't quite sober. It had taken that much to dull the sharp edge of pain.

"You didn't come," he said when she answered.

She hadn't expected him to notice. She swallowed, hard. "The invitation was all for show," she said, her voice husky. "You didn't expect me."

There was a pause. "Did you go out with Brody after all?" he drawled sarcastically. "Is that why you didn't show up?"

"No, I didn't," she muttered. "I'm not spending another minute of my life trying to fit into your exalted social class," she added hotly. "Cheating wives, consciousless husbands, social climbing friends…that's not my idea of a party!"

He sat back in his chair. "You might not believe it, but it's not mine, either," he said flatly. "I'd rather get a fast food hamburger and talk shop with the guys."

That was surprising. But she didn't quite trust him. "That isn't Kirry's style," she pointed out.

He laughed coldly. "It would become her style in minutes if she thought it would make me propose. I'm rich. Haven't you noticed?"

"It's hard to miss," she replied.

"Kirry likes life in the fast lane. She wants to be decked out in diamonds and taken to all the most expensive places four nights a week. Five on holidays."

"I'm sure she wants you, too."

"Are you?"

"I'm folding clothes, Alexander. Was there anything else?" she added formally, trying to get him to hang up. The conversation was getting painful.

"I never knew that you heard me the night of our last party, Jodie," he said in a deep, husky, pained sort of voice. "I'm more sorry than I can say. You don't know what it was like when my mother had parties. She drank like a fish..."

So Margie had told him. It wasn't really a surprise. "I had some champagne," she interrupted. "I don't drink, so it overwhelmed me. I'm very sorry for the way I behaved."

There was another pause. "I loved it," he said gruffly.

Now she couldn't even manage a reply. She just stared at the receiver, waiting for him to say something else.

"Talk to me!" he growled.

"What do you want me to say?" she asked unsteadily. "You were right. I don't belong in your class. I never will. You said I was a nuisance, and you were ri—"

"Jodie!" Her name sounded as if it were torn from his throat. "Jodie, don't! I didn't mean what I said. You've never been a nuisance!"

"It's too late," she said heavily. "I won't come back to the ranch again, ever, Alexander, not for you or even for Margie. I'm going to live my own life, make my own way in the world."

"By pushing us out of it?" he queried.

She sighed. "I suppose so."

"But not until I solve this case," he added after a minute. "Right?"

She wanted to argue, but she kept seeing the little boys' faces in that photograph he'd shown her. "Not until then," she said.

There was a rough sound, as if he'd been holding his breath and suddenly let it out. "All right."

"Alexander, where are you?!" That was Kirry's voice, very loud.

"In a minute, Kirry! I'm on the phone!"

"We're going to open the presents. Come on!"

Jodie heard the sound Alexander made, and she laughed softly in spite of herself. "I thought it was your birthday?" she mused.

"It started to be, but my best present is back in Houston folding clothes," he said vehemently.

Her heart jumped. She had to fight not to react. "I'm nobody's present, Alexander," she informed him. "And now I really do have to go. Happy birthday."

"I'm thirty-four," he said. "Margie is the only family I have. Two of my colleagues just had babies," he remarked, his voice just slightly slurred. "Their desks are full of photographs of the kids and their wives. Know what I've got in a frame on my desk, Jodie? Kirry, in a ball gown."

"I guess the married guys would switch places with you…"

"That's not what I mean! I didn't put it there, she did. Instead of a wife and kids, I've got a would-be debutante who wants to own Paris."

"That was your choice," she pointed out.

"That's what you think. She gave me the framed picture." There was a pause. "Why don't you give me a photo?"

"Sure. Why not? Who would you like a photo of, and I'll see if I can find one for you."

"You, idiot!"

"I don't have any photos of myself."

"Why not?"

"Who'd take them?" she asked. "I don't even own a camera."

"We'll have to do something about that," he murmured.

"Do you like parks? We could go jogging early Monday in that one near where you live. The one with the goofy sculpture."

"It's modern art. It isn't goofy."

"You're entitled to your opinion. Do you jog?"

"Not really."

"Do you have sweats and sneakers?"

She sighed irritably. "Well, yes, but…"

"No buts. I'll see you bright and early Monday." There was a pause. "I'll even apologize."

"That would be a media event."

"I'm serious," he added quietly. "I've never regretted anything in my life more than knowing you heard what I said to Margie that night."

For an apology, it was fairly headlong. Alexander never made apologies. It was a red letter event.

'Okay," she said after a few seconds.

He sighed, hard. "We can start over," he said firmly.

"Alexander, are you coming out of there?" came Kirry's petulant voice in the background.

"Better tell Kirry first," she chided.

"I'll tell her…get the hell out of my study!" he raged abruptly, and there was the sound of something heavy hitting the wall. Then there was the sound of a door closing with a quick snap.

"What did you do?" Jodie exclaimed.

"I threw a book in her general direction. Don't worry. It wasn't a book I liked. It was something on Colombian politics."

"You could have hit her!"

"In pistol competition, I hit one hundred targets out of a hundred shots. The book hit ten feet from where she was standing."

"You shouldn't throw things at people."

"But I'm uncivilized," he reminded her. "I need someone to mellow me out."

"Kirry's already there."

"Not for long, if she opens that damned door again. I'll see you Monday. Okay?"

There was a long hesitation. But finally she said, "Okay."

She put down the receiver and stared at it blankly. Her life had just shifted ten degrees and she had no idea why. At least, not right then.

Seven

Jodie had just changed into her sweats and was making breakfast in her sock feet when Alexander knocked on the door.

He was wearing gray sweats, like hers, with gray running shoes. He gave her a long, thorough appraisal. "I don't like your hair in a bun," he commented.

"I can't run with it down," she told him. "It tangles."

He sniffed the air. "Breakfast?" he asked hopefully.

"Just bacon and eggs and biscuits."

"Just! I had a granola bar," he said with absolute disdain.

She laughed nervously. It was new to have him in her apartment, to have him wanting to be with her. She didn't understand his change of attitude, and she didn't really trust it. But she was too enchanted to question it too closely.

"If you'll feed me," he began, "I'll let you keep up with me while we jog."

"That sounds suspiciously like a bribe," she teased, moving toward the table. "What would your bosses say?"

"You're not a client," he pointed out, seating himself at the table. "Or a perpetrator. So it doesn't count."

She poured him a mug of coffee and put it next to his plate, frowning as she noted the lack of matching dishes and even silverware. The table—a prize from a yard sale—had noticeable scratches and she didn't even have a tablecloth.

"What a comedown this must be," she muttered to herself as she fetched the blackberry jam and put it on the table, along with another teaspoon that didn't match the forks.

He gave her an odd look. "I'm not making comparisons, Jodie," he said softly, and his eyes were as soft as his deep voice. "You live within your means, and you do extremely well at it. You'd be surprised how many people are mortgaged right down to the fillings in their teeth trying to put on a show for their acquaintances. Which is, incidentally, why a lot of them end up in prison, trying to make a quick buck by selling drugs."

She made a face. "I'd rather starve than live like that."

"So would I," he confessed. He bit into a biscuit and moaned softly. "If only Jessie could make these the way you do," he said.

She smiled, pleased at the compliment, because Jessie was a wonderful cook. "They're the only thing I do well."

"No, they aren't." He tasted the jam and frowned. "I didn't know they made blackberry jam," he noted.

"You can buy it, but I like to make my own and put it up," she said. "That came from blackberries I picked last summer, on the ranch. They're actually your own blackberries," she added sheepishly.

"You can have as many as you like, if you'll keep me supplied with this jam," he said, helping himself to more biscuits.

"I'm glad you like it."

They ate in a companionable silence. When she poured their second cups of strong coffee, there weren't any biscuits left.

"Now I need to jog," he teased, "to work off the weight

I've just put on. Coffee's good, too, Jodie. Everything was good.''

"You were just hungry."

He sat back holding his coffee and stared at her. "You've never learned how to take a compliment," he said gently. "You do a lot of things better than other people, but you're modest to the point of self-abasement."

She moved a shoulder. "I like cooking."

He sipped coffee, still watching her. She was pretty early in the morning, he mused, with her face blooming like a rose, her skin clean and free of makeup. Her lips had a natural blush, and they had a shape that was arousing. He remembered how it felt to kiss her, and he ached to do it again. But this was new territory for her. He had to take his time. If he rushed her, he was going to lose her. That thought, once indifferent, took on supreme importance now. He was only beginning to see how much a part of him Jodie already was. He could have kicked himself for what he'd said to her at the ill-fated party.

"The party was a bust," he said abruptly.

Her eyes widened. "Pardon?"

"Kirry opened the presents and commented on their value and usefulness until the guests turned to strong drink," he said with a twinkle in his green eyes. "Then she took offense when a former friend of hers turned up with her ex-boyfriend and made a scene. She left in a trail of flames by cab before we even got to the live band."

She was trying not to smile. It was hard not to be amused at Kirry's situation. The woman was trying, even to people like Margie, who wanted to be friends with her.

"I guess there went Margie's shot at fashion fame," she said sadly.

"Kirry would never have helped her," he said carelessly, and finished his coffee. "She never had any intention of risking her job on a new designer's reputation. She was stringing Margie along so that she could hang out with us. She was wearing thin even before Saturday night."

"Sorry," she said, not knowing what else to say.

"We weren't lovers," he offered blatantly.

She blushed and then caught her breath. "Alexander…!"

"I wanted you to know that, in case anything is ever said about my relationship with her," he added, very seriously. "It was never more than a surface attraction. I can't abide a woman who wears makeup to bed."

She wouldn't ask, she wouldn't ask, she wouldn't…! "How do you know she does?" she blurted out.

He grinned at her. "Margie told me. She asked Kirry why, and Kirry said you never knew when a gentleman might knock on your door after midnight." He leaned forward. "I never did."

"I wasn't going to ask!"

"Sure you were." His eyes slid over her pretty breasts, nicely but not blatantly outlined under the gray jersey top she was wearing. "You're possessive about me. You don't want to be, but you are."

She was losing ground. She got to her feet and made a big thing of checking to see that her shoelaces were tied. "Shouldn't we go?"

He got up, stretched lazily, and started to clear the table. She was shocked to watch him.

"You've never done that," she remarked.

He glanced at her. "If I get married, and I might, I think marriage should be a fifty-fifty proposition. There's nothing romantic about a man lying around the apartment in a dirty T-shirt watching football while his wife slaves in the kitchen." He frowned thoughtfully. "Come to think of it, I don't like football."

"You don't wear dirty T-shirts, either," she replied, feeling sad because he'd mentioned marrying. Maybe there was another woman in his life, besides Kirry.

He chuckled. "Not unless I'm working in the garage." He came around the table after he'd put the dishes in the sink and took her gently by the shoulders, his expression somber. "We've never discussed personal issues. I know less about you than a stranger does. Do you like children? Do you want to have them? Or is a career primary in your life right now?''

The questions were vaguely terrifying. He was going from total indifference to intent scrutiny, and it was too soon. Her face took on a hunted look.

"Never mind," he said quickly, when he saw that. "Don't worry about the question. It isn't important."

She relaxed, but only a little. "I...love children," she faltered. "I like working, or I would if I had a challenging job. But that doesn't mean I'd want to put off having a family if I got married. My mother worked while I was growing up, but she was always there when I needed her, and she never put her job before her family. Neither would I." She searched his eyes, thinking how beautiful a shade of green they were, and about little children with them. Her expression went dreamy. "Fame and fortune may sound enticing, but they wouldn't make up for having people love you." She shrugged. "I guess that sounds corny."

"Actually, it sounds very mature." He bent and drew his mouth gently over her lips, a whisper of contact that didn't demand anything. "I feel the same way."

"You do?" She was unconsciously reaching up to him, trying to prolong the contact. It was unsettling that his lightest touch could send her reeling like this. She wanted more. She wanted him to crush her in his arms and kiss her blind.

He nibbled her upper lip slowly. "It isn't enough, is it?"

"Well...no..."

His arms drew her up, against the steely length of his body, and his mouth opened her lips to a kiss that was consuming with its heat. She moaned helplessly, clinging to him.

He lifted his mouth a breath away. His voice was strained when he spoke. "Do you have any idea what those little noises do to me?" he groaned.

"Noises?" she asked, oblivious, as she stared at his mouth.

"Never mind." He kissed her again, devouring her soft lips. The sounds she made drugged him. He was measuring the distance from the kitchen to her bedroom when he realized how fast things were progressing.

He drew back, and held her away from him, his jaw taut with an attempt at control.

"Alexander," she whispered, her voice pleading as she looked up at him with misty soft eyes.

"I almost never get women pregnant on Monday, but this could be an exception," he said in a choked tone.

Her eyes widened like saucers as she realized what he was saying.

He burst out laughing at her expression. He moved back even more. "I only carry identification and twenty dollars on me when I jog," he confessed. "The other things I keep in my wallet are still in it, at my apartment," he added, his tone blatantly expressive.

She divined what he was intimating and she flushed. She pushed back straggly hair from her face as she searched for her composure.

"Of course, a lot of modern women keep their own supply," he drawled. "I expect you have a box full in your medicine cabinet."

She flushed even more, and now she was glaring at him.

He chuckled, amused. "Your parents were very strict," he recalled. "And deeply religious. You still have those old attitudes about premarital sex, don't you?"

She nodded, grimacing.

"Don't apologize," he said wistfully. "In ten minutes or so, the ache will ease and I can actually stand up straight... God, Jodie!" he burst out laughing at her horrified expression. "I'm kidding!"

"You're a terrible man," she moaned.

"No, I'm just normal," he replied. "I'd love nothing better than a few hours in bed with you, but I'm not enough of a scoundrel to seduce you. Besides all that—" he sighed "—your conscience would kill both of us."

"Rub it in."

He shrugged. "You'd be surprised how many women at

my office abstain, and make no bones about it to eligible bachelors who want to take them out,'' he said, and he smiled tenderly at her. ''We tend to think of them as rugged individualists with the good sense not to take chances.'' He leaned forward. ''And there are actually a couple of the younger male agents who feel the same way!''

''You're kidding!''

He shook his head, smiling. ''Maybe it's a trend. You know, back in the early twentieth century, most women and men went to their weddings chaste. A man with a bad reputation was as untouchable as a woman with one.''

''I'll bet you never told a woman in your life that you were going to abstain,'' she murmured wickedly.

He didn't smile back. He studied her for a long moment. ''I'm telling you that I am. For the foreseeable future.''

She didn't know how to take that, and it showed.

''I'm not in your class as a novice,'' he confessed, ''but I'm no rake, either. I don't find other women desirable lately. Just you.'' He shrugged. ''Careful, it may be contagious.''

She laughed. Her whole face lit up. She was beautiful.

He drew her against him and kissed her, very briefly, before he moved away again. ''We should go,'' he said. ''I have a meeting at the office at ten. Then we could have lunch.''

''Okay,'' she said. She felt lighthearted. Overwhelmed. She started toward the door and then stopped. ''Can I ask you a question?''

''Shoot.''

''Are you staking out my company because you're investigating Brody for drug smuggling?''

He gave her an old, wise look. ''You're sharp, Jodie. I'll have to watch what I say around you.''

''That means you're not going to tell me. Right?''

He chuckled. ''Right.'' He led the way into the hall and then waited for her to lock her door behind them.

She slipped the key into her pocket.

"No ID?" he mused as they went downstairs and started jogging down the sparsely occupied sidewalk.

"Just the key and five dollars, in case I need money for a bottle of water or something," she confessed.

He sighed, not even showing the strain as they moved quickly along. "One of our forensic reconstruction artists is always lecturing us on carrying identification. She says that it's easier to have something on you that will identify you, so that she doesn't have to take your skull and model clay to do a reconstruction of your face. She helps solve a lot of murder victims' identities, but she has plenty that she can't identify. The faces haunt her, she says."

"I watched a program about forensic reconstruction on educational television two weeks ago."

"I know the one you mean. I saw it, too. That was our artist," he said with traces of pride in his deep voice. "She's a wonder."

"I guess it wouldn't hurt to carry my driver's license around with me," she murmured.

He didn't say another word, but he grinned to himself.

The meeting was a drug task force formed of a special agent from the Houston FBI office, a Houston police detective who specialized in local gangs, a Texas Ranger from Company A, an agent from the U.S. Customs Service and a sheriff's deputy from Harris County who headed her department's drug unit.

They sat down in a conference room in the nearest Houston police station to discuss intelligence.

"We've got a good lead on the new division chief of the Culebra cartel in Mexico," Alexander announced when it was his turn to speak. "We know that he has somebody on his payroll from Ritter Oil Corporation, and that he's funneling drugs through a warehouse where oil regulators and drilling equipment are kept before they're shipped out all over the southwest. Since the parking lot of that warehouse is locked by a key code, the division chief has to have someone on the inside.''

''Do we know how it's being moved and when?'' the FBI agent asked.

Alexander had suspicions, but no concrete evidence. ''Waiting for final word on when. But we do have an informant, a young man who got cold feet and came to U.S. Customs with information about the drug smuggling. I interviewed the young man, with help from Customs,'' he added, nodding with a smile at the petite brunette customs official at the table with them.

''That would be me,'' she said with a grin.

''The informant says that a shipment of processed cocaine is on the way here, one of the biggest in several years. It was shipped from the Guajira Peninsula in Colombia to Central America and transshipped by plane to an isolated landing site in rural Mexico. From there it was carried to a warehouse in Mexico City owned by a subsidiary of an oil company here in Houston. It was reboxed with legitimate oil processing equipment manufactured in Europe, in boxes with false bottoms. It was shipped legally to the oil company's district office in Galveston where it was inspected briefly and passed through customs.''

''The oil company is one that's never been involved in any illegal activity,'' the customs representative said wistfully, ''so the agent didn't look for hidden contraband.''

''To continue,'' Alexander said, ''it's going to be shipped into the Houston warehouse via the Houston Ship Canal as domestic inventory from Galveston.''

''Which means, no more customs inspections,'' the Texas Ranger said.

''Exactly,'' Alexander agreed.

The brunette customs agent shook her head. ''A few shipments get by our inspectors, but not many. We have contacts everywhere, too, and one of those tipped us off about the young man who was willing to inform on the perpetrators of an incoming cocaine shipment," she told the others. "So we saved our bacon."

"You had the contacts I gave you, don't forget," the blond lieutenant of detectives from Houston reminded her with a smile, as she adjusted her collar.

"Do we even have a suspect?" the customs agent asked.

Alexander nodded. "I've got someone on the inside at Ritter Oil, and I'm watching a potential suspect. I don't have enough evidence yet to make an accusation, but I hope to get it, and soon. I'm doing this undercover, so this information is to be kept in this room. I've put it out that we have another company, Thorn Oil, under surveillance, as a cover story. Under no circumstances are any of you to discuss any of this meeting, even with another DEA agent—*especially* with another DEA agent—until further notice. That's essential."

The police lieutenant gave him a pointed look. "Can I ask why?"

"Because the oil corporation isn't the only entity that's harboring an inside informant," Alexander replied flatly. "And that's all I feel comfortable saying."

"You can count on us," the Texas Ranger assured him. "We won't blow your cover. The person you're watching, can you tell us why you're watching him?"

"In order to use that warehouse for storage purposes, the drug lord has to have access to it," Alexander explained. "I'm betting he has some sort of access to the locked gate and that he's paying the night watchman to look the other way."

"That would make sense," the customs agent agreed grimly. "These people know how little law enforcement personnel make. They can easily afford to offer a poorly paid night watchman a six figure 'donation' to just turn his head at the appropriate time."

"That much money would tempt even a law-abiding citizen," Alexander agreed. "But more than that, very often there's a need that compromises integrity. A sheriff in another state had a wife dying of cancer and no insurance. He got fifty thousand dollars for not noticing a shipment of drugs coming into his county.''

"They catch him?'' the policewoman asked.

"Yes. He wasn't very good at being a crook. He confessed, before he was even suspected of being involved.''

"How many people in your agency know about this?'' the deputy sheriff asked Alexander.

"Nobody, at the moment,'' he replied. "It has to stay that way, until we make the bust. I'll depend on all of you to back me up. The mules working for the new drug lord carry automatic weapons and they've killed so many people down in Mexico that they won't hesitate to waste anyone who gets in their way.''

"Good thing the president of Mexico isn't intimidated by them,'' the customs agent said with a grin. "He's done more to attack drug trafficking than any president before him.''

"He's a good egg,'' Alexander agreed. "Let's hope we can shut down this operation before any more kids go down.''

"Amen to that,'' the FBI agent said solemnly.

Alexander showed up at Jodie's office feeling more optimistic than he had for weeks. He was close to an arrest, but the next few days would be critical. After their meeting, the task force had gleaned information from the informant that the drug shipment was coming into Houston the following week. He had to be alert, and he had to spend a lot of time at Jodie's office so that he didn't miss anything.

He took her out to lunch, but he was preoccupied.

"You're onto something,'' she guessed.

He nodded, smiling. "Something big. How would you like to be part of a surveillance?''

"Me? Wow. Can I have a gun?''

He glared at her. "No.''

She shrugged. "Okay. But don't expect me to save your life without one.''

"Not giving you one might save my life," he said pointedly.

She ignored the jibe. "Surveillance?" she prodded. "Of what?"

"You'll find out when we go, and not a word to anybody."

"Okay," she agreed. "How do you do surveillance?"

"We sit in a parked car and drink coffee and wish we were watching television," he said honestly. "It gets incredibly boring. Not so much if we have a companion. That's where you come in," he added with a grin. "We can sit in the car and neck and nobody will guess we're spying on them."

"In a Jaguar," she murmured. "Sure, nobody will notice us in one of those!"

He gave her a long look. "We'll be in a law enforcement vehicle, undercover."

"Right. In a car with government license plates, four antennae and those little round hubcaps..."

"Will you stop?" he groaned.

"Sorry!" She grinned at him over her coffee. "But I like the necking part."

He pursed his lips and gave her a wicked grin. "So do I."

She laughed a little self-consciously and finished her lunch.

They were on the way back to his Jaguar when his DEA agent, Kennedy, drove up. He got out of his car and approached them with a big smile.

"Hi, Cobb! How's it going?" he asked.

"Couldn't be better," Alexander told him complacently. "What's new?"

"Oh, nothing, I'm still working on that smuggling ring." He glanced at Alexander curiously. "Heard anything about a new drug task force?"

"Just rumors," Alexander assured him, and noticed a faint reaction from the other man. "Nothing definite. I'll let you know if I hear anything."

"Thanks." Kennedy shrugged. "There are always rumors."

"Do you have anybody at Thorn Oil, just in case?" Alexander asked him pointedly.

Kennedy cleared his throat and laughed. "Nobody at all. Why?"

"No reason. No reason at all. Enjoy your lunch."

"Sure. I never see you at staff meetings lately," he added. "You got something undercover going on?"

Alexander deliberately tugged Jodie close against his side and gave her a look that could have warmed coffee. "Something," he said, with a smile in Kennedy's direction. "See you."

"Yeah. See you!"

Kennedy walked on toward the restaurant, a little distracted.

Jodie waited until they were closed up in Alexander's car before she spoke. "You didn't tell him anything truthful," she remarked.

"Kennedy's got a loose tongue," he told her as he cranked the car. "You don't tell him anything you don't want repeated. Honest to God, he's worse than Margie!"

"So that's it," she said, laughing. "I just wondered. Isn't it odd that he seems to show up at places where we eat a lot?"

"Plenty of the guys eat where we do," he replied lazily. "We know where the good food is."

"You really do," she had to admit. "That steak was wonderful!"

"Glad you liked it."

"I could cook for you, sometime," she offered, and then flushed at her own boldness.

"After I wind up this case, I'll let you," he said, with a warm smile. "Meanwhile, I've got a lot of work to do."

She wondered about that statement after he left her at the office. She was still puzzling over it when she walked right into Brody when she got off the elevator at her floor.

"Oh, sorry!" she exclaimed, only then noticing that Cara was with him. "Hello," she greeted the woman as she stopped to punch her time card before entering the cubicle area.

Cara wasn't inclined to be polite. She gave Jodie a cold look and turned back to Brody. "I don't understand why you can't do me this one little favor," she muttered. "It isn't as if I ask you often for anything."

"Yes, but dear, it's an odd place to leave your car. There are garages…"

"My car is very expensive," she pointed out, her faint accent growing in intensity, like the anger in her black eyes. "All I require is for you to let me in, only that."

Jodie's ears perked up. She pretended to have trouble getting her card into the time clock, and hummed deliberately to herself, although not so loudly that she couldn't hear what the other two people were saying.

"Company rules…" he began.

"Rules, rules! You are to be an executive, are you not? Do you have to ask permission for such a small thing? Or are you not man enough to make such decisions for yourself?" she added cannily.

"Nice to see you both," Jodie said, and moved away— but not quickly. She fumbled in her purse and walked very slowly as she did. She was curious to know what Cara wanted.

"I suppose I could, just this once," Brody capitulated. "But you know, dear, a warehouse isn't as safe as a parking garage, strictly speaking."

Jodie's heart leaped.

"Yours certainly is, you have an armed guard, do you not? Besides, I work for a subsidiary of Ritter Oil. It is not as if I had no right to leave my car there when I go out of town for the company."

"All right, all right," Brody said. "Tomorrow night then. What time?"

"At six-thirty," she told him. "It will be dark, so you must flash your lights twice to let me know it is you."

They spoke at length, but Jodie was already out of earshot. She'd heard enough of the suspicious conversation to wonder about it. But she was much too cautious to phone Alexander from her work station.

She would have to wait until the end of the day, even if it drove her crazy. Meanwhile she pretended that she'd noticed nothing.

Brody came by her cubicle later that afternoon, just before quitting time, while she was finishing a letter he'd dictated.

"Can I help you?" she asked automatically, and smiled.

He smiled back and looked uncomfortable. "No, not really. I just wondered what you thought about what Cara asked me?"

She gave him a blank look. "What she asked you?" she said. "I'm sorry, I'd just come from having lunch with Alexander." She smiled and sighed and lowered her eyes demurely. "To tell you the truth, I wasn't paying attention to anything except the time clock. What did she ask you?" She opened her eyes very wide and looked blank.

"Never mind. She phoned and made a comment about your being there. It's nothing. Nothing at all."

She smiled up at him. "Did you enjoy the concert that night?"

"Yes, actually I did, despite the fact that Cara went out to the powder room and didn't show up again for an hour." He shook his head. "Honestly, that woman is so mysterious! I never know what she's thinking."

"She's very crisp, isn't she?" she mused. "I mean, she's assertive and aggressive. I guess she's a good marketer."

"She is," he sighed. "At least, I guess she is. I haven't heard much from the big boss about her work. In fact, there was some talk about letting her go a month or two ago, because she lost a contract. Funny, it was one she was supposedly out of town negotiating at the time, but the client said he'd never seen her. Mr. Ritter talked him into staying, but he had words with Cara about the affair.''

"Could that have been when her mother was ill?" she asked.

"Her mother hasn't ever been ill, as far as I know," he murmured. "She did move from Peru to Mexico, but you know about that." He put his hands in his pockets. "She wants me to do something that isn't quite acceptable, and I'm nervous about it. I'm due for a promotion. I don't want to get mixed up in anything the least bit suspicious."

"Why, Brody, what does she want you to do?" she asked innocently.

He glanced at her, started to speak, and then smiled sheepishly. "Well, it's nothing, really. Just a favor." He shrugged. "I'm sure I'm making a big deal out of nothing. You never told me that your boyfriend works for the Drug Enforcement Administration."

"He doesn't advertise it," she stammered. "He does a lot of undercover work at night," she added.

Brody sighed. "I see. Well, I'll let you finish. You and Cobb seem to get along very well," he added.

"I've known him a long time."

"So you have. You've known me a long time, too, though," he added with a slow smile.

"Not really. Only three years."

"Is it? I thought it was longer." He toyed with his tie. "You and Cobb seem to spend a lot of time together."

"Not as much as we'd like," she said, seeing a chance to help Alexander and throw Cara off the track. "And I have a cousin staying with me for a few days, so we spend a lot of time in parked cars necking," she added.

Brody actually flushed. "Oh." He glanced at his watch and grimaced. "I've got a meeting with our vice president in charge of human resources at four, I'd better get going. See you later."

"See you, Brody."

She was very glad that she'd learned to keep what she

knew to herself. What Brody's girlfriend had let slip was potentially explosive information, even if it was only circumstantial. She'd have a lot to tell Alexander when she saw him. Furthermore, she'd already given Alexander some cover by telling Brody about the company car, and the fact that they spent time at night necking in one. He was going to be proud of her, she just knew it!

Eight

The minute she got to her apartment, Jodie grabbed the phone and called Alexander.

"Can you come by right away?" Jodie asked him quickly.

He hesitated. "To your apartment? Why?"

She didn't know if her phone might be bugged. She couldn't risk it. She sighed theatrically. "Because I'm wearing a see-through gown with a row of prophylactics pinned to the hem…!"

"Jodie!" He sounded shocked.

"Listen, I have something to tell you," she said firmly.

He hesitated again and then he groaned. "I can't right now…"

"Who's on the phone, Alex?" came a sultry voice from somewhere in the background.

Jodie didn't need to ask who the voice belonged to. Her heart began to race with impotent fury. "Sorry I interrupted," she said flatly. "I'm sure you and Kirry have lots to talk about."

She hung up and then unplugged the phone. So much for any feeling Alexander had for her. He was already seeing Kirry again, alone and at his apartment. No doubt he was only seeing Jodie to avert suspicion at Ritter Oil. The sweet talk was to allay any suspicion that he was using her. Why hadn't she realized that? The Cobbs were always using her, for one reason or another. She was being a fool again. Despite what he'd said, it was obvious now that Alexander had no interest in her except as a pawn.

She fought down tears and went to her computer. She might as well use some of her expertise to check out Miss Cara Dominguez and see if the woman had a rap sheet. With a silent apology to the local law enforcement departments, she hacked into criminal files and checked her out.

What she found was interesting enough to take her mind off Alexander. It seemed that Cara didn't have a lily-white past at all. In fact, she'd once been arrested for possession with intent to distribute cocaine and had managed to get the charges dropped. Besides that, she had some very odd connections internationally. It was hinted in the records of an international law enforcement agency—whose files gave way to her expertise also—that her uncle was one of the Colombian drug lords. She wondered if Alexander knew that.

Would he care? He was with Kirry. Damn Kirry! She threw a plastic coffee cup at the wall in impotent rage.

Just as it hit, there was a buzz at the intercom. She glowered at it, but the caller was insistent. She pushed the button.

"Yes?" she asked angrily.

"Let me in," Alexander said tersely.

"Are you alone?" she asked with barely contained sarcasm.

"In more ways than you might realize," he replied, his voice deep and subdued. "Let me in, Jodie."

She buzzed him in with helpless reluctance and waited at her opened door for him to come out of the elevator.

He was still in his suit. He looked elegant, expensive, and

very irritated. He walked into the apartment ahead of her and went straight to the kitchen.

"I was going to take you out to eat when Kirry showed up, in tears, and begged to talk to me," he said heavily, examining pots until he found one that contained a nice beef stew. He got a bowl out of the cupboard and proceeded to fill it. "Any corn bread?" he asked wistfully, having sniffed it when he entered the apartment.

"It's only just getting done," she said, reaching around him for a pot holder. She opened the oven and produced a pone of corn bread.

"I'm hungry," he said.

"You're always hungry," she accused, but she was feeling better.

He caught her by the shoulders and pulled her against him, tilting her chin up so that he could see into her mutinous eyes. "I don't want Kirry. I said that, and I meant it."

"Even if you didn't, you couldn't say so," she muttered. "You need me to help you smoke out your drug smuggler."

He scowled. "Do you really think I'm that sort of man?" he asked, and sounded wounded. "I'll admit that Margie and I don't have a good track record with you, but I'd draw the line at pretending an emotion I didn't feel, just to catch crooks."

She shifted restlessly and didn't speak.

He shook his head. "No ego," he mused, watching her. "None at all. You can't see what's right under your nose."

"My chin, and no, I can't see it…"

He chuckled, bending to kiss her briefly, fiercely. "Feed me. Then we might watch television together for a while. I'll be working most evenings during the week, but Friday night we could go see a movie or something."

Her heart skipped. "A movie?"

"Or we could go bowling. I used to like it."

Her mind was spinning. He actually wanted to be with her! But cold reality worked its way between them again. "You haven't asked why I wanted you to come over,'' she began as he started for the table with his bowl of stew.

"No, I haven't. Why?'' he asked, pouring himself a cup of freshly brewed coffee and accepting a dish of corn bread from her.

She put coffee and corn bread at her place at the table and put butter next to it before she sat down and gave Alexander a mischievous smile. ''Cara talked Brody into letting her into the warehouse parking lot after hours tomorrow—about six-thirty in the evening. She said she wanted to park her car there, but it sounded thin to me.''

He caught his breath. ''Jodie, you're a wonder.''

"That's not all,'' she added, sipping coffee and adding more cream to it. ''She was arrested at the age of seventeen for possession with intent to distribute cocaine, and she got off because the charges were dropped. There's an unconfirmed suspicion that her uncle is one of the top Colombian drug lords.''

"Where did you get that?''

She flushed. ''I can't tell you. Sorry.''

"You've hacked into some poor soul's protected files, haven't you?'' he asked sternly, but with twinkling eyes.

"I can't tell you,'' she repeated.

"Okay, I give up.'' He ate stew and corn bread with obvious enthusiasm. ''Then I guess you and I will go on stakeout tomorrow night.''

She smiled smugly. ''Yes, in your boss's borrowed security car, because my cousin is visiting and we can't neck in the apartment. I told Brody that, and he'll tell Cara that, so if we're seen near my office, they won't think a thing of it.''

"Sheer genius,'' he mused, studying her. ''Like I said; you're a natural for law enforcement work. You've got to get your expert computer certification and change professions, Jodie. You're wasted in personnel work.''

"Human resources work,'' she reminded him.

"New label, same job.''

She wrinkled her nose. ''Maybe so.''

They finished their supper in pleasant silence, and she produced a small loaf of pound cake for dessert, with peaches and whipped cream.

"If I ate here often, I'd get fat," he murmured.

She laughed. "Not likely. The cake was made with margarine and reduced-fat milk. I make rolls the same way, except with light olive oil in place of margarine. I don't want clogged arteries before I'm thirty," she added. "And I especially don't want to look like I used to."

He smiled at her warmly. "I like the way you used to look," he said surprisingly. "I like you any way at all, Jodie," he continued softly. "That hasn't changed."

She didn't know whether or not to trust him, and it showed in her face.

He sighed. "It's going to be a long siege," he said enigmatically.

Later, they curled up together on the couch to watch the evening news. There was a brief allusion to a drug smuggling catch by U.S. Customs in the Gulf of Mexico, showing the helicopters they used to catch the fast little boats used in smuggling.

"Those boats go like the wind," Jodie remarked.

He yawned. "They do, indeed. The Colombian National Police busted an operation that was building a submarine for drug smuggling a couple of years ago."

"That's incredible!"

"Some of the smuggling methods are, too, like the tunnel under the Mexican border that was discovered, and having little children swallow balloons filled with cocaine to get them through customs."

"That's barbaric," she said.

He nodded. "It's a profitable business. Greed makes animals of men sometimes, and of women, too."

She cuddled close to him. "It isn't Brody you were after, is it? It's his girlfriend."

He chuckled and wrapped her up in his arms. "You're too sharp for me."

"I learned from an expert," she said, lifting her eyes to his handsome face.

He looked down at her intently for a few seconds before he bent to her mouth and began to kiss her hungrily. Her arms slid up around his neck and she held on for dear life as the kiss devoured her.

Finally he lifted his head and put her away from him, with visible effort. "No more of that tonight," he said huskily.

"Spoilsport," she muttered.

"You're the one with the conscience, honey," he drawled meaningfully. "I'm willing, but you'd never live it down."

"I probably wouldn't," she confessed, but her eyes were misty and wistful.

He pushed back her hair. "Don't look like that," he chided. "It isn't the end of the world. I like you the way you are, Jodie, hang-ups and all. Okay?"

She smiled. "Okay."

"And I'm not sleeping with Kirry!"

The smile grew larger.

He kissed the tip of her nose and got up. "I've got some preparations to make. I'll pick you up tomorrow at 6:20 sharp and we'll park at the warehouse in the undercover car." He hesitated. "It might be better if I had a female agent in the car with me…"

"No, you don't," she said firmly, getting to her feet. "This is my stakeout. You wouldn't even know where to go, or when, if it wasn't for me."

"True. But it could be very dangerous," he added grimly.

"I'm not afraid."

"All right," he said finally. "But you'll stay in the car and out of the line of fire."

"Whatever you say," she agreed at once.

The warehouse parking lot was deserted. The night watchman was visible in the doorway of the warehouse as he opened the door to look out. He did that twice.

"He's in on it," Alexander said coldly, folding Jodie

closer in his arms. "He knows they're coming, and he's watching for them."

"No doubt. Ouch." She reached under her rib cage and touched a small hard object in his coat pocket. "What is that, another gun?"

"Another cell phone," he said. "I have two. I'm leaving one with you, in case you see something I don't while I'm inside," he added, indicating a cell phone he'd placed on the dash.

"You do have backup?" she worried.

"Yes. My whole team. They're well concealed, but they're in place."

"Thank goodness!"

He shifted her in his arms so that he could look to his left at the warehouse while he was apparently kissing her.

"Your heart is going very fast," she murmured under his cool lips.

"Adrenaline," he murmured. "I live on rushes of it. I could never settle for a nine to five desk job."

She smiled against his mouth. "I don't like it much, either."

He nuzzled her cheek with his just as a car drove past them toward the warehouse. It hesitated for a few seconds and then sped on.

"That's Brody's car," she murmured.

"And that one, following it?" he asked, indicating a small red hardtop convertible of some expensive foreign make.

"Cara."

"Amazing that she can afford a Ferrari on thirty-five thousand a year," he mused, "and considering that her mother is poor."

"I was thinking the same thing," she murmured. "Kiss me again."

"No time, honey." He pulled out a two-way radio and spoke into it. "All units, stand by. Target in motion. Repeat, target in motion. Stand by."

Several voices took turns asserting their readiness. Alexander watched as Brody's car suddenly reappeared and he drove away. The gates of the warehouse closed behind his car. He paused near Alexander's car again, and then drove off down the road.

As soon as he was out of sight, a van came into sight. Cara appeared at the parking lot entrance, inserted a card key into the lock, opened the gate and motioned the van forward. The gate didn't close again, but remained open.

Alexander gave it time to get to a loading dock and its occupants to exit the cab and begin opening the rear doors before he took out the walkie-talkie again.

"All units, move in. I repeat, all units, move in. We are good to go!"

He took the cell phone from the dash and put it into Jodie's hands. "You sit right here, with the doors locked, and don't move until I call you on that phone and tell you it's safe. Under no circumstances are you to come into the parking lot. Okay?"

She nodded. "Okay. Don't get shot," she added.

He kissed her. "I don't plan to. See you later."

He got out of the car and went toward a building next door to the warehouse. He was joined by another figure in black. They went down an alley together, out of sight.

Jodie slid down into her seat, so that only her eyes and the top of her head were visible in the concealing darkness, barely lit by a nearby street light. She waited with her heart pounding in her chest for several minutes, until she heard a single gunshot. There was pandemonium in the parking lot. Dark figures ran to and fro. More shots were fired. Her heart jumped into her throat. She gritted her teeth, praying that Alexander wasn't in the line of fire.

Then, suddenly, she spotted him, with another dark figure. They had two people in custody, a man and a woman. They were standing near another loading dock, apparently conversing with the men, when Jodie spotted a solitary figure outside the gates, on the sidewalk, moving toward the open gate. The figure was slight, and it held what looked like an automatic weapon. She'd seen Alexander with one of those, a rare time when he'd been arming himself for a drug bust.

She had a single button to push to make Alexander's cell phone ring, but when she pressed in the number, nothing happened. The phone went dead in her hand.

The man with the machine gun was moving closer to where Alexander and the other man stood with their prisoners, their backs to the gate.

The key was in the car. She only saw one way to save Alexander. She got behind the wheel, cranked the car, put it in gear and aimed it right for the armed man, who was now framed in the gate.

She ran the car at him. He whirled at the sudden noise of an approaching vehicle and started spraying it with machine gun fire.

Jodie ducked down behind the wheel, praying that the weapon didn't have bullets that would penetrate the engine block as easily as they shattered the windshield of the car she was driving. There was a loud thud.

She had to stop the car, because she couldn't see where she was going, but the windshield didn't catch any more bullets. Now she heard gunshots that didn't sound like that of the small automatic her assailant was carrying.

The door of the car was suddenly jerked open, and she looked up, wide-eyed and panicky, into Alexander's white face.

"Jodie!" he ground out. "Put the car out of gear!"

She put it into Park with trembling hands and cut off the ignition.

Alexander dragged her out of it and began going over her with his hands, feeling for blood. She was covered with little shards of glass. Her face was bleeding. So were her hands. She'd put them over her face the instant the man started firing.

Slowly she became aware that Alexander's hands had a faint tremor as they searched her body.

"I'm okay," she said in a thin voice. "Are you?"

"Yes."

But he was rattled, and it showed.

"He was going to shoot you in the back," she began.

"I told you to use the cell phone!" he raged.

"It wouldn't work!"

He reached beside her and picked it up. His eyes closed. The battery was dead.

"And you stop yelling at me," she raged back at him. "I couldn't let him kill you!"

He caught her up in his arms, bruisingly close, and kissed her furiously. Then he just held her, rocked her, riveted her to his hard body with fierce hunger. "You crazy woman," he bit off at her ear. "You brave, crazy, wonderful woman!"

She held him, too, content now, safe now. Her eyes closed. It was over, and he was alive. Thank God.

He let her go reluctantly as two other men came up, giving them curious looks.

"She's all right," he told them, moving back a little. "Just a few cuts from the broken windshield."

"That was one of the bravest things I've ever seen a woman do," one of the men, an older man with jet black hair and eyes, murmured. "She drove right into the bullets."

"We'd be dead if she hadn't," the other man, equally dark-haired and dark-eyed, said with a grin. "Thanks!"

"You're welcome," she said with a sheepish smile as she moved closer to Alexander.

"The car's a total write-off," the older man mused.

"Like you've never totaled a car in a gun battle, Hunter," Alexander said with a chuckle.

The other man shrugged. "Maybe one or two. What the hell. The government has all that money we confiscate from drug smugglers to replace cars. You might ask your boss for that cute little Ferrari, Cobb."

"I already drive a Jaguar," he said, laughing. "With all due respect to Ferrari, I wouldn't trade it for anything else."

"I helped make the bust," Jodie complained. "They should give it to me!"

"I wouldn't be too optimistic about that," came a droll remark from the second of the two men. "I think Cobb's boss is partial to Italian sports cars, and he can't afford a Ferrari on his salary."

"Darn," Jodie said on a sigh. "Just my luck."

"You should take her to the hospital and have her checked," Hunter told Alexander. "She's bleeding."

"She could be dead, pulling a stunt like that," Alexander said with renewed anger as he looked at her.

"That's no way to thank a person for saving your life," Jodie pointed out, still riding an adrenaline high.

"You're probably right, but you took a chance you shouldn't have," Alexander said grimly. "Come on. We'll hitch a ride with one of my men."

"Your car might still be drivable," she said, looking at it. The windshield was shattered but still clinging to the frame. She winced. "Or maybe not."

"Maybe not," Alexander agreed. "See you, Hunter. Lane. Thanks for the help."

"Any time," Hunter replied, and they walked back toward the warehouse with Alexander and Jodie. "Colby Lane was in town overnight and bored to death, so I brought him along for the fun."

"Fun!" Jodie exclaimed.

The older man chuckled. "He leads a mundane nine-to-five life. I've talked him into giving it up for international intrigue at Ritter Oil."

"I was just convinced," the man named Colby Lane said with a chuckle.

"Good. Tomorrow you can tell Ritter you'll take the job. See you, Cobb."

"Sure thing."

"Who were those two guys you were talking to?" Jodie asked when the hospital had treated her cuts and Alexander had commandeered another car to take her home in.

"Phillip Hunter and Colby Lane. You've surely heard of Hunter."

"He's a local legend," she replied with a smile, "but I didn't recognize him in that black garb. He's our security chief."

"Lane's doing the same job for the Hutton corporation, but they're moving overseas and he isn't keen on going. So Hunter's trying to get him to come down here as his second-in-command at Ritter Oil."

"Why was Mr. Lane here tonight?"

"Probably just as Phillip said—Lane just got into town, and Hunter volunteered him to help out. He and Hunter are old friends."

"He looked very dark," she commented.

"They're both Apache," he said easily. "Hunter's married to a knockout blond geologist who works for Ritter. They have a young daughter. Lane's not married."

"They seem to know each other very well."

Alexander chuckled. "They have similar backgrounds in black ops. Highest level covert operations," he clarified. "They used to work for the 'company.'"

"Not Ritter's company," she guessed.

He chuckled. "No. Not Ritter's."

"Did you arrest Cara?"

"Our Houston policewoman made the actual arrest, so that Cara wouldn't know I headed the operation. Cara was arrested along with two men she swears she doesn't know," he replied. "We had probable cause to do a search anyway, but I had a search warrant in my pocket, and I had to use it. We found enough cocaine in there to get a city high, and the two men in the truck had some on them."

"How about Cara?"

He sighed. "She was clean. Now we have to connect her." He glanced at her apologetically. "That will mean getting your boss involved. However innocently, he did let her into a locked parking lot."

"But wasn't the night watchman working for them? Couldn't he have let them in?"

"He could have. But I have a feeling Cara wanted Brody involved, so that he'd be willing to do what she asked so that she didn't give him away for breaking a strict company rule," he replied. He saw her expression and he smiled. "Don't worry. I won't let him be prosecuted."

"Thanks, Alexander."

He moved closer and studied the cuts on her face and arms. He winced. "You poor baby," he said gently. "I wouldn't have had you hurt for the world."

"You'd have been dead if I hadn't done something," she said matter-of-factly. "The phone went dead and you were too far away to hear me if I yelled. Besides," she added with a chuckle, "I hate going to funerals."

"Me, too." He swept her close and kissed the breath out of her. "I have to go back to work, tie up loose ends. You'll need to come with me to the nearest police precinct and give a statement, as well. You're a material witness." He hesitated, frowning.

"What's wrong?" she asked.

"Cara knows who you are, and she can find out where you live," he said. "She's a vengeful witch. Chances are very good that she's going to make bond. I'm going to arrange some security for you."

"Do you think that's necessary?"

He nodded grimly. "I'm afraid it is. Would you like to know the estimated street value of the cocaine we've just confiscated?"

"Yes."

"From thirty to thirty-five million dollars."

She whistled softly. "Now I understand why they're willing to kill people. And that's just one shipment, right?"

"Just one, although it's unusually large. There's another drug smuggling investigation going on right now involving Colombian rebels, but I can't tell you about that one. It's top secret." He smoothed back her hair and looked at her as if she were a treasure trove. "Thank you for what you did," he said after a minute. "Even if it was crazy, it saved my life, not to mention Lane's and Hunter's."

She reached up a soft hand to smooth over his cheek, where it was slightly rough from a day's growth of beard. "You're welcome. But you would have done the same thing, if it had been me, or Margie."

"Yes, I'm afraid I would have."

He still looked worried. She tugged his head down and kissed him warmly, her body exploding inside when he half-lifted her against him and kissed her until her lips were sore.

"I could have lost you tonight," he said curtly.

"Oh, I'm a weed," she murmured into his throat. "We're very hard to uproot."

His arms tightened. "Just the same, you watch your back. If Brody asks what you know, and he will, you tell him nothing," he added. "You were with me when things started happening, you didn't even know what was going on until bullets started flying. Right?"

"Right."

He sighed heavily and kissed her one last time before he put her back onto her own feet. "I've got to go help the guys with the paperwork," he said reluctantly. "I'd much rather be with you. For tonight, lock your doors and keep your freedom phone handy. If you need me, I'm a phone call away. Tomorrow, you'll have security."

"I've got a nice big heavy flashlight like the one you keep in your car," she told him pertly. "If anybody tries to get in, they'll get a headache."

Unless they had guns, he added silently, but he didn't say that. "Don't be overconfident," he cautioned. "Never underestimate the enemy."

She saluted him.

He tugged her face up and kissed her, hard. "Incorrigible," he pronounced her. "But I can't imagine life without you, so be cautious!"

"I will. I promise. You have to promise, too," she added.

He gave her a warm smile. "Oh, I have my eye on the future, too," he assured her. "I don't plan to cash in my chips right now. I'll phone you tomorrow."

"Okay. Good night."

"Good night. Lock this," he added when he went out the door.

She did, loudly, and heard him chuckle as he went down the hall. Once he was gone, she sank down into her single easy chair and shivered as she recalled the feverish events of the evening. She was alive. He was alive. But she could still hear the bullets, feel the shattering of the windshield followed by dozens of tiny, painful cuts on her skin even through the sweater she'd been wearing. It was amazing that she'd come out of a firefight with so few wounds.

She went to bed, but she didn't sleep well. Alexander phoned very early the next morning to check on her and tell her that he'd see her at lunch.

She put on her coat and went to work, prepared for some comments from her co-workers, despite the fact that she was wearing a long-sleeved, high-necked blouse. Nothing was going to hide the tiny cuts that lined her cheeks and chin. She knew better than to mention where she got them, so she made up a nasty fall down the steps at her apartment building.

It worked with everyone except Brody. He came in as soon as she'd turned on her computer, looking worried and sad.

"Are you all right?" he asked abruptly. "I was worried sick all night."

Her wide-eyed look wasn't feigned. "How did you know?" she faltered.

"I had to go and bail Cara out of jail early this morning," he said coolly. "She's been accused of drug smuggling, can you imagine it? She was only parking her car when those lunatics opened fire!"

Nine

Remembering what Alexander had cautioned her about, Jodie managed not to laugh out loud at Brody. How could a man be so naive?

"Drug smuggling?" she exclaimed, playing her part. "Cara?"

"That's what they said," he replied. "Apparently some of Ritter's security people had the warehouse staked out. When the shooting started, they returned fire, and I guess they called in the police. In fact, your friend Cobb was there when they arrested Cara."

"Yes, I know. He heard the shooting and walked right into it," she said, choosing her words carefully. "We were parked across the street…"

"I saw you when I let Cara into the parking lot," Brody said, embarrassed. "One of the gang came in with a machine gun and they say you aimed Cobb's car right at him and drove into a hail of bullets to save his life. I guess you really do care about him."

"Yes," she confessed. "I do."

"It was a courageous thing to do. Cara said you must be crazy about the guy to do that."

"Poor Cara," she replied, sidestepping the question. "I'm so sorry for the trouble she's in. Why in the world do they think she was involved? She was just in the wrong place at the wrong time."

Brody seemed to relax. "That's what Cara said. Uh, Cobb wasn't in on that bust deliberately, was he?"

"We were in a parked car outside the gate. We didn't know about any bust," she replied.

"So that's why he was there," he murmured absently, nodding. "I thought it must be something of the sort. Cara didn't know any of the others, but one was a female detective and another was a female deputy sheriff. The policewoman arrested her."

"Don't mess with Texas women," Jodie said, adding on a word to the well-known Texas motto.

He laughed. "So it seems. Uh, there was supposed to be a DEA agent there as well. Cara has a friend who works out of the Houston office, but he's been out of town a lot lately and she hasn't been able to contact him. She says it's funny, but he seems to actually be avoiding her." He gave her an odd look. "I gather that it wasn't Cobb. But do you know anything about who the agent was?"

"No," she said straight-faced. "And Alexander didn't mention it, either. He tells me everything, so I'd know if it was him."

"I see."

She wondered if Cara's friend at the DEA was named Kennedy, but she pretended to know nothing. "What's Cara going to do?" she asked, sounding concerned.

"Get a good lawyer, I suppose," he said heavily.

"I wish her well. I'm so sorry, Brody."

He sighed heavily. "I seem to have a knack for getting myself into tight corners, but I think Cara's easily superior to me in that respect. Well, I'd better phone the attorney whose name she gave me. You're sure you're all right?''

"I'm fine, Brody, honestly." She smiled at him.

He smiled back. "See you."

She watched him go with relief. She'd been improvising widely to make sure he didn't connect Alexander with the surveillance of the warehouse.

When Alexander phoned her, she arranged to meet him briefly at the café downstairs for coffee. He was pushed for time, having been in meetings with his drug unit most of the day planning strategy.

"You've become a local legend," he told her with a mischievous smile when they were drinking cappuccino.

"Me?" she exclaimed.

He grinned at her. "The oil clerk who drove through a hail of bullets to save her lover."

She flushed and glared at him. "Point one, I am not a clerk, I'm an administrative assistant. And point two, I am not your—!"

"I didn't say I started the rumor." He chuckled. His eyes became solemn as he studied her across the table. "But the part about being a heroine, I endorse enthusiastically. That being said, would you like to add to your legend?"

She paid attention. "Are you kidding? What do you want me to do?"

"Cara made bond this afternoon," he told her. "We've got a tail on her, but she's sure to suspect that. She'll make contact with one of her subordinates, in some public place where she thinks we won't be able to tape her. When she does, I'm going to want you to accidentally happen upon her and plant a microphone under her table."

"Wow! 'Jane Bond' stuff!"

"Jane?" he wondered.

She shrugged. "A woman named James would be a novelty."

"Point taken. Are you game?"

"Of course. But why wouldn't you let one of your own people do it?"

His face was revealing. "The last hearty professional we sent to do that little task stumbled over his own feet and pitched headfirst into the table our target was occupying. In the process he overturned a carafe of scalding coffee, also on the target, who had to be taken to the hospital for treatment."

"What if I do the same thing?" she worried.

He smiled gently. "You don't have a clumsy bone in your body, Jodie. But even if you did, Cara knows you. She might suspect me, but she won't suspect you."

"When do I start?"

"I'll let you know," he promised. "In the meantime, keep your eyes and ears open, and don't..."

Just as he spoke, there was a commotion outside the coffee shop. A young woman with long blond hair was trailing away a dark-haired little girl with a shocked face. Behind them, one of the men Jodie recognized from the drug bust—one of Alexander's friends—was waving his arms and talking loudly in a language Jodie had never heard before, his expression furious.

The trio passed out of sight, but not before Jodie finally recognized the man Alexander had called Colby Lane.

"What in the world...?" she wondered.

"It's a long story," Alexander told her. "And I'm not at liberty to repeat it. Let's just say that Colby has been rather suddenly introduced to a previously unknown member of his family."

"Was he cursing—and in what language?" she persisted.

"You can't curse in Apache," he assured her. "It's like Japanese—if you really want to tick somebody off in Japan, you say something about their mother's belly button. But giving them the finger doesn't have any meaning."

"Really?" She was fascinated.

He chuckled. "Anyway, Native Americans—whose origins are also suspected to be Asian—don't use curse words in their own language.''

"Mr. Lane looked very upset. And I thought I recognized that blond woman. She was transferred here from their Arizona office just a few weeks ago. She has a little girl, about the same age as Mr. Hunter's daughter.''

"Let it lie,'' Alexander advised. "We have problems of our own. I meant to mention that we've located one of Cara's known associates serving as a waiter in a little coffeehouse off Alameda called 'The Beat'…''

"I go there!'' she exclaimed. "I go there a lot! You can get all sorts of fancy coffees and it's like a retro 'beatnik' joint. They play bongos and wear all black and customers get up and read their poetry.'' She flushed. "I actually did that myself, just last week.''

He was impressed. "You, getting up in front of people to read poetry? I didn't know you still wrote poetry, Jodie.''

"It's very personal stuff,'' she said, uneasy.

He began to look arrogant. "About me?''

She glared at him. "At the time I wrote it, you were my least favorite person on the planet,'' she informed him.

"Ouch!'' He was thinking again. "But if they already know you there, it's even less of a stretch if you show up when Cara does—assuming she even uses the café for her purposes. We'll have to wait and see. I don't expect her to arrange a rendezvous with a colleague just to suit me.''

"Nice of you,'' she teased.

He chuckled. He reached across the table and linked her fingers with his. His green eyes probed hers for a long moment. "Those cuts are noticeable on your face,'' he said quietly. "Do they hurt?''

"Not nearly as much as having you gunned down in front of me would have,'' she replied.

His eyes began to glitter with feeling. His fingers contracted around hers. "Which is just how I felt when I saw those bullets slamming into the windshield of my car, with you at the wheel.''

Her breath caught. He'd never admitted so much in the past.

He laughed self-consciously and released her hand. "We're getting morose. A miss is as good as a mile, and I still have paperwork to finish that I haven't even started on." He glanced at his watch. "I can't promise anything, but we might see a movie this weekend."

"That would be nice," she said. "You'll let me know...?"

He frowned. "I don't like putting you in the line of fire a second time."

"I go to the coffee shop all the time," she reminded him. "I'm not risking anything." Except my heart, again, she thought.

He sighed. "I suppose so. Just the same, don't let down your guard. I hope you can tell if someone's tailing you?"

"I get goose bumps on the back of my neck," she assured him. "I'll be careful. You do the same," she added firmly.

He smiled gently. "I'll do my best."

Having settled down with a good book the following day after a sandwich and soup supper, it was a surprise to have Alexander phone her and ask her to go down to the coffee shop on the double.

"I'll meet you in the parking lot with the equipment," he said. "Get a cab and have it drop you off. I'll reimburse you. Hurry, Jodie."

"Okay. I'm on my way," she promised, lounging in pajamas and a robe.

She dashed into the bedroom, threw on a long black velvet skirt, a black sweater, loafers, and ran a quick brush through her loosed hair before perching her little black beret on top of her head. She grabbed her coat and rushed out the door, barely pausing except to lock it. She was at the elevator before she remembered her purse, lying on the couch. She dashed back to get it, cursing her own lack of preparedness in an emergency.

* * *

Minutes later, she got out of the cab at the side door of The Beat coffeehouse.

Alexander waited by his company car while Jodie paid the cab. She joined him, careful to notice that she was unobserved.

He straightened at her approach. In the well-lit parking lot, she could see his eyes. They were troubled.

"I'm here," she said, just for something to say. "What do you want me to do?"

"I'm not sure I want you to do anything," he said honestly. "This is dangerous. Right now, she has no reason to suspect you. But if you bug her table for me, and she finds out that you did, your life could be in danger."

"Hey, listen, you were the one who told me about the little boys being shot by her henchmen," she reminded him. "I know the risk, Alexander. I'm willing to take it."

"Your knees are knocking," he murmured.

She laughed, a little unsteadily. "I guess they are. And my heart's pounding. But I'm still willing to do it. Now what exactly do I do?"

He opened the passenger door for her. "Get in. I'll brief you."

"Is she here?" she asked when they were inside.

"Yes. She's at the table nearest the kitchen door, at the left side of the stage. Here." He handed her a fountain pen.

"No, thanks," she said, waving it away. "I've got two in my purse…"

He opened her hand and placed the capped pen in it. She looked at it, surprised by its heaviness. "It's a miniature receiver," he told her. He produced a small black box with an antenna, and what looked like an earplug with a tiny wire sticking out the fat end. "The box is a receiver, linked to a tape recorder. The earplug is also a receiver, which we use when we're in close quarters and don't want to attract attention. Since the box has a range of several hundred feet, I'll be able to hear what comes into the pen from my car."

"Do you want me to accidentally leave the pen on her table?"

"I want you to accidentally drop it under her table," he said. "If she sees it, the game's up. We're not the only people who deal in counterespionage."

She sucked in her breath. She was getting the picture. Cara was no dummy. "Okay. I'll lean over her table to say hello and make sure I put it where she won't feel it with her foot. How will that do?"

"Yes. But you have to make sure she doesn't see you do it."

"I'll be very careful."

He was having second thoughts. She was brave, but courage wasn't the only requirement for such an assignment. He remembered her driving through gunfire to save him. She could have died then. He'd thought about little else, and he hadn't slept well. Jodie was like a silver thread that ran through his life. In recent weeks, he'd been considering, seriously, how hard it would be to go on without her. He wasn't certain that he could.

"Why are you watching me like that?" she wanted to know, smiling curiously. "I'm not a dummy. I won't let you down, honest."

"It wasn't that." He closed her fingers around the pen. "Are you sure you want to go through with this?"

"Very sure."

"Okay." He hesitated. "What are you going to give as an excuse for being there?"

She gave him a bright smile. "I phoned Johnny—the owner—earlier, just after you phoned me and told him I had a new poem, but I was a little nervous about getting up in front of a big crowd. He said there was only a small crowd and I'd do fine."

"You improvise very well."

"I've been observing you for years," she teased. "But it's true. I do have a poem to read, which should throw Cara off the track."

He tugged her chin up and kissed her, hard. "You're going to be fine."

She smiled at him. "Which one of us are you supposed to be reassuring?"

"Both of us," he said tenderly. He kissed her again. "Go to work."

"What do I do when she leaves?"

"Get a cab back to your apartment. I'll meet you there. If anything goes wrong," he added firmly, "or if she acts suspicious, you stay in the coffeehouse and phone my cell number. Got that?" He handed her a card with his mobile phone number on it.

"I've got it."

She opened the car door and stepped out into the cool night air. With a subdued wave, she turned, pulled her coat closer around her and walked purposefully toward the coffeehouse. What she didn't tell Alexander was that her new poem was about him.

She didn't look around noticeably as she made her way through the sparse crowd to the table where she usually sat on her evenings here. She held the pen carefully in her hand, behind a long fold of her coat. As she pulled out a chair at the table, her eyes swept the room and she spotted Cara at a table with another woman. She smiled and Cara frowned.

Uh-oh, she thought, but she pinned the smile firmly to her face and moved to Cara's table.

"I thought it was you," she said cheerily. "I didn't know you ever came here! Brody never mentioned it to me."

Cara gave her a very suspicious look. "This is not your normal evening entertainment, surely?"

"But I come here all the time," Jodie replied honestly. "Johnny's one of my fans."

"Fans." Cara turned the word over on her tongue as if she'd never heard it.

"Aficionados," Jodie persisted. "I write poetry."

"You?"

The other woman made it sound like an insult. The woman

beside her, an even older woman with a face like plate steel, only looked.

Jodie felt a chill of fear and worked to hide it. Her palm sweated against the weight of the pen hidden in her hand. As she hesitated, Johnny came walking over in his apron.

"Hey, Jodie!" he greeted. "Now don't worry, there's only these two unfamiliar ladies in here, you know everybody else. You just get up there and give it your best. It'll be great!"

"Johnny, you make me feel so much better," she told the man.

"These ladies friends of yours?" he asked, noticing them—especially Cara—with interested dark eyes.

"Cara's boyfriend is my boss at work," Jodie said.

"Lucky boyfriend," Johnny murmured, his voice dropping an octave.

Cara relaxed and smiled. "I am Cara Dominguez," she introduced herself. "This is my *amiga,* Chiva."

Johnny leaned over the table to shake hands and Jodie pretended to be overbalanced by him. In the process of righting herself and accepting his apology, she managed to let the pen drop under the table where it lay unnoticed several inches from either woman's foot.

"Sorry, Jodie, meeting two such lovely ladies made me clumsy." He chuckled.

She grinned at him. "No harm done. I'm not hurt."

"Okay, then, you go get on that stage. Want your usual French Vanilla cappuccino?"

"You bet. Make it a large one, with a croissant, please."

"It'll be on the house," he informed her. "That's incentive for you."

"Gee, thanks!" she exclaimed.

"My treat. Nice to meet you ladies."

"It is for us the same," Cara purred. She glanced at Jodie, much less suspicious now. "So you write poetry. I will enjoy listening to it."

Jodie chuckled. "I'm not great, but people here are generally kind. Good to see you."

Cara shrugged. The other woman said nothing.

Jodie pulled off her coat and went up onto the stage, trying to ignore her shaking knees. Meanwhile she prayed that Alexander could hear what the two women were saying. Because the minute she pulled the microphone closer, introduced herself, and pulled out the folded sheet of paper that contained her poem, Cara leaned toward the other woman and started speaking urgently.

Probably exchanging fashion tips, or some such thing, Jodie thought dismally, but she smiled at the crowd, unfolded the paper, and began to read.

Apparently her efforts weren't too bad, because the small crowd paid attention to every line of the poem. And when she finished reading it, there was enthusiastic applause.

Cara and her friend, however, were much too intent on conversation to pay Jodie any attention. She went back to her seat, ate her croissant and drank her cappuccino with her back to the table where Cara and the other woman were sitting, just to make sure they knew she wasn't watching them.

A few minutes later, Johnny came by her table and patted her on the back. "That was some good work, girl!" he exclaimed. "I'm sorry your friend didn't seem to care enough to listen to it."

"She's not into poetry," she confided.

"I guess not. She and that odd-looking friend of hers didn't even finish their coffee."

"They're gone?" she asked without turning.

He nodded. "About five minutes ago, I guess. No great loss, if you ask me."

"Thanks for the treat, Johnny, and for the encouragement," she added.

"Um, I sure would like to have a copy of that poem."

Her eyes widened. "You would? Honestly?"

He shrugged. "It was really good. I know this guy. He works for a small press. They publish poetry. I'd like to show it to him. If you don't mind."

"Mind!" She handed him the folded paper. "I don't mind! Thanks, Johnny!"

"No problem. I'll be in touch." He turned, and then paused, digging into his apron pocket. "Say, is this yours? I'm afraid I may have stepped on it. It was under that table where your friend was sitting."

"Yes, it's mine," she said, taking it from him. "Thanks a lot."

He winced. "If I broke it, I'll buy you a new one, okay?"

"It's just a pen," she said with determined carelessness. "No problem."

"You wait, I'll call you a cab."

"That would be great!"

She settled back to wait, her head full of hopeful success, and not only for Alexander.

"Is it broken?" she asked Alexander when she was back at her apartment, and he was examining his listening device.

"I'll have the lab guys check it out," he told her.

"Could you hear anything?"

He grinned hugely. "Not only did I hear plenty, I taped it. We've got a lead we'd never have had without you. There's just one bad thing."

"Oh?"

"Cara thinks your poetry stinks," he said with a twinkle in his eyes.

"She can think what she likes, but Johnny's showing it to a publisher friend of his. He thought it was wonderful."

He searched her face. "So did I, Jodie."

She felt a little nervous, but certainly he couldn't have known that he was the subject of it, so she just thanked him offhandedly.

"Now I'm sure I'm cut out for espionage," she murmured.

"You may be, but I don't know if my nerves could take it."

"You thought I'd mess up," she guessed.

He shook his head, holding her hand firmly in his. "It

wasn't that. I don't like having you at risk, Jodie. I don't want you on the firing line ever again, even if you did save my skin last night.''

She searched his green eyes hungrily. ''I wouldn't want to live in a world that didn't contain you, too,'' she said. Then, backtracking out of embarrassment, she laughed and added, ''I really couldn't live without the aggravation.''

He laughed, as he was meant to. ''Same here.'' He checked his watch. ''I don't want to go,'' he said unexpectedly, ''but I've got to get back to my office and go through this tape. Tomorrow, I'll be in conference with my drug unit. You pretend that nothing at all was amiss, except you saw Cara at your favorite evening haunt. Right?''

''Right,'' she assured him.

''I'll call you.''

''That's what they all say,'' she said dryly.

He paused at the door and looked at her. ''Who?''

''Excuse me?''

''Who else is promising to call you?'' he persisted.

''The president, for my advice on his foreign policy, of course,'' she informed him.

He laughed warmly. ''Incorrigible,'' he said to himself, winked at her, and let himself out. ''Lock it!'' he called through it.

She snicked the lock audibly and heard him chuckle again. She leaned back against the door with a relieved sigh. It was over. She'd done what he asked her, and she hadn't fouled it up. Most of all, he was pleased with her.

She was amazed at the smiles she got from him in recent weeks. He'd always been reserved, taciturn, with most other people. But he enjoyed her company and it showed.

The next day, Brody seemed very preoccupied. She took dictation, which he gave haltingly, and almost absently.

''Are you okay?'' she wanted to know.

He moved restively around his office. He turned to stare

at her curiously. "Are you involved in some sort of top secret operation or something?"

Her eyes popped. "Pardon?"

He cleared his throat. "I know you were at a coffeehouse where Cara went last night with a friend. I wondered if you were spying on her…?"

"I go to The Beat all the time, Brody," she told him, surprised. "Alexander's idea of an evening out is a concert or the theater, but my tastes run to bad poetry and bongos. I've been going there for weeks. It's no secret. The owner knows me very well."

He relaxed suddenly and smiled. "Thank goodness! That's what Cara told me, of course, but it seemed odd that you'd be there when she was. I mean, like you and your boyfriend showed up at the restaurant where we had lunch that day, and then you were at the concert, too. And your friend does work for the DEA…"

"Coincidences," she said lazily. "That's all. Unless you think I've been following you," she added with deliberate emphasis, demurely lowering her eyes.

There was a long, shocked pause. "Why, I never thought… considered…really?"

She crossed her legs. "I think you're very nice, Brody, and Cara treats you like a pet dog," she said with appropriate indignation. She peered at him covertly. "You're too good for her."

He was obviously embarrassed, flattered, and uncertain. "My gosh…I'm sorry, but I knew about Cobb working for the DEA, and then the drug bust came so unexpectedly. Well, it seemed logical that he might be spying on Cara with your help…"

"I never dreamed that I looked like a secret agent!" she exclaimed, and then she chuckled. "As if Alexander would ever trust me with something so dangerous," she added, lowering her eyes so that he couldn't see them.

He sighed. "Forgive me. I've had these crazy theories. Cara thought I was nuts, especially after she told me the owner of that coffeehouse knew you very well and encouraged you to read...well...very bad poetry. She thought maybe he had a case on you.''

"It was not bad poetry! And he had a case on Cara, not me,'' she replied with just the right amount of pique.

"Did he!''

"I told him she was your girlfriend, don't worry,'' she said, and managed to sound regretful.

"Jodie, I'm very flattered,'' he faltered.

She held up a hand. "Let's not talk about it, Brody, okay? You just dictate, and I'll write.''

He sighed, studying her closely. After a minute, he shrugged, and began dictating. This time, he was concise and relaxed. Jodie felt like collapsing with relief, herself. It had been a close call, and not even because Cara was suspicious. It was Brody who seemed to sense problems.

Ten

It was a relief that Cara didn't suspect Jodie of spying, but it was worrying that Brody did. He was an intelligent man, and it wouldn't be easy to fool him. She'd have to mention that to Alexander when she saw him.

He came by the apartment that evening, soon after Jodie got home from work, taciturn and worried.

"Something happened," she guessed uneasily.

He nodded. "Got any coffee?"

"Sure. Come on into the kitchen."

He sat down and she poured him a cup from the pot full she'd just made. He sipped it and studied her across the table. "Kennedy came back to town today. He's Cara's contact."

"Oh, dear," she murmured, sensing that something was very wrong.

He nodded. "I called him into my office and told him I was firing him, and why. I have sworn statements from two witnesses who are willing to testify against him in return for reduced sentences." He sighed. "He said that he knew you were involved, that you'd helped me finger Cara, and that he'd tell her if I didn't back down.''

"Don't feel bad about it,'' she said, mentally panicking while trying not to show it. "You couldn't let him stay, after what he did.''

He looked at her blankly. "You're a constant surprise to me, Jodie. How did you know I wouldn't back down?''

She smiled gently. "You wouldn't be Alexander if you let people bluff you.''

"Yes, baby, but he's not bluffing.''

The endearment caught her off guard, made her feel warm inside, warm all over. "So what do we do now?'' she asked, a little disconcerted.

He noted her warm color and smiled tenderly. "You go live with Margie for a few days, until I wrap up this case. Our cover's blown now for sure.''

"Margie can shoot a gun, but she's not all that great at it, Alexander,'' she pointed out.

"Our foreman, Chayce, is, and so is cousin Derek,'' he replied. "He was involved in national security work when he was just out of college. He's a dead shot, and he'll be bringing his two brothers with him.'' He chuckled. "Funny. All I had to say was that Margie might be in danger along with you, and he volunteered at once.''

"You don't like him,'' she recalled.

He shrugged. "I don't like the idea of Margie getting involved with a cousin. But Derek seemed to know that, too, and he told me something I didn't know before when I phoned him. He wasn't my uncle's son. His mother had an affair with an old beau and he was the result. It was a family secret until last night. Which means,'' he added, "that he's only related to us by marriage, not by blood.''

"He told you himself?'' she asked.

"He told me. Apparently, he told you, too. But he didn't tell Margie.''

"Have you?'' she wondered.

"That's for him to do,'' he replied. "I've interfered

enough." He checked his watch. "I've got to go. I have a man watching the apartment," he added. "The one I told you about. But tomorrow, you tell Brody you're taking a few days off to look after a sick relative and you go to Margie. Got that?"

"But my job…!"

"It's your life!" he shot back, eyes blazing. "This is no game. These people will kill you as surely as they killed those children. I am not going to watch you die, Jodie. Least of all for something I got you into!"

She caught her breath. This was far more serious than she'd realized.

"I told you," he emphasized, "Cara knows you were involved. The secret's out. You leave town. Period."

She stared at him and knew she was trapped. Her job was going to be an afterthought. They'd fire her. She was even afraid to take a day off when she was sick, because the company policy in her department was so strict.

"If you lose that job, it will be a blessing," Alexander told her flatly. "You're too good to waste your life taking somebody else's dictation. When this is over, I'll help you find something better. I'll take you to classes so that you can get your expert computer certification, then I'll get an employment agency busy to find you a better job."

That was a little disappointing. Obviously he didn't have a future with her in mind, or he wouldn't be interested in getting her a job.

He leaned back in his chair, sipping coffee. "Although," he added suddenly, his gaze intent, "there might be an alternative."

"An alternative?"

"We'll talk about that later," he said. He finished his coffee. "I have to go."

She got up and walked him to the door. "You be careful, too," she chided.

He opened his jacket and indicated the .45 automatic in its hand-tooled leather holster.

"It won't shoot itself," she reminded him pertly.

He chuckled, drew her into his arms, and kissed her until her young body ached with deep, secret longings.

He lifted his head finally, and he wasn't breathing normally. She felt the intensity of his gaze all the way to her toes as he looked at her. "All these years," he murmured, "and I wasted them sniping at you."

"You seemed to enjoy it at the time," she remarked absently, watching his mouth hover over hers.

"I didn't want a marriage like my parents had. I played the field, to keep women from getting serious about me," he confessed. He traced her upper lip with his mouth, with breathless tenderness. "Especially you," he added roughly. "No one else posed the threat you did, with your old-fashioned ideals and your sterling character. But I couldn't let you see how attracted to you I was. I did a pretty good job. And then you had too much champagne at a party and did what I'd been afraid you'd do since you graduated from high school."

"You were afraid…?"

He nibbled her upper lip. "I knew that if you ever got close, I'd never be able to let you go," he whispered sensuously. "What I spouted to Margie was a lot of hot air. I ached from head to toe after what we did together. I wanted you so badly, honey. I didn't sleep all night thinking about how easy it would have been."

"I didn't sleep thinking that you hated me," she confessed.

He sighed regretfully. "I didn't know you'd overheard me, but I said enough when I left you at your bedroom. I felt guilty when I went downstairs and saw your face. You were shamed and humiliated, and it was my fault. I only wanted a chance to make amends, but you started backing away and you wouldn't stop. That was when I knew what a mistake I'd made."

She toyed with his shirt button. "And then you needed help to catch a drug smuggler," she mused.

There was a pause long enough to make her look up. "You're good, Jodie, and I did need somebody out of the agency to dig out that information for me. But…"

"But?"

He smiled sheepishly. "Houston P.D. owes me a favor. They'd have been glad to get the information for me. So would the Texas Rangers, or the county sheriff."

"Then why did you ask me to do it?" she exclaimed.

His hands went to frame her face. They felt warm and strong against her soft skin. "I was losing you," he whispered as he bent again to rub his lips tenderly over her mouth. "You wouldn't let me near you any other way."

His mouth was making pudding of her brain. She slid her arms up around his neck and her hands tangled in the thick hair above his nape. "But there was Kirry…"

"Window dressing. I didn't even like her, especially by the time my birthday rolled around. I gave Margie hell for inviting her to my birthday party, did she tell you?"

She shook her head, dazed.

He caught her upper lip in his mouth and toyed with it. His breathing grew unsteady. His hands on her face became insistent. "I got drunk when Margie told me you'd overheard us," he whispered. "It took two neat whiskeys for me to even phone you. Too much was riding on my ability to make an apology. And frankly, baby, I don't make a habit of giving them."

She melted into his body, hungry for closer contact. "I was so ashamed of what I'd done…"

His mouth crushed down onto hers with passionate intent. "I loved what you did," he ground out. "I wasn't kidding when I told you that. I could taste you long after I went to bed. I dreamed about it all night."

"So did I," she whispered.

His lips parted hers ardently. "I thought you were hung up on damned Brody," he murmured, "until you aimed that car at the gunman. I prayed for all I was worth until I got to you and knew that you were all right. I could have lost you forever. It haunts me!''

''I'm tougher than old cowboy boots,'' she whispered, elated beyond belief at what he was saying to her.

''And softer than silk, in all the right places. Come here.'' He moved her against the wall. His body pressed hers gently against it while he kissed her with all the pent-up longing he'd been suppressing for weeks. When she moaned, he felt his body tremble with aching need.

''You're killing me,'' he ground out.

''Wh…what?''

He lifted his head and looked down into soft, curious brown eyes. ''You haven't got a clue,'' he muttered. ''Can't you tell when a man's dying of lust?''

Her eyebrows arched as he rested his weight on his hands next to her ears on the wall and suddenly pressed his hips into hers, emphatically demonstrating the question.

She swallowed hard. ''Alexander, I was really only kidding about having a dress with prophylactics pinned to the hem.…''

He burst out laughing and forced his aching body away from hers. ''I've never laughed as much in my life as I do with you,'' he said on a long sigh. ''But I really would give half an arm to lay you down on the carpet right now, Jodie.''

She flushed with more delight than fear. ''One of us could run to the drugstore, I guess,'' she murmured dryly.

''Not now,'' he whispered wickedly. ''But hold that thought until I wind up this case.''

She laughed. ''Okay.''

He nibbled her upper lip. ''I'll pick you up at work about nine in the morning,'' he murmured as he lifted his head. ''And I'll drive you down to Jacobsville.''

''You're really worried,'' she realized, when she saw the somber expression.

''Yes, Jodie. I'm really worried. Keep your doors locked and don't answer the phone.''

''What if it's you?'' she worried.

"Do you still have the cell phone I loaned you?"

"Yes."

She produced it. He opened it, turned it on, and checked the battery. "It's fully charged. Leave it on. If I need to call you, I'll use this number. You can call me if you're afraid. Okay?"

"Okay."

He kissed her one last time, gave her a soulful, enigmatic look, and went out the door. She bolted it behind him and stood there for several long seconds, her head whirling with the changes that were suddenly upsetting her life and career. Alexander was trying to tell her something, but she couldn't quite decide what. Did he want an affair? He certainly couldn't be thinking about marriage, he hated the whole thought of it. But, what did he want? She worried the question until morning, and still had no answers.

"You're going to leave for three days, just like that?" Brody exploded at work the next morning, his face harder than Jodie had ever seen it. "How the hell am I going to manage without a secretary?" he blustered. "I can't type my own letters!"

The real man, under the facade, Jodie thought, fascinated with her first glimpse of Brody's dark side. She'd never seen him really angry.

"I'm not just a secretary," she reminded him.

"Oh, hell, you do mail and requisition forms," he said coldly. "Call it what you like, it's donkey work." His eyes narrowed. "It's because of what you did to Cara, isn't it? You're scared, so you're running away!"

Her face flamed with temper. She stood up from her desk and gave him a look that would have melted steel. "Would you be keen to hang around if they were gunning for you? You listen to me, Brody, these drug lords don't care who dies as long as they get their money. There are two dead little children who didn't do a thing wrong, except stand between a drug dealer and their mother, who was trying to shut down drug dealing in her neighborhood. Cara is part of that sick trade, and if you defend her, so are you!''

He gaped at her. In the years they'd worked together, Jodie had never talked back to him.

She grabbed up her purse and got the few personal belongings out of her desk. "Never mind holding my job open for me. I quit!'' she told him flatly. "There must be more to life than pandering to the ego of a man who thinks I'm a donkey. One more thing, Brody,'' she added, facing him with her arms full of her belongings. "You and your drug-dealing girlfriend can both go to hell, with my blessing!''

She turned and stalked out of her cubicle. She imagined a trail of fire behind her. Brody's incredulous gasp had been music to her ears. Alexander was right. She was wasted here. She'd find something better, she knew it.

On her way out the door, she almost collided with Phillip Hunter. He righted her, his black eyebrows arching.

"You're leaving, Miss Clayburn?'' he asked.

"I'm leaving, Mr. Hunter,'' she said, still bristling from her encounter with Brody.

"Great. Come with me.''

He motioned with his chin. She followed him, puzzled, because he'd never spoken to her before except in a cordial, impersonal way.

He led her into the boardroom and closed the door. Inside was the other dark man she'd met briefly during the drug bust at the warehouse, Colby Lane, and the owner of the corporation himself, Eugene Ritter.

"Sit down, Ms. Clayburn,'' Ritter said with a warm smile, his blue eyes twinkling under a lock of silver hair.

She dropped into a chair, with her sack full of possessions clutched close to her chest.

"Mr. Ritter,'' she began, wondering what in the world she was going to do now. "I can explain…''

"You don't have to,'' he said gently. "I already know everything. When this drug case is wrapped up—and Cobb assures me it will be soon—how would you like to come back and work for me in an area where your skills won't be wasted?''

She was speechless. She just stared at him over her bulging carry-all.

''Phillip wants to go home to Arizona to work in our branch office there, and Colby Lane here—'' he indicated the other dark man ''—is going to replace him. He knows about your computer skills and Cobb's already told him that you're a whiz with investigations. How would you like to work for Lane as a computer security consultant? It will pay well and you'll have autonomy within the corporation. The downside,'' he added slowly, ''is that you may have to do some traveling eventually, to our various branch offices, to work with Hunter and our other troubleshooters. Is that a problem?''

She shook her head, still grasping for a hold on the situation.

''Good!'' He rubbed his hands together. ''Then we'll draw up a contract for you, and you can have your attorney read and approve it when you come back.'' He was suddenly solemn. ''There are going to be a lot of changes here in the near future. I've been coasting along in our headquarters office in Oklahoma and letting the outlying divisions take care of themselves, with near-disastrous results. If Hunter hadn't been tipped off by Cobb about the warehouse being used as a drug drop, we could have been facing federal charges, with no intentional involvement whatsoever on our part, on international drug smuggling. Tell Cobb we owe him one for that.''

She grinned. ''I will. And, Mr. Ritter, thank you very much for the opportunity. I won't let you down.''

''I know that, Ms. Clayburn,'' he told her, smiling back. ''Hunter will walk you outside. Just in case. Not that I think you need too much protection,'' he added, tongue-in-cheek. ''There aren't a lot of people who'll drive into gunfire to save another person.''

She laughed. ''If I'd had time to think about it, I probably wouldn't have done it. Just the same, I won't mind having an escort to the front entrance,'' she confessed, standing. "I'm getting a cab to my apartment."

"We'll talk again," Ritter assured her, standing. He was tall and very elegant in a gray business suit. "All right, come on, Lane. We'll inspect the warehouse one last time."

"Yes, sir," Lane agreed.

"I'm just stunned," Jodie murmured when they reached the street, where the cab she'd called was waiting. She'd also phoned Cobb to meet her at her apartment.

"Ritter sees more than people think he does," Hunter told her, chuckling. "He's sharp, and he doesn't miss much. Tell Cobb I owe him one, too. My wife and I have been a little preoccupied lately—we just found out that we're expecting again. My mind hasn't been as much on the job as it should have been."

"Congratulations!"

He shrugged. "I wouldn't mind another girl, but Jennifer wants a son this time, a matched set, she calls it. She wants to be near her cousin Danetta, who's also expecting a second child. She and Cabe Ritter, the old man's son, have a son but they want a daughter." He chuckled. "We'll see what we both get. Meanwhile, you go straight to your apartment with no stops," he directed, becoming solemn. He looked over the top of the cab, saw something, and nodded approvingly. "Cobb's having you tailed. No, don't look back. If anyone makes a try for you, dive for cover and let your escort handle it, okay?"

"Okay. But I'm not really nervous about it now."

"So I saw the other night," he replied. "You've got guts, Ms. Clayburn. You'll be a welcome addition to security here."

She beamed. "I'll do my best. Thanks again."

"No problem. Be safe."

He closed the door and watched the taxi pull away. Her escort, in a dark unmarked car, pulled right out behind the cab. She found herself wishing that Cara and her group would make a try for her. It wouldn't bother her one bit to have the woman land in jail for a long time.

Alexander was waiting for her at her apartment. He picked up the suitcase she'd packed and then he drove her down to the Jacobsville ranch. She didn't have time to tell him about the changes in her life. She was saving that for a surprise. She was feeling good about her own abilities, and her confidence in herself had a surprising effect on her friend Margie, who met her at the door with faint shock.

Margie hugged her, but her eyes were wary. "There's something different about you," she murmured sedately.

"I've been exercising," she assured the other woman amusedly.

"Sure she has." Alexander chuckled. "By aiming cars at men armed with automatic weapons."

"What!" Margie exclaimed, gasping.

"Well, they were shooting at Alexander," Jodie told her. "What else could I do?"

Margie and her brother exchanged a long, serious look. He nodded slowly, and then he smiled. Margie beamed.

"What's that all about?" Jodie wondered aloud.

"We're passing along mental messages," Margie told her with wicked eyes. "Never mind. You're just in time to try on the flamenco dress I made you for our Halloween party."

"Halloween party." Jodie nodded blankly.

"It's this Saturday," Margie said, exasperated. "We always have it the weekend before Halloween, remember?"

"I didn't realize it was that far along in the month," Jodie said. "I guess I've been busier than I realized."

"She writes poetry about me," Alexander said as he went up the staircase with Jodie's bag.

"I do not write poetry about you!" Jodie called after him.

He only laughed. "And she reads it on stage in a retro beatnik coffeehouse."

"For real?" Margie asked. "Jodie, I have to come stay with you in Houston so you can take me there. I love cof-

feehouses and poetry!'' She shook her head. ''I can't imagine
you reading poetry on a stage. Or driving a car into bullets,
for that matter.'' She looked shocked. ''Jodie, you've
changed.''

Jodie nodded. ''I guess I have.''

Margie hugged her impulsively. ''Are we still friends?''
she wondered. ''I haven't been a good one, but I'm going to
try. I can actually make canapés!'' she added. ''I took lessons. So now you can come to parties when Jessie's not here,
and I won't even ask you to do any of the work!''

Jodie burst out laughing. ''This I have to see.''

''You can, Friday. I expect it will take all day, what with
the decorating, and I'm doing all that myself, too. Derek
thinks I'm improving madly,'' she added, and a faint flush
came to her cheeks.

''Cousin Derek's here already?'' she asked.

''He's not actually my cousin at all, except by marriage,
although I only just found out,'' Margie said, drawing Jodie
along with her into the living room. ''He's got two brothers
and they're on the way here. One of them is a cattle rancher
and the other is a divorced grizzly bear.''

''A what?''

Margie looked worried. ''He's a Bureau of Land Management enforcement agent,'' she said. ''He tracks down poach-
ers and people who deal in illegal hunting and such. He's the
one whose wife left him for a car salesman. He's very bitter.''

''Is Derek close to them?''

''To the rancher one,'' Margie said. ''He doesn't see the
grizzly bear too often, thank goodness.''

''Thank goodness?'' Jodie probed delicately.

Margie flushed. ''I think Cousin Derek wants to be much
more than my cousin.''

''It's about time,'' Jodie said with a wicked smile. ''He's
just your type.''

Margie made a face. ''Come on into the kitchen and we'll
see what there is to eat. I don't know about you, but I'm

hungry.'' She stopped suddenly. ''Don't take this the wrong way, but why are Derek and his brothers moving in and why are you and Alexander here in the middle of the week?''

''Oh, somebody's just going to try to kill me, that's all,'' Jodie said matter-of-factly. ''But Alexander's more than able to handle them, with Cousin Derek's help and some hard work by the DEA and Alexander's drug unit.''

''Trying to kill you.'' Margie nodded. ''Right.''

''That's no joke,'' Alexander said from the doorway. He came into the room and pulled Jodie to his side, bending to kiss her gently. ''I have to go. Derek's on the job, and his brothers will be here within an hour or two. Nothing to worry about.''

''Except you getting shot,'' Jodie replied worriedly.

He opened his jacket and showed her his gun.

''I know. You're indestructible. But come back in one piece, okay?'' she asked softly.

He searched her eyes and smiled tenderly. ''That's a deal. See you later.'' He winked at Margie and took one last look at Jodie before he left.

''How people change,'' Margie murmured dryly.

But Jodie wasn't really listening. Her eyes were still on Alexander's broad back as he went out the door.

Alexander and his group met somberly that evening to compare notes and plan strategy. They knew by now where Cara Dominguez was, who her cohorts were, and just how much Brody Vance knew about her operation. The security guard on the job at the Ritter warehouse was linked to the organization as well, but thought he was home free. What he didn't know was that Alexander had a court order to wiretap his office, and the agent overseeing that job had some interesting information to impart about a drug shipment that was still concealed in Ritter's warehouse. It was one that no one knew about until the wiretap. And it was a much bigger load than the one the drug unit had just busted.

The trick was going to be catching the thieves with the

merchandise. It wasn't enough to know they were connected with it. They had to have hard evidence, facts that would stand up in court. They had to have a chain of evidence that would definitively link Cara to the drug shipment.

Just when Alexander thought he was ready to spring the trap, Cara Dominguez disappeared off the face of the earth. The security guard was immediately arrested, before he could flee, but he had nothing to say under advice of counsel.

When they went to the Ritter warehouse, with Colby Lane and Phillip Hunter, to appropriate the drug shipment, they found cartons of drilling equipment parts. Even with drug-sniffing dogs, they found no trace of the missing shipment. And everybody connected with Cara Dominguez suddenly developed amnesia and couldn't remember anything about her.

The only good thing about it was that the operation had obviously changed locations, and there was no further reason for anyone to target Jodie. Where it had moved was a job for the DEA to follow up on. Alexander was sure that Kennedy had something to do with the sudden disappearance of Cara, and the shipment, but he couldn't prove a thing. The only move he had left was to prosecute Kennedy for giving secret information to a known drug dealer, and that he could prove. He had Kennedy arraigned on charges of conspiracy to distribute controlled substances, which effectively removed the man from any chance of a future job in law enforcement—even if he managed to weasel out of a long jail term for what he'd already done.

Alexander returned to the Jacobsville ranch on Friday, to find Margie and Jodie in the kitchen making canapés while Cousin Derek and two other men sat at the kitchen table. Derek was sampling the sausage rolls while a taller dark-eyed man with jet-black hair oiled his handgun and a second dark-haired man with eyes as green as Alexander's sat glaring at his two companions.

"She's gone," Alexander said heavily. "Took a powder.

We can't find a trace of her, so far, and the drug shipment vanished into thin air. Needless to say, I'm relieved on your behalf," he told a radiant Jodie. "But it's not what I wanted to happen."

"Your inside man slipped up," the green-eyed stranger said in a deep bass voice.

"I didn't have an inside man, Zeke," Alexander said, dropping into a chair with the other men. "More's the pity."

"Don't mind him," the other stranger said easily. "He's perfect. He never loses a case or misses a shot. And he can cook."

Zeke glared at him. "You could do with a few lessons in marksmanship, Josiah," he returned curtly. "You can't even hit a target."

"That's a fact," Derek agreed at once, dark eyes dancing. "He tried to shoot a snake once and took the mailbox down with a shotgun."

"I can hit what I aim at when I want to," Josiah said huffily. "I hated that damned mailbox. I shot it on purpose."

His brothers almost rolled on the floor laughing. Josiah sighed and poured himself another cup of coffee. "Then I guess I'm on a plane back to Oklahoma."

"And I'm on one to Wyoming." Zeke nodded.

Derek glared at them. "And I'm booked for a rodeo in Arizona. Listen, why don't we sell up and move down here? Texas has lots of ranches. In fact, I expect we could find one near here without a lot of trouble."

"You might at that," Alexander told them as he poured his own cup of coffee, taking the opportunity to ruffle Jodie's blond hair and smile tenderly down at her. "I hear the old Jacobs place is up for sale again. That eastern dude who took it over lost his shirt in the stock market. It's just as well. He didn't know much about horses anyway."

"It's a horse farm?" Josiah asked, interested.

Alexander nodded. "A seed herd of Arabians and a couple of foals they bred from racing stock. He had pipe dreams about entering a horse in the Kentucky Derby one day."

"Why'd he give it up?"

"Well, for one thing, he didn't know anything about horses. He wouldn't ask for advice from anybody who did, but he'd read this book. He figured he could do it himself. That was before he got kicked out of the barn the first time," he added in a droll tone.

Zeke made a rough sound. "I'm not keen on horses. And I work in Wyoming."

"You're a little too late, anyway," Margie interrupted, but she was watching Derek with new intensity. "We heard that one of Cash Grier's brothers came down here to look at it. Apparently, they're interested."

"Grier has brothers?" Jodie exclaimed. "What a horrifying thought! How many?"

"Three. They've been on the outs for a long time, but they're making overtures. It seems the ranch would get them close enough to Cash to try and heal the breach."

"That's one mean hombre," Derek ventured.

"He keeps the peace," Alexander defended him. "And he makes life interesting in town. Especially just lately."

"What's going on lately?" Derek wanted to know.

Alexander, Jodie and Margie exchanged secretive smiles. "Never mind," Alexander said. "There are other properties, if you're really interested. You might stop by one of the real estate agencies and stock up on brochures."

"He'll never leave Oklahoma," Derek said, nodding toward Josiah. "And Wyoming's the only place left that's sparsely populated enough to appeal to our family grizzly." He glanced at Margie and grinned. "However, I only need a temporary base of operations since I'm on the road so much. I might buy me a little cabin nearby and come serenade Margie on weekends when I'm in town."

Margie laughed, but she was flushed with excitement. "Might you, now?"

"Of course, you're set on a designing career," he mused. "And you're hooked on breaking bones and spraining muscles in the rodeo circuit."

"We might find some common ground one day," Derek replied.

Margie only smiled. "Are you all staying for my Halloween party?" she asked the brothers.

Zeke finished his coffee and got up. "I don't do parties. Excuse me. I have to call the airline."

"I'm right behind you," Josiah said, following his brother with an apologetic smile.

"Well, I guess it's just me," Derek said. "What do you think, Marge, how about if I borrow one of Alex's suits and come as a college professor?"

She burst out laughing.

Alexander caught Jodie by the hand and pulled her out of the kitchen with him.

"Where are we going?" she asked.

"For a walk, now that nobody's shooting at us," he said, linking her fingers into his.

He led her out the front door and around to the side of the house, by the long fences that kept the cattle in.

"When do you have to go back to work?" he asked Jodie reluctantly.

"That wasn't exactly discussed," she confessed, with a secret smile, because he didn't know which job she was returning to take. "But I suppose next week will do nicely."

"I still think Brody Vance is involved in this somehow," he said flatly, turning to her. "I can't prove it yet, but I'm certain he's not as innocent as he's pretending to be."

"That's exactly what I think," she agreed, surprising him. "By the way," she added, "I quit my job before we came down here."

"You quit...good for you!" he exclaimed, hugging her close. "I'm proud of you, Jodie!"

She laughed, holding on tight. "Don't be too proud. I'm still working for Mr. Ritter. But it's going to be in a totally different capacity."

"Doing what?" he asked flatly.

"I'm going to be working with Colby Lane as a computer security consultant," she told him.

"What about Hunter?" he asked.

"He's going back to Arizona with his wife. They're expecting a second child, and I think they want a little less excitement in their life right now," she confided with a grin. "So Colby Lane is taking over security. Mr. Ritter said I might have to do some traveling later on as a troubleshooter, but it wouldn't be often."

He was studying her with soft, quiet eyes. "As long as it's sporadic and not for too long, that's fine. You'll do well in security," he said. "Old man Ritter isn't as dense as I thought he was. I'm glad he's still keeping an eye on the company. Colby Lane will keep his security people on their toes just as well as Hunter did."

"I think Mr. Hunter is irritated that Cara managed to get into that warehouse parking lot," she ventured.

"He is. But it could have happened to anyone. Brody Vance is our wild card. He's going to need watching. And no, you can't offer to do it," he added firmly. "Let Lane set up his own surveillance. You stick to the job you're given and stop sticking your neck out."

"I like that!" she exclaimed. "And who was it who encouraged me to stick my neck out in the first place planting bugs near people in coffeehouses?"

He searched her eyes quietly. "You did a great job. I was proud of you. I always thought we might work well together."

"We did, didn't we?" she mused.

He pushed back wispy strands of loose hair from her cheek and studied her hungrily. "I have in mind another opportunity for mutual cooperation," he said, bending to her mouth.

Eleven

"**W**hat sort of mutual cooperation?" she whispered against his searching lips. "Does it involve guns and bugs?"

He smiled against her soft mouth. "I was thinking more of prophylactics…"

While Jodie was trying to let the extraordinary statement filter into her brain, and trying to decide whether to slug him or kiss him back, a loud voice penetrated their oblivion.

"Jodie!" Margie yelled. "Where are you?"

Alexander lifted his head. He seemed as dazed as she felt.

"Jodie!" Margie yelled more insistently.

"On my way!" Jodie yelled back.

"Sisters are a pain," he murmured on a long sigh.

She smiled at him. "I'm sure it's a minor disaster that only I can cope with," she assured him.

He chuckled. "Go ahead. But tonight," he added in a deep, husky tone, "you're mine."

She flushed at the way he said it. She started to argue, but Margie was yelling again, so she ran toward the house instead.

* * *

Alexander stared hungrily at Jodie when she came down the stairs just before the first party guest arrived the next evening. They'd spent the day together, riding around the ranch and talking. There hadn't been any more physical encounters, but there was a new closeness between them that everyone noticed.

Jodie's blond hair was long and wavy. She was wearing a red dress with a long, ruffled hem, an elasticized neckline that was pushed off the shoulders, leaving her creamy skin visible. She was wearing high heels and more makeup than she usually put on. And she was breathtaking. He just shook his head, his eyes eating her as she came down the staircase, holding on to the banister.

"You could be dessert," he murmured when she reached him.

"So could you," she replied, adoring him with her eyes. "But you aren't even wearing a costume."

"I am so," he argued with a wry smile. "I'm disguised as a government agent."

"Alexander!" she wailed.

He chuckled and caught her fingers in his. "I look better than Derek does. He's coming as a rodeo cowboy, complete with banged-up chaps, worn-out boots, and a championship belt buckle the size of my foot."

"He'll look authentic," she replied.

He smiled. "So do I. Don't I?"

She sighed, loving the way he looked. "I suppose you do, at that. There's going to be a big crowd, Margie says."

He tilted her chin up to his eyes. "There won't be anyone here except the two of us, Jodie," he said quietly.

The way he was looking at her, she could almost believe it.

"I think Margie feels that way with Derek," she murmured absently. "Too bad his brothers wouldn't stay."

"They aren't the partying type," he said. "Neither are we, really."

She nodded. Her eyes searched his and she felt giddy all over at the shift in their relationship. It was as if all the arguments of years past were blown away like sand. She felt new, young, on top of the world. And if his expression was anything to go by, he felt the same way.

He traced her face with his eyes. "How do you feel about short engagements?" he asked out of the blue.

She was sure that it was a rhetorical question. "I suppose it depends on the people involved. If they knew each other well…"

"I've known you longer than any other woman in my life except my sister," he interrupted. His face tightened as he stared down at her with narrow, hungry eyes. "I want to marry you, Jodie."

She opened her mouth to speak and couldn't even manage words. The shock robbed her of speech.

He grimaced. "I thought it might come as a shock. You don't have to answer me this minute," he said easily, taking her hand. "You think about it for a while. Let's go mingle with the guests as they come in and spend the night dancing. Then I'll ask you again."

She went along with him unprotesting, but she was certain she was hearing things. Alexander wasn't a marrying man. He must be temporarily out of his mind with worry over his unsolved case. But he didn't look like the product of a deranged mind, and the way he held Jodie's hand tight in his, and the way he watched her, were convincing.

Not only that, but he had eyes for her alone. Kirry didn't come, but there were plenty of other attractive women at the party. None of them attracted so much as a glance from Alexander. He danced only with Jodie, and held her so closely that people who knew both of them started to speculate openly on their changed relationship.

"People are watching us," Jodie murmured as they finished one dance only to start right into another one.

"Let them watch," he said huskily. His eyes fell to her soft mouth. "I'm glad you work in Houston, Jodie. I won't have to find excuses to commute to Jacobsville to see you."

"You never liked me before," she murmured out loud.

"I never got this close to you before," he countered. "I've lived my whole life trying to forget the way my mother was, Jodie," he confessed. "She gave me emotional scars that I still carry. I kept women at a safe distance. I actually thought I had you at a safe distance, too," he added on a chuckle. "And then I started taking you around for business reasons and got caught in my own web."

"Did you, really?" she murmured with wonder.

"Careful," he whispered. "I'm dead serious." He bent and brushed his mouth beside hers, nuzzling her cheek with his nose. "It's too late to go back, Jodie. I can't let go."

His arm contracted. She gasped softly at the increased intimacy of the contact. She could feel the hunger in him. Her own body began to vibrate faintly as she realized how susceptible she was.

"You be careful," she countered breathlessly. "I'm on fire! You could find yourself on the floor in a closet, being ravished, if you keep this up."

"If that's a promise, lead me to a closet," he said, only half joking.

She laughed. He didn't.

In fact, his arm contracted even more and he groaned softly at her ear. "Jodie," he said in a choked tone, "how do you feel about runaway marriages?"

"Excuse me?"

He lifted his head and looked down into her eyes with dark intensity. "Runaway marriage. You get in a car, run away to Mexico in the middle of somebody's Halloween party and get married." His arm brought her closer. "They're binding even in this country. We could get to the airport in about six minutes, and onto a plane in less than an hour."

"To where?" she burst out, aghast.

"Anywhere in Mexico," he groaned, his eyes biting into hers as he lifted his head. "We can be married again in Jacobsville whenever you like."

"Then why go to Mexico tonight?" she asked, flustered.

His hand slid low on her spine and pulled her hips into his with a look that made her blush.

"That is not a good reason to go to Mexico on the spur of the moment," she said, while her body told her brain to shut up.

"That's what you think." His expression was eloquent.

"But what if I said yes?" she burst out. "You could end up tied to me for life, when all you want is immediate relief! And speaking of relief, there's a bedroom right up the stairs…!"

He stopped dancing. His face was solemn. "Tell me you wouldn't mind a quick fling in my bed, Jodie," he challenged. "Tell me your conscience wouldn't bother you at all."

She sighed. "I'd like to," she began.

"But your parents didn't raise you that way," he concluded for her. "In fact, my father was like that," he added quietly. "He was old-fashioned and I'm like him. There haven't even been that many women, if you'd like to know, Jodie," he confessed. "And right now, I wish there hadn't been even one."

"That is the sweetest thing to say," she whispered, and pulled his face down so that she could kiss him.

"As it happens, I mean it." He kissed her back, very lightly. "Run away with me," he challenged. "Right now!"

It was crazy. He had to be out of his mind. But the temptation to get him to a minister before he changed his mind was all-consuming. She was suddenly caught up in the same excitement she saw in his face. "But you're so conventional!"

"I'll be very conventional again first thing tomorrow," he promised. "Tonight, I'm going for broke. Grab a coat. Don't tell anybody where we're going. I'll think up something to say to Margie."

She glanced toward the back of the room, where Margie was watching them excitedly and whispering something to Derek that made him laugh.

"All right. We're both crazy, but I'm not arguing with you. Tell her whatever you like. Make it good," she told him, and dashed up the staircase.

He was waiting for her at the front door. He looked irritated.

"What's wrong?" Jodie asked when she reached him. Her heart plummeted. "Changed your mind?"

"Not on your life!" He caught her arm and pulled her out the door, closing it quickly behind them. "Margie's too smart for her own good. Or Derek is."

"You can't put anything past Margie," she said, laughing with relief as they ran down the steps and toward the garage, where he kept his Jaguar.

"Or Derek," he murmured, chuckling.

He unlocked the door with his keyless entry and popped out the laser key with his thumb on the button. He looked down at her hesitantly. "I'm game if you are," he told her. "But you can still back out if you want to."

She shook her head, her eyes full of dreams. "You might never be in the mood again."

"That's a laugh." He put her inside and minutes later, they were en route to the airport.

Holding hands all the way during the flight, making plans, they arrived in El Paso with bated breath. Alexander rented a car at the airport and they drove across the border, stopping at customs and looking so radiant that the guard guessed their purpose immediately.

"You're going over to get married, I'd bet," the man said with a huge grin. *"Buena suerte,"* he added, handing back their identification. "And drive carefully!"

"You bet!" Alexander told him as he drove off.

They found a small chapel and a minister willing to perform the ceremony after a short conversation with a police officer near a traffic light.

Jodie borrowed a peso from the minister's wife for luck

and was handed a small bouquet of silk flowers to hold while the words were spoken, in Spanish, that would make them man and wife.

Alexander translated for her, his eyes soft and warm and possessive as the minister pronounced them man and wife at last. He drew a ring out of his pocket, a beautiful embossed gold band, which he slid onto her finger. It was a perfect fit. She recognized it as one she'd sighed over years ago in a jewelry shop she'd gone to with Margie when they were dreaming about marriage in the distant future. She'd been back to the shop over the years to make sure it was still there. Apparently Margie had told Alexander about it.

They signed the necessary documents, Alexander paid the minister, and they got back into the car with a marriage license.

Jodie stared at her ring and her new husband with wide-eyed wonder. "We must be crazy," she commented.

He laughed. "We're not crazy. We're very sensible. First we have an elopement, then we have a honeymoon, then we have a normal wedding with Margie and our friends." He glanced at her with twinkling eyes. "You said you didn't have to be back at work until next week. We'll have our honeymoon before you go back."

"Where, exactly, did you have in mind for a honeymoon?" she asked.

Three hours later, tangled with Alexander in a big king-size bed with waves pounding the shore outside the window, she lay in the shadows of the moonlit Gulf of Mexico. The hotel was first class, the food was supposed to be the best in Galveston, the beach was like sugar sand. But all she saw was Alexander's face above hers as her body throbbed in the molasses slow rhythm of his kisses on her breasts on cool, crisp sheets.

"You taste like candy," he whispered against her belly.

"You never said I was sweet before," she teased breathlessly.

"You always were. I didn't know how to say it. You gave me the shakes every time I got near you." His mouth opened on her diaphragm and pressed down, hard.

She gasped at the warm pleasure of it. Her hands tangled in his thick, dark hair. "That was mutual, too." She drew his face to her breasts and coaxed his mouth onto them. "This is very nice," she murmured unsteadily.

"It gets better." His hands found her in a new and invasive way. She started to protest, only to find his mouth crushing down over her parted lips about the same time that his movements lifted her completely off the bed in a throbbing wave of unexpected pleasure.

"Oh, you like that, do you?" he murmured against her mouth. "How about this…?"

She cried out. His lips stifled the sound and his leg moved between both of hers. He kissed her passionately while his lean hips shifted and she felt him in an intimacy they hadn't yet shared.

He felt her body jerk as she tried to reject the shock of invasion, but his mouth gentled hers; his hands soothed her, teased her, coaxed her into allowing the slow merging of their bodies.

She gasped, her hands biting into his back in mingled fear and excitement.

"It won't hurt long," he whispered reassuringly, and his tongue probed her lips as he began a slow, steady rhythm that rippled down her nerves like pure joy on a roller coaster of pleasure.

"That's it," he murmured against her eager lips. "Come up against me and find the pressure and the rhythm that you need. That's it. That's…it!"

She was amazed that he didn't mind letting her experiment, that he was willing to help her experience him. She'd heard some horror stories about wedding nights from former friends. This wasn't one. She'd found a man who wanted eager participation, not passive acceptance. She moved and shifted and he laughed roughly, his deep voice throbbing with pleasure, as her seeking body kindled waves of delight in his own.

She was on fire with power. She moved under him, invited him, challenged him, provoked him. And he went with her, every step of the way up the ladder to a mutual climax that groaned out at her ear in ripples of satiation. She clung to him, shivering in the explosive aftermath of an experience that exceeded her wildest hopes.

"And now you know," he whispered, kissing her eyelids closed.

"Now I know." She nose-dived into his damp throat and clung while they slowly settled back to earth again.

"I love you, baby," he whispered tenderly.

Joy flooded through her. "I love you, too!" she whispered breathlessly.

He curled her into his body with a long yawn and with the ocean purring like a wet kitten outside the windows, they drifted off into a warm, soft sleep.

"Hey."

She heard his voice at her ear. Then there was an aroma, a delicious smell of fresh coffee, rich and dark and delicious.

Her eyes didn't even open, but her head followed the retreat of the coffee.

"I thought that would do it. Breakfast," Alexander coaxed. "We've got your favorite, pecan waffles with bacon."

Her eyes opened. "You remembered!"

He grinned at her. "I know what you like." His lips pursed. "Especially after last night."

She laughed, dragging herself out of bed in the slip she'd worn to bed, because it was still too soon to sleep in nothing at all. She was shy with him.

He was completely dressed, right down to his shoes. He gave her an appreciative sweep of his green eyes that took in her bare feet and her disheveled hair.

"You look wonderful like that," he said. "I always knew you would."

"When was that, exactly?" she chided, taking a seat at the table facing the window. "Before or after you accused me of being a layabout?"

"Ouch!" he groaned.

"It's okay. I forgive you," she said with a wicked glance. "I could never hold a grudge against a man who was that good in bed."

"And just think, I was very subdued last night, in deference to your first time."

She gasped. "Well!"

His eyebrows arched. "Think of the possibilities. If you aren't too delicate after last night, we could explore some of them later."

"Later?"

"I had in mind taking you around town and showing you off," he said, flipping open a napkin. "They have all sorts of interesting things to see here."

She sipped coffee, trying to ignore her body, which was making emphatic statements about what *it* wanted to do with the day.

He was watching her with covert, wise eyes. "On the other hand," he murmured as he nibbled a pancake, "if you were feeling lazy, we could just lie around in the bed and listen to the ocean, while we…"

Her hand poised over the waffle. "While we…?"

He began to smile. She laughed. The intimacy was new and secret, and exciting. She rushed through the waffle and part of the bacon, and then pushed herself away from the table and literally threw herself into his arms across the chair. He prided himself on his control, because they actually almost made it to the bed….

Two days later, worn-out, and not because of any sightseeing trip, they dragged themselves into the ranch house with a bag full of peace offerings for Margie which included seashells, baskets, a pretty ruffled sundress and some taffy.

Margie gave them a long, amused look. "There is going to have to be a wedding here," she informed them. "It won't do to run off to Mexico and get married, you have to do it in Jacobsville before anybody will believe you're really man and wife."

"I don't mind," Alexander said complacently, "but I'm not making the arrangements."

"Jodie and I can do that."

"But I have to go back to work," she told Margie, and went forward to hand her the bag and hug her. "And I haven't even told you about my new job!"

"What about your new husband?" Alexander groaned. "Are you going to desert me?"

She gave him a wicked glance. "Don't you have to talk to somebody about ranch business? Margie doesn't even know that I'm changing jobs!"

He sighed. "That's all husbands are good for," he murmured to himself. "You marry a woman, and she runs off and leaves you to gossip with a girlfriend."

"My sister-in-law, if you please," Jodie corrected him with a grin. "I'll cook you a nice apple pie for later, Alexander," she promised.

"Okay, I do take bribes," he had to confess. He grinned at her. "But now that we're married, couldn't you find something else to call me? Something a little less formal?"

She thought about it for a minute. "Darling," she said.

He looked at her with an odd expression, smiled as if he couldn't help himself, and made a noise like a tiger. He went out the back door while they were still laughing.

Jodie moved into her new job with a little apprehension, because of what she'd said to Brody Vance, but he was as genial as if no cross words had ever been spoken between them. Cara Dominguez still hadn't been heard from or seen, neither had her accomplice. There was still a shipment of drugs missing, that had to be in the warehouse somewhere, but guards and stepped up surveillance assured that the drug dealers couldn't get near the warehouse to search for it.

One of Cara's rivals in the business was arrested in a guns-for-drugs deal in Houston that made national and international headlines. Alexander told Jodie about it just before the wire services broke the story, and assured her that Cara's organization was going to be next on the list of objectives for his department.

Meanwhile, Jodie learned the ropes of computer security and went back to school to finish her certification, with Alexander's blessing. Margie came up to see her while she was arranging a showing of her new designs with a local modeling agency and a department store that Kirry didn't work for.

Alexander kept shorter hours and did more delegating of chores, so that he could be at home when Jodie was. They bought a small house on the outskirts of Houston. Margie arranged to help Jodie with the decorating scheme. She was still amazed at the change in her best friend, who was now independent, strong-willed, hardworking and nobody's doormat.

There was still the retro coffeehouse, of course, and one night Jodie had a phone call from the owner, Johnny. She listened, exploded with delight, and ran to tell Alexander the news.

"The publisher wants to buy my poems!" she exclaimed. "He wants to include them in an anthology of Texas poetry! Isn't it exciting?"

"It's exciting," he agreed, bending to kiss her warmly. "Now tell the truth. They're about me, aren't they?"

She sighed. "Yes, they're about you. But I'm afraid this will be the only volume of poetry I ever create."

"Really? Why?"

She nibbled his chin. "Because misery is what makes good poetry. And just between us two," she added as her fingers went to his shirt buttons, "I'm far too happy to write good poetry ever again."

He guided her fingers down his shirt, smiling secretively. "I have plans to keep you that way, too," he murmured deeply.

And he did.

* * * * *

THORN'S CHALLENGE
by
Brenda Jackson

BRENDA JACKSON

is a die-'heart' romantic who married her childhood
sweetheart and still proudly wears the ring he gave her
when she was fifteen. Because she's always believed in
the power of love, Brenda's stories always have happy
endings. In her real-life love story, Brenda and her
husband of thirty years live in Jacksonville, Florida,
and have two sons at university.

An award-winning author of ten romance titles,
Brenda divides her time between family, writing and
working in management at a major insurance company. You may write to Brenda at PO Box 28267,
Jacksonville, Florida 32226, USA, or visit her website
at www.brendajackson.net

To my friend India Catrett, 'Motorcycle Lady' extraordinaire. The only woman I know who owns her own Harley. Thanks for all the information you provided on motorcycles, Bike Week and motorcycle racing. This book is definitely for you.

Love endures long and is patient and kind…
it takes no account of the evil done to it—
pays no attention to a suffered wrong.
—I Corinthians 13: 4-5

Prologue

Tara Matthews hated weddings.

She had done a pretty good job of avoiding them until she had met the Westmorelands. Since then she had attended two weddings within an eighteen-month period. She'd had even been maid of honor when her good friend, Delaney Westmoreland, had married a desert sheikh almost a year and a half ago.

And today, like everyone else in the grand ballroom of the Sheraton Hotel in downtown Atlanta, she had come to celebrate the wedding of Delaney's brother, Dare Westmoreland to the woman he loved, Shelly Brockman.

The worst part, Tara thought as she glanced around her, was that she couldn't really complain about having to attend the weddings. Not when the Westmorelands had become the closest thing to a family she'd had since that fateful day in June two years ago. It was to have been her wedding day, but she had stood at the altar in complete shock after the groom, the man she had loved, who she thought had loved her, had announced to all three hundred guests that he couldn't go through with the wedding because he was in love with her maid of honor—the woman she'd considered her best friend for over fifteen years. That day Tara had left Bunnell, Florida, hurt and humiliated, and vowing to her family that she would never return.

And so far she hadn't.

A few days later she'd accepted a position as a resident pediatrician at a hospital in Bowling Green, Kentucky. Leaving her hometown had destroyed her and her father's dream of working together in his pediatric practice.

While working at the hospital in Kentucky, she had met Delaney Westmoreland, another pediatrician, and they had become the best of friends. She had also become good friends with four of Delaney's five older brothers, Dare, Stone and the twins, Chase and Storm. The initial meeting between her and the fifth brother, Thorn, had been rather rocky. She'd "gone off" on him about his unpleasant mood. Since then, they had pretty much avoided each other, which suited her just fine. At six foot-four, thirty-five-years of age, ruggedly handsome and sexy as sin, Thorn Westmoreland was the last man she needed to be around; especially since whenever she saw him she thought of scented candles, naked bodies and silken sheets.

"I'm going to the ladies' room," she whispered to Delaney, who turned to her, nodded and smiled. Tara smiled back, understanding that the older woman Delaney was talking to wasn't letting her get a word in. Glancing at her watch to see how much longer she needed to put in an appearance, Tara made her way down a long, empty hallway to the restrooms.

Her thoughts drifted to the fact that next month she would be moving from Kentucky to the Atlanta area. She was moving because an older married doctor with clout at the Kentucky hospital had been obsessed with having her in his bed. When she'd rebuffed his advances, he'd tried making her work environment difficult. To avoid the sexual harassment lawsuit she'd threatened to file, the hospital had decided to relocate her and Atlanta had been her first choice.

Tara was so busy putting her lipstick case back in her purse after leaving the restroom that she didn't notice the man coming out of the men's room at the same time, until they collided head on.

"Oh, I'm so sorry. I wasn't looking where I was—"

Any further words died on her lips when she saw that the man she had bumped into was Thorn Westmoreland. He seemed as surprised to see her as she was to see him.

"Thorn."

"Tara."

He returned her greeting in an irritated tone as his intense dark eyes held her gaze. She frowned, wondering what he was upset about. He hadn't been looking where he was going any more than she had, so the blame wasn't all hers. But she decided to be cordial for once where he was concerned. "I apologize for not looking where I was going."

When he didn't say anything, but frowned and narrowed his eyes at her, Tara decided not to wait for a response that undoubtedly wasn't coming. She made a move to pass him, and it was then that she noticed he had not removed his hand from her arm. She looked down at his hand and then back at him.

"Thanks for keeping me from falling, Thorn, but you can let go of me now."

Instead of releasing her, his hold tightened and then he muttered something deep in his throat, which to Tara's ears sounded pretty much like, "I doubt if I can." Then, sud-

denly, without any warning, he leaned down and captured
her lips with his.

The first thought that came to Tara's mind was that she
had to resist him. But a second thought quickly followed;
she should go ahead and get him out of her system since
he had been there from the day they'd met. Shamefully she
admitted that the attraction she'd felt for him was stronger
than any she'd ever felt for a man, and that included Derrick Hayes, the man she had planned to marry.

The third thought that whipped through her mind was
that Thorn Westmoreland definitely knew how to kiss. The
touch of his tongue to hers sent a jolt through her so intense, her midsection suddenly felt like a flaming torch.
Emotions, powerful and overwhelming, shot through her,
and she whimpered softly as he deepened the kiss with bold
strokes of his tongue, seizing any sound she made, effectively and efficiently staking a claim on her mouth.

A claim she didn't want him to make, but one he was
making anyway.

He used his hands to cup her bottom boldly and instinc-
tively she moved closer to him, coming into contact with
his straining arousal. When she placed her arms around his
neck, he arched his back, lifted her off the floor and brought
her more snugly to him, hip-to-hip, thigh-to-thigh, and
breast-to-breast. His taste, tinged with the slight hint of
champagne, went right to her head, and a dizzy rush of
need she couldn't explain sent blood rushing through all
parts of her.

When he finally released her mouth and placed her back
down on solid ground, they were both breathless. He didn't
let go of her. He continued to hold her in his arms, nibbling
on her neck, her chin and her lips before recapturing her
mouth with his for another bone-melting kiss.

He sucked on her tongue tenderly, passionately, slowly,

as though he had all the time in the world to drive her mad with desire. It was a madness that flooded her insides and made her moan out a pleasure she had never experienced before. Potent desire, stimulating pleasure, radiated from his hands, his tongue and the hard body pressed to hers. When he finally broke off the kiss, she slumped weakly against his chest thinking that in all her twenty-seven years, she had never been kissed like that.

She slowly regained her senses as she felt him remove his hands from her. She slid her hands from his shoulders and looked up into his eyes, seeing anger radiating there. He apparently was mad at himself for having kissed her, and even madder with her for letting him. Without saying a word he turned and walked off. He didn't look back. When he was no longer in sight she breathed deeply, still feeling the heat from his kiss.

Tara nervously moistened her lips as she tried to regain control of her senses. She felt it was fairly safe to assume, after a kiss like that, that Thorn was now out of her system. In any case, she was determined more than ever to continue to avoid him like the plague.

Two years ago she had learned a hard lesson; love, the happily-ever-after kind, was not meant for her.

One

Three months later

She had a body to die for and Thorn Westmoreland was slowly drawing his last breath.

A slow, easy smile spread across his face. She was exquisite, every man's fantasy come true. Everything about her was a total turn-on, guaranteed to get your adrenaline flowing, and his blood was so incredibly fired up he could barely stand it.

He took his time and studied every magnificent line of her. The sight lured him closer for an even better inspection. She was definitely a work of art, sleek, well built with all the right angles and curves, and tempted him beyond belief. He wanted to mount her and give her the ride of her life…or possibly get the ride of his.

He felt a distinct tingle in his stomach. Reaching out, his fingers gently touched her. She was ready for him.

As ready as he was for her...

"Hey, Thorn, you've been standing there salivating over that bike for at least ten minutes. Don't you think you should give it a rest?"

The smile on Thorn's face faded and without turning around to see who had spoken he said. "The shop's closed, Stone."

"You're here, so that means it's open," Stone Westmoreland said, coming into his brother's line of vision. Thorn was standing ogling the motorcycle he had built, his latest creation, the Thorn-Byrd RX1860. Rumors were spreading like wildfire that a Harley couldn't touch the Thorn-Byrd RX1860 for style and a Honda had nothing on it for speed. Stone didn't doubt both things were true. After all, this was another one of Thorn's babies. It had taken Thorn an entire year to build it; five months longer than it usually took him to put together one of his motorcycles. People came from all over the country to special order a Thorn-Byrd. They were willing to pay the hefty price tag to own the custom-built style and class only Thorn could deliver. You got what you paid for and everyone knew Thorn put not only his reputation and name behind each bike he built, but also his heart and soul.

"And why are you closing up early?" Stone asked, ignoring his brother's deep frown. He knew Thorn well enough to overlook his grouchiness.

"I thought I would be getting a few moments of privacy. I regret the day I gave all of you keys to this place."

Stone grinned, knowing Thorn was referring to him and their three brothers. "Well, it was best that you did. No telling when we might drop in and find you trapped beneath a pile of chrome and metal."

Thorn raised his eyes to the ceiling. "Has the thought

ever occurred to you that you could also find me in bed with a woman?''

''No.''

''Well, there is that possibility. Next time try knocking first instead of just barging in,'' Thorn snapped. Because he spent so many hours at the shop, his office had all the comforts of home including a room in the back with a bed. He also had a workout room that he used regularly to stay in shape.

''I'll try and remember that,'' Stone said, chuckling. His brother was known for his bark as well as his bite. Thorn could be a real pain in the rear end when he wanted to. There was that episode with Patrice Canady a few years back. It seemed Thorn had been mad at the whole world because of one woman. On top of that, there was Thorn's policy of not indulging in sex while training for a race. And since he'd been involved in a number of races so far this year, he'd been grouchier than usual. Like a number of athletes, Thorn believed that sex before an event would drain your body and break your concentration. As far as Stone was concerned, race or no race, to improve his mood Thorn definitely needed to get laid.

''What are you doing here, Stone? Don't you have a book to write?'' Thorn asked. Stone, at thirty-three, was a nationally known bestselling author of several action-thriller novels. He wrote under the pen name of Rock Mason.

Thorn's question reminded Stone why he had dared enter the lion's den. ''No, I just finished a book and mailed it to my publisher this morning. I'm here to remind you about tonight's card game at seven-thirty.''

''I remember—''

''And to let you know the location has changed. It's not going to be over at Dare's place as planned since AJ's camping trip was cancelled. The last thing we need is for Storm to be cursing all over the place when he starts losing and tempting our nephew to add a few of those choice words to his vocabulary.''

Thorn nodded in agreement. "So where will it be?''

"Tara's place.''

Thorn turned and narrowed his gaze at his brother. "Why the hell are we playing cards at Tara's place?''

Stone hoped the amusement dancing in his eyes didn't show. He and the other brothers had taken Tara up on her offer to have the card game at her place mainly because they knew it would rile Thorn. They were well aware of how hard he went out of his way to avoid her. "The reason we're having the card game at her place is because she invited us over as a way to thank us for helping her move in.''

"I didn't help.''

"Only because you were out of town for a race that weekend.''

Thorn propped his hip against a table and decided not to tell Stone that even if he'd been in town he would not have helped. Being around Tara Matthews was pure torture and the last thing he wanted to remember was the time he'd lost his head and gotten a real good taste of her at Dare's wedding. If his brothers knew the two of them had kissed, he would never hear the last of it.

Sighing deeply, Thorn slanted his brother a hard look. "Why can't we play cards at your place?''

"It's being painted.''

"What about Chase's place?'' He asked about the brother who owned a soul food restaurant in downtown Atlanta. Chase was a twin to his brother Storm.

"Too junky.''

"And Storm's?''

"There'll be too many interruptions from women calling him on the phone."

Thorn sighed deeply. At thirty-two, Storm, who was the younger of the twins, was a fireman by day and a devout ladies' man at night.

"Then what about my place?"

Stone laughed and shook his head. "Forget it. You never have any food in the fridge or enough beer to drink. So are you coming?"

Thorn frowned. "I'll think about it."

Stone inwardly smiled. It was hard for Thorn to miss a Westmoreland card game "Okay, if we see you, that's fine, and if we don't see you that will be fine, too. I'll just win all of Storm's money by myself."

Thorn's frown deepened. "Like hell you will."

Stone smile. "And like hell you would even if you're there," he said throwing out the challenge, knowing just how much Thorn liked challenges. Whether Thorn admitted it or not, his brothers knew that his biggest challenge was a good-looking woman by the name of Tara Matthews.

The buzzing of Tara Matthews's intercom captured her attention. "Yes, Susan?"

"Mrs. Lori Chadwick is here to see you, Dr. Matthews."

Tara lifted a brow, wondering what had brought Lori Chadwick to her office. Her husband, Dr. Martin Chadwick, was Head of Pediatrics and a very important man around the hospital. He was also her boss. "Please send her in."

Tara smiled when the door opened and Lori Chadwick walked in. As usual the older woman looked stunning. It was a known fact that Lori Chadwick enjoyed raising money for the hospital, and if the new children's wing was any indication, she was very good at it.

"Mrs. Chadwick," Tara greeted respectfully, offering her hand.

"Dr. Matthews, it's good seeing you again, dear."

"Thanks," Tara said, gesturing to a chair across from her desk. "It's good seeing you again, too." The last time she'd seen Mrs. Chadwick had been at a charity function a few weeks ago. It had been the first such function she had attended since moving to Atlanta and joining the staff at Emory University Hospital.

Lori Chadwick smiled. "I know how busy you are, Dr. Matthews, so I'll get straight to the point. I'm here to solicit your help in a fundraiser I'm planning."

Tara sat down behind her desk and returned Lori Chadwick's smile, flattered that the older woman had sought her assistance. One of the first things she'd been told by the other doctors when she had first arrived was not to get on Lori Chadwick's bad side. The woman loved her pet projects and expected everyone else to have the same enthusiasm for them as well. "I'd be glad to help. What sort of project do you have in mind?"

"I thought a charity calendar would be nice and would generate a lot of interest. The money that we'll make from the sale of the calendars will help Kids' World."

Tara nodded. Kids' World was a foundation that gave terminally ill children the chance to make their ultimate dream—such as a visit to any place in the world—come true. All proceeds for the foundation came from money raised through numerous charity events.

"Any ideas for this calendar?" Tara asked, thinking she really liked what Mrs. Chadwick was proposing.

"Yes. It will be a calendar of good-looking men," the older woman said chuckling. "I'm not too old to appreciate a fine masculine physique. And a 'beef-cake' calendar, tastefully done of course, would sell like hotcakes. But I want a variety of men from all walks of life,'' she added excitedly. ''So far, I've already gotten a number of firm commitments. But there are still a few spots open and that's why I'm here. There's one name that keeps popping up as a suggestion from a number of the women I've talked to, and from what I understand he's a friend of yours.''

Tara raised a brow. ''A friend of mine?''

''Yes.''

''Who?''

''Thorn Westmoreland, the motorcycle racer. I understand that he's something of a daredevil, a risk-taker on that motorcycle of his. He would definitely do the calendar justice.''

Before Tara could gather her wits and tell Lori Chadwick that Thorn was definitely not a friend of hers, the woman smiled radiantly and said. ''And I'm counting on you, Dr. Matthews, to convince Mr. Westmoreland to pose for the charity calendar. I know you won't let me and Kids' World down.''

Later that evening Tara glanced up at a knock at her front door. Wiping the cookie dough from her hands she looked at the clock on the stove. It was only a little past seven and the card game wouldn't start until nine. She crossed her living room to the door and peeped out.

Thorn!

She thought Stone had said that Thorn wouldn't be coming tonight. Her heart suddenly began pounding fast and furious. Adrenaline mixed with overheated hormones gave her a quick rush, and the first thought that entered her mind was of the kiss she and Thorn had shared at his brother's wedding three months before; a kiss she'd been certain would get him out of her system.

But it hadn't.

In fact he was more in her thoughts than ever before.

She slowly opened the door, wondering why, if he had come to play cards, he had arrived so early. There was just something about the way he stood there with his helmet in his hand that really did crazy things to Tara's entire body. She felt breathless and her pulse actually ached low in her stomach as he adopted the sexiest pose she had ever seen in a man. It was a stance that would have any woman salivating if it was captured on a calendar; especially the kind Lori Chadwick proposed.

The thumb of his right hand was in his pocket and his left hand held his helmet by his side. He had shifted most of his weight to his right leg which made his jeans stretch tight, firmly across his thighs. They were masculine thighs, lean and powerful looking. The broad shoulders under the leather bomber jacket revealed a beautiful proportioned upper body and from the first, she had been acutely conscious of his tall, athletic physique. He was so devilishly handsome she could barely stand it. She lowered her gaze to his black leather motorcycle boots before returning to his eyes. The man was definitely gorgeous with his brooding good looks. There was no other way to describe him.

His gaze made intense heat settle in the pit of her stomach, and her heart began pounding even harder. She tried not to concentrate on his tight jeans, his leather bomber jacket or the diamond stud earring in his left ear. But that only left his face, which in itself was a total turn-on. His hair was cut close to his head and his skin was a smooth coppery brown. His eyes were so dark they appeared to be black satin. His nose was firm and his cheekbones chiseled. But it was his mouth that had her full attention. She was flooded with memories of how that mouth had felt against hers and how it had tasted. It was full, generously curved, and enticing with a capital *E*. It suddenly occurred to her that she had never seen him smile. Around her he always wore a frown.

Even now.

Even that night he had kissed her.

She sighed, not wanting to remember that night although she knew she'd never forget it. "Thorn, what are you doing here?" she cleared her throat and asked.

"Isn't there a card game here tonight?" he responded in a voice too good to be real. A deep huskiness lingered in its tone and the throaty depth of it held a sensuality that was like a silken thread wrapping all around her, increasing the rhythm of her heart.

She cleared her throat again when he raised his brow, waiting for her response. "Yes, but you're early. It doesn't start until nine."

"Nine?" he lifted a dark, brooding brow. "I could have sworn Stone said the game started at seven-thirty." He glanced down at his watch. "All right, I'll be back later," he said curtly and turned to leave.

"Thorn?"

He turned back around and met her gaze. He was still frowning. "Yes?"

Tara knew that now would be a good time to talk to him about the Lori Chadwick's calendar. She had mentioned it to Chase Westmoreland when he'd stopped by the hospital after Mrs. Chadwick's visit, and he'd said there was no reason for her not to ask Thorn if he'd do it. After all, the calendar was for charity. He had warned her upfront, however, that she had her work cut out for her in persuading Thorn to do the calendar. Thorn, he'd said, detested a lot of publicity about himself. According to Chase, the last time Thorn had been involved in a publicity stunt had ended up being a love affair from hell. No amount of further probing had made Chase give her any more information than that. He had said that if she wanted to know the whole story, Thorn would have to be the one to tell her.

"You're welcome to hang around until the others arrive if you'd like. You won't have that long to wait. It's only an hour and a half," she said.

"No thanks," he didn't hesitate in saying. "In fact, tell my brothers that I've changed my mind and won't be playing cards tonight after all."

Tara watched as walked over to his bike, straddled his thighs over it, placed the shiny black helmet over his head, started the engine and took off as if the devil himself was chasing him.

This, Thorn thought, *is the next best thing to making love to a woman.*

Bearing down, he leaned onto the bike as he took a sharp curve. The smooth humming sound of the bike's engine soothed his mind and reminded him of a woman purring out her pleasure in bed. It was the same purring sound he would love to hear from Tara Matthews's lips.

Even with Atlanta's cool January air hitting him, his body felt hot, as a slow burning sensation moved down his spine. He was experiencing that deep, cutting, biting awareness he encountered every time he saw Tara. His hands tightened their grip on the handlebars as he remembered how she had looked standing in the doorway wearing a pair of jeans and a tank top. He found her petite, curvy body, dark mahogany skin, light brown eyes and dark brown shoulder-length hair too distracting on one hand and too attracting on the other. It rattled him to no end that he was so physically aware of everything about her as a woman.

Even when she'd lived in Kentucky she had invaded his sleep. His dreams had been filled with forbidden and invigorating sex. Cold showers had become a habit with him.

No woman had been able to invade his space at work, but she had been there too, more times than he could count. Building motorcycles and preparing for races had always gotten his total concentration—until he'd met Tara Matthews.

He'd constantly been reminded of the first time they had met. He had arrived at his sister Delaney's apartment late one night with his four brothers playing cards and no one had a clue where Delany had gone or when she would return. At least no one had felt the need to tell him. He had lost his cool and had been one step away from murdering his brothers. Tara had stormed out of Delaney's kitchen, with all her luscious curves fitting snugly in a short denim skirt, sexier than any woman had a right to be. And with more courage than anyone had a right to have, she had gotten all in his face. She had straightened her spine, lifted her chin and read him the riot act about the way he had questioned his brothers over Delaney's whereabouts. She'd told him in no uncertain terms what she thought of his foul mood. All the while she'd been setting him straight, his lust had stirred to maximum proportions, and the only thing he could think about was getting her to the nearest bedroom and zapping her anger by making love to her.

The quick intensity of his desire had frightened the hell out of him, and he had resented feeling that way. After Patrice, he had vowed that no woman would be his downfall again and he'd meant it. He wasn't having any of that.

An ache suddenly gripped his mid-section when he thought of just what he *would* like to have. A piece of Tara would do him just fine; just enough so that he could get her out of his system, something the kiss hadn't accomplished. He wanted to bury himself inside her as deeply as he could and not come out until he had gotten his fill, over and over again. Such a feat might take days, weeks, even months. He had never been in this predicament before and was working hard not to let his brothers know. If they had any idea that he had the hots for their baby sister's best friend, they would give him pure hell and he would never hear the last of it. Even now the reminder of Tara's taste was causing his mouth to water.

And to think she had invited him to hang around her place for an hour and a half and wait for his brothers tonight. He couldn't imagine himself alone with her for any length of time and especially not for longer than an hour. There was no way he could have done that and kept his sanity. That would have been asking for even more trouble than he had gotten into with her at Dare's wedding.

Squaring his shoulders he leaned onto his bike as he took another sharp curve with indulgent precision, relishing the freedom and thrill of letting go in a totally uninhibited way. It was the same way he wanted to take Tara when he made love to her.

The way he *would* take her.

That simple acceptance strengthened his resolve and made the decision he'd just made that much easier to deal with. The restraint and control he'd tried holding on to since first meeting Tara was slowly loosening. A completely physical, emotionally free affair is what he wanted with her. It was time to stop running and meet his challenge head-on.

His next race was during Bike Week in Daytona Beach and was only seven weeks from now. Seven more weeks of celibacy to go.

While waiting he intended to get Tara primed, ripe and ready, much like this very machine he was riding. However, even with all the similarities, there was no doubt in his mind that getting Tara in his bed would be a unique experience. He would get the ride of his life and centrifugal force would definitely be the last thing on his mind.

He smiled. Yes, it was time he and Tara stopped avoiding each other and started making plans to put all that wasted energy to good use.

Two

Tara heard the doorbell ring the minute she opened the oven to take out another batch of cookies. "Stone, can you get that for me, please?" she called out to one of the men busy setting up the card table in her dining room.

"Sure thing," Stone said, making his way to Tara's front door.

Opening the door, Stone lifted a brow when he saw Thorn standing on the other side. "I thought you told Tara that you'd changed your mind about tonight," he said, stepping aside to let his brother enter.

"And I changed it back," Thorn said curtly, meeting Stone's curious gaze. "Why are you the one opening the door instead of Tara?"

Stone smiled. It was hard getting used to Thorn's jealous streak; especially since it was a streak Thorn wasn't even aware he had. "Because she's busy in the kitchen. Come on. You can help get the card table set up in the dining room.''

"And didn't you tell me the card game started at seventy-thirty instead of nine?" Thorn asked meeting his brother's gaze.

Keeping a straight face, Stone said. "I don't think so. You must have misunderstood me.''

The moment Thorn walked into the kitchen, Tara turned away from the sink and met his gaze. Surprise flared in her eyes and increased the rhythm of her heart. She swallowed deeply and looked at him for a moment then said. "I thought you weren't coming back.''

Thorn leaned against a kitchen counter and stared at her. It was apparent seeing him again had rattled her. The way she was pulling in a ragged breath as well as the nervous way she was gripping the dish towel were telling signs. "I changed my mind," he said, not taking his gaze from hers, beginning to feel galvanized by the multitude of sensations coursing through him.

Now that he had decided that he would no longer avoid her, he immediately realized what was happening between them and wondered if she realized it, too. He inwardly smiled, feeling that she did. She broke eye contact with him and quickly looked down at the kitchen floor, but it hadn't been quick enough. He had seen the blush coloring her cheeks as well as the contemplative look in her eyes.

"There's a lot of money to be won here tonight and I decided that I may as well be the one to win it," he added.

Stone rolled his eyes to the ceiling. "Are you going to help set up the table or are you going to stay in here and engage in wishful thinking?''

Thorn turned to his brother and frowned slightly. "Since you want to be such a smart-mouth, Stone, I'm going to make sure your money is the first that I win, just to send you home broke.''

''Yeah, yeah, whatever,'' Stone said.

Thorn's gaze then moved back to Tara with a force he knew she felt. He could feel her response all the way across the room. Satisfied with her reaction, he followed Stone out of the kitchen.

As soon as Thorn and Stone left the room, Tara leaned back against the kitchen counter feeling breathless, and wondered if Stone had picked up on the silent byplay that had passed between her and Thorn. Staring at him while he had stared at her had almost been too much for her fast-beating heart. The intensity of his gaze had been like a physical contact and she hadn't quite yet recovered from it.

But she would.

Ever since Derrick, she had instituted a policy of not letting any man get too close. She had male friends and she hadn't stopped dating altogether, but, as soon as one showed interest beyond friendship she hadn't hesitated to show him the door. She'd been aware from the first that Thorn was dangerous. Even though her intense attraction to him had set off all kinds of warning signs, she had felt pretty safe and in control of the situation.

Until their kiss a few months back.

Now she didn't feel safe and wasn't sure she was in control of anything. The man was temptation at its finest and sin at its worse. There was something about him that was nothing short of addictive. She had no plans to get hooked on him and knew what she needed to do, but more importantly, she also knew what she needed *not* to do; she couldn't let Thorn Westmoreland think she was interested in him.

Curious, yes. Interested, no.

Well, that was partly true. She *was* interested in him for Mrs. Chadwick's calendar, but Tara was determined not to let her interest go any further than that.

Where is she?

Thorn glanced around the room once again and wondered where Tara had gone. After they had gotten things set up in her dining room, she had shown them her refrigerator filled with beer, and the sandwiches and cookies she had placed on the kitchen counter. Since then he had seen her only once, and that was when she had come into the room to tell them she had also made coffee.

That had been almost two hours ago.

He couldn't help but think about what had transpired between them in her kitchen, even in Stone's presence, although he felt certain his brother hadn't had a clue as to what had been going on. Stone had a tendency sometimes to overlook the obvious. And the obvious in this case was the fact that just being in the same room with Tara made him hot and aroused. Judging from her reaction to him, she'd also been affected. Since it seemed they were on the same wave length, he saw no reason to fight the attraction any longer.

He wanted her, plain and simple.

First he wanted to start off kissing her, to reacquaint himself with her mouth until he knew it just as well as he knew his own. Then he wanted to get to know her body real well. He had always admired it from a distance, but now he wanted to really get into it, literally. He'd had nearly two years to reconcile himself to the reality that Tara Matthews was not just a bump-and-grind kind of woman. He hadn't needed to get up close and personal with her to realize that fact. He could easily tell that she was the kind of woman who could stimulate everything male about him, and fate had given him the opportunity to discover what it was about her that made his senses reel and heated up his blood. The relationship he wanted to share with her would be different than the one he had shared with any woman, including Patrice. This time his heart would not be involved, only certain body parts.

"Are you in this game or not, Thorn?"

Dare's question captured his attention and judging from his brother's smile, Dare found Thorn's lack of concentration amusing. Dare, the oldest brother at thirty-seven, was sheriff of College Park, a suburb of Atlanta, and didn't miss much. "Yes, I'm in the game," Thorn stated with annoyance, studying the cards he held in his hand once more.

"Just thought I'd ask, since you've lost a whole lot of money tonight."

Dare's words made him suddenly realized that he *had* lost a lot of money, three hundred dollars, to Stone who was looking at him with a downright silly grin on his face.

"It seems Thorn's mind is on other things tonight," Stone said chuckling. "You know what they say—you snooze, you lose—and you've been snoozing a lot tonight, bro."

Thorn leaned back in his chair and glared at his brother. "Don't get too attached to my money. I'll recoup my losses before the night's over." He pushed back his chair and stood. "I think I'll stretch my legs by walking to the living room and back."

"Tara's not in there, Thorn. She's upstairs reading," his brother Storm said smiling as he threw out his last card. At Thorn's frown he chuckled and said. "And please don't insult my intelligence by giving me that, I-don't-know-what-you're-talking-about look. We're not stupid. We all know you have this thing for her."

Thorn's frown deepened. He wondered how long they'd known. His brothers were too damn observant for their own goods. Even Stone, whom he'd always considered the less observant one, seemed to have sensed the tension between him and Tara. "So what if I do?" he snapped in an agitated voice. "Any of you have a problem with it?"

Dare leaned back in his chair. "No, but evidently you do since you've been fighting it for nearly two years now," he said, meeting Thorn's frown with one of his own. "We knew from the beginning that she was your challenge and even told you so. It's about time you come to terms with it."

Thorn leaned forward, both palms on the table, and met his brothers' gazes. "I haven't come to terms with anything," he snapped.

"But you will once you put that nasty episode with Patrice behind you," Dare responded. "Damn, Thorn, it's been three years since that woman. Let it go. To my way of thinking you never actually loved her anyway, you just considered her your possession and got pissed to find out you weren't the only man who thought that. As far as I'm concerned she was bad news and I'm glad you found out her true colors when you did. You're a smart man and I don't think you're into self-torture, so relax and stop being stubborn and uptight and get over what she did to you. And for Pete's sake, please do something about your sexual frustrations. You're driving us crazy and it's gotten so bad we hate to see you coming."

Chase laughed. "Yeah, Thorn, it's obvious you haven't gotten laid in a while. Don't you think that rule you have of not indulging in sex while racing is a bit much? By my calculations it's been way over a year, possibly two. Don't you think you're carrying this celibacy thing a bit too far?"

"Not if he's waiting on a particular woman that he's set

his sights on and he wants with a fierce Westmoreland hunger," Stone said smiling, knowing the others knew the gist of his meaning. "Since we all have a good idea what he wants from Tara, maybe now would be a good time to tell Thorn just what Tara wants from him, Chase."

The room got quiet and all eyes turned to Chase. But the ones that unsettled Chase more than the others belonged to Thorn as he sat back down. Chase smiled, seeing Thorn's annoyance as well as his curiosity. He had shared the news with Stone about Tara wanting Thorn to pose for the charity calendar but hadn't gotten around to telling the others yet.

"I stopped by the hospital today to visit Ms. Amanda, who's had hip surgery," he said, mentioning the older woman who worked as a cook at his soul food restaurant. "While I was there I decided to drop in on Tara to see if there was anything she needed for tonight. She mentioned that some lady who's a big wheel around the hospital had stopped by her office earlier asking about you, Thorn. The lady wants you to pose for a charity calendar," Chase said in a calm voice, explaining things to everyone.

"After talking to Tara, I got the distinct impression that somehow the lady found out Tara knew you. She wanted Tara to use her influence to get you to do it," Chase added.

"Thorn doesn't 'do it,'" Storm said, chuckling. "Didn't we just establish the fact that he's still celibate?"

Chase frowned and swung his glance toward his twin. "Can't you think about anything but sex, Storm? I'm talking about posing for the calendar."

"Oh."

Chase refocused his gaze on Thorn. "So, will you do it?"

Thorn frowned. "Are you asking me on Tara's behalf?"

"No. But does it matter? If Tara were to ask you, would you do it?"

"No," Thorn said without hesitation while throwing a card out, remembering how he and Patrice had first met. She was a photographer who had wanted to do a calendar of what she considered sexy, sweaty, muscle-bound hunks, and in the process had ended up being his bed partner. His and a few others, he'd later found out.

Chase frowned. "It's for a good cause."

"All charities are," Thorn said, studying his hand.

"This one is for children, Thorn."

Thorn looked up and met Chase's gaze. Anyone knowing Thorn knew that on occasion he might give an adult pure hell, but when it came to children, he was as soft as a marshmallow. "The racing team I'm affiliated with already works closely with the Childrens' Miracle Network, Chase."

Chase nodded. "I know that, Thorn, but that's on a national level. This is more local and will benefit Kids' World."

Everyone living in the Atlanta area was familiar with Kids' World and the benefits it provided to terminally ill children. "All I'm asking is for you to think about it and be prepared when Tara finally gets up enough nerve to ask you," Chase added.

Thorn frowned. "Why would she need to get up nerve to ask me anything?"

It was Dare who chuckled. "Well, ahh, it's like this, Thorn," he said throwing a card out. "You aren't the friendliest person toward her, but we all know the reason why, even if you refuse to acknowledge it."

Glancing around the room to make sure Tara hadn't come back downstairs, Dare continued. "The plain and simple fact is that you have a bad case of the hots for her and it's been going on now for almost two solid years. And as far as I'm concerned, you need to do something about it or learn to live with it. And if you choose to live with it, then please adjust your attitude so the four of us can live with you."

Thorn glared at Dare. "I don't need an attitude adjustment."

"The hell you don't. Face it, Thorn. You're not like the rest of us. Storm, Chase, Stone and I can go a long time without a woman and it doesn't bother us. But if you go without one for too long, it makes you hornier than sin, which for you equates to being meaner than hell. And it seems that you're deliberately holding out while deciding what to do about Tara, and it's making you worse than ever. Don't you think that in two years you should have made some decisions?"

Thorn's intense dark eyes held his brothers'; they were all watching him like hawks, waiting for his response. "I *have* made decisions regarding what I'm going to do about Tara," he said slowly, seeing the looks of comprehension slowly unfolding in their eyes.

"About damn time you stop backing away from the inevitable," Storm said, smiling broadly. "I knew you would come to your senses sooner or later."

"Uh, I hate to be the voice of reason at a time like this," Chase said grinning. "But I'd think twice about whatever decisions you've made about Tara without her consent, Thorn. She's quite a handful. I've seen her rebellious side and bringing her around won't be easy. Personally, I don't think you can handle her."

"Neither do I," Stone chimed in.

Thorn's face darkened as he gazed at all of them. "I can handle Tara."

"Don't be so sure about that," Stone said smiling. "Her first impression of you wasn't a good one, and I don't think she likes you much, which means you'll definitely have your hands full trying to win her over. I'm not so sure you're up for the challenge.''

''I bet you any amount of money that he is,'' Storm said grinning. ''Thorn can do anything he wants to do, including taming Tara.''

''Don't hold your breath for that to happen,'' Chase said chuckling. ''Have you ever really noticed the two of them around each other? They're both stubborn and strong-willed. I say he can't hang.''

''Okay you guys, pull back,'' Storm said, slowly stroking his chin. ''Thorn's a smart man who plans his strategies well. Hell, look how he has trained for those races he's won. If he goes after Tara with the same determination, then there won't be anything to it. Therefore, I say taming Tara will be a piece of cake for Thorn.''

''No, it won't,'' Chase said chuckling. ''In fact, I'll be willing to bet a case of Jack Daniels that it won't.''

''And I bet you a new set of tools that it won't be, too,'' Stone added shaking his head with a grin.

''And I bet you a day's wage and work for no pay in your restaurant as a waiter that it will, Chase. And I also bet you that same set of tools that it will, Stone. Thorn can handle any challenge he faces,'' Storm said, with confidence in his voice as he gathered up everyone's cards to start a new game.

Thorn had been sitting back listening to his brothers make their bets. He looked over at Dare who just shrugged his shoulders. ''Making those kinds of bets aren't legal, and since as a sheriff I'm duty-bound to uphold the law, I'll pass,'' he said jokingly. ''However, if I *were* a betting man, I'd say you *could* pull it off, but it wouldn't be as easy as Storm thinks. Calendar or no calendar, Tara's not going to let you just waltz in and sweep her off her feet. You'll have to set yourself up on a mission,'' he said, grinning, as he remembered the tactic he'd used to win the heart of the woman he'd loved. "Then you can't play fair," he added, thinking of the technique his brother-in-law, Prince Jamal Ari Yasir, had used to woo their baby sister, Delaney.

Thorn nodded. *Set myself up on a mission and then play unfair.* He could handle that. He'd put his plans into action later tonight when everyone left. Tara wouldn't know what had hit her until it was too late.

Way too late.

Three

Tara's heart, beating twice as fast as it should have, slammed against her rib cage when, after the card game was over, it became obvious that, unlike his brothers, Thorn had no intentions of leaving.

She closed the door and turned to him. The air in the room suddenly seemed charged. "Aren't you leaving?" she asked, as she leaned against the closed door.

"No. I think we need to talk."

Tara inhaled deeply, wondering what he thought they needed to discuss. While upstairs in her bedroom she had managed to get her thoughts and her aroused senses under control after convincing herself that her earlier reaction to Thorn had been expected. After all, from the first she had been physically attracted to him and memories of the kiss they had shared a few months back hadn't helped matters. Then there was the way he always looked at her with that penetrating gaze of his. After thinking things through logically, she felt confident that the next time he looked at her as if he would love to gobble her up in one scrumptious bite, things would be different. She would be more in control of the situation as well as her senses.

"What do you want to talk about?" she asked, wondering if Chase had mentioned anything to him about the charity calendar.

He met her gaze. "About us."

She lifted an arched brow. There was no "us" and decided to tell him so. "There's no us, Thorn. In fact I've always gotten the distinct impression that you don't even like me."

Boy, was she wrong, Thorn thought. If anything he liked her too damn much. There were several emotions he'd always felt toward Tara Matthews from the first and dislike hadn't been one of them.

He took a couple of steps forward, bringing him right in front of her. "I've never disliked you, Tara."

She swallowed deeply against the timbre in his voice and the look of melting steel in his eyes. That's the same thing his brothers had claimed when she'd told them how she felt last year. They had argued that Thorn was just a moody person and told her not to take it personally. But a part of her *had* taken it personally.

"My brothers think you're my challenge," he added, not taking his eyes off her.

"Why would they think that?" she asked. She had wondered about it the first time the brothers had mentioned that very same thing to her. But none of them had given her any further explanation.

"Because they don't think I can handle you."

She frowned. "Handle me? In what way?"

His gaze ran provocatively down her full length before coming back to meet hers. "Evidently not the way I originally thought," he said, thinking just how much he had underestimated his brothers' cleverness. They had set him up from the first.

"Of the five of us, I'm the one who'd always had a better handle on Laney than anyone, so I assumed they meant that I couldn't handle you because you were as headstrong, willful and unmanageable as she could be at times. And although you seem to have those traits, too, I now believe they meant you were my challenge for a totally different reason. I think they meant that I couldn't handle you as a woman. There's a big difference in the two."

They gazed at each other for a long, intense moment and then she asked. "And what's the difference?" She knew she might be asking for trouble, but at the moment she didn't care.

The room crackled and popped with what she now recognized as sexual tension and physical attraction. It hadn't been dislike the two of them had been battling since they'd met. It had been primal animal lust of the strongest kind.

He took another step closer. "If I were to group you in the same category as Laney, I'd have no choice but to think of you with brotherly affections since I'm almost eight years older than you. But if I were to forget about the age thing and place you in the same category as I do any other woman, then that would make you available."

Tara frowned. "Available?"

"Yes, available for me."

Tara swallowed again and ran her sweaty palms down over her slender waist to settle on her hips. She wondered what his reaction would be if he knew that in all her twenty-seven years she had never been available for any man. Although she and Derrick had dated for a number of years, they had never slept together, which meant she was probably the oldest living virgin in the state of Georgia.

But that certainly didn't make her open game and she resented any man thinking she was his for the taking. Derrick had taught her a lesson and she had no desire to forget it any time soon. "Sorry to burst your bubble, but I'm not available for any man, Thorn."

Thorn continued to stare at her. Yes, she was definitely his challenge, and he liked challenges. "I think differently," he finally said.

Tara blinked once, then twice when she actually saw the corners of Thorn's lips move and his mouth suddenly creased into a smile. It was definitely a rare Kodak moment and she would have given anything to capture it on film. He had the most irresistibly, devastating smile she had ever seen. It contained a spark of eroticism that sent her pulses racing.

"You are definitely my challenge, Tara," he added in a raspy voice.

Too late she realized he had taken another step forward, bringing her thigh-to-thigh, chest-to-chest with him. Her breath caught when the sexy sound of his voice and the heat from his smile set her body on fire. But she fought to hold on to every ounce of control she had and refused to go up in flames. "I'm not anyone's challenge, Thorn," she said, barely above a whisper.

He began lowering his head toward hers and said huskily, "You are definitely *mine,* Tara."

The impact of Thorn's statement, his words of possession, made a degree of lust, stronger and more potent than she'd ever experienced before, fill the air; the room suddenly felt hot. A distinct, seductive warmth flooded the area between her legs. She wanted to fight him and the emotions he was causing her to feel. She tried convincing herself that he was just a man and she had promised herself that she would never lose her head over a man again. She had to admit that Thorn was the type of man who would make it hard to keep that promise, but she was determined to do so.

The one thing Thorn didn't know about her was that she didn't need a man, physically or mentally. As far as she was concerned, you couldn't miss what you'd never had. Besides, like most men who didn't have marriage on their minds, the only thing Thorn would ever give her was a whirlwind, meaningless affair that centered on sex.

Feeling more in control she took a step back, away from him, out of the way of temptation. "The hour is late and we're through talking."

"Yes, we're through talking."

Tara swallowed deeply, suddenly aware that his tone of voice was a low, seductive whisper and the intensity of his gaze had darkened. She stood rooted in place as he slowly recovered the distance she had put between them. He was so close that she could actually see her reflection in his eyes. So close she was sure that he heard the irregular beat of her heart.

She swallowed deeply. He was staring at her and his face was filled with such intense desire, that even a novice like herself could recognize it for what it was. It then occurred to her that her earlier assumption that you couldn't miss what you'd never had had no meaning when it came to basic human nature, and tonight, between them, animal magnetism was at an all-time high. Other than the kiss they had shared before, she had never felt so wired, so hungry for something she'd never had and so ripe for the picking.

The part of her that made her a woman felt thick, pouty and naughty. It was as if it had a mind of its own and was responding to Thorn as though he had some sort of mysterious telepathic connection to it. The absurdity of such a thing made her want to take a step back but she couldn't.

His gaze was holding her still. Her entire concentration was on him and his was centered on her.

"I should probably get the hell out of here," he whispered in a low, sexy rumble of a voice as he placed his arms at her waist and shifted his gaze to her lips.

"Yes, you should," she whispered back, as a shiver passed from his touch at her waist all the way to her toes. She shifted her gaze to his lips as well and felt the intensity, the desires that were building up within her. Blood rushed to every part of her body.

"And I will," he said in a sensually charged voice, bringing her body closer to his. "After I've gotten a real good taste of you again."

Tara blinked and her mouth fell open. Thorn swiftly descended on it like an eagle swooping down on its prey. The feel of his mouth closing on hers was warm, startling, a direct hit. His lips were seductive against hers and gently yet thoroughly coaxed her into a response, a response she had no trouble giving him.

The sensations, acute and volatile, were a replay of the last time they had kissed, but, as she settled against him, she immediately decided that this kiss was destined to be in a class by itself. If he was bold before, this time he was confidently assertive. There was nothing timid about the way he was feasting on her mouth. The intensity of it made her body tremble. It was heat and sensuality rolled into one and her body tightened in hunger unaccustomed to such nourishment. Her pulse points pounded, right in sync with the turbulent beating of her heart.

When she felt his hands moving over her body with an expertise that overwhelmed her, Tara knew she had to put a stop to this madness and slowly, regretfully, she eased her lips from Thorn's.

But he continued to touch her, gently rubbing her back.

For the longest time neither of them said anything. They couldn't. The act of breathing alone took too much effort.

When she found the ability to lift her head, she met his gaze. It was so intense it nearly made the words she was about to say catch in her throat. She swallowed then forced herself to speak. ''Why?''

She saw comprehension in the dark eyes that were locked with hers. He knew what she was asking and understood her need to know. ''Because I want you and have from the first time I saw you. I tried denying it but I can't any longer. You may not accept it or acknowledge it, but your response proves to me that you want me just as much as I want you, Tara.''

She knew his words were true, but she wasn't ready to accept what he was saying. ''But I don't want this.''

He nodded. ''I know, but I refuse to give up or walk away. I want you more than I've wanted any woman in a long time.''

A spark of anger lit her features. ''And I'm supposed to feel good about that?''

Thorn lifted a brow. ''I would hope that you do.''

''Well, I don't. The last thing I want is an involvement with a man.''

Thorn's frown deepened. ''You're saying one thing but your kiss said another.''

Her eyes filled with anger. ''Imagine what you want, but I prefer doing the solo act. There's less chance of being played a fool that way. Once bitten you have a tendency to avoid a second bite.''

Thorn sighed deeply, remembering what one of his brothers had told him about how Tara's fiancé had hurt and humiliated her on what was supposed to have been their wedding day. Tara's words touched a part of him that hadn't been touched in a long time. He reached out and caressed her cheek tenderly, mesmerized by the smoothness of her flesh and the pained yet angry look in her eyes.

He wanted to kiss her again but forced himself to speak instead. "You will never get a bite of pain from me, Tara. But you will get nibbles of passion and pleasure of the most profound kind. That I promise you." Walking away while he had the mind to do so, he picked his helmet up off the table.

He paused before opening the door, seeing the confused look on her face. As he'd hoped, he had her thinking. The Tara that been feeding his nightly fantasies for almost two years was a woman who was as turbulent as the storm of sensations she stirred within him. Now that he'd finally admitted to himself that he wanted her, he intended to have her. And if she thought she was going to put distance between them then she had another thought coming.

"I'll be by tomorrow," he said calmly. He could tell by the way she narrowed her eyes that she intended to rebuild that wall between them. Little did she know he had every intention of keeping it torn down. He watched as she folded her arms beneath her breasts. They were breasts he intended to know the taste of before too long.

"You have no reason to come by tomorrow, Thorn."

"Yes I do," he responded easily. "I want to take you for a ride on my bike." He saw something flicker in her eyes. First surprise, then stubbornness, followed by unyielding resistance.

She lifted her chin. "I have no intention of doing anything with you."

Thorn sighed good-naturedly, thinking that she liked talking tough, and a part of him couldn't help but admire her spunk, which was something you rarely saw in a woman these days. Most were too eager to please. But even with all her feistiness, in good time she would discover that he was a man who appreciated a good fight more often then most people, so her willfulness didn't bother him any. In fact it made her just that much more desirable.

"And I intend to see that you do anything and everything with me, Tara," he said throatily, assuredly, before opening the door, walking out and closing it behind him.

Tara leaned against the closed door as the soft hum of Thorn's motorcycle faded into the distance. Taking a deep breath she tried to get her pulse rate and heartbeat back to normal. There was no denying that Thorn Westmoreland had the ability to rock her world. But the problem was that she didn't want her world rocked. Nor did she want the changes he was putting her through. And she definitely didn't want to remember the kiss they had just shared. The memory of it sent a tingling feeling through every part of her body. She had discovered three months ago that the man was an expert kisser and had a feeling he was probably an expert at making love as well. And she believed if given the chance he would do whatever it took to get her mind and body primed for sex.

She pulled in a deep breath trying to get her mind back in focus. It was late, but she doubted she would be able to sleep much tonight. She thought that it was a good thing she didn't have to work tomorrow. She was having lunch with Delaney and was looking forward to it.

Pushing away from the door she headed for the kitchen hoping she would find something there to keep her busy. She stopped in the doorway. There was nothing for her to do since the Westmoreland brothers had left everything spotless. But one brother in particular had gone a step further. Tonight Thorn had invaded her space and gotten closer to her than any man since Derrick had dumped her. That realization disturbed her. Her fantasies of Thorn had been rather tame compared to the real thing and she hated to admit it but she had found kissing him the most exciting thing she had done since leaving Bunnell.

As she climbed the stairs to her bedroom, it suddenly dawned on her that she hadn't mentioned anything about the calendar to Thorn, which meant she would have to see him again this week. And since he claimed he would be coming by tomorrow she would bring it up then.

Thorn had a difficult time sleeping that night. Whenever he tried closing his eyes, memories of his kiss with Tara were so vivid he could still actually taste her. Tonight's kiss had been much better than the previous one. That kiss had had an element of surprise. Tonight their kiss had been fueled by desire—basic and fundamental.

Muttering something unintelligible, he rolled out of bed knowing that sleep was out of the question. Making his way through the living room and into the kitchen he opened the refrigerator, needing a beer. With his present state of mind, he might need more than one.

As he pulled a beer from the six-pack and popped the tab, a low moan formed in his throat. He took a long, pleasurable gulp. At that moment, unexpectedly, huge drops of rain splattered on his rooftop and he was glad he had made it home before the downpour. He had gotten caught on his bike during storms enough times to know it wasn't something he relished.

A smile worked at his mouth when he thought of something he did relish. Thorn couldn't wait until he saw Tara again. The thought that she would try to avoid him made the challenge that much more sweet.

Tonight he had made a decision and it hadn't been easy, but kissing her had helped to put things into the right perspective. Tara was a pure challenge if he'd ever seen one, and although she had fought what they shared and would continue to fight it, he was convinced more than ever that she was just the woman he needed.

They had been attracted to each other from the first, and tonight had exposed numerous possibilities, all of them definitely worth pursuing.

Finishing off his beer and placing the empty can in the bin, he headed back up the stairs to the bedroom. He was hot. He was hard. He was horny. And the sound of the rain pounding against his roof didn't help matters. It only made him want to pound his body into Tara's with the same steady yet urgent rhythm. The thought of doing so made his gut clench with need. A vivid, sensuous scene flashed in his mind. The impact almost took his breath away. Thorn quickly sucked in air. This was not good. Tara Matthews fascinated him. She intrigued him and filled him with intense desire and made him think of unbridled passion.

Unless he did something about his predicament, she would be the death of him and he wasn't ready to die just yet.

Four

"There's only one word to describe your brother, Laney, and that's stubborn."

The two women were sitting at a table on the terrace of the restaurant. They had enjoyed lunch and were now enjoying a glass of wine. A smile tilted the corners of Delaney's lips and her eyes sparkled as she glanced over at her friend. "Let me guess. You must be referring to brother number two, none other than Thorn Westmoreland."

Tara couldn't help but return Delaney's smile. "Yes. Who else? Your other brothers are simply adorable and don't have a grumpy bone in their bodies. But that Thorn…"

Delaney chuckled. "I don't know why you continue to let him get next to you, Tara," she said, taking another sip of her wine, although she had a pretty good idea. She had been keeping a close eye on Thorn and Tara since they'd met and knew better than anyone that the spark of annoyance flying between two individuals was a sure sign of attraction. She and her husband Jamal could certainly attest to that. When they'd first met there had been sparks, too, but then the sparks had turned into fiery embers that had fed another kind of fire. Delaney hated that she hadn't been around more to prod Thorn and Tara in the right direction. She and Jamal had spent more time in his homeland during their son Ari's first year of life. They had returned to the States a few months ago so that she could complete the rest of her residency at a hospital in Kentucky. They would be remaining in the States for at least another year.

"I know I shouldn't let him get under my skin, Laney, but I can't help it. For instance, last night, when the others left my house after the card game, Thorn hung back just to rattle me."

Delaney lifted a brow. "Thorn hung back? I'm surprised he wasn't the first to leave."

Tara had been surprised, too. Usually, he avoided her like the plague. "Well, for once he decided to stick around."

"And?"

"And he said we needed to talk."

Delaney shook her head. "About Mrs. Chadwick wanting him to do that calendar?"

"No, I never got around to mentioning that."

"Oh. Then what did the two of you have to talk about?"

A rush of color suffused Tara's mahogany skin when she thought of just what they had done in addition to talking. Aftereffects of their kiss still had her feeling warm and tingly in certain places.

"Tara?"

Tara met Delaney's gaze. "Ahh…he wants to take me bike-riding today and we talked about that," she said, not telling Delaney everything because she figured she really didn't have to. No doubt there was a telltale sign all over her face that Thorn had kissed her.

"Are you?"

Tara blinked as Delaney's question broke into her thoughts. "Am I what?"

"Are you going bike-riding with Thorn?"

Tara shrugged. "I told him I wouldn't, but that didn't mean a thing to him since he indicated he would drop by today anyway. At first I had planned to make sure I wasn't home when he arrived, but then I remembered Mrs. Chadwick and that darned calendar."

"So, you're going?"

Tara breathed in a deep sigh. "I guess so, I'm only going so that I can ask him about the charity calendar."

Delaney smiled. It seemed things were finally beginning to happen between Thorn and Tara; after two years it was definitely about time. But still she decided she needed to leave her friend with a warning. "Look, Tara, I know my brothers probably better than anyone and Thorn is the one I can read the best. He was involved in an affair a few years back that left him with a bad taste in his mouth, and heaven knows that was the last thing Thorn needed, since he was moody enough. He's an ace when it comes to doing whatever it takes to get whatever it is he wants. He'll pull out all stops and take any risks necessary if the final result suits him. There's only one way I know to get the best of him."

"And what way is that?"

Delaney smiled, her eyes crinkling attractively as she thought of the brother who loved being a thorn in everyone's side most of the time. "Don't try beating Thorn at his game, since he's a pro. What you should do is to come up with a game plan of your own."

Tara lifted an arch eyebrow. "A game plan of my own?"

Delaney nodded. "Yes. One that will get you what you want, while making him think he has accomplished his goal—getting whatever it is he wants from you."

Tara frowned. For the past two years Thorn had avoided her space and now suddenly he was determined to invade it. She didn't have to think twice as to what he wanted from her since he had pretty much spelled things out last night. He wanted her! "A game plan of my own. Umm, I think that's a wonderful idea."

Thorn sat astride his motorcycle and gazed at Tara's house, wondering if she was home. He had heard from Stone that she had had lunch with Laney earlier that day.

He should have called first but he hadn't wanted to give her the chance to refuse his invitation. He'd figured that the best thing to do was to catch her with her guard down since chances were she probably thought she had made herself clear and he wouldn't show up today.

Shutting off the engine he began walking toward her door with two helmets in his hands. He was determined that they would go today. He hadn't slept most of the night for thinking of how it would feel when she leaned into his back with her arms wrapped around him, while the vibrations of the motorcycle's powerful engine hummed through her.

He rang the doorbell and heard the faint sound of footsteps approaching. Moments later Tara opened the door. And she was smiling.

"I was beginning to wonder if you were going to show up, Thorn. I've been ready for over an hour."

He blinked and a look of indecision filled his eyes. The woman certainly looked like Tara but the one standing before him didn't appear surprised to see him. In fact, from her statement it seemed she had been expecting him. His gaze darkened dangerously as he wondered just what the hell she was up to.

"I thought you weren't going riding with me," he said, meeting her gaze and holding it with an intensity that should have made her nervous. Instead she waved her hand, dismissing his words and stood aside to let him enter.

"If you really thought that then why are you here?" she asked, closing the door behind him and leaning against it to look at him. The suspicious look on his face, his pensive and forever brooding expression had Tara wanting to go up to him and wrap her arms around his neck and assure him that he wasn't imagining things, and that she had thrown him a curve. She had a feeling that few people did that to him. And she had another feeling that she should savor this rare moment of having the upper hand with Thorn.

Then, to her astonishment and complete surprise, the corner of his mouth quirked into a seductive grin. "Because I've learned when most women say one thing they really mean another."

She frowned. "When I say I won't do something, usually I won't. The only reason I changed my mind is because I remembered I needed to talk to you about something."

Thorn continued to meet her gaze. He knew just what she wanted to talk to him about—that charity calendar. He quickly decided he would prefer turning her down after their bike ride rather than before it. "All right. I plan for us to have dinner at a restaurant I think you'll like. We'll be able to talk then."

She raised a brow. "Dinner? You didn't mention anything about dinner."

He shrugged. "Didn't I? It must have slipped my mind."

He then studied her outfit, a pair of jeans, a lightweight pullover sweater and a pair of short leather boots. It was the perfect riding attire and the outfit looked perfect on her.

"It may get chilly later so you might want to grab a jacket," he suggested.

Tara sighed. He had intentionally not mentioned dinner to her last night. A part of her thought of resisting, but she quickly decided not to start fighting him just yet. There would be plenty of time for that later. There was no doubt in her mind that after telling him what she needed from him, he would prove to be difficult. "Okay, I'll be right back."

Thorn went completely still and held his breath when Tara passed him to go up the stairs. He'd seen her in jeans a number of times before and always thought she knew how to wear them well, but today he couldn't help but pay close attention to how the jeans fit her, especially the way the denim cupped her curvy backside.

And she was wearing her hair down and he liked that. He wanted to know how the silken strands would feel blowing in the wind as he tore up the road with her clinging to him.

"All right, I'm ready."

He glanced back to the stairs and watched her come down. He looked at her intently before saying. "So am I."

"Here, let me help you with that," Thorn said, easing the helmet on Tara's head and adjusting the straps to keep it firmly in place. "Have you ever ridden on a motorcycle before?" he asked as he tried to ignore how his body was responding to her closeness. As usual, whenever he was around her, a deep, sexual hunger stirred to life in his mid-section. It was only at times like these that he remembered just how long he had been celibate, which didn't help matters.

"No, I've never ridden on one before."

He swallowed deeply. The low, seductive tone of her voice was only adding to his misery.

"But I have ridden on a moped. Does that count?" she asked.

He shook his head. "No, that doesn't count, so consider this your first experience," he said as he assisted her in straddling the seat behind him. He tried not to think of how good she looked with her legs spread wide across the padded seat or how well her body fit onto it. Today he was riding the Thorn-Byrd 1725, a huge bike that had a passenger armrest and backrest to give a second rider added comfort.

"You, okay?" he asked as he placed his own helmet on his head and strapped it on.

"Yes, I'm fine, just a little nervous. This bike is huge."

He chuckled. "Yeah, and I prefer building them that way."

"I'm truly amazed."

"About what?"

"The skill and craftsmanship that went into building this bike. You truly have gifted hands."

A pleased smile curved the corners of his lips. He was glad she thought so and intended that she find out real soon just how gifted his hands were. But at the moment his main thoughts were on *her* hands. "Place your arms around me and hold on tight with your hands. And don't hesitate to lean into me for an easier ride. Okay?"

"Why would leaning into you provide an easier ride?" she asked, in a confused tone of voice.

"You'll see."

Tara nodded, preferring to try and sit up straight with her arms around Thorn's waist. But when he turned on the engine to a low, rumbling purr that escalated to a much louder growl, she automatically leaned forward, tightened her grip around him and pressed her body against the wide expanse of his back. His leather bomber jacket felt warm, cushiony, and so much a part of him. Pressing her face against his solid back, she breathed in the scent of leather and the scent of man. It was masculine and a mixture of shaving cream and a real nice-smelling cologne. This wasn't the first time she had been aware of his scent. That first time he had kissed her at Dare's wedding she had gone to bed later that night with his scent embedded in her nostrils. It had been both alluring and arousing.

It still was.

"Ready?" she heard him ask her over his shoulder.

She sighed deeply and closed her eyes. "Yes, I'm ready." The next thing she knew he shifted gears and the two of them went flying into the wind.

Tara opened her eyes as her nervousness began easing away. It was plain to see that in addition to being a gifted craftsman, Thorn was also a skilled biker. He took the sharp curves with ease as he expertly controlled the large and powerful machine.

Her breasts felt tight and achy, so she leaned forward and pressed her body even more to his. He'd been right. This was the best position. She wondered if, with her sitting so close, he could feel the frantic pounding of her heart. But that question and others were suddenly zapped from her mind when she took a look at the countryside they passed. Instead of traveling on the busy interstate, Thorn had maneuvered the bike onto a scenic two-lane road that had very few cars. She liked the view. And she liked the feel of the man she was clutching for dear life.

"Am I holding you too tight?" she decided to ask. She wondered if he heard her question or if the sound of her voice had been swept away with the wind.

"No."

She smiled. He *had* heard her, and she was glad she hadn't caused him any discomfort.

Thorn tried to keep his concentration on the road ahead of him and not on the woman behind him, but her breasts were pressing against his back and arousing him no end. Everything about her was arousing. He had ridden other women on his bike but never had he felt such excitement and exhilaration before. Riding with Tara was seduction at its best, temptation at its finest.

He pulled his concentration back in as he maneuvered the bike around a curvy mountain road. This was the part of Atlanta that he loved seeing on his bike and he wanted to share the view with Tara. It was a part of the city that had escaped the developer's bulldozer. The Westmoreland family intended to keep it that way.

He slowed the bike as he left the highway and steered to a single-lane gravel road that led to a huge lake in a wooded area surrounded by large overhanging trees. Moments later, he brought the motorcycle to a stop and shut off the engine. Before she could ask, he said. "I think this is one of the most beautiful spots in Atlanta and thought you might enjoy seeing it."

Tara glanced around and her breath caught. He was right. It *was* breathtaking. She gazed back at him. She would never have guessed that he was a man in sync with nature, but from the look in his eyes as he glanced around, she could tell that he was.

"You come here often," she said. It wasn't a question but a statement. She could detect deep appreciation in his gaze as he viewed his surroundings.

"Yes. This is Westmoreland land. The ruins of my grandparents' house isn't far from here and we visited this place a lot while growing up. My father's youngest brother, the one who has never been married, Corey Westmoreland, spent a lot of his time teaching us to appreciate the natural world and its environment here. I believe you've met my uncle."

Tara nodded. "Yes, twice—at both Laney's and Dare's weddings. He's the one who's a park ranger at Yellowstone National Park. Right?"

Thorn nodded. "Yes, and so is my cousin Durango. In fact when Durango finished high school he decided to move to Montana to attend college to be near our uncle. Now I doubt you could get either of them to return here to live. They're Montana men through and through."

He kicked down the motorcycle stand and removed his helmet. "Come on, let's take a walk."

Tara slowly slid off the bike and had to steady herself so she wouldn't lose her balance. Thorn appeared at her side to assist and to help her take off her helmet. He stared down at her when he held her helmet in his hand.

"What?" she asked, wondering if she had something on her face since he was looking at her so intently.

"Nothing. I'd been wondering why your hair hadn't been blowing in the wind. I had forgotten that the helmet would hold it in place."

She lifted a brow. He had been thinking of her hair blowing in the wind? Before she could think about that further, he took her hand in his. "Come on, let me show you around."

Tara knew she was seeing another side of Thorn Westmoreland. For some reason he wasn't his usual grumpy self, and she decided to take full advantage of his current kinder and gentler disposition. She knew it would probably be best for the both of them if they were to continue to avoid each other, but then she thought of Mrs. Chadwick's request.

Somehow and someway she had to get Thorn to agree to pose for that calendar.

Together they silently walked the surrounding land. She saw more wild animals than she had ever seen before. There was a family of deer, numerous rabbits and wild turkeys. There was even a fox skirting across the overbrush. In soft tones Thorn pointed out to her the spot where he had learned to ride his first motorcycle. His grandparents had bought it for him when he was twelve years old. It had been a dirt bike, one not meant for the road.

"Ready to go?" he finally asked her.

Tara glanced up at him. "Yes, I'm ready."

Thorn leaned toward her to place her helmet back on her head and suddenly he stopped. He traced her jawline with the tip of his finger and met her gaze. She took a slow, deep breath to calm the erratic beating of her heart when it became crystal-clear what he was about to do. He was going to kiss her and she couldn't form the words to tell him not to.

Instead, a need, a hunger, flared to life inside her when her gaze settled on his lips as his gaze had settled on hers. Memories filled her mind of the last two kisses they had shared. Hot. Mind-boggling kisses.

She quickly decided that she would question the sensibility of her actions later, but for now she needed this kiss as much as she needed her next breath.

She shuddered when she thought of the intensity of that need and felt a quickening in her stomach when he lowered his mouth to hers. Her lips automatically parted the second their mouths touched, and she breathed a sigh of pleasure as her arms reached out to hold him.

As it had been the other times, his mouth was skillful, and another soft sigh escaped her lips when he deepened the kiss and thoroughly explored the warm recesses of her mouth with his tongue. Then he captured hers and gently mated with it, the sensations rocking her all the way to her toes.

She knew the taste of him, had never forgotten it and refused to consider the possibility it was becoming addictive. However, she did concede that this kiss, the hunger behind it and all the enticements in front of it, were causing a deep ache between her legs. This open-mouthed exploration of tongues and teeth was flooding her with sensations she had never felt before. She heard one of them whimper and moan and realized the sounds were coming from her. She shouldn't expect any less when the blood was running so hot and heavy in her veins.

She felt his hand run provocatively down her back to settle on her hips, then slowly to her backside, and she moved her body closer to the fit of his. Her belly was pressed against his front and she could feel an incredible hardness straining against the crotch of his jeans. For the moment, she didn't care. The only thing she did care about was the fact that she was enjoying kissing him. Their tongues continued to tangle and their breaths steadily mingled.

Reluctantly, he ended the kiss, struggling for control. She saw his jaw tense and knew he was regretting kissing her already. Without saying anything he placed her helmet back on her head, adjusted the straps and help her straddle the bike.

He had gone from tender to moody in just that instant and she didn't like it. When he got back on the bike and had his own helmet in place, she asked, in a fairly angry voice. "Why did you kiss me if you're going to get all huffy and puffy about it? Next time keep your mouth to yourself, Thorn Westmoreland."

For the longest moment he didn't say anything, then finally he turned to her on the bike and said. "That's the problem, Tara. When it comes to you I don't think I can keep my mouth to myself. It seems to always wants to find its way to yours."

He sighed deeply and added. "My brothers think you're my challenge, but now I'm beginning to think you're something else all together."

She lifted a brow. "What?"

"My sweetest temptation."

Five

"So what did you want to talk to me about?"

Tara nervously nibbled on her bottom lip. She and Thorn had just finished the best chili she had ever eaten. The building that housed the restaurant was rustic, made of logs with tall, moss-covered oak trees surrounding it. The place resembled a roadside café more than a restaurant and was positioned almost in seclusion off the two-lane highway.

Due to its lack of visibility, Tara could only assume that those who frequented the restaurant were regular customers since the place was taking in a high degree of business. It also appeared that a lot of those customers were bikers. She found the atmosphere comfortable and had almost forgotten the discussion she needed to have with Thorn.

"I want to ask a favor of you."

He met her gaze over his cup of coffee. "What kind of favor?"

She sighed. "Have you ever heard of Lori Chadwick?"

He frowned as if searching his brain, then moments later said, "No."

Tara nodded. "Well, she is well-known around the city for her charity work. Mrs. Chadwick has come up with this great idea for a project to raise funds for Kids' World. You have heard of Kids' World haven't you?"

"Yes."

"Well, she has decided what she wants to do to raise money for that particular charity this year. She wants to do a calendar of good-looking men from different professions, and would like you to be one of the models. She wanted me to ask you about it."

He placed his coffee cup down. "You can go back and let her know that you asked me."

She met his gaze. "And?"

"And that I turned you down."

Tara narrowed her eyes. "I think it was wonderful that you were one of the men she wanted."

"Then I'm flattered."

"From what I understand, they will pay you."

"It's not about the money."

"Then what is it about, Thorn? I know for a fact you're involved with a number of charities for children. Why not this one?"

He leaned back in his chair. "I don't like having my picture taken."

She frowned. "That's a crock and you know it, considering the number of times newspaper photographers have taken your picture when you've won a motorcycle race or built a bike for some celebrity."

He shrugged. "Newspapers reporters are different. I don't like having my picture taken in a private session, in a studio or anything like that."

"In that case you won't have anything to worry about.

It's my understanding they want to capture you in your element—probably outside standing next to your bike.''

"The answer is still no, Tara."

She glared at him. "Why are you being so difficult, Thorn?''

"I have my reasons," he said, glaring back at her as he threw money on the table for their meal. "It's getting late so we should head back."

Tara sighed. He had to be the most stubborn man she had ever met. "I need to make a pit stop at the ladies' room before we leave," she said softly, disappointed that he had flatly refused to do the calendar.

Moments later, when she walked outside to where he stood next to the bike, she couldn't help but wonder why he didn't want to be photographed by a professional photographer. "I'm ready now."

Without saying anything, he helped put her helmet on again and adjusted the straps. She swung her legs across the huge bike without his help and glared up at him. "I said I was ready, Thorn."

He stood there and looked at her for a few moments before finally getting on the bike in front of her, revving the engine and riding off.

Tara was mad and he knew it, but there was nothing he could do about it since he would *not* be doing the calendar. The sooner she accepted that the better.

"You're in la-la land again, Thorn. Are you in this game or not?''

Thorn glared at Chase. "Yes, I'm in."

Chase chuckled as he studied his hand. "Yes, you may be in this game but from what I hear you're definitely out with Tara since you turned her down for that calendar."

Thorn tossed out a card. "She'll get over it."

"Possibly. However, it may take a while since she feels she let someone down."

Thorn decided not to ask, but curiosity got the best of Storm and he did the asking. "Who did Tara let down?"

"The children."

"Oh." Storm glared at Thorn after throwing out a card. "I'd forgotten about Kids' World. So I guess that also means I'm going to lose the bet. Thorn will never make any points with Tara by pissing her off."

Thorn decided he needed a break and placed his cards face-down on the table. "Where is Shelly, Dare? I need a drink of water."

Dare didn't look up from studying his hand. "She's probably upstairs watching a movie or something, but you know where the refrigerator is. Help yourself. There's beer and soda in there as well."

Thorn stood up from the dining room table as all of the brothers except for Dare glared at him. He walked into the kitchen and pulled out a pitcher of water from the refrigerator. He'd reached the max for beers he could consume and still ride his bike.

After reaching into the cabinet for a glass, he filled it with cold water and glanced across the way at a framed photograph that was on Dare and Shelly's living-room table. It was a photograph of Shelly, Tara and Delaney taken during a shopping trip the three women had taken to New York a few months ago.

Tara.

He hadn't seen her or talked to her since the day of their bike ride almost a week ago, but there hadn't been a day that passed when she hadn't crossed his mind. He had called her and left her a couple of messages, but she hadn't returned his calls, not that he had really expected her to. He hated admitting it, but Storm was right. It would be hard for him to garner any points with her because she was totally pissed off with him. But still, the thought of standing in front of a camera, posing for a photographer—as he'd done for Patrice—was something he was hell-bent against doing.

"Thorn! If you're still in the game, we need you out here!"

He recognized Stone's voice. "Keep your underwear on. I'm coming."

As he went back to the card game, Thorn returned his brothers' glares.

"I don't like losing, Thorn," Storm said as he watched him intently.

Thorn knew Storm was talking about the bet his brothers had made and not about the card game. He sighed. He knew what Tara wanted from him, and he knew what he wanted from her. Suddenly, he had an idea how they could both get what they wanted. Satisfied he had come up with a workable plan, one he thought was strategically sound, he met Storm's intense stare. "Don't give up on me yet, bro."

Storm's lips eased into a relieved smile. "Thanks, Thorn. I knew I could count on you."

Thorn pulled his bike to a stop in front of Tara's apartment. A number of lights were still on inside which must mean she hadn't gone to bed yet. He quickly shut off the bike's engine and made his way to her door, wondering if she would agree to the offer he intended to make.

He rang her doorbell and waited for her to answer. He didn't wait long. First he registered her surprise and then her frown. "Thorn. What are you doing here?"

He leaned against the doorjamb. "I needed to talk to you about something."

He saw the lifting of her brow. He also noticed that although she hadn't gone to bed, she was wearing a white velour bathrobe. He couldn't help but wonder what, if anything, she wore underneath the robe.

"Talk to me about what?"

"The possibility of me doing that calendar."

She met his gaze and he saw uncertainty. "You've changed your mind about doing it?"

He shook his head. "No, not yet. However, I think the two of us can work something out where I might be able to swing it."

The uncertainty in her gaze changed to hope. "All right. Come in," she invited, opening the door to him and standing back.

He entered and closed the door behind him. More than anything, he wanted to take her into his arms and kiss her senseless. He had missed her taste, her scent and every damn thing about her. But he didn't think she would appreciate him touching her just yet.

"Would you like something to drink?"

Her voice, soft and delicate, captured his attention. "No, I just left a card game at Dare's. I'm on the bike and don't want anything else to drink."

She nodded. "I was sitting in the kitchen drinking a cup of coffee while reading a medical report if you want to join me there."

"All right."

He'd always thought her kitchen was large...until the two of them were in it alone. Now it seemed small. And for some reason her kitchen table seemed to have shrunk.

"Are you sure I can't at least pour you a cup of coffee?"

He sighed as he sat down. "Now that I think about it, a cup of coffee would be nice."

"And how would you like it?"

"Black with two sugars."

Silence closed around them as she stood at the counter and prepared his coffee. "I called you a couple of times and you never returned my calls," he decided to say to break the silence in the room.

"I really didn't think we had anything to say, Thorn."

He nodded. Yes, he could see her thinking that way.

She came back to the table with his cup of coffee. He took a slow sip. He was particular about how he liked his coffee but found that she had made it just right. "Ahh, this is delicious."

"Thanks. Now if you'll excuse me, I need to slip into some clothes."

He slowly looked her up and down. He liked what she was wearing. "Don't go to any trouble on my account."

"It's no trouble. Please excuse me, I'll be back in a few minutes."

When she left him in the kitchen he glanced over at the medical journal she'd been reading. After making sure she had marked the page where she had left off, he closed it. When she came back he wanted her full attention. He had given his proposal much thought and didn't know how she would take it but he hoped she would keep an open mind. He intended to be honest with her, up-front, and not to pull any punches. He needed to make sure she understood just what he expected from her...if she went along with things.

"Okay, Thorn. What did you want to talk to me about?"

He turned in his seat. She was back already. He met her gaze after checking out her outfit; a pair of capri pants and a midriff top. She looked good, he thought. But what really grabbed his attention was the portion of her bare belly that showed beneath the short top. Damn if her navel didn't look good enough to taste. He cleared his throat to get his mind back to the business at hand. "I have a proposition for you," he said, barely able to get the words out of his mouth.

He watched as she arched a brow. He leaned back in the chair when she came to stand in the middle of the kitchen, a few feet from him and propped her hips against the counter near the sink. "What sort of a proposition?"

He had to force his attention away from her navel and back to the subject at hand. He cleared his throat again. "You still want me to do that calendar?"

"Yes, that would be nice."

He nodded. "Then I hope what I'm proposing will be acceptable."

She inclined her head and tilted it somewhat as a cautious smile touched her lips. "You still haven't told me just what this proposition is, Thorn."

He slowly stood and walked over to her. He leaned forward, braced his hands on the counter behind her, trapping her in. He moved his face close to hers. "I will agree to do the calendar if you do a favor for me, Tara."

He watched as she nervously licked her lips. "What kind of favor, Thorn?"

He felt his pulse quicken as desire for what he wanted from her filled his entire being. "I've been without a woman for over two years."

She blinked. He saw her throat move as she swallowed deeply. "You have?"

"Yes."

"Why?"

"Because I always take an oath of celibacy right before a race, and during the past couple of years I've been involved in a number of races. But I have to admit that had I really wanted to, I could have found the time to squeeze a woman or two in during the off season when there were no races, but I didn't."

She nervously licked her lips again. "Why not?"

"Because I had met you and from the first time I laid eyes on you I wanted you and no one else."

Tara shook her head as if what he was saying didn't make much sense. "But—but you didn't like me. You avoided me. You were downright moody and grumpy."

He smiled. "Yes, I was. I'm usually moody and grumpy whenever I've gone without sex for a long period of time. My bad moods have become a habit and most people who know me get used to them. I avoided you because I had no intention of getting involved with you. But now I've changed my mind."

She swallowed again. "How so?"

"I want to make a deal. I'll give you what you want from me if you'll give me what I want from you."

Tara stared at him. "And just what is it that you want from me?"

He leaned closer. "My next race is in Daytona during Bike Week, five weeks from now. Once the race is over, I want you to share my bed for a week."

He saw the startled look in her eyes. He then saw that look turn to anger. He quickly placed his finger to her lips to shut off whatever words she was about to say. "One week is all I'm asking for, one week in a completely physical and emotionally free affair. I need to get you out of my system as well as make up for what I haven't had in over two years."

He felt her breathing become unsteady as what he was proposing became crystal clear in her mind. For one week they would share a bed and take part in nothing short of a sexual marathon. He decided not to worry her mind by also telling her that during the five weeks leading up to the race, he intended to use that time to get her primed, ripe and ready for what he planned to do. By the time they slept together, she would want him just as much as he wanted her.

Just to prove a point he removed his finger from her lips and quickly placed his mouth there, swiping away any words she wanted to say. In no time at all he had her panting and whimpering under the onslaught of his mouth as he kissed her with everything he had inside him, mating relentlessly with her tongue.

He placed a hand on the bare section of her belly, feeling the warmth of her skin, smooth as silk, and felt her shudder from his touch. Deciding to take things farther, his fingers breached the elastic of her capri pants and went deeper until he could feel the silky material of her underpants.

He didn't stop there.

While he continued to make love to her mouth, he slipped his fingers past the elastic of her panties until he found just what he was seeking, that part of her that was hot, plump and damp.

Inhaling the very essence of her womanly scent, he let his fingers go to work as he centered on that part of her that he knew would bring her pleasure. She had told him last week that she thought he had gifted hands and she was about to experience just how gifted his hands were. He intended to use his fingers to drive her over the edge.

Desire was blatant in their kiss, the way their tongues mingled, fused, mated, as his fingers entered her. Her body felt extremely tight but that didn't stop him from using his fingers to make her shudder, tremble, shiver. Then there were those sounds she was making that were driving him insane.

He felt her knees weaken as though she could no longer stand, and, with his other hand he held on to her, keeping her upright while his fingers worked inside her. Then he felt her scream into his mouth, shudder in his arms, as an orgasm rocked her body, shaking her to the core.

He pulled his mouth away and looked at her, wanting to see her in the throes of passion, but she quickly pulled his mouth back down to hers, needing the contact. He didn't let his fingers stop what they were doing. He intended to keep going until it was all over for her. Until he heard her very last sigh of ecstasy.

When he saw she was gradually coming back down to earth, he slowly removed his hand and spread her dampness on her bare belly, letting it get absorbed into her skin. He inhaled deeply, loving her scent and knowing the next five weeks would be tortuous for him, but definitely well worth the wait.

He took a step back and watched as she slowly opened her eyes and met his gaze, realizing that he had just given her an orgasm while she stood in the middle of her kitchen. He knew she wanted to say something, but no words came from her mouth. So he leaned forward and placed a kiss on her lips.

"That's just a sample, Tara," he whispered softly. "Agree to have an affair with me for a week and I'll do the calendar thing for you. Think about it and let me know your decision."

Without saying anything else, he turned and left.

As soon as Thorn got home he went straight to the kitchen, grabbed a beer from the refrigerator and sank into the nearest chair. He quickly popped open the can and took a sip. Hell, he took more than a sip; he took a gulp. He needed it.

No other woman had ever affected him the way Tara did. Even now the potent scent of her still clung to him and he had an erection so huge it was about to burst out of his jeans. The only thing his mind could remember, the only thing his mind could not forget was the sound of her letting go; the sound of her reaching the pinnacle of pleasure under his hands.

He took another gulp of beer. He had almost lost it as a result of the sounds she had made. He knew she wasn't dating anyone. In fact, according to one of his brothers, after what had happened with her and that jerk she was supposed to marry, she had pretty much sworn off men.

And although no one had given him the full story, he knew she had moved to Atlanta because some married doctor with clout at her last job had gotten obsessed with her and had tried to force her to become his mistress. Although he hadn't tried forcing her, Thorn had to admit that he had pretty much made her the same offer. He hoped like hell that she would see the difference between his pursuit and that doctor's harassment. They would be good together in bed; tonight she'd got a sample of just how good they would be. From the way she had come apart against him, he had a feeling she had not even been aware of the full extent of her sensuality as a woman. She hadn't known the desires of the body could be so intense, so strong or so damn stimulating. And there had been something else he had found rather strange, but tonight he didn't want to think about that possibility.

The only thing he wanted to think about was the fact that he wanted her.

That was the bottom line. He wanted her in a way he had never wanted another woman. He wanted her in positions his mind was creating; in ways he had taken her in his dreams, his fantasies. And as he had told her, had blatantly warned her, by the time the motorcycle race was over in Daytona, he would have more than two years worth of pent-up sexual needs.

He hadn't wanted to scare her, but he had wanted her to know up front just what she would be facing. He owed her that piece of honesty.

He groaned, feeling himself get harder, straining even more against his jeans at the thought of them making love. If she agreed to what he wanted, he would make all the plans. He wanted a hotel for a week, in seclusion, in privacy and all he would need was food, something to drink and Tara in his bed.

Tara in his bed.

What he had told her last week was true. She had become his sweetest temptation and, he hoped, in a few weeks she would also be his greatest pleasure.

Six

Tara got to the hospital almost thirty minutes later than usual after enjoying the best sleep she remembered ever having. It was only with the brightness of morning that she had allowed herself to think of Thorn's proposition. Last night, after he'd left, she had been too exhausted and too satiated to do anything but strip naked, take a shower, slip into a nightgown and get into bed.

That morning while she had taken another shower, brushed her teeth, dressed for work and grabbed a small carton of apple juice as she raced out of the door, she was feeling angry all over again.

First it was Derrick, then Dr. Moyer and now Thorn. Did she have a sign on her forehead that said, Go Ahead And Use Me?

Not that she was even considering Thorn's ridiculous offer, but if she did go with him to Daytona, she would be close to home. Her hometown of Bunnell, Florida, was less than an hour from Daytona Beach, and it had been two years since she'd been home. She frequently talked to her family on the telephone, but she hadn't visited them. Luckily they had understood her need to stay away from the place that conjured up such painful memories. Instead of her going home, her family often visited her. Since Bunnell was a small town, everyone knew what had happened with Derrick on their wedding day.

Her thoughts shifted back to Thorn. Funny, but no matter how mad she got, she could not discount the pleasure Thorn had given her last night. A penetrating heat settled deep in her stomach just thinking about it, and she still felt this awesome tingle between her legs. She knew all about climaxes and orgasms, although she had never experienced one before last night. But still, a part of her couldn't help but think that if Thorn could make her orgasm so explosively with his hands, what would happen when they really made love?

And she hated admitting it, but a part of her was dying to find out.

She sighed deeply, getting as mad with herself as she was with Thorn. He should never have introduced her to something like that. All this time she had been operating under the premise that you couldn't miss what you never had, and now that he had given her a sampling, she couldn't get it out of her mind. Already she was anticipating the possibility of a repeat performance.

"Doctor Matthews, Mrs. Chadwick left a message asking that you give her a call," Tara's secretary informed her the moment she stepped off the elevator.

She briefly closed her eyes, having a good guess what the woman wanted. She needed to know if Thorn would be posing for the calendar. Oh, he would be posing, Tara thought, as she opened the door to her office and placed her medical bag on her desk. He would willingly pose if she agreed to his "completely physical, emotionally free affair."

Only a man could assume there was such a thing!

And what was this nonsense about him not engaging in sexual activities while training for a race? Not to mention his claim that he hadn't slept with a woman in over two years. Could that really be true? If it was then no wonder he was in a bad mood most of the time.

She had read enough medical books to know how the lack of intimate physical contact could play on some people's mind. No doubt Thorn was expecting a sexual marathon once his long, self-imposed wait was over. He had even mentioned he wanted to get her out of his system.

Tara's head began spinning and she sat down at her desk knowing she had to make decisions and soon. Suddenly, Delaney's words came back to her mind… *Don't try to beat Thorn at his game since he's a pro. What you should do is to come up with a game plan of your own.*

Tara sighed deeply. She had tried that very thing the day they had gone bike-riding and had failed, miserably. Maybe it was time she made another attempt.

Thorn thought he could hold out and not sleep with her until after the race. She couldn't help but wonder just how far he would go not to yield to temptation. Chances were if his willpower and control were tested or pushed to the limit, he would go away and leave her alone. There was no way he would let his sexual need for her interfere with the possibility of him losing a race. And if he really believed that nonsense that he needed to remain celibate before a race, then she would make it hard on him and do everything in her power to try and un-celibate him.

If he thought he was the one calling all the shots he

needed to think again. Thorn Westmoreland would soon
discover that he had met his match.

Tara shook her head as she entered what Stone had re-
ferred to as "the lion's den."

She slipped the key he had given her back into her purse
as she stepped inside and glanced around. According to the
brothers, this is where Thorn spent most of his evenings.
He would usually close shop and work on the special bike
he was building. And in this case, he was putting together
a dirt bike that he planned to give his nephew, AJ. AJ was
the son Dare hadn't known he had until last year when both
mother and son had moved back into town. Now Dare,
Shelly and AJ were a very happy family.

At first Tara hadn't wanted to take the key Stone had
offered her, but he had assured her that it was all right and
that Thorn could probably use the company. But they had
warned her to watch out for his bark as well as his bite.
The closer the time got to a race, the moodier he became.

After what Thorn had told her the other night, she now
understood why.

It had been three days since she had seen Thorn. Even
now, the episode in her kitchen was still on her mind and
was the cause of many sleepless nights. She would wake
up restless. Agitated. Hot.

And Thorn was to blame.

But somehow, she had found the courage to brave the
lion in his den to let him know of her decision about his
proposition. She hoped like the dickens she wasn't making
a mistake and the plan she had concocted wouldn't backfire
on her.

She glanced around after quietly closing the door. Inside
the building, the side entrance led into a huge office area
with file cabinets on both sides of the wall. There was also

a huge desk that was cluttered with metal and chrome instead of with paper. But what caught her attention were the framed photographs hanging on the wall. She walked farther into the room to take a closer look.

The first was a photo of Thorn and former president Bill Clinton. In the photo the two men were smiling as they stood beside a beautiful motorcycle. Tara then remembered that Thorn had built a motorcycle for the former president last year.

She then glanced at the other photographs, all of Thorn and Hollywood and sports celebrities. She couldn't stop the feeling of pride that suddenly flooded her as she viewed the evidence of Thorn's accomplishments. What she had told him the day they had gone bike-riding was true. He had gifted hands.

A shudder ran through her when she thought that the same hands that skillfully shaped chrome and metal into a motorcycle could also bring a woman to the epitome of sexual release. She shook her head, not wanting to go there, but remembering that the main reason she was here was because she *had* gone there…too many times lately. There wasn't a single day that went by that she didn't think of her and Thorn's kitchen encounter. She wanted to believe that although he had kept his control, he had been just as affected as she had been.

With that belief, she had made a decision to show him that he had bitten off more than he could chew and she was more trouble than she was worth. She intended to turn up the heat by tempting him so badly that he would want to break things off with her before their relationship interfered with his race.

She saw it as the battle of wills, Mr. Experience against Miss Innocence. Thorn's brothers thought she was his challenge. He thought she was his sweetest temptation. She was determined to become Thorn's ultimate downfall.

The screwdriver Thorn was using to tighten a bolt on the bike's fender nearly slipped from his fingers. His nostrils flared and his entire body went on alert. He swore he'd picked up Tara's scent although he knew that wasn't possible. But still, the mere thought of her had blood pumping into every part of his body and shoved the beating of his heart into overdrive.

He couldn't help but groan under a tightly held breath. Boy, did he have it bad! He hadn't seen her in three days and already he was imagining her presence and inhaling the essence of her scent.

He had tried not to think about her; tried not to wonder what she'd been doing since he'd last seen her, and if she'd given any thought to his proposal. A light shudder raced down his spine at the possibility that she would consider it. The very idea of Tara in his bed for a week nearly made it impossible for him to breathe.

He placed his work tools aside. With her so deeply embedded in his mind, it would be impossible to get any work done. He decided to call it quits for the night and grab a beer. And he may as well spend the night at the shop since there was definitely no one waiting for him at home.

Thorn had turned and headed toward the refrigerator that sat on the other side of the room when he thought he heard something. He stopped and his gaze took a slow scan of the room, lingering on the area where the hallway led to his office.

Only his brothers had keys to his shop. He wondered if one of them had dropped by. It wouldn't be the first time one of them had found refuge in his office to read his latest issue of *Cycle World* magazine and raid his candy jar.

He suddenly caught Tara's scent again. The smell was both alluring and seductive. He narrowed his eyes curiously as he began walking toward his office.

The air inside the building began to sizzle with each step he took. His skin began to get warm, his hands felt damp and pressure began escalating deep in his chest. Tension within him mounted at the sheer possibility, the inkling of any notion that Tara had stepped into his domain. His shop was more than just his place of business. It was more than somewhere he hung out most of the time. It was his lair. His sphere. His space.

The sharp edge of that thought cut deep into his brain. But not for one moment did it cut into his increasing desire. If anything, his body was struggling to get back the cool it had lost a while ago. He tried to keep his face solemn as he slowly and quietly rounded a corner. Tara's scent was becoming more overpowering.

And then he saw her.

Tara Matthews. His challenge. His sweetest temptation. Thorn watched as she studied the pictures he had hanging on the wall, not believing she was really there.

He wondered which one of his brothers had given her a key, not that it mattered. However, they had been with him earlier and knew the state of his mind...and his body. They were very well aware that lately he had been a man on the edge, a man in a state of pure funk with an attitude that was more biting and cutting than they had seen in a long time. Yet they had sent Tara here! At least, they hadn't tried talking her out of coming. If this was their idea of a joke, then he didn't see a damn thing funny about it. He just had to keep his mind on the prize. At the moment his mind was slightly foggy about whether that prize was the trophy he sought in Daytona or the woman standing across the room from him.

He shook his head, not believing he had thought such a thing. No woman, and that included Patrice, had ever come between him and his motorcycle, his desire to win, his need to take risks.

The corners of his lips quirked upward, as he admitted that Tara came pretty damn close to ruining his focus. His gaze took her in from head to toe, from behind, since her back was to him as she continued to study the pictures on his office wall. But that was okay. Checking out the back of her was just fine. He'd always like the shape of her backside anyway.

Her head was thrown back as she tried viewing a photograph that was positioned at a high angle. That made her hair fan across her shoulders, and the way the light in the room was hitting it gave the strands a brilliant glow.

She was wearing a dress. A rather short one but her curves were meant for the dress and the dress was meant for her curves. His gaze roamed down her body to her legs. They were long, shapely and he bet they would feel like heaven wrapped around his waist, holding him inside her real tight while he made love to her with no intention of ever stopping.

Something made her go still. He could tell the exact moment she knew he was in the room although she didn't turn around. It didn't matter to him that she wasn't ready to acknowledge his presence. Eventually she would have to. What really mattered to him was that she was there. Alone with him and looking sexier than any woman had a right to look.

But he inwardly admitted that there was a lot more to Tara than her being pleasing to the eyes. There were things about her that went beyond the physical. There was the way she had captured the love, admiration and respect of his family, especially his four brothers. For some reason, none of them had taken a liking to Patrice; however, with Tara it was an entirely different story. Then there was the love and dedication she had for her job as a pediatrician. He happened to be at the hospital one day and had seen first hand what a warm, loving and caring approach she had with a sick child. He had known at that moment while watching her that she would make a fantastic mother to any man's child…even his.

A warning bell went off in his head and he got the uneasy feeling that he was losing control and shouldn't be thinking such thoughts, even if Tara was proving to be the most captivating woman he'd ever met.

He drew in a deep breath. The coming weeks would test his willpower, his determination and definitely his control. The only thing that would make any of it worth a damn was the possibility of her being his, completely his, in the end. And that was what he needed to know more than anything. He had to know if she would accept the proposal he had offered her.

"If I'd known you were stopping by, I would have tidied up the place," he finally said as moments continued to tick by.

She turned slightly and gestured around the room that all of a sudden looked small and felt cramped. "I wouldn't have wanted you to go to any trouble on my account. Besides, I don't plan to stay that long anyway. I only stopped by to let you know of my decision."

He pushed away from the door and walked into the center of the room, needing to be closer to her. "And what is your decision, Tara?"

She turned and met his inquiring gaze. Damn, she looked good, and he fought the urge to reach out and pull her into his arms, to taste her in a kiss that had his mouth watering at the thought of it.

Awareness flashed in her eyes. They were heated, compelling, and he watched as emotions flickered through them. For a long moment the two of them stood in the center of his office feeding off each other's needs, wants and desires. And the sad thing about it was that they couldn't control their reactions to each other. It seemed they were both suffering from a unique brand of animal lust.

Thorn let out a deep breath and took a step back. Nothing of this magnitude had ever happened to him. He was within a few feet of jumping her bones. He had a mind to take her right there in his office, on his desk. Right then, at that moment, he saw her as a means to an end, a way to get intense pleasure and a way to give pleasure as well.

He shook his head, reminding himself that he would have to wait another five weeks, until after the race. He cursed inwardly. As far as he was concerned the first week of March couldn't get there soon enough.

He then remembered he was assuming things. She hadn't said she would go along with what he had proposed. For all he knew she could have come to tell him to go to hell and to take his proposal with him.

He swallowed deeply. The suspense was killing him as much as his lust was. "What's it going to be?" he had to ask her.

He watched her study him with dark eyes before saying, "I want to make sure I understand what you're proposing, Thorn. You will pose for the calendar if I agree to sleep with you in a completely physical, emotional free affair once your race at Bike Week is over. I'm supposed to be at your disposal, your beck and call for a week."

He smiled. Everything she had said sounded pretty damn right to him. It had also painted one hell of a tempting picture in his mind. "Yeah, that about sums it up."

"And you won't touch me until *after* the race?" she said, as if to clarify.

Thorn crossed his arms over his chest. "Oh, I will touch you, I just won't make love to you in the traditional sense until *after* the race. As far as I'm concerned, anything else is game."

Tara lifted a brow. "Anything…like what?"

Now it was Thorn's turn to lift a brow. "A variety of things, and I'm surprised you would have to ask."

Tara nodded, deciding to leave well enough alone before he become suspicious about just how much experience she had. Knowing she was a virgin would really scare him off and probably anger him to the point of not posing for the calendar. "I fully understand my part in all of this."

Thorn inwardly smiled. He doubted that she fully understood anything, especially her part in it. But her duties would be clearly defined over the coming weeks. "So what's your answer?"

Tara prayed things worked out as she had planned. "Yes. I'll go along with your proposition."

Thorn released a deep breath, relieved.

"So how soon can you be available to do the calendar?"

Her question broke into his thoughts, just as well, since they were about to go somewhere they shouldn't be going. "How soon would they want me?"

"Probably within the next couple of weeks."

He nodded. "Just let me know when and where and I'll be there."

She blinked, and he could tell she couldn't believe he was being so accommodating. "What are your plans for this weekend?" he asked her.

She raised a brow before answering. "I'm working at the hospital on Saturday but I'll be off on Sunday. Why?"

"Chase is having a Super Bowl party at his restaurant Sunday evening. I'd like you to go with me."

She blinked again. "Me? You? As a couple?" she asked, as if clearly amazed.

"Yes. Don't you think we should let my family get used to seeing us together as a couple? Otherwise, what will they think when we take off for Daytona together?" he asked.

In all honesty, Thorn really didn't give a hoot what his brothers thought, since they assumed they had things pretty much figured out to suit their fancy anyway. His main concern was his parents. They considered Tara as another daughter and would give him plenty of hell if they thought for one minute his intentions toward her weren't honorable. Since his intentions weren't honorable, he had to at least pretend they were for his parents' benefit. Then there was Delaney to consider. She definitely wouldn't like it if she knew his plans for Tara.

He watched as she nervously bit her bottom lip before saying. "Yes, I guess you're right. In that case, yes, I'll go to Chase's party with you on Sunday."

He nodded, pleased with himself.

"It's getting late and I'd better go."

Her leaving wasn't such a bad idea considering his body's reaction to her presence. There was only so much temptation he could handle. "All right. I'll walk you to your car." He thought of something. "How did you get in here anyway?"

"Stone let me use his key. He told me it would be best to come in quietly through the side door and not the front so as not to disturb you."

Thorn nodded, knowing that wasn't the true reason Stone had told her that. He had wanted him to be surprised by her presence; he definitely had been.

They didn't talk as he walked her to her car. A couple

of times he came close to asking her to stay and let him show her around his shop. But he couldn't do that. He had to play by the rules he had established to keep his sanity, and at the moment the temptation to bed her was too great. After she left he would spend time working out, getting his blood flowing to all the parts of his body, especially to his brain.

He had to think clearly and tread lightly with Tara. Now that she had agreed to his proposal, he had to make sure he was the one in the driver's seat and she was only along for the ride. And in the end, he intended to give her the ride of her life.

But temptation being what it was, he couldn't stop himself from inching closer to her as they walked toward her car, intentionally allowing his thigh and hip occasionally to brush against hers. Her sharp intake of breath at each contact sent shivers down his spine. When they did sleep together, there was no doubt in his mind they would go up in smoke. They were just that hot.

He stood back and watched her open the door to her compact sedan. She turned to him before getting inside. "Thanks for walking me to my car, Thorn."

"Don't mention it." His gaze was devouring her but he couldn't help it. He blew out a long breath before taking a step toward her. He could tell that she was ready for his kiss, and he was more than happy to oblige her. He leaned forward and placed his mouth on hers, lightly tracing the tip of his tongue along the line of her lips, repeating the gesture several times before she easily parted her lips and drew his tongue inside her mouth with her own. His heart thudded deep in his chest at the way she was eager for the mating with his tongue, something that seemed a necessity for both of them. At this moment in time, it all made sense. He would probably think he was crazy later, but for now, standing in the middle of his parking lot, devouring her mouth like there was no tomorrow seemed perfectly normal to him. As far as he was concerned, it was the sanest thing he had done in a long time.

Her taste seduced him. It made his mind concentrate on things it shouldn't be thinking about this close to competition time. He needed to pull back, but he was steadily convincing himself otherwise.

He only brought the kiss to an end when he detected her need to breathe and wondered just how long their mouths had been joined. He stared into her eyes, watching the play of emotions that crossed her face. Confusion? Curiosity? Caution?

He took a step back. They had shared enough for tonight. The next time they were together they would be around family and friends who would serve as the buffer he needed between them.

"Drive home safely, Tara," he said, deciding she needed to leave now so he could pull himself together before he was tempted to do something he would later regret.

She nodded and without saying anything, she got into the car. His heart skipped a beat when he got a glimpse of her thighs. The hem of her dress inched up as she slid into the driver's seat. Forcing breath into his lungs, he watched as she slowly drove off, all the while thinking, that he had five weeks of pure hell to endure. Five whole weeks he somehow intended to survive.

Seven

"Okay, Mr. Westmoreland, I only need a few more shots and then this session will be all over," the photographer said as she adjusted the lighting.

Thank God, Thorn thought as he sat astride his bike once again. He had plenty of work to do back at the shop and had been at this photo session for three hours. The photographer, Lois Kent, had decided the best place to shoot the photos was outside to better show the man, his bike and the open road.

They had taken over a hundred shots already and Thorn's patience was beginning to wear thin. The only thing that kept him going was knowing that he was living up to his end of the bargain, which meant he could make damn sure Tara lived up to hers. This past week he'd been restless, agitated and moodier than ever.

"It will only take a minute while I reload the film."

Thorn nodded. Things hadn't gone as badly as he'd

thought they would. Lois Kent was strictly a professional, unlike Patrice. To Lois this was a job and nothing more and he appreciated that.

He glimpsed behind her and saw a car pull up. His heart quickened when he recognized the driver.

He watched as Tara got out of her car and walked toward them. She was wearing a pair of white slacks and a pull-over blue sweater.

And as usual she looked good.

It had been a week since he had seen her; a week since he had taken her to his brother's restaurant for the Super Bowl party. Even surrounded by family and friends, he hadn't been able to keep his eyes off her. His interest in Tara hadn't gone unnoticed by his brothers. And they had been teasing him about it ever since, which only pissed him off even more.

He raised a brow, wondering why she was here, not that he had any complaints. It was only that he had been trying to keep his distance from her so that he could retain his sanity and his control. He had decided it would only take a week or two to get her primed to the level he wanted her to be. He now had four weeks left.

He watched as she spoke to Lois, and then she glanced over at him. "Hi Thorn."

"Tara," he acknowledged, taking a deep breath. He had been the perfect gentleman that Super Bowl Sunday, even when he had taken her home. He had kissed her on her doorstep, made sure she had gotten safely inside and left. Doing more than that would have been suicide.

"I'm surprised to see you here," he said, not taking his eyes off her as he drank in her beauty. It was one of those days when the air was brisk with a slight chill although the sun was shining high overhead. The sun's rays made her look that much more gorgeous.

"Today was my day off. I wasn't doing anything special so I thought I would come and check things out. I had lunch at Chase's place, and when I asked about you, he told me where you were."

Thorn nodded. He just bet his brother was happy to give her any information about him that she wanted. They would do anything to get him out of his foul mood. But what surprised him was that Tara had asked Chase about him. Thorn wondered if perhaps she had sought him out about anything in particular. He sighed, deciding he would find out soon enough.

"All right, Mr. Westmoreland, I'm ready to start shooting again," Lois said, recapturing his attention.

He slid his gaze from Tara's to Lois's. "Okay," he said, ready to get the photo session over with. "Let your camera roll."

Tara's breath got lodged in her throat as she watched Thorn before the camera. He looked magnificent.

Thorn and his motorcycle.

Together they were a natural, and she knew that he would be the highlight in any woman's calendar as Mr. July. In a month that was known to be hot anyway, he would definitely make things explosive.

She should have her head examined even for being here. She had known that today was the day for Thorn's photo session and when Chase had mentioned just where it would be, she couldn't help being pulled to this place to seek him out. On the drive over she kept asking herself why she needed to see him, but she hadn't come up with an answer.

"That's right, Mr. Westmoreland, give me another one of those sexy smiles for the camera. That's it. Just think about all those women who'll be looking at you on that calendar and panting. I'm sure some of them will even find a way to contact you. You'll certainly have your pick of any of them," Lois said, as she moved around in front of Thorn and snapped picture after picture.

Tara frowned. The photographer's words didn't sit too well with her. Just the thought of other women contacting Thorn after seeing the calendar bothered her. It shouldn't have. She met his gaze and saw he was watching her intently. Had he read the displeasure on her face when the photographer had mentioned other women?

She sighed deeply, getting aggravated with herself. What Thorn did with his free time did not concern her. At least it shouldn't, but it did.

"Okay, that's it, Mr. Westmoreland. You were a wonderful subject to capture on film and I can't wait for the calendar to come out. I know it will be a huge success and will benefit Kids' World greatly."

Lois then added. "And not to impose but I have a friend who asked me to give you her phone number. She is a huge fan of yours and would love to get together with you some time. She's a flight attendant who usually attends Bike Week in Daytona each year and was wondering if perhaps—"

"Thanks, but I'm not interested," Thorn said, getting off his bike. He didn't even glance at the surprised look on Lois's face when he walked toward Tara. "I have all the woman I need right here."

Thorn saw surprise in Tara's face just seconds before he leaned down and kissed her in a full open-mouth caress that left no one guessing about their relationship. At least no one other than Tara.

"Oops, sorry," Lois said when Thorn released Tara's mouth from his. "I didn't know the two of you were an item, Dr. Matthews." She smiled apologetically. "I assumed you had dropped by as a member of the committee to see how things were going. Besides, from everything I'd always heard or read, Thorn Westmoreland has never made a claim on any woman," she said, chuckling. "Evidently, I'm wrong."

Before Tara could open her mouth, the one that had just been thoroughly kissed by Thorn, to tell Lois that she had not been wrong and had misread things, Thorn spoke up.

"Yeah, you were wrong because I'm definitely staking a claim on this woman."

Tara raised a brow and decided that now was not the time or the place to set Thorn straight. No man staked a claim on her. "I gather things went well," she found herself saying instead.

"Better than I thought they would. Lois is good at her job. I just hope all those photographs she took come out the way she wants them to."

Tara nodded. There was no doubt in her mind they would. What Lois had said was true. Thorn was definitely a wonderful subject to capture on film. "Well, I'd better go. I dropped by out of curiosity," she said easing away.

He nodded. "What are your plans for the rest of the day?"

Tara's heart thudded in her chest with his question. "I don't have any. Why?"

"Would you like go to bike-riding with me and have dinner at that restaurant again?"

Tara really would have liked that but wondered if it was wise. But then, if she planned to seduce Thorn into breaking his vow of celibacy, she had to get things rolling.

"All right. Just give me an hour to go home and change clothes."

His gaze was steadily focused on hers when he said, "Okay."

* * *

Thorn didn't have to encourage Tara this time to lean into him. Her body automatically did so after straddling the bike behind him and fitting her rear end comfortably on the seat. She placed her chest against his back, delighting in the feel of her body pressed against his. She inhaled the pleasant scent of him as she rested her head against his jacket, and, at the moment, without understanding what was going on with her, she felt being this close to him was a necessity to her very existence. It didn't make sense. She had vowed never to feel that way about any man again.

But she admitted that Thorn was her challenge.

Although she knew a future wasn't in the cards for them, and any involvement would be just as he wanted—completely physical and emotionally free she still couldn't help but be cautious. There was something about Thorn that could become addictive. But then she reminded herself quickly that she didn't intend things to go that far between them. Thorn would have to choose between her and the race, and she was banking that it would be the race. It was an ego thing. He could get another woman in his bed any time, but a chance to be victorious at Bike Week, to reign supreme, was something he had been working years to achieve.

So she decided to do whatever was needed to increase his physical craving and make sure he was tempted beyond his control. She scooted closer to him and leaned more into him. Her arms around his waist tightened. She planted her cheek against his back and again inhaled his scent—manly, robust and sensual.

Closing her eyes, she remembered that night in her kitchen, the skill of his exploring fingers and the sensations he had made her feel. She then imagined how things might be if they were to make it beyond the four weeks, although she knew they wouldn't. But still she decided there was nothing wrong with having wild fun in her imagination.

What would happen if her plan to seduce Thorn failed? He would probably win the race—only because he was arrogant and cocky enough to do so—and then he would celebrate his victory, but not for long. He would turn his attention to her with one thought on his mind; taking her to bed.

The thought of that happening was almost too much to think about. But she did so anyway. In the dark recesses of her mind, she could picture the two of them wrapped in silken sheets in a huge bed, making out like there was no tomorrow.

For an entire week.

She opened her eyes and tried to shove the thoughts away. Too late. There were too many of them firmly planted in her mind. After two years of going without he would no doubt take her at a level that bordered on desperation. He would be like a starving man eating his favorite meal for the first time in a long while. She shuddered slightly as she imagined how his first thrust would feel. Probably painful, considering her virginal state. But then, any that followed would be...

She blinked, noticing Thorn had slowed the bike down. She glanced around, wondering if they had arrived at their destination, and was surprised to see he had brought her back to the wooded area he had said was Westmoreland land. Why? They had taken a walk around the property the last time they were here a couple of weeks ago. Why was he bringing her back here?

Thorn breathed in deeply as he brought his bike to a stop. All he had planned to do was take Tara out to eat and then back home. But the feel of her arms wrapped tightly around his waist, the feel of her pressed so close to his back and the scent of her surrounding him had been too much.

He angled his head over his shoulder and came very close to her face. "We need to talk."

Tara lifted a brow. "Couldn't we have waited until we got to the restaurant?"

He shook his head. "No, it's rather private and not a topic we would want to discuss over dinner."

"Oh," she said, wondering just what topic that could be.

She climbed off the bike and stood back as he turned off the engine, kicked down the motorcycle stand and then swung his leg over the bike. She tried not to look at how tightly stretched his jeans were across his body, especially over his midsection, as he slowly covered the distance that separated them. She met his gaze. He had said that he wanted to talk, but the look in his eyes told another story.

She swallowed when he came to a stop in front of her. "What did you want to talk about?"

Thorn blinked. For a moment he had completely forgotten just what he had wanted to discuss with her. His concentration had gone to her mouth and his desire to devour it. Savor it. Taste it.

"It's about birth control," he finally said.

Now it was Tara's turn to blink. "Birth control?"

"Yes," Thorn answered in a husky voice. "I need to know if you're using any?"

Tara blinked again. "Excuse me?"

Thorn's voice got huskier when he explained. "I need to know if you plan on using birth control when we make love because I don't intend to use anything."

Tara stared at him, momentarily speechless. Never in a million years would she have thought that he was the kind of man who would be the selfish type in the bedroom. They were men who thought all they had to do was to enjoy the act of making love and not contribute to the responsibility of making sure there was not an unwanted pregnancy. She had heard about such men and couldn't believe that Thorn was one of them. She couldn't believe he was actually standing in front of her dumping something like that in her lap.

Looking him squarely in the eye she placed her hands on her hips. "No, I'm not on any type of birth control," she said, deciding not to add that she had started taking the pill six months before her wedding was to take place. She had stopped when the marriage hadn't happened and had not given any thought to going back on them since there had not been a need. As far as she was concerned there still was no need since she had no intention of sleeping with Thorn, although he didn't know that.

Her gaze sharpened and angry fire appeared in her eyes. The expression on her face would probably have killed lesser men. "So if you plan to sleep with me, Thorn Westmoreland, then it will be up to you to wear a condom."

Thorn crossed his arms over his chest. Oh, he intended to sleep with her all right. But sleep was only a portion of what they would do, a very small portion. He watched her glare at him. Damn, but he liked her feistiness and had from the first time they had met. He knew he had ventured into territory that was probably off limits by the way she was acting, but the sooner she knew the score, the better. First he had to clarify things with her.

"Don't misunderstand me, Tara. If it were any woman other than you, I wouldn't even dream of taking them to bed without my own brand of protection no matter what type of protection they claimed to be using. In addition to that, I would make sure we both knew the state of our health. Safe sex means a lot to me, and I need to be certain it also means a lot to the woman I'm sleeping with. When it comes to bed partners, I'm extremely selective. Because of racing, I routinely take physicals, and I'm sure since you're involved in the medical field, things are probably the same way with you. I apologize if I came off just now as being a man who leaves the responsibility of birth control strictly in the hands of the woman. That is far from the truth. I'm not that selfish nor am I that stupid.''

Confusion clouded Tara's eyes. ''Then why did you ask me that? I still don't understand.''

He decided it was time to make her understand. ''Because I have wanted you for so long, and my desire for you is so great, I want to explode inside you and know it's happening and actually feel it happening. I want to be skin to skin with you when it happens. More than anything, I desire it to be that way with you.''

Tara's chest rose as she took a deep breath, removed her hands from her hips and clenched them by her sides. She met the eyes that bored into hers and whispered in a soft voice the single word that immediately came to her mind. ''Why?''

He took a step closer. ''Because I want to share more pleasure with you than I've ever shared with another woman. For one solid week I don't want to know where your body begins and where mine ends. And at that moment when I am inside of you, making love to you over and over again, I want to be able to feel, actually feel, you getting wet for me. I want the full effect of reaching the ultimate climax with you.''

He reached out and touched her waist and felt the tremors that his words had caused. He pulled her to him, wanting her to feel just what he was feeling too. She was the reason for his constant state of arousal and had been the reason for quite some time. No other woman had been able to do this to him. Only her. He had two years of pent-up

sexual frustrations to release and he wanted to do it inside
of her. He could think of making love to no one else.

He saw an involvement with someone else as a sexual
act that would be empty, meaningless and unfulfilling.
Maybe it was a mind game he had gotten caught up in, but
there was no help for it. He was convinced that Tara was
not only his challenge and his sweetest temptation, he truly
believed that she was also his passion and the two of them
would connect in bed in a special way. They would be
fantastic together. He had no illusions that they would not
be.

Tara licked her bottom lip. She wondered what Thorn
would say if she told him she was a virgin. And better yet,
what would he say if she told him she didn't intend to get
on any type of birth control just for a week that wouldn't
happen? But she couldn't tell him either of those things.

Instead, she said. "And what if I told you I couldn't take
the pill due to medical reasons and that I don't feel comfortable using any other type of birth control? Would you
use a condom then?"

Without hesitating he said. "Yes."

She nodded, believing that he would. But then, after what
he had just told her, she knew that if they ever made love—
although there was a very slim chance of that happening—
they both knew what it would take to give him the ultimate
in sexual satisfaction when he slept with her. He wanted it
all and had engrained into his mind that he wanted things
to be different with her than they had been with any other
woman he had been with.

Tara didn't know whether to be flattered or frightened.

A part of her knew she had nothing to fear from Thorn.
Even when he had come across as moodier than hell, she
hadn't been afraid of him. The reason she had avoided him

for the past two years was for the very thing he was talking to her about now.

Wants and desires.

She had always wanted him, from the first. Even now she wanted him. She was woman enough to admit that. But wanting something and having something were two totally different things. Derrick had pretty much killed her emotions, but Thorn had easily brought them back to life. If she was afraid of anything, it was of losing her heart to someone else and getting hurt once more. But she couldn't think about any of that when Thorn was looking at her as if she was a treat he wanted to savor, over and over again.

"Thanks for letting me know what I'm up against, Thorn," she said softly. She watched a slow smile touch the corners of his lips. Everyone knew Thorn's smiles were infrequent, and whenever he smiled, especially at her, pleasant emotions always flooded her body.

"That's not the only thing you will be up against, Tara."

She heard the little hitch in his voice and followed the path of his gaze downward as it settled on his midsection. She shuddered when she saw his arousal straining against the zipper of his jeans.

"But there's no doubt in my mind that you can handle me."

Tara blinked. She wasn't so sure when she saw how large he was. A mixture of desire and anticipation rammed through her mind as well as her body. It didn't do any good to try and convince herself that she didn't have a thing to worry about since she and Thorn would never make love. Seeing him standing before her with a determined look on his face made her realize just what she really *was* up against. His mind was pretty made up. He would be competing in the race, and he would have her at the end of four weeks and nothing would deter him from his goals.

She would have to see about that. She needed to test his control and let him know just what he was up against as well.

Determined to make a point, she leaned up on tiptoe and placed her mouth to his. After overcoming his surprise, he immediately captured her lips with his. At the first touch of his tongue to hers she began to shudder, and he placed his arms around her and brought her closer into the fit of him to thoroughly taste her and devour her mouth. A keen ache throbbed deep within her. She slipped her arms around his neck and held on as his kiss became more demanding. Arching against him she felt the hardness of his erection more firmly against her belly, igniting heat and a deep sense of yearning.

He was giving her just what she wanted, and she suddenly pushed aside her need to make a point. At the moment nothing mattered to her, except the sensation of him against her stomach, and the feel of his hands cupping her backside to secure a closer fit.

Breath whooshed from her lungs the moment he broke off the kiss, and he held her in his arms as they both panted their way back to reality. For the longest moment, neither of them moved. Instead they stood there, on Westmoreland land, with their arms wrapped around each other trying their best to breathe and regain control of their minds and bodies.

Doing so wasn't easy and they both knew, for totally different reasons, they were in deep trouble.

"I understand you were once engaged to be married."

Tara stopped eating abruptly and glanced up at Thorn, startled by his statement. There was a serious glint in the depths of the dark eyes looking at her. Trying to keep her features expressionless, she met his gaze and asked. "Who told you that?"

Thorn contemplated her for a long moment before saying. "One of my brothers. I can't remember which one, though. Was it supposed to have been a secret?"

Tara gave him a considering glance. "No."

He studied her. "So, what happened?"

Tara figured he already knew the full story and wondered why he was asking. The night of Delaney's wedding she had been the one to catch the bouquet, and when the Westmoreland brothers had remarked that she would be next, she'd immediately told them she would never marry and had ended up telling them why.

She sighed. "Derrick, the man I was to marry decided on my wedding day at the church, in front of over three hundred guests, that he loved my maid of honor instead of me. So he stopped the wedding, asked for my forgiveness and he and the woman I'd always considered my best friend took off. They drove to Georgia and got married that same day."

"He was a fool," Thorn didn't hesitate in saying before taking a sip of his coffee. He met her gaze then asked, "Are you over him?"

His question and the way he was looking at her quickened her pulse. "Yes. Why?"

"Curious."

Tara continued eating, wondering why Thorn would be curious about her feelings for Derrick. Deciding she had given him enough information about her past, she decided she wanted to know about the woman who'd been in his past. The one who'd made him leery of getting serious about a woman.

"What about you, Thorn? Have you ever been in love?"

He met her gaze over the rim of the coffee cup he held to his lips. "Why do you ask?"

"Curious."

He set down his cup. "I don't know. I may have thought I was at one time, but when I take the time to analyze the situation, I don't think I've ever been in love."

Tara nodded. "But a woman has hurt you." It was more a statement than a question.

"I think it was more disappointment than hurt. It's hard for anyone to discover they were deceived by someone they cared about, Tara."

She of all people knew how right he was on that one. She thought of how many times Derrick and Danielle had written to her, asking her forgiveness for deceiving her, and how many times she had tossed their letters in the trash.

"But she meant a lot to you?"

He picked up his cup and took another sip before answering. "Yes, at the time I thought she did, but I can say it was nothing but lust. What disappointed me the most was finding out I wasn't the only man she was sleeping with, and I'm glad I used protection to the max with her. I make it a point to stay away from women who routinely have multiple bed partners."

Tara nodded. "What did she do for a living?"

He signaled for a waitress to refill his coffee. "She's a freelance photographer."

"Oh." No wonder he hadn't been anxious to do that photo shoot, she thought. "And are you over her?"

He chuckled. Evidently he thought she had scored with that question. She was following the same line of questioning he had used on her earlier.

"Yes, I am definitely over her." He leaned over the table, closer to her and whispered. "You, Tara Matthews, are the only woman on my agenda, and I'm counting the days until I have you in bed with me while I do all kinds of wild and wicked things to you."

Tara swallowed as her pulse rate increased. She dropped her gaze to her plate, but the sensations that swept through her with his words forced her to meet his gaze again. The look he was giving her was dark, sexy and brooding and she knew that if things worked out the way he planned, he would have her in his bed after the race so fast it would make her head spin.

She lowered her gaze and began eating her food again. Thorn was seducing her and she couldn't let him do that. They had already played their love games for the day. She needed to think smart and stay in control. She decided to maneuver their conversation to a safer topic.

"Why do you race?"

His mouth twitched, and a smile appeared. She knew he saw through her ploy but decided to go along with her. "I like the excitement of taking risks. I've always liked to compete. Motorcycle racing stimulates that side of me."

For the next twenty minutes she listened while he talked about racing and what benefits, promotions and recognition his company would receive if he won the first race of the year, the one during Bike Week at the Daytona Speedway. He also told her about his desire one day to compete on the European circuit.

"Do you race a lot?"

"I do my share. Last year I was in a total of twelve races. That averaged out to be a race a month, so I was on the road quite a bit. The men who're my crew chief and mechanic are the best in the business. And I also have the best damn wrench around."

"Wrench?"

"Yeah, just like a wrench is a mechanic's basic tool, the same holds true of a human wrench in racing. He's the person I most depend on. I have an eighteen-wheeler that transports my bikes from race to race and wherever I go, my wrench travels with me. Racing is a team sport and if I win, my team wins.''

By the time the evening was over, Tara had received a very extensive education on motorcycle racing. For most of an hour, they had avoided bringing sex into their conversation and when they left the restaurant to head home, Tara looked at Thorn and smiled before getting on the motorcycle. Unlike the last time, when they had ended their meal with tempers flaring, tonight she had thoroughly enjoyed the time she had spent with him.

Later that night, as she lay in bed, half asleep with thoughts of Thorn running through her head, she couldn't help but remember their conversation about birth control.

She inhaled a lengthy, deep, fortifying breath when she thought of what Thorn wanted to do to her. Closing her eyes she thought of the picture Thorn had painted at the restaurant of them in bed together. She imagined him climbing on her, straddling her and burying himself deep within her, stroking her insides, making it last while his desire raged for her at a level that wasn't normally possible. Then finally, as she imagined him climaxing inside her, with nothing separating them, feeling everything, the complete essence of him, she felt the area around the juncture of her legs get hot and sensitive.

Tara opened her eyes. She'd better play it safe. Just in case there was a slim possibility that she and Thorn ever actually did make love, she knew she would want it just as he described. Tara decided to make an appointment with her gynecologist this week.

Eight

Tara glanced at the clock on the wall. Thorn would be arriving any minute.

She had called him at the shop asking if he knew anything about repairing a leaking faucet. It was the perfect ploy since his brothers had gone on a camping trip for the weekend. Had they been available, he would wonder why she had summoned him instead of one of them.

She nearly jumped at the sound of the doorbell. It had been a couple of days since she had seen him, and today she had a plan. She was intent on testing his control to the limit, with the hope that he would finally see that was more trouble than she was worth and a threat to his winning his race; especially if he strongly believed in this celibacy thing.

She looked down at herself before walking to the door. Although her outfit wasn't outright provocative, she thought it would definitely grab his attention. After glancing out of the peephole in the door, she opened it.

"Thorn, thanks for coming. I really hated to bother you but that dripping faucet was driving me crazy and I knew if I didn't get it taken care of, I wouldn't be able to sleep tonight."

"No problem," he said, stepping inside with a toolbox in his hand. "I'm sure this will only take a minute."

His gaze traveled down the length of her, taking in her very short cut-off jeans and her barely-there, thin tank top. It wasn't transparent but it might as well have been the way her nipples showed through. It left very little to the imagination.

His face turned into a frown. "You went somewhere dressed like that?"

She glanced down at herself. "What's wrong with the way I'm dressed?"

"Nothing, unless you're looking for trouble."

She thought about telling him that the only trouble she was looking for was standing right in front of her. Instead she rolled her eyes. "Back off, Thorn. You're beginning to sound like Stone."

He raised a brow. "Stone?"

"Yes, Stone. He's on this big-brother kick."

Thorn met her gaze. "I'm sure he is concerned about your welfare."

"Trust me, I can take care of myself. Now, if you don't mind, will you take a look at my faucet?"

He sighed. "Lead the way."

Thorn wished he could take back those three words when she walked off in front of him. His blood raced fast and furiously through all parts of his body when his gaze slid to her backside. Damn, her shorts were short. Way too short. And they were as tight as tight could be. She would probably get arrested if she wore something that short and tight out in public. They stopped barely at the end of her cheeks and each step she took showed him a little of a bare behind. When she headed up the stairs he decided to stop her.

"Hey, wait. Where are we going?"

She stopped and glanced back at him over her shoulder. "Up to my room."

He swallowed. "Why?"

Tara turned around and tried to keep her expression bland and innocent. "To fix the leaking faucet in the master bathroom."

Thorn didn't move. He had assumed she needed the faucet in her kitchen fixed. Hell, his control would be tested to the limit if he had to go anywhere near her bedroom.

"Is there something wrong, Thorn?"

Yes, there's a lot of things wrong, and two years of abstinence heads the list, he thought. He reached down within to drum up some self-control that he didn't think he had. "No, there's nothing wrong. Show me the way," he said.

He inhaled slowly as he followed her up the stairs and almost choked on his own breath when he walked into her bedroom. It was decorated in black, silver-gray and mauve, and everything matched—the floral print on the bedcovers, curtains and the loveseat. The room looked like her, feminine and sensuous. Even the huge bed looked like a bed intended for lovemaking more than for sleeping. He could imagine rolling around the sheets with her in that bed.

"The bathroom is this way."

He quickly pushed the thoughts out of his mind as he followed her into the connecting bathroom.

"Do you need my help with anything?" she asked, leaning against the vanity.

His gaze moved from her face to her chest, settling on

what could be seen of her breasts through the thin material of her top. At the moment, the only thing she could do for him was to give him breathing space. "No, I'll be fine. Just give me a couple of minutes."

"All right. I'll be in my bedroom if you need anything."

He lifted a brow. He'd much prefer it if she went downstairs to the kitchen, as far away from him as she could, but he decided not to tell her that. After all, it wasn't her fault that he wanted to jump her bones.

As soon as she left, he went about checking out her faucet while trying to ignore the sound of her moving around in the bedroom. It didn't take him any time at all to repair the faucet and he was glad of that. Now he could concentrate on getting the hell out of here. He worked his way from under her sink and stood. It had been rather quiet in her bedroom for the past couple of minutes and he hoped she was downstairs.

Wrong.

He walked out of the bathroom and saw her standing on the other side of the room wearing nothing but her skimpy top and a pair of black thong panties. Her back was to him, and as soon as he cleared his throat she snatched a short silk robe off the bed and quickly put it on.

Too late. He had seen more than he should have.

"Sorry. I thought you would be a while and decided to change into something comfortable," she said, apologetically, looking down as she tied the belt of her robe around her waist.

He didn't say anything. He couldn't say anything. All he could think about was just how much of her naked skin he had seen. Damn, she looked good in a thong. His entire body began aching.

"Is it fixed?"

Her question reminded him why he was there, but

couldn't quite bring him back around. His mind was still glued to the bottom part of her although she was now decently covered. But nothing could erase from his memory what he had seen.

"Well, is it?"

He slowly moved his gaze up to her face, and without thinking twice about what he was doing, he placed his toolbox on the table in her room and quickly crossed the space separating them. He stood staring at her then took her mouth with his, and she didn't try to resist when he thrust his tongue between her lips, tasting her with a force that shook him to the very core. And when he felt her return his kiss, mating her tongue with his, he totally lost it and began feasting greedily on her mouth.

He felt her tremble as he slid his hand down her body, reached under the short robe, spread her legs apart and then begin moving his hand between them, needing to touch her in the same intimate way he had done before.

Moments later he discovered that wasn't enough. He had to have her. He needed to ease his thick, hot arousal into the very place he was touching.

With his free hand he began undoing his zipper while his mouth continued to plunder hers. Suddenly, she broke off the kiss.

"Thorn, we can't. No protection. The race."

Sanity quickly returned to Thorn with her words. He breathed in deeply and took a step back and rezipped his pants. For a moment he hadn't cared about anything. Nothing had mattered, definitely not the fact he didn't have any protection with him or the fact that he had completely forgotten about his vow of celibacy.

He raked a hand down his face then wished he hadn't done that. She had been primed, ready and wet; her scent was on his hand and made his nostrils flare with wanting and desire. Her scent was woman. Hot, enticing woman.

He closed his eyes for a moment then reopened them as he slowly began backing toward the door. He picked his toolbox off the table. "Your faucet should be working just fine now," he said, huskily. "I'll call you."

And as quick as she could bat an eye, he was gone.

During the following weeks, Tara threw her heart and soul into her work.

After that first attempt, she had discovered that getting Thorn to break his vow of celibacy—finding an opportunity to put her plan into action and getting him to cooperate was not easy.

He had taken her out to dinner several times and they had even gone to the movies together twice, but whenever he returned her home, he deposited her on her doorstep, kissed her goodnight and quickly got on his bike or into his car and took off. Getting under Thorn's skin was turning out to be a monumental task.

A stomach virus that was going around kept her busy as frantic mothers lined the emergency room seeking medical care for their little ones. Twice during the past week she had worked longer hours than she normally did, but Tara was grateful to stay busy.

Nighttime for her was torture at its best. She was restless, her mind returned to the kiss she'd shared with Thorn again and again. In an effort to help her sleep or just to occupy her mind, Delaney had given her plenty of reading materials in the way of romance novels.

That only made matters worse.

She enjoyed reading about how the hero and heroine found their way to everlasting love, but the searing passion and profound intimacy the fictional characters shared always left Tara breathless, wondering if things like that could really happen between two people.

Pushing the covers aside, Tara got out of bed. Tonight was one of those nights she felt restless. She had gone to bed early, before eight o'clock, with a book to read, and had tried falling asleep. Instead, it was almost midnight and she was still wide awake.

It was a good thing that she was off work tomorrow. She knew Thorn was spending a lot of time at his shop working on his nephew's motorbike. Tara couldn't wait to see the expression on AJ's face when he received the sporty dirt bike Thorn was building especially for him. She hadn't seen it yet, but according to the brothers it was a sweet piece of machinery. All the Westmoreland men owned motorcycles. At eleven it was time AJ got his.

More than once Tara had thought of using the pretense of wanting to see the dirt bike as an excuse to drop by Thorn's shop unexpectedly again, but each time she got in her car and headed in that direction, she would change her mind and turn around. She'd had lunch with the brothers at Chase's restaurant earlier in the week and they had joked among themselves about how Thorn's mood had gone from bad to worse.

She had sat quietly, eating her meal while listening to their chatter. It seemed they knew the reason for Thorn's mean disposition these days and openly said they wished like hell that Bike Week would hurry up and come before he drove them, as well as himself, crazy.

From the conversation around her it appeared Thorn hadn't mentioned to his brothers that she would be going with him to Bike Week, because no one, including Delaney, had mentioned it.

Tara headed for the kitchen, deciding to get a glass of

the iced tea she had made earlier that day. Maybe the drink would cool her off because tonight her body definitely felt hot.

Thorn brought his motorcycle to complete stop and shut off the engine. The lights were still on in Tara's home, which meant she hadn't gone to bed yet. He had worked at the shop until he couldn't get his mind to concentrate on what he was doing. He kept thinking of Tara and what he wanted to do to her.

He'd never gone into a race this tense and restless over a woman before. Usually, one was the last thing on his mind this close to competition. This time that was not the case. Now that he knew how she tasted, he couldn't get the sweet flavor of her mouth and her body from his mind. And a day didn't go by when he didn't think about what they'd almost done that day in her bedroom. He had zipped down his pants, been ready to take her right then and there had her words not reclaimed his senses.

And his brothers were making matters worse with that stupid bet of theirs. He had refused to tell them anything; his relationship with Tara was not up for discussion. No one knew about their agreement, and other than the time they'd been seen together at Chase's Super Bowl party, no one knew what was going on with them. He wanted to keep it that way for as long as he could. The family would find out soon enough that she was going to Bike Week.

Earlier, when he'd seen he would not get any work done, he had tossed his tools aside, stripped off his clothes and had taken a shower to cool off his heated body. That hadn't worked. He got dressed and decided to go for a ride on his bike to let the wind and the chilly night air cool him down and take the edge off. But that hadn't worked either.

There was only one way he could relieve what ailed him and he couldn't risk going that far. Breaking his vow of

celibacy before the race was not an option. Therefore, with
Bike Week only a couple of weeks away, he needed to put
as much distance between himself and Tara as possible. She
was becoming too much of a temptation. That was why he
had made the decision tonight to leave for Daytona earlier
than planned and have Tara ride down later with one of his
brothers.

The most important thing was that she be in Daytona
when the race was over. There was no way he could hang
around and run the risk of making love to her. But he was
determined to leave them both with something to anticipate
while he was gone.

Moments later he walked up to her door and rang the
doorbell. He knew it was late but he had to see her. His
body pulsed with something he had never felt before...urgency.

The sound of her soft voice hummed through the door.
"Who is it?"

He took a deep breath and responded. "Thorn."

He watched as the door slowly opened, exposing the surprise on her features. "Thorn, what are you doing here?"

He swallowed as his gaze took in all of her. She was
wearing a short silk nightgown that only covered her to
midthigh. Her hair was in disarray—as if she had tossed
and turned while trying to sleep, and one of the spaghetti
straps of her gown hung down off her shoulder. The total
picture was ultra-sexy, enticing, a product of any man's
fantasy.

"Thorn?"

He blinked, realizing he hadn't answered her question.
"There's been a change in my plans about Bike Week and
I thought I should share it with you."

He saw the indecision that appeared in her features. It
was as if she was trying to make up her mind about whether

to let him in. She was probably wondering why he hadn't picked up a phone and called her instead of dropping by unexpectedly.

"I apologize for showing up without calling first, but I wanted to tell you about the change in person," he added, hoping that would explain things to her although he was still confused as to what had driven him to seek her out tonight. All he knew was that he had to be alone with her if only for a few minutes. Hell, he would take a few seconds if that were all she would spare.

"All right, come in," she said, then stood aside to let him enter.

The moment he walked into her home and closed the door behind him, he was engulfed with desire so thick he was having difficulty breathing. He had to force air through his lungs.

This wasn't normal, but nothing, he reasoned, had been normal for him since he had first laid eyes on Tara. His life hadn't been the same since that day. And watching her bare legs and the way her hips swayed under the nightgown she was wearing as she walked across the room before turning around to face him wasn't helping matters.

For two years he had battled what he had felt for her, his desire, but most importantly, his growing affection. He hadn't wanted to care about her. He hadn't wanted to care about any woman for that matter. Other than his family, his love for motorcycles was the only thing he felt that he needed in his life. But Tara had come into it and messed up things really well. The more he'd found himself attracted to her, the more he had tried to resist, but to no avail.

"Thorn, what is the change in your plans?"

He leaned back against the closed door. "I've decided to leave for Daytona early."

Tara raised an arched brow. "How early?"

"I'm leaving Sunday if I can arrange everything."

"This Sunday?" When he nodded, she said. "That's only three days away. I can't take off work and—"

"And I don't expect you to. I'll talk to one of my brothers about you coming down with them later at the beginning of Bike Week."

"But—but why are you leaving so early?" she asked.

He shifted his helmet to his other hand, thinking there was no way he could tell her the absolute truth. So instead he said. "There are a few things I need to do to get ready for the race, like getting my mind in check," he said, which wasn't a total lie. With any type of race, concentration was the key and he couldn't do it here, not in the same town where she lived.

He placed his helmet on the table. "Tara?"

She met his gaze. "Yes?"

He held out his hand to her. "Come here," he said in a voice he didn't recognize as his own. The only thing he did recognize and acknowledged was his need to touch her, to taste her and hold her in his arms. Two weeks without seeing her would be absolute torture for him.

He watched her stare at his outstretched hand, moments longer than he had hoped, before she slowly closed the distance that separated them, taking his fingers and entwining them with her smaller ones. The heat from her touch was automatic. Sensual heat moved from his hand and quickly spread throughout his body. Even his blood simmered with their touch. He gently pulled her to him, letting her body come to rest against the hardness of his.

"Do you have any idea how much I want you, Tara?" he asked huskily, his lips only a few inches from hers.

Desire formed in her eyes before she said softly, "Yes, I think I do."

''I want you to know for certain. The moment you step foot in Daytona I want you to know just what to expect after the race is over and I turn my full attention to you. I don't want you to be surprised at the magnitude of my hunger and desire, and I want to give you a sample of what is to come. May I?''

As far as she was concerned he had given her plenty of samples already and she had a pretty good idea what she was in for. But still, the very thought that he asked permission almost made Tara come apart then and there. With all his roughness, and even when he'd been in his worse mood, Thorn had always remained a gentleman in his dealings with her. Sensuous, irresistible and sexy, yet a gentleman just the same.

Tara swallowed the lump in her throat, not knowing what she should do or more importantly, what she should say. If she granted him what he wanted, it wouldn't help matters where she was concerned. She was in the thick of things and didn't see a way out, not with Thorn hightailing it out of town on Sunday. With him leaving for Daytona earlier than planned, there was no way she could tempt him the way she needed in order to get him to call off their agreement. He would expect her to keep her end of the bargain and give him the week she had promised him.

But then she decided she had to be completely honest with herself and admit that she wanted that week, as well. Thorn Westmoreland had needs and a part of her could not imagine him making love to another woman. She refused to think about that. And standing before him now, she knew why.

She was in love with him.

The thought that he could end up hurting her the way Derrick had made her want to cover her heart and protect it from pain, to escape into her bedroom and hide. But it was too late for that. She had tried avoiding Thorn for two years, had tried protecting her heart and her soul from him. Yet in the end, he had gotten them anyway. He had asked her if she knew how much he wanted her; well she had a question for him. Did he have any idea how much she loved him?

However, that was a question she couldn't ask him.

Before getting lost in deep thoughts of how much she loved him, she decided to turn her attention back to the issue at hand. She met his gaze and knew he was waiting for an answer to his question of whether or not he could give her a sample of what was to come. And she would give him the only answer she could; there was no way she could deny his request. "Yes, you may."

Wordlessly, without wasting any time, in the next moment, the next breath, he covered her lips with his. He immediately deepened the kiss and she automatically draped her arms around his neck for support. He pulled her closer to him, molding both his mouth and his body to hers as his hands stroked downward, cupping her behind and pulling her closer.

Thorn's mouth fed off hers; he was like the hungriest of men, ravaging, taking possession. In a way this was different from all their other kisses, and for a second she felt his control slipping as the kiss became more intense. When she felt weak in the knees, he picked up her into his arms and carried her over to the sofa and sat down with her in his lap.

Tara looked up at the man holding her gently in his arms. Her gaze took in his dark brooding eyes, his chiseled jaw and the firmness of his lips. His breathing was irregular and he was staring down at her as if she was a morsel he wanted to devour. Now. Tonight.

She swallowed. She was cradled in his lap practically

naked. She wasn't wearing a bra or panties, just a night-gown, a short one at that. And she knew that even if he wasn't fully aware of it before, he was now aware of the state of her dress since she was sitting in his lap and her bare bottom was coming into contact with his aroused body.

Tara felt the air surrounding them heighten to full sexual awareness as she stared at Thorn the same way he was staring at her. She saw a muscle tick in his jaw as if he was fighting hard for control. She realized just how hard this had to be for him—a man who had gone without sex for two years—and she knew the only way to make things easier for him was to send him away, but she couldn't do that.

She licked her bottom lip and decided to tell him without words just how much she wanted his touch, how much she desired it. Her body was aching for him. And when she thought she couldn't stand it any longer, he leaned down and kissed her again.

Her breath caught when she felt his hand beneath her nightgown, touching her at the juncture of her thighs. And then he began stroking her. She whimpered her pleasure into his mouth as her body came alive to his intimate touch. She remembered how it had been the last time he had touched her this way, and she clutched at the front of his shirt while his mouth made love to hers and his skillful fingers stroked her until she thought she would scream.

He suddenly broke off the kiss, and before she could let out a whimper of protest, he eased her gown down from her shoulders, giving him a good view of her neck and exposing her breasts. His hand lightly caressed her neck and then he leaned forward, and slowly lowered his head. He captured a budding dark nipple in his mouth and began licking and sucking.

"Thorn," was the only word she could think to say as pleasure beyond her control vanquished any further words. The only thing she could do was close her eyes and savor the moment in Thorn's arms. She moaned as his mouth continued to greedily taste her breasts and his hands stroked her wetness.

"I want to taste you," he mouthed against her breast, and she didn't get the full meaning of just what he meant until he gently laid her down on the sofa.

"Close your eyes, baby," he said in a deep, husky voice kneeling over her.

She met his gaze and saw the deep desire lodged in their dark depths. She couldn't help but wonder how much control he had left and knew she couldn't do this to him. She couldn't do anything to jeopardize his chance of winning the race. "Thorn, we can't," she managed to get out the words. "Remember, no birth control."

His hand was still touching her between the legs. His fingers were stroking her, entering her, driving her mad with desire. "Shh, I know, sweetheart, but we don't need protection for what I want to do. I need this for good luck. Taking your taste with me makes me a sure winner in more ways than one. This is what I need right now more than anything."

And then he lifted her gown, dipped his head and kissed her stomach at the same moment that she closed her eyes to concentrate on what he was doing. Her breath caught when his mouth lowered to replace his stroking fingers.

"Thorn!"

She cried out his name then sucked in a deep breath, never having been kissed this way before. Her mind went blank of all conscious thought except for him and what he was doing to her. She felt pleasure, deep and profound, all the way to her bones. She groaned aloud when he deepened the intimate kiss. His tongue, she discovered, was just as skillful as his hands, and was drugging her into an intimacy she had never shared with any man. Sensations beyond belief with his seductive ministrations were making her realize and accept the extent and magnitude of her love for him.

She whimpered deep within her throat when the first wave of ecstasy washed over her, more powerful than the last time, and she cried out as she held his head to her, his tongue increasing its strokes and tasting her greedily while tremor after tremor raced through her body. Her body shook with the pleasure he was giving her, and moments later, when the tremors had stopped and her body had quieted, he picked her up and cradled her back in his lap while gently stroking her back.

"Thank you," she heard him whisper in her ear.

She shifted in his arms slightly and pulled back, wondering why he was thanking her when she should be the one thanking him. From the feel of his arousal it was evident that he still was in a state of need, but had pushed his need aside to take care of hers.

"But—but you didn't—"

He placed a finger to her lips to seal off any further words. "That's okay. My day will come, trust me. I'm thanking you for giving me something to look forward to, something to anticipate, and whether I win the race or not, I have the prize I desire the most right here in my arms."

His words touched her deeply, and before she could find her voice to respond, he kissed away any words she was about to say, and she knew that the man who held her so tenderly in his arms would have her heart for always.

The next morning, Tara stirred then rolled over in bed. She slowly opened her eyes as she remembered last night.

After Thorn had kissed her, he had taken her upstairs and placed her in bed, then he had left.

She moaned deep in her throat as she recalled what they had done. He had created more passion in her than she had thought was possible, and he had unselfishly satisfied a need she didn't know she had. Even now, the memory sent delicious tremors all the way down to her womanly core. Thorn had branded a part of her as his in the most provocative and intimate way.

She loved him, and no matter how things turned out in Daytona, she knew that she would always love him.

The four men crossed their arms over their chests and glared at the one who stood before them, making a request they intended to refuse.

"What do you mean you're not in love with Tara? If that's the case then there's no way one of us will bring her to you, Thorn. We won't allow you to take advantage of her that way," Stone Westmoreland said angrily. "And you can forget the damn bet."

Thorn inhaled deeply, deciding not to knock the hell out of his brother just yet. He was about to leave for Daytona and had found all four of them having breakfast at Storm's house as they got ready to head out to go fishing. He had merely asked that one of them bring Tara to Bike Week. When Stone had grinned and asked him how it felt being in love, he'd been quick to set him straight and had told him he wasn't in love, and that what he and Tara shared was a completely physical, emotional-free affair. That's when all hell had broken loose.

"That bet wasn't my idea and shouldn't have been made in the first place. And regardless of what you say, Stone, one way or the other, Tara will be coming to Bike Week," Thorn said, barely holding on to his anger.

"No, she won't. I agree with Stone," Chase Westmoreland said with a frown on his face. "When we made that bet we thought it was to make you see how much you cared for Tara. But instead, you've concocted some plan to use her. Dammit man, if Tara was Laney, we would beat the crap out of any man with your intentions. So whatever plans you've made for Tara you can scrap them until you fall in love with her."

"I won't be using her," Thorn growled through gritted teeth. Ready to knock the hell out of Chase as well. Other than Dare, he didn't see any of them falling in love with anyone, so why were they trying to shove this love thing down his throat?

Storm chuckled. "And you want us to believe that? Hell, you haven't had a woman in over two years and you want us just to stand aside while you get your fill knowing you don't care a damn thing about her?"

Thorn felt steam coming out of his ears. "I do care about Tara. I just don't love her. Besides, what Tara and I do is our business and none of you have a damn thing to say about it."

"That's where you are wrong, Thorn," Stone said angrily, rolling up his sleeves and taking a step forward.

Dare Westmoreland decided it was time to intercede before there was bloodshed. "It seems you guys are a little hot under the collar. Keep it up and I'll be forced to throw all four of you behind bars just for the hell of it, so back up, Stone."

He then turned his full attention to Thorn. "And as far as Tara goes, I'll bring her to Daytona when Shelly and I drive up."

"What!"

Dare ignored the simultaneous exclamations from his

brothers, as well as the cursing. Instead his gaze stayed glued to Thorn, who was visibly relieved.

"Thanks, Dare," Thorn said, and without giving his other brothers a parting glance, he turned and walked out of the house.

It didn't take long for the other three Westmoreland brothers to turn on Dare.

"Sheriff or no sheriff, we ought to kick your ass, Dare," Chase said angrily. "How can you even think about doing that to Tara? Thorn doesn't mean her any good and she doesn't deserve something like this. Thorn is planning on using her and—"

"He loves her too much to use her," Dare said softly, as he heard the roar of Thorn's motorcycle pulling off.

"Love? Dammit, Dare, weren't you listening to anything Thorn said? He said he wasn't in love with Tara," Stone said angrily.

Dare smiled. "Yes, I heard everything he said. But I believe differently. Take it from someone who's been there, who's still there. Thorn is so much in love with Tara that he can't think straight. However, he needs total concentration for that race, which is why I'm glad he's leaving for Daytona early. Thorn needs Tara at that race, but once the race is over there is no doubt in my mind he'll begin seeing things clearly. It won't take long for him to realize just how much he loves her."

Chase frowned. "We all know just what a stubborn cuss Thorn can be. What if he never realizes it? Where does that leave Tara?"

Dare chuckled. "Right where she's been for the past two years, deeply embedded in Thorn's heart. But it's my guess that Tara's not going to settle for being any man's bed partner and will force Thorn to face his feelings."

"And if he doesn't?" Storm asked, still not convinced.

A smile tilted the corners of Sheriff Dare Westmoreland's lips. "Then we beat the crap out of him. One way or the other, he's going to accept that Tara is no longer his challenge. She's the woman he loves. But I don't think we have to take things that far. Rumor has it that he's sent Tara flowers for Valentine's Day.

Chase raised a shocked brow. "Flowers? Thorn?"

Dare chuckled. "Yes, Thorn. You know Luanne Coleman can't hold water, and word is out that Thorn went into her florist shop yesterday, ordered flowers for Tara and wrote out the card himself. I heard he even sealed it before nosey Luanne could take a peek at it."

"Damn," Stone said, with disbelief on his face. He'd never known his brother to send flowers to any woman before, and that included Patrice. Everyone knew Thorn hadn't really loved Patrice, but had merely considered her as his possession, and when it came to the things Thorn considered his, he had a tendency to get downright selfish and wasn't into sharing. Being in love was a totally new avenue for Thorn, and Stone couldn't help wondering how his brother would handle things once the discovery was made. Knowing Thorn, he would be a tough nut to crack, but he agreed with Dare; Tara was just the woman to set him straight. In Thorn's case she might need a full-fledged nutcracker.

"Hey, guys, I bet there will be a wedding in June," Stone said to his brothers.

"I think it will be before June. I doubt he'll wait that long. I'll say sometime in May, close to his birthday," Chase threw in.

Storm rolled his eyes. "Love or no love, Thorn is going to kick and scream all the way down the aisle. He's going to be difficult, that's just his nature, so I bet he won't be tying the knot before September."

All three glanced at Dare to see what he had to say about it. "All of you know I'm not a betting man." A smile touched his lips. "But if I were to bet, I'd have to agree with Chase. Thorn won't last until June."

Tara walked down the busy hospital corridor, glad she was finally able to take a break in her hectic schedule. It only took a few minutes to slip into the small chamber that led away from the crowded hallway lined with patients, as she made her way toward her office.

Once inside she closed the door behind her, walked across the room and collapsed into the chair behind her desk. She had been at the hospital since six that morning and had agreed to make it a fourteen-hour day instead of a ten. One of her fellow doctors had asked her to cover for her while she treated her husband to a special dinner for Valentine's Day. Since Tara hadn't made any plans for the evening herself, she decided she could be flexible and help her co-worker out.

She leaned back against her chair and closed her eyes and immediately remembered what had happened two nights ago when Thorn had come to see her to let her know of his change of plans.

After days of little sleep, her body had needed the release he had given to it, and she had been sleeping like a baby since. But now she was feeling downright guilty at the thought that in a few weeks, after the race, she would be letting him down. He thought he would be getting an experienced woman in his bed, when in truth he would be getting the complete opposite.

Twice she had thought of calling him before he left to tell him the truth, so he could make additional changes in his plans if he needed to make them. Chances were, after a two-year abstinence, he would want to share a bed with a woman who would know what she was doing. And the truth of the matter was that she didn't know squat. At least not enough to handle a man like Thorn Westmoreland.

He would be leaving sometime tomorrow for Daytona, so today was her last chance to come clean. Somehow she had to tell him that she'd never thought things would actually get this far. She'd assumed from the get-go that she would get him to the point where he would have to choose between her and celibacy.

That day in her bedroom hadn't even put a dent in the situation. He had merely given them a couple of days' breathing space then he had called to take her out, but he'd made sure the two of them had never been completely alone in her house again. And except for the other night, they hadn't been.

Okay, so she'd been stupid to count on such a thing happening, but she *had* counted on it, and now she was in a real fix. Delaney would be just the person to talk to about her dilemma, and to help her look at things more objectively, but unfortunately, Jamal had whisked her friend off to Rome where Valentine's Day was reputed to have originated. No doubt the prince intended to wine and dine his wife in style.

Tara smiled, thinking how much in love the couple were, as were Dare and Shelly. Love always seemed to radiate between them, and she always felt strong affectionate emotions whenever she was around them. On Super Bowl Sunday at Chase's restaurant it had been hard not to notice the intimate smiles the couples had exchanged, as well as the discreet touches.

She often wondered whether, if things had gone according to plan, she and Derrick would have shared that kind of loving relationship. For some reason she believed they would eventually have become a divorce statistic. It was only after she had finally stopped wallowing in bitterness and self-pity that she had decided not marrying Derrick had really been for the best. Still, she could not let go of the fact that he had betrayed and humiliated her the way he had.

Her thoughts shifted back to Thorn. When she had met him two years ago, her heart was recovering from being brutally battered. But still she knew, just as sure as she knew there were still a lot of patients yet to be seen, that she had fallen in love with Thorn that night they'd first met. It had been the same night she had stormed out of Delaney's kitchen to give him a piece of her mind. Instead, he had gotten a piece of her heart, a pretty big chunk. She had known the exact moment it had happened. At that time she had fled to the safety of her apartment.

Now she had nowhere to run to. The die was cast. A bargain made. He had kept his end of things and now she had to keep hers.

She loved him.

And the sad thing about it was that he had done nothing to encourage her emotional involvement. In fact, he had been more than up-front with her by letting her know he only wanted a physical relationship. She had known from the very beginning that his attraction to her had been based on lust and not love, and although it had been her intentions never to fall in love with another man after Derrick, she had done so anyway.

She opened her eyes at the sound of the knock on her office door. "Yes? Come in."

A fellow pediatrician, Dr. Pamela Wentworth, walked in carrying a huge vase of the most beautiful flowers Tara had ever seen. Tara smiled. "Wow, Pam, those are gorgeous. Aren't you special?"

Pam grinned. "No, in fact, you are, since these are for you."

Tara sat up straight in her chair. Her eyes instantly widened. "Excuse me. Did you say those were for me?"

"Yes. They were just delivered at the nurses' station, and I told Nurse Meadows that I would bring them to you myself," she said, setting the huge container in the middle of Tara's desk. "Hey, girlfriend, whatever you're doing, you must be doing it right to get flowers like these." She smiled brightly. "Well, I've got to get back. It's like a zoo out there so enjoy your break while it lasts."

Pam breezed out of her office just as quickly as she had breezed in, leaving Tara to stare at the huge arrangement of flowers sitting in the middle of her desk.

She frowned. "Who on earth would send these?" Tara wondered, leaning forward and pulling off the card that was attached. What man would remember her on Valentine's Day by sending her something like this?

She quickly opened the envelope and blinked at the message, then reread it again.

Be mine, Thorn.

A knot formed in Tara's throat. Be his what? His lover? His one-night stand? His bedmate for a week? His true love? His baby's mommy? What?

She sighed deeply. Only Thorn knew the answer to that question, and she intended to ask him when she saw him again.

Nine

Tara scanned all the activities through Dare's SUV's window as the vehicle rolled into the heart of Daytona Beach where Bike Week would be held. Squinting against the glare of the sun shining brightly through the window, she was amazed at what she saw billed as the World's Largest Motorcycle Event. And to think that Thorn was a major part of it.

It had been a little more than two weeks since she had seen him and she couldn't forget the night he had shown up unexpectedly at her house. It had been the same night she had come to terms with her feelings for him. It had also been the same night he had given her a sample of what he had in store for her.

But what had arrived two days after his visit still weighed more heavily on her mind—the flowers he had sent her for Valentine's Day. The message on the card had been personal, and she still found herself wondering just what he'd meant.

"Ready to get settled so we can do some shopping, Tara?"

Shelly's question got her attention. She had enjoyed the company of Dare and his wife during the seven-hour drive from Atlanta. Since school was still in session in Atlanta, their son AJ had not been able to make the trip. He was staying with Dare's parents.

"I'm always ready to shop," Tara said, smiling. When she glanced out the window and saw the numerous vendors, she wondered if there was anything for sale other than bike wear and leather.

"As soon as we get settled into our hotel rooms we can hit the malls," Shelly said, turning around in her car seat to smile at Tara.

Tara nodded her head in agreement. A few months ago, before Shelly's wedding, she, Shelly and Delaney had flown to New York for a girls' weekend and had enjoyed themselves immensely. The one thing the three of them discovered they had in common was their obsession with shopping.

"I hope I see Thorn sometime today," she said honestly, not caring what Shelly or Dare thought, although she did wonder whether they thought she was making a mistake even coming here to spend time with Thorn. However, if they thought such a thing, neither said so. Even Delaney hadn't tried talking her out of coming, nor had Thorn's other brothers.

"It shouldn't be too hard to find Thorn," Dare said, meeting her gaze in the rear-view mirror. "He rode his bike from Atlanta, but his work crew arrived by eighteen-wheeler a few days ago to set up shop and put his Thorn-Byrds on display. You wouldn't believe the number of people who're here to buy bikes. But then, within a few days of the race, be prepared not to see Thorn for a while. He usually goes off by himself to train. Going more than 180 mph while tackling the high banks of Daytona International Speedway on two wheels is no joke. Thorn needs total concentration for what he'll be doing, and I mean *total* concentration.''

Tara nodded, understanding what Dare was saying. She had talked enough with the brothers over the past two weeks to know that what Thorn would be doing was risky. But she couldn't allow her mind to think about that. She had to believe that he would be fine.

She sighed deeply. From what Stone had told her, beside the races, the other activities lined up for the week included motorcycle shows and exhibits and concerts. There would be vendors at practically every corner who would try to sell anything they thought you needed, even a few things you didn't need.

When Dare pulled into the parking lot of their hotel, the only thing Tara could think about was Thorn and her need to see him before he went into seclusion.

Storm glanced down at his watch. ''Dare, Shelly and Tara have probably arrived by now. Aren't you going over to the hotel to see them?''

Thorn was crouched down in front of one of his motorcycles and didn't miss a beat as he continued to put a shine on the immaculate machine. ''Not now. Maybe later.''

Storm frowned, thinking Thorn was definitely not acting like the man Dare had painted him to be, a man deeply in love. In fact he hadn't even mentioned Tara since Storm, Stone and Chase had arrived a few days ago.

Storm decided to try something. ''Maybe it's just as well.''

Thorn glanced up. "Why is that?"

Storm shrugged. "There's a chance Tara didn't come,"
he lied. "The last I heard she hadn't made up her mind
whether she was coming or not."

Thorn frowned and he immediately stopped what he was
doing. "What do you mean she hadn't made up her mind
about coming? The last time I talked to her it was a sure
thing."

"And how long ago was that, Thorn?"

Thorn's frown deepened as he tried to remember. Moments later he said, "A couple of days before I left town."

Storm shook his head. "Damn Thorn, that was over two
weeks ago. You mean to say that you haven't called or
spoken to her since you left Atlanta?"

"No."

Storm crossed his arms over his chest. "Then it would
serve you right if she didn't come. Even I know that women
don't like being ignored."

"I wasn't ignoring her. I was giving both of us space."

"Space? Hell, there's nothing wrong with space if you
keep in touch and let them know you're thinking about
them. Women like to know they're on your mind at least
every once in a while. I hate to say it, man, but you may
have blown it. What on earth were you thinking about?"

Thorn stood and threw down the cloth in his hand. "How
to keep my sanity." He grabbed his helmet off the seat of
his bike and quickly put it on. "I'll be back later."

Storm chuckled as he watched his brother take off with
the speed of lightning. He shook his head. Damn, Dare had
been right. Thorn was in love and didn't even know it yet.

Tara had taken a shower and changed into comfortable
clothing. Dare and Shelly's room was on the tenth floor
and, like her hotel room, it had a beautiful ocean view.

Stepping out on the balcony, she decided the sight was breathtaking. Down below, the boardwalk was filled with people having a good time.

She and Shelly had decided to postpone their trip to the mall. It was quite obvious that Dare wanted to spend time with his wife alone for a while, and Tara couldn't find fault with that. The two were still newlyweds. They wanted to put to good use their week without having to worry about AJ popping up unexpectedly.

Stepping back inside her hotel room, Tara glanced at the clock, wondering why Thorn hadn't at least called to make sure she had arrived. She knew he was probably busy and all, but still, she would have thought he'd have made time to see her, especially since they hadn't talked to or seen each other in over two weeks. Evidently, she'd been wrong.

She had to face the fact that as far as he was concerned, her sole purpose in being there took place *after* the race and not before. The hotel room she'd been given was in his name and he had seen to her every comfort by providing her with a suite, a suite he would eventually share with her. The bedroom was enormous and the bed was king-size. She could just imagine the two of them in that bed making love.

She nervously licked her lips. She needed to talk to Thorn and let him know before things went too far that she was not the experienced woman he thought she was. Chances were when he found out she was a twenty-seven-year-old virgin, he would put a quick halt to his plans and run for cover. She had overheard enough conversations between the single male doctors to know that most men preferred experienced women. No man wanted to waste time teaching a woman how to please him in bed.

Tara sighed. She'd intended to tell Thorn the truth when she saw him, but after hearing what Dare had said about Thorn needing total concentration, she'd decided not to tell him until after the race. That wouldn't be the best time but there was nothing she could do about it.

She glanced around when she heard a knock at the door. Thinking Shelly had changed her mind about going shopping, she quickly crossed the room to the door and glanced out the peephole.

"Thorn!"

She didn't waste any time in opening the door, and he didn't waste any time in stepping inside the room and closing the door behind him. Nor did he waste any time in pulling her into his arms and kissing her.

And she didn't waste any time in kissing him back.

His tongue was stroking hers with relentless precision and his hands were roaming all over her body as if to make sure she was really there. And when she wrapped her arms around him, he deepened the kiss.

She held on to him tight as he evoked sensations within her that were beyond anything she could have ever imagined from a kiss.

She thought he tasted of desire so hot she could feel it in the pit of her stomach, and pleasure points spread throughout every limb in her body. His kiss was overpowering, and she felt their controls slipping. Tara knew she should pull away from the kiss before they got carried away, but the more their tongues dueled and feasted, the more her mouth refused to do anything but stay put and get everything that Thorn was offering. Thorn was laying it on thick and she was enjoying every single minute of it.

Moments later, he pulled back, but didn't end the kiss completely. Instead he continued to torture her with tiny flicks of his tongue on her mouth. A moan escaped her lips and he captured it with his.

"I missed you," Thorn's voice whispered throatily as a hot throbbing sensation settled in her midsection. "Damn this celibacy thing. I want you now. Hell, I might not be around later. Anything could happen.''

Thorn's words reminded her of the danger inherent in Sunday's race. She groaned as she pulled back from his touch. She could not, she would not, be responsible for him losing the race or possibly getting hurt. She loved him too much for that. One of them had to see reason and it seemed it would have to be her at the moment.

She exhaled a bone-deep sigh when they stood facing each other. Her heart was beating way out of control as her gaze took in everything about him, from the jeans and T-shirt that he wore to the biker boots on his feet. But she mostly zeroed in on his desire-glazed gaze that hadn't yet left hers.

For the longest time he didn't say anything, but neither did she. They continued to stand there, looking at each other, until finally, Thorn spoke in a voice that was husky and deep. "I want you, Tara. Not after the race but *now*."

She swallowed. Lust had temporarily taken over Thorn's mind, and it was up to her to put it back on track. If they did what he wanted and he lost the race, he would despise her for the rest of his days, and she couldn't handle that. She knew her next words would sound cold and indifferent, but he'd left her no choice.

She tilted her head back and frowned up at him. "It doesn't matter what you want now. Need I remind you that we have an agreement, Thorn? My purpose for being here is to fill your needs *after* the race and not before. I think it would be best if you kept your hands and lips to yourself until then."

He didn't say anything but stared at her with a look that went from desire to anger in a second, and seeing the transformation made Tara's heart thump so hard in her chest that it hurt. Her tone of voice had intentionally been like a dose of ice water on a burning flame, and the effect was unmistakably scorching.

Thorn took a step forward and looked Tara squarely in the eye. "Thanks for reminding me of your purpose for being here, Tara, and you won't have to worry about me keeping my hands and mouth to myself. But make no mistake about it, I've kept my end of the deal, and after the race I fully expect you to keep yours."

Without saying anything else he turned and walked out the door, slamming it behind him.

Gravel flew from the tires of Thorn's motorcycle as he leaned into a sharp curve, tearing up the road in front of him. He shuddered from the force of the anger consuming him as he tightened his grip on the handlebars.

Tara's words had burned, although quite frankly, he supposed he should be grateful that she had helped him to come to his senses before he'd done something he would later regret. But instead of wanting to thank her he felt the need to throttle her instead.

Damn, just like that day in her bedroom, he'd been ready to zip down his pants and have his way with her, race or no race. He'd been that hungry for sex. No, it wasn't just about sex. It was about her. He had been just that hungry for her. But leave it to her to remind him of their arrangement and to make him remember the only thing between them would be a no-strings-attached affair.

His spine tightened as he took another curve. Damn the agreement, he wanted more. During the past two weeks he had come to realize just how much Tara meant to him. He had discovered she was goodness and sweetness all rolled into one—on her good days—and tart and tingly on her bad days, but he enjoyed her just the same.

Letting her get under his skin had definitely not been

part of the plan. But it had happened anyway. His thoughts
went back to the harsh words she'd spoken. Did she really
see her sole reason for being here as she had described it?
But then, how could she not, when he had pretty much
spelled out why he wanted her here?

He wondered just when his thoughts on the matter had
changed. When had he decided that he wanted more from
Tara than a week in bed? When had he decided he wanted
more from her than sex?

He sighed deeply. He had been in denial for two long
years, but he wouldn't lie to himself any longer. It had
taken him long enough to come to grips with his feelings
for her. He could now admit that he loved her and had
from the first time he'd seen her. He had lied through his
teeth when he'd told his brothers he didn't love her. At this
very moment he was faced with the truth. He desperately
loved her and didn't want her to pick now to start getting
temperamental and difficult.

The last of his pent-up anger floated away in the wind
as he rounded another curve at high speed. Now was not
the time to get mad; he would get even and teach a certain
doctor a lesson. Tara would soon discover that Thorn the
celibate was moodier and grumpier than hell, but Thorn in
love was a force to be reckoned with.

"Enjoying yourself, Tara?"

Tara glanced up from her drink and met Stone Westmoreland's curious stare. She then glanced around the table
and met the gazes of the other Westmoreland brothers and
smiled. It seemed every one of them was interested in her
response.

"Yes, I'm enjoying myself," she responded cheerfully.
She knew they weren't fooled and were well aware she was
having a lousy time. The only thing she enjoyed was seeing

Dare and Shelly and how they interacted with each other. The two were so much in love they practically glowed. Even now she couldn't help but watch as they danced together. It was a slow number and Dare was holding his wife as though she meant the world to him.

It touched Tara's heart deeply, the thought of a woman being loved that much by a man. She sighed. No man had ever loved her that much, certainly not Derrick.

"You want to dance, Tara?"

She glanced up at Chase. She wasn't fooled either. She was well aware that the brothers knew the one person she wanted to dance with wasn't around. What they probably didn't know was that she was intentionally keeping Thorn at bay.

"No, but thanks for asking." They were all seated around a table in a nightclub that had live entertainment. All the Westmoreland brothers were present except for Thorn.

She hadn't seen him since he had paid her a visit at the hotel three days ago. Each day she had made it a point to drop by the booth where his Thorn-Byrds were on display, hoping that he would be there, but he never was. According to Dare, Thorn was keeping a low profile and would probably be doing so until the day of the race.

"Tara?"

She smiled and glanced around, wondering what question one of the Westmoreland brothers had for her now, when suddenly she realized it hadn't been one of them who had called her name. Her name had been spoken by the man who stood next to their table.

Derrick!

Surprised, she met his gaze and wondered what on earth Derrick was doing in Daytona during Bike Week. Although Bunnell was less than sixty miles away, she had never known him to show an interest in motorcycles. But then she had to remember many people came to Bike Week just to check out the festivities.

She had planned to rent a car and drive to Bunnell to see her family tomorrow. It had been two years and it was time she finally went home for a visit. The main reason she had stayed away was now standing next to her table.

She plastered a smile on her face as she reached for the glass of soda in front of her. "Derrick, what are you doing here? This is certainly a surprise."

He was nervous, she could tell. But then after glancing around the table she understood why. Stone, Chase and Storm were glaring, facing him down, and letting Derrick know without saying a word that they didn't appreciate his presence. Evidently, it hadn't taken much to figure out who he was and to remember what he had done.

"Yes, well, me and a couple of the guys from town decided to come check things out," he said after nervously clearing his throat.

Tara nodded. She couldn't help but be openly amused by his nervousness. "And how is Danielle?"

Derrick cleared his throat again. "She's fine. She's expecting. Our baby is due to be born in a few weeks."

Surprisingly, that bit of news didn't have the effect on her it would have had a year ago. She found herself genuinely smiling. "Congratulations. I'm glad the two of you are happy and have decided to add to your family and wish you both the best."

Derrick nodded and then asked. "What about you, Tara? Are you happy?"

Tara opened her mouth to answer, but instead a deep male voice sounded from the shadows behind where Derrick stood.

"Yes, she's happy."

When the person came into view, Tara's heart began beating fast. She held her breath as Thorn moved around Derrick and came straight to her, leaned down and placed an open-mouthed kiss on her lips, publicly declaring before Derrick, his brothers and anyone who saw him, that Tara was his.

After releasing her mouth Thorn straightened to his full height and turned back to Derrick. He glared at the man. "I make it my business to see that she's happy."

Tara wanted to scream out "Since when?" but decided to go along with whatever game Thorn was playing. Besides, what he'd done had effectively squashed any notion Derrick might have that there was a chance she was still pining away for him. She was grateful for that. According to her parents, the rumor still floating around Bunnell was that she hadn't been home because she hadn't gotten over Derrick.

Derrick met Thorn's stare. "I'm glad to know that." He then blinked as recognition hit. "Hey, aren't you Thorn Westmoreland?"

"Last I heard." Thorn crossed his arms over his chest and studied the man who'd had the nerve to betray and humiliate Tara on her wedding day. As far as Thorn was concerned, this man's loss was certainly his gain.

A look of adoration appeared in Derrick's eyes and a smile tipped the corners of his mouth. "Wow. Your bikes are the bomb."

Usually Thorn was appreciative of anyone who admired his work, but not this man. "Thanks. Now if you don't mind, I'd like to dance with my lady. The race is in two days and I want to spend as much time with her as I can before then."

"Oh, sure, man," Derrick said awkwardly. He then met

Tara's gaze again. "Take care, Tara, and I'll tell your family that I saw you."

Tara shrugged. "There's really no need since I plan to visit them tomorrow. There's no reason to be this close and not visit."

Derrick nodded. "Yeah, right. I'll be seeing you." He then moved on.

"Glad you could find the time to grace us with your presence tonight, Thorn," Dare said sarcastically to his brother when he and Shelly sat down at the table after dancing. He then glanced across the room at Derrick's retreating back after seeing his brothers' glares. "Who was that?"

Thorn met his brother's gaze. "Some fool who didn't know a good thing when he had it."

Without waiting for Dare, or anyone else for that matter, to make another comment, Thorn reached out and gave Tara's hand a gentle tug and brought her to her feet. "Dance with me."

Whatever words Tara wanted to say died in her throat the moment Thorn touched her. She offered no resistance when he led her to the dance floor where a slow number had just started. An uncomfortable glance over her shoulder verified that Derrick was sitting at a table with his friends, staring at her and Thorn. She quickly glanced around the crowded room. It seemed everyone was staring, especially the Westmoreland brothers. But they were doing more than just staring; they were all grinning from ear to ear. Why?

"Okay, what's going on with your brothers?" she asked Thorn the moment he pulled her into his arms.

He glanced over at the table where his four brothers sat, then back at her, meeting her gaze. "I have no idea. They tend to act ignorant while out in public. Ignore them."

That wouldn't be hard to do, Tara thought, since her concentration was mainly on him. "What are you doing here, Thorn? I thought with only two days left before the race you would be somewhere in seclusion."

Thorn frowned. "Yeah, you would probably think that. But don't worry, I'm more than ready for the race." He met her stare and his hands moved gently down to the small of her back and drew her closer into his arms. "In fact, I'm looking forward to it being over. And I don't want you to worry your pretty little head any, because I'm also ready for you after the race."

His words gave her pause, and she nervously licked her bottom lip with the tip of her tongue. Maybe now was a good time to tell him about her virginal state. She opened her mouth to speak, but before she would get any words out, he kissed her. In the middle of the dance floor he gave her a full-blown, nothing-held-back, full-mouth kiss, just the thing to make her lose all rational thought.

She ignored the catcalls she heard, the whistles, as well as the flashing bulbs from several sport reporters' cameras. Instead, she held on to Thorn to receive the mind-blowing kiss he was giving her.

He reluctantly pulled away when someone tapped him on his shoulder. He glared and turned to meet Dare's amused features. He and Shelly had returned to the dance floor. "You're making a scene, Thorn, and your song stopped playing moments ago. Maybe you ought to take that outside."

"No problem," Thorn said, and without waiting for Tara to say anything, he pulled her across the room and out the door.

Tara snatched her hand from Thorn's the moment Florida's night air hit her in the face, returning her to her senses. "Hold on, Thorn. What do you think you're doing?"

"Taking you somewhere," he said, pulling her out of the doorway to a secluded area.

She refused to move an inch. "Where?"

"To show you my bike."

Tara frowned. "I've seen your bike. I've even ridden on it, remember?"

He smiled. "Not this one. The bike I want to show you is the one I'll be using in the race."

For a moment it seemed as though Tara had forgotten to breathe. She had been around the Westmorelands enough to know how they joked with Thorn about not letting anyone see the bike he would race. Since he owned so many for racing, it was anyone's guess as to which one he would use to compete in any given race.

"But I thought that other than your racing team, no one is supposed to know about which bike you'd be using."

He gave a small shrug as he leaned one shoulder against a brick wall. "Usually that's true, but I want you to see it." He met her gaze. "In fact, I want you to christen it."

Tara lifted a brow. "Christen it? You want me to hit it with a bottle of champagne or something?"

Thorn shook his head and smiled. "No, that would put a dent in it. There's more than one way to christen something. If you come with me, I'll show you another way."

Indecisively, Tara just stared at him, not knowing what she should do. Being somewhere alone with Thorn was not a good idea, especially when he had told her just two days ago that he would be keeping his hands and his lips to himself. Already tonight he had touched her and had kissed her twice and there was no telling what else he had in store.

Evidently she took too long to say anything because he covered the distance separating them, took her face in his hands and lowered his head to capture her lips with his.

Kiss number three, Tara thought, closing her eyes as his

mouth totally devoured hers. She shuddered when she felt his hands pull her T-shirt from her shorts and slowly began caressing her bare skin underneath. Her tongue automatically mated with his, relishing in the taste of him.

Moments later, when he released her mouth, she pressed her face to his chest and sighed deeply into his T-shirt. The manly scent of him made her groan at the same time her midsection became flooded with warmth. She felt his hands gently caressing her back as he pulled her closer to him, letting him feel the hardness of the erection that stirred against her belly.

She forced her eyes upward and met his. They were so dark and filled with so much desire it made her tremble. "I thought you said you wouldn't touch me or kiss me, Thorn, until *after* the race."

He sighed deeply and reached up to thread his fingers through her hair, pushing it away from her face. "Lord knows I tried, but I don't think I can not touch you or kiss you, Tara," he said truthfully.

A part of him wanted to tell her more. He wanted to let her know that he loved her and that no matter whether he won the race or not, he knew his most valued prize was standing right here in front of him. But he couldn't tell her any of that yet. He would wait and tell her later, when he felt the time was right.

He inclined his head to take a good look at her and let her take a good look at him. "Will you come with me, Tara? I won't do anything you don't want me to do."

Oh, hell, Tara thought. Didn't he know she was human, and so far, whatever he'd done to her had been just fine and dandy with her. She couldn't imagine turning him down for anything unless it meant going all the way. She would not allow him to break his vow of celibacy two days before the race, but he was definitely testing her control.

"Tara? Will you come with me?"

Tara heaved an enormous sigh. If he thought she was his sweetest temptation, then he was her most tantalizing weakness. A chocolate bar with almonds had nothing on him.

She leaned back far enough to gaze into his eyes. And she knew at that moment that no matter what he claimed, he intended to do more than show her his bike. But heaven help her, she didn't have the strength to turn and walk away.

Instead she gave him the only answer she could. "Yes, Thorn. I'll go with you."

Tara glanced around, not believing that she was standing in the back of an eighteen-wheeler. Thorn had explained that he used the fifty-three-foot-long semi-tractor trailer whenever he traveled with his bikes. The back of the trailer had been separated into three sections. The back section, the one closer to the ramp style door, was where the bikes were stored. The middle section served as Thorn's office and work area. The third section, the one closest to the cab of the truck, was set up like a mini motor home and included a comfortable-looking bed, a bathroom with a shower, a refrigerator, microwave, television and VCR—all the comforts of home.

After being shown around, Tara decided to play it safe and remain in the section where the motorcycles were stored. She moved around the trailer admiring all the bikes; some she had seen before and others she had not.

"This is the one I'll be racing," Thorn said, getting her attention.

She walked over to stand next to him to check out the motorcycle he was showing her. It was definitely a beauty and she told him so.

"Thanks. I began building it last year." He met her gaze. "It reminds me a lot of you."

Tara lifted a brow. She'd never been compared to a motorcycle before and was curious why it had reminded him of her. "Would you like to explain that one, Thorn?"

He smiled. "Sure. This beauty was designed to be every man's dream as well as fantasy. So were you. She's well-built, with all the right angles and curves, temptation at its best. And so are you." His eyes held hers, shining with blatant desire when he added, "And she gives a man a good, hard ride and there's no doubt in my mind that you'll do the same."

Tara swallowed thickly. She wasn't sure about that. The only riding she'd ever done was on her bicycle, and even then she could have used a lot more practice. She had preferred staying inside the house, playing doctor on her baby dolls.

Having no idea what comment she could make to Thorn's statement, she cleared her throat and pretended to give the immaculate riding machine her full attention.

"Tara?"

The sound of her name from Thorn's lips was like a warm caress, and it sent sensations flowing through her body. "Yes?"

His gaze held hers and the look in his eyes was dark, intense. "Do you want to ride?"

She blinked, wondering if this was a trick question. "Ride?"

He nodded, not breaking eye contact with her. "Yes, ride."

She swallowed again, thickly, then said. "But you've already put your bikes up for the night."

He nodded again. "Yes, but there's another way we can ride while my bike stays right here. I want you to christen it for me. Then there's no doubt in my mind that I'll be a sure winner on Sunday."

Tara released a deep sigh. He was confusing her, which wasn't hard to do when the subject was about sex, considering how little she knew. But she was smart enough to have an idea of what he was suggesting. "You want us to make out on your bike?"

He smiled. "Yes."

Her stomach clenched from his smile and his answer. "Call me crazy for not knowing the answer to this, but is such a thing possible?"

His smile widened. "Anything is possible with us, Tara, and I promise we won't go all the way. I'll take you part of the way, just like the other times." He took a step toward his bike and reached out his hand. "Let me do that, baby."

Tara wondered if he was into self-torture, because any time they made out, it was she who was left satisfied and not he. She couldn't help but wonder what Thorn was getting out of this. "But I won't be doing anything for you. Why are you doing this to yourself? Whenever we come together that way I'm the only one who's satisfied."

He thought about her question, trying to decide the best way to answer it, and decided to be as honest with her as he could. "I get my satisfaction from watching you reach an orgasm in my arms, Tara. I get a natural stone high knowing that under my ministrations you come apart, lose control and soar to the stars. And right now that's all the satisfaction I need. My time will come later."

There was a question she had to ask him. "When you sent those flowers to me for Valentine's Day, the card read, Be mine. What did you mean?"

In the confines of the trailer, Thorn smelled the way she thought a man was supposed to, masculine, robust and sexy. The warm solid strength of him surrounded her, touched her, and made a foreign need tingle at the juncture of her legs. She swallowed deeply when he reached out and curled a finger beneath her chin and tipped her head back to meet his gaze.

For a moment they just stood there, staring at each other. Then he finally said, "Even if it's for only a week, Tara, I won't take the time we spend together lightly. I know I have no right to ask for exclusiveness beyond that point, but until then, I want to know that no other man is on your mind, in your heart or a part of your soul. When I make love to you, I want you to be mine in every way a woman can belong to a man." And then he lowered his head, and Tara's mouth became his.

She melted into him, into his kiss, into everything that was essentially Thorn Westmoreland. He opened his mouth wider over hers, absorbing any and every sound of pleasure she made. Disregarding the warning bells going off in her head, she clung to him thinking this was where she wanted to be, in his arms, and at the moment, that was all that mattered.

Thorn broke the kiss and lifted her into his arms. She didn't resist him when he sat her in the bike's passenger seat. Instead of straddling his seat with his back to her, he straddled it facing her, then leaned forward and kissed her.

His hands touched her everywhere before going to her T-shirt. He pulled it off over her head and looked down. He had discovered she wasn't wearing a bra while dancing with her and had been anticipating this moment since then. The sight of her hard little nipples thrusting upward made him moan.

Taking her legs he wrapped them around his waist as he eased her back while leaning over and capturing a tight dark bud between his lips, letting his tongue caress it, then sucking greedily, enjoying the taste of her breasts.

But there was another taste he wanted. Another taste he needed.

Easing back up he slowly pulled down the zipper of her shorts, then, lifting her hips, he slid them down her body, taking them off completely. He gave an admiring glance to her sexy, black lace panties before taking them off as well.

He reached out and caressed her inner thigh with his fingers, then slowly traced a path across her feminine folds, already wet and hot for him. He lifted her, removed her legs from around his waist and lifted them high on his shoulders.

Then Thorn lifted her to him and leaned forward toward her body, seeking what he wanted the most. No matter how loudly Tara moaned and groaned, his mouth refused to let up as he gave her soul deep pleasure. Her body began trembling uncontrollably while his tongue thrust back and forth inside her, sending her over the edge.

"Thorn—"

"It's okay, baby, let it go," he said, as his fingers momentarily replaced his mouth. "I need to have you this way. When I'm taking the curves with this bike on Sunday, I'm going to remember just how it felt loving you like this. My pleasure is knowing I've given you pleasure."

And he did give her pleasure. Moments after his mouth once again replaced his fingers, she let out a mind-blowing scream and came apart, lost control and soared to the stars in his arms.

Ten

Tara glanced around at the many spectators in the grand-stands. Excitement was all around as everyone waited for the race to begin. She nervously bit her bottom lip as the scent of burnt rubber and fuel exhaust permeated the air. The weather was picture-perfect with sunny skies. It was a beautiful day for a motorcycle race.

The Westmoreland brothers had talked to her that morning and had gone out of their way to assure her that Thorn would be fine. But a part of her still felt antsy. She'd seen the preliminary races and knew how fast the riders would be going. Any incorrect riding technique of braking, cornering, sliding and passing could mean injury to a rider.

She tried not to think about the numerous laps around the speedway that Thorn and his bike would be taking, as well as the sharp curves; instead she tried to think about what had happened that night she had "christened" his bike. Even now she blushed thinking about it. Afterward,

Thorn had taken her to the hotel and had walked her to her room. He hadn't come inside. Instead he had kissed her tenderly in front of her door before turning to leave.

The next morning he had surprised her when he'd unexpectedly shown up to take her to breakfast. The meal had been delicious and she had enjoyed his company. They avoided discussing anything about the previous night; instead, he had listened while she did most of the talking. She had told him of her plans to visit her family, and he'd said he thought it would be a good idea.

She smiled when she remembered how glad her family had been to see her. Derrick hadn't wasted any time calling everyone he knew to let them know he had seen her at Bike Week with Thorn Westmoreland. Since Thorn was something of a racing celebrity, her parents, siblings and many of their friends in Bunnell, had had a lot of questions about their alleged affair. Her two brothers were still in college and were home for the weekend, and her baby sister was a senior in high school.

In a way she was glad everyone's attention had shifted from her and Derrick and was now focused on her and Thorn's relationship. She'd told anyone who asked—and it seemed just about everybody did—that she and Thorn were seeing each other and had left it at that. She'd let them draw their own conclusions.

Sighing deeply, she glanced down below at Pit Road where the Westmoreland brothers had become part of Thorn's racing team. She couldn't help but admire how they had made this a family affair with each helping out any way he could. Everyone, including her, was sporting a black T-shirt with the colorful huge Thorn-Byrd emblem on the front and back, as well as a matching black Thorn-Byrd cap. Like the other riders, Thorn was dressed in leather. She had seen him from a distance and thought he looked good in his riding outfit.

She thought it would be best if she remained out of sight for now. He had spent the last two days getting psychologically prepared for today's race and she didn't want to do anything to mess with his concentration.

Tomorrow she and Thorn would be heading for West Palm Beach for a week and she didn't want to think about what he had in store for her. Already his luggage had been delivered to her suite. He had told her that night in his eighteen-wheeler that he intended to spend tonight with her at the hotel with a Do Not Disturb sign on the door. And there was no doubt in her mind that he would do that very thing…if he decided to keep her.

She couldn't help remembering what Delaney had told her about Jamal's reaction when he'd discovered she was a virgin right in the middle of their lovemaking. Delaney had decided not to tell Jamal beforehand, but let him find out for himself. According to Delaney, Prince Jamal Ari Yasir had been angrier than hell, but had soon gotten over it with a little female persuasion.

Tara couldn't help wondering if Thorn would get over it. Unlike Delaney, Tara planned to remove the element of surprise and tell him before anything got started. Considering his current state of mind after having being celibate for almost two years, she prayed he wouldn't be too upset by her news.

The announcer's loud voice over the intercom drowned out any further thoughts, and she settled back in her seat and smiled at Shelly, who was sitting next to her. Nervousness and anxiety laced with excitement raced down her spine. The green flag was dropped and the race began.

Everyone was on their feet as the cyclists rounded the curve, making the last lap around Lake Lloyd. Tara and

Shelly had left their seats in the stands to join the Westmoreland brothers on Pit Road. Thorn's bike had performed
with the precision that everyone had expected. There had
been no mechanical problems such as those that had caused
a number of other riders to drop from competition.

Thorn was three bikes behind, but the Thorn-Byrd was
holding its own as the bikers made their way down the final
stretch. Coming in fourth wouldn't be so bad, Tara thought,
although according to Chase, this was Thorn's sixth time
competing in this particular race, and he was determined to
come home a winner this time.

All of a sudden Dare let out a humongous yell of excitement and started jumping up and down. The other Westmoreland brothers joined him, screaming at the tops of their
lungs.

Tara squinted against the glare from the sun to see what
had caused all the commotion. Using the binoculars she'd
borrowed from Storm, she watched the proceedings unfold.
Thorn was beginning to gain ground in a big way. He began
moving forward as the bikers headed toward the finish line.
The grandstands erupted into pure exhilaration as everyone
focused their attention on motorcycle number thirty-four,
Thorn and the Thorn-Byrd, as man and machine took center
stage and eased past the bikes holding the second and third
position coming neck to neck with the cyclist in the lead.

"Come on, Thorn, you can do it," Dare screamed, as if
his brother would be able to hear him across the width of
the track.

And then it happened: Thorn appeared to be giving the
Thorn-Byrd all he had as man and machine inched past
bike one and took the lead.

Tara's breath caught in her throat. Thorn had given the
spectators at Daytona International Speedway something to

talk about for years to come. Everyone was screaming as Thorn crossed the finish line, becoming the winner of this year's Bike Week.

Thorn barely had time to bring the Thorn-Byrd to a stop when everyone descended upon him. A reporter from CNN was there with the first question after a round of congratulations.

"Thorn, after six years of competing, you've finally won your first Daytona Speedway Bike Week, how do you feel?"

Thorn smiled. Thinking it wouldn't be appropriate to answer, "still horny," instead, he said, "It feels wonderful." He glanced around for Tara; though he didn't see her anywhere, somehow he felt her presence and knew Dare would follow his instructions to the letter.

"That was an excellent display of skill and sportsmanship when you took over the lead. What was the main thing on your mind as you inched your way across the finish line?"

Again, Thorn thought it wouldn't be kosher to give a truthful answer, at least not one with all the full details. His thoughts and emotions were too consumed with a certain woman. He smiled at the reporter and responded truthfully. "My woman."

"Thorn asked me to make sure you got back to the hotel, Tara," Dare Westmoreland said, smiling cheerfully. It was evident that he and his brothers were proud of Thorn.

"All right."

From the number of reporters crowding around Thorn, Tara knew it would be a while before he would be free. In a way that was good. She needed time to think. A proud smile touched her lips as she watched from a distance as

Thorn was presented the winning trophy. He was happy and she was happy for him. She was glad she'd been able to share this special moment with him.

As she began walking away with Dare and Shelly, she couldn't help but think that her moment of reckoning had arrived.

Tara nervously paced her hotel room waiting for Thorn. The race had been over more than two hours. Because she had felt hot and sticky, she had showered and changed into a floral sundress with spaghetti straps.

The air conditioning in the room was set at a reasonable temperature, but still she felt hot and was about to step outside on the balcony when she heard the sound of the door opening.

She turned and met Thorn's gaze the moment he stepped into the room. He had also showered and changed clothes. Gone was the leather outfit he had competed in. He was wearing a pair of jeans, a blue denim shirt and his biker boots.

Tara stood rooted in place and watched him watch her. A part of her wanted to go to him and kiss him and tell him just how proud she was of him, but another part of her held back. There was a possibility that Thorn wouldn't want to have anything to do with her after what she had to say. But still, she had to let him know of her pride in him.

"Congratulations, Thorn. I was so proud of you today."

He leaned against the closed door and continued to stare at her. His hands were pushed deep into his denim pockets and from the look on his face, winning the race, although a major accomplishment, was not at the moment what his thoughts were on.

His full attention was focused on her.

His next statement proved she was right. "You still have clothes on."

His words caught her off guard and for a moment she didn't know what to say. "Oh, boy," she finally whispered on an uneven sigh. "Did you really expect to find me here naked waiting for you?"

A slow, cocky smile curved his lips. "Yes, that would have been nice."

Tara couldn't help but return his smile. She guessed after a two-year abstinence, for him that *would* have been nice. "We need to talk, Thorn," she said, deciding not to beat around the bush.

She swallowed when he moved away from the door and walked toward her, like a hawk eyeing its prey. When he came to a stop less than a foot away, she inhaled his scent. He smelled of soap and shampoo as well as the manly fragrance that was so much a part of him.

He reached out and touched her chin with his finger. "We'll talk tomorrow."

Tara raised a brow. *Tomorrow?* Did he think he would be keeping her so busy this afternoon and tonight that she would have neither the time nor the strength to get a word out? She couldn't help it when the thought of that sent a tremor throughout her body.

She was suddenly swamped with memories of all the dreams she'd ever had of him, her need for him as well as her love for him. But still, none of that mattered if there was not complete honestly between them. He was entitled to know the truth about her.

"What I have to tell you can't wait until tomorrow." *After what I have to say there might not be a tomorrow for us,* she thought.

"Okay, you talk," he said huskily. And if he needed to touch her as much as he needed to breathe, he reached out and placed his hand at her waist, then slowly began caressing her side, flooding her sensitive flesh with sensations through the material of her dress. She didn't bother to resist him since she wanted his touch as much as it seemed that he wanted hers.

She cleared her throat and covered his hand with hers to stop the movement so she could think straight. "There's something I think you ought to know about me, Thorn. Something that will determine whether you want to take this any further."

While she held fast to his one hand, before she realized what he was about to do, his free hand reached out and pushed the straps of her dress completely off her shoulders, exposing her black lace bra.

He stood quietly for a moment, not saying anything but just looking at her. "I don't think there's anything you can say that would make me think of not taking this any further, Tara," he said huskily, not taking his eyes off her.

Tara wasn't so sure of that. Thorn was an experienced man and more than likely he wouldn't want a novice in his bed.

Moving with the speed he'd displayed on the speedway, he flicked the front closure of her bra and bared her breasts. Just as quickly he moved his hand to her naked flesh, cupped her breast in his hand and muttered the word, "Nice."

Tara's breathing escalated and she felt her body go limp at his touch. Her entire being was becoming a feverish heat. She leaned back and tipped her head, suddenly realizing that at some point Thorn had backed her against a wall. Literally. It was a solid wall that prevented her from going any further, neatly trapping her. She was caught, it seemed, between a rock and a hard place.

And when he leaned down and clamped his damp open

mouth to a nipple and began caressing it gently with the tip of his tongue, she lost her train of thought.

Almost, but not quite. She had to have her say.

"Thorn?"

"Umm?"

She swallowed hard and drew in a deep breath. She closed her eyes, not wanting to see his expression when she said the words. "I'm a virgin."

She braced, waited for his fury and when minutes passed and he didn't say anything, she opened her eyes. He seemed not to have heard her since he had left one nipple and was now concentrating on the other. She inhaled a long, fortifying breath at the way his mouth was nibbling her as though she was a treat he had gone without for too long.

"Thorn? Did you hear what I said?" She finally decided to ask, fighting against the astounding sensations that were running through her body.

He lifted his head and met her gaze. "Yes, I heard you."

Tara lifted a brow, thinking that if he had heard her, he was taking her news rather well. Too well. She frowned as things became obvious to her. "You knew, didn't you?" The question was a scant whisper in the room.

He gazed at her for a long moment before saying. "Yes, I knew."

Tara's eyebrows bunched. How had he known? She hadn't told another soul other than Delaney, and she knew his sister would not have shared that information with him. "But—but how…?" she asked, barely able to speak.

He shrugged. "I touched you there, several times, and on that first night I found you extremely tight and when my fingers couldn't go any farther, I suspected as much. But the next time when I touched you, I knew for sure."

She blinked. You asked Thorn a question and he would definitely give you a straight answer. She then felt a spark of anger that he'd known all this time and she had worried for nothing. But her anger was replaced by curiosity when she wondered why he wasn't upset. "But aren't you mad?"

He quirked a brow. "No, I'm not mad, Tara...I'm horny," he said with a sly chuckle.

"Yes, but I thought most men preferred experienced women in their beds."

He let out a frustrated sigh. "I want *you* in my bed, Tara, experienced or not. And as far as you being a virgin, I guess there's a good reason you waited this long, and I guess there's a good reason why it was meant for me to do the honor."

She looked up at him. "And you're sure about this? Are you sure this is what you want?"

He breathed in deeply. "Baby, this is what I want," he said, before exhibiting another quick move by placing his hand beneath her dress and gently clutching her feminine mound through the silky material of her panties. "This is what I need."

He leaned down and their lips touched and Tara knew at that very moment that she loved him more than she thought was humanly possible.

"I promise to be gentle the first time," he whispered against her moist lips. "And I promise to be gentle the second time. But all the times after that, I plan to ride you hard."

"Oh," she said in a soft and tremulous voice, moments before being swept effortlessly up into his arms.

Thorn placed Tara on the bed and his gaze swept down the full length of her half-clad body. She was still wearing her sundress, but barely. The straps were off her arms and the dress was bunched up to her waist showing her panties and her hips and thighs.

He began removing his shirt. When that was done, he met her gaze again and simply said, "I want you."

She swallowed and decided to be honest with him. "And I want you, too."

He smiled, seemingly pleased with what she had said and slowly unbuckled his belt. She blinked. She hadn't expected him to be this bold, to take off his clothes in front of her, but should not have been surprised. He was Thorn Westmoreland, a man who took risks, a man who lived on the edge, the man she loved.

Tara continued watching as he removed his boots then eased his jeans down his hips. She was enjoying this striptease show he had started. When he kicked his jeans aside and stood before her in a pair of black low-rise briefs that were contoured for a snug fit and supported his over-aroused erection, she almost lost her breath.

He was perfect in every way.

His body exemplified everything she had come to expect of him: power, endurance and strength. Lifting slowly, she eased toward the end of the bed where he was standing, wanting to touch his firm stomach. She knew his scent was masculine and robust, but she needed to know the texture of his skin under her fingers and her mouth.

Making a move before she lost her nerve, she felt her own cheeks become heated as she reached out and touched his belly, marveling at how his skin felt, solid and hard. She heard his sharp intake of breath and glanced up and met his gaze.

Potent desire pooled in his eyes and she felt her body become completely hot. Wanting to taste the texture of his skin she leaned forward and with the tip of her tongue traced a path around his navel.

"Oh, man," he uttered, tangling his hand in her hair as she continued laving her tongue across his stomach.

She knew what she was doing was torture, but he hadn't seen anything yet. She might be new at this, but those romance novels Delaney had given her to read had educated as well as entertained her. And tonight she felt bold enough to go for it, to show Thorn just what he meant to her.

Thorn was losing control and he knew had to slow down. When he felt Tara's tongue inch lower and she scooted her hand inside his briefs and touched him, he knew he had to take control.

Aroused beyond belief, he pulled her up to him and claimed her mouth, kissing her with the urgency of a starving man as their mouths mated intensely, on the edge of total madness. It was the taste of forbidden fruit, the sweetest temptation and the ultimate fulfillment.

He pulled back from the kiss, his gaze full of desire. He was driven with the need to remove her clothes and gently tumbled her back on the bed while pulling the dress from her body, and carelessly tossing it aside. Next he reached for the waistband of her panties, nearly ripping them from her in the process.

Before she could react to what he'd done, he quickly maneuvered his body on the bed with her and, like a starving man, grabbed her hips and pulled her to his mouth as if the need to taste her was paramount to the preservation of his sanity.

"Thorn!"

He wanted to make this time different from the times before and went about tasting her with an intensity that made her buck under the demand of his mouth, crying out and thrashing about as he absorbed himself in her womanly flavor. And when he felt her body come apart in a climax that sent shudders even through him, he intensified the intimate kiss and sampled each and every shiver that rocked her body.

Moments later, still dazed as fragments of ecstasy raced through her, Tara watched as Thorn stood and removed his briefs. Her breath caught upon seeing his naked body. She blinked, wondering how they would fit together and said a silent prayer that they would.

He reached down and picked up his jeans, then fumbled in the back pocket to retrieve his wallet. He withdrew a condom packet. He was about to tear it open when she stopped him.

"That's not necessary, Thorn."

He glanced up and met her gaze. "It isn't?"

She shook her head. "No."

He stared at her for a long moment before asking. "Why not?"

A long silence stretched between them before she finally gave him an answer. "I'm on birth control. The pill."

He lifted a brow. "But I thought you said that you couldn't take the pill for medical reasons."

Tara shook her head. "No, I asked you what would you do if I couldn't take the pill for medical reasons. I had to know that you cared enough to do the responsible thing."

He nodded. "Is the pill in your system real good?"

She certainly hoped so, otherwise there was a good chance that with all their heat, combustion and raging hormones they would be making a baby tonight. But the thought of him getting her pregnant didn't bother her one bit. "Yes, I've been on it long enough."

Thorn stared at her, thinking just how much he loved her. Because he had expressed a desire not to use a condom, she had unselfishly taken the necessary precautions.

He would show his love and appreciation in the only way he knew—by loving her totally and completely with his heart, body and soul. He eased onto the bed with her, over her, knowing he had to take things slow and be gentle, no matter how driven he was to do otherwise. His need for her was strong, desperate.

He touched the dampness at the juncture of her legs. She was sufficiently wet for him, primed, ripe and ready. But even so, their first joining would be painful for her. There was no way for it not to be.

When he had placed his body over hers, he gazed down at her, saw desire and trust shining in the depths of her eyes and knew he would keep his word, even if it killed him. A part of him wanted her to know just how affected he was with what they were about to do.

"I think I've wanted you, I've wanted *this,* from the first time I saw you that night, Tara," he admitted honestly. "I've dreamed about this moment, fantasized about it and desired it with a vengeance, and I want you to know I won't take what you're about to give me and what we're about to do lightly."

And since he knew that being on the pill wasn't a hundred-percent full proof, he said, "And although you're on the pill, if you get pregnant anyway, I take full responsibility for any child we make together."

Before Tara could say anything, Thorn began placing kisses all over her mouth, and her heart pounded, full of love. Ever since they had started seeing each other, he had made her feel feminine and desired and she was ready for any sensual journey he wanted to take her on.

And then she felt him, the tip of him, touching her womanly folds, and their gazes locked. He bore down slowly as he began easing into her gently, and although it was tight, she felt her body automatically stretch for him, open to receive him.

Sweat beaded Thorn's forehead. Tara was tight and

damp. Entering her body sent a ripple of pleasure through him, from the tip of his toes to the top of his head. He held her hips firmly in his hands as he went deeper, feeling the muscles of her body clamp down on him as he slowly eased inside her and felt her opening her legs wider to smooth the progress of his entry.

He saw that quick moment of pain that flashed across her features when he broke through the barrier overwhelmed by what was taking place. He was her first lover, the first man to venture into her body like this and a part of him was deeply touched by the magnitude of what that meant.

He had never been the first with a woman before, and in the past that fact hadn't mattered. But with Tara it did matter. She didn't know it yet, but she was the woman he planned to marry. The woman who would have his children. The woman who would always be there for him. The woman he planned to grow old with and love until the last breath was exhaled from his body.

Moments later he was deeply embedded inside her as far as it was humanly possible for him to go. It was tight, a snug fit, and the thought that he was joined to her this way sent a shudder racing up his spine. For a long moment he didn't move; he just wanted to savor their joining. Their union. Neither of them spoke, but each recognized this as a very profound and meaningful moment.

"You okay?" he whispered just seconds before dipping his head and kissing her gently on the lips.

She nodded. "Yeah, what about you?"

He smiled. "I'm fine. I wish I could stay locked to you, stay inside you, forever." He removed his hands from her hips, clasped their hands together and whispered. "Now, I take things slow."

And he did.

With slow, gentle precision, he began withdrawing then reentering her body, over and over again, thrusting gently, firmly, deeply, establishing a rhythm that she immediately followed.

Tara closed her eyes, savoring their lovemaking, wanting Thorn never to stop what he was doing to her, how he was making her feel. Every time he reentered her, the sensations were heightened and shivers of pleasure raced all through her.

Overwhelmed, feeling herself losing control, she reached up and brought his mouth to hers when she felt him increase their rhythm in a beat so timeless it intensified the passion between them. Explosive, flashing heat surrounded them, making her dig her fingertips into his shoulders and whisper his name over and over, revelling in the feel of flesh against flesh.

And then Tara felt herself go. Her body shook beneath the force of his firm hips locking her body to his as sensations poured through her.

"Look at me, baby."

She opened her eyes and did as Thorn requested. She met his gaze when she felt her body come apart and watched as his own body stiffened while waves of pleasure washed through him. He increased the pace of their rhythm and whispered, "mine," at the exact moment he threw his head back and spilled inside her, his release flooding her insides.

"Thorn!"

Her body responded yet again as another climax tore into her, this one more volatile, eruptive and explosive than all others, triggering him into another orgasm as well. He tightened his hold on her as his body devoured her, mated with hers, and loved her.

In Tara's mind and heart this was more than sex. It was the most beautiful and profound joining, and she knew in her heart that for the rest of her life she would love Thorn Westmoreland.

Eleven

His woman was asleep.

After they had made love twice, he had cuddled her into his arms and watched as her eyes had drifted closed. And he had been watching her since.

She was lying facing him, her front to his, her face just a breath away from his. She was a silent sleeper, barely making a sound as she inhaled and exhaled.

Damn, she looked and smelled good.

His arousal stirred and the need to have her again sent tremors through his body. This would be the third time, but he couldn't ride her hard the way he had planned. She was sore, and he knew that only a selfish person would put her through a vigorous round of lovemaking after what they'd just shared.

He would go slow and gentle. Reaching out, he slid his hand up and down her body, his caresses lingering on her breasts, the curves of her waist before moving lower to her belly. He pushed aside the sheet that covered her, and, moving his hand even lower, he gently touched her feminine folds, inhaling the sensuous scent, a combination of sex and Tara.

His heartbeat raced, knowing that this part of her, whether she realized it or not, was now his, lock, stock and barrel. He had taken ownership of it. Her body was her body and her body was also *his*. No other man would have the opportunity to sample the treasures that she had entrusted to him.

Feeling the need to join with her once again, he leaned forward and kissed her awake. She slowly opened her eyes and a sultry, tempting smile touched the corners of her lips.

"You want more?" she asked sleepily, coming fully awake.

He smiled. "What gave you that idea?"

She glanced down and saw his aroused body. "That."

A chuckle escaped his lips. "Yeah, *that* is certainly a giveaway." He then reached out and placed her on top, straddling him. From the expression on her face, he knew she was surprised by the move. "This way you control everything," he whispered, explaining.

The hard length of him was standing at attention, which made it easy for her body to move over it and sink down upon it, taking him within her. It felt hot as it penetrated the depths of her.

She smiled. Thorn had been right. This position gave her more sexual freedom and definitely provided him with visual pleasure. Her breasts were right there in front of his eyes…as well as his mouth, and he quickly took full advantage.

He sucked and licked her nipples to his heart's content while she slowly moved back and forth, up and down over him, establishing the rhythm and speed of his thrusting. She looked down and watched him devour her breasts, the sight making her go faster and deeper, stimulating her mind as well as her body in a way she hadn't thought was possible.

And then it happened again, she became absorbed with pleasure so deep and profound she couldn't help but cry out as she increased their rhythm. Her climax triggered his and he moved his lips from her breasts to her mouth, as waves of pleasure drowned them, leaving them swirling in a sensuous aftermath.

"Are you sure you want to go to the victory party?"

Tara glanced up from putting the finishing touches on her makeup. "Of course I want to go. This is a big moment for you and I'm glad to be able to share in it. Besides, how would it look if the honoree didn't make an appearance?"

Thorn chuckled as he buttoned up his shirt. "I'm sure my brothers would come up with an excuse."

Tara exhaled deeply. That's what she was worried about since she was certain his brothers were well aware of what they'd been doing closed up in a hotel room for the past four hours. Still she didn't want anyone to think of their intimate activities as something meaningless and degrading.

Thorn had assured her that he hadn't told them about the deal they'd made and she was grateful for that. It would be bad enough seeing them tonight knowing they knew, or had a pretty good idea of, just what she and Thorn had been doing.

She was sure that most of the time the winner of such a publicized event didn't disappear behind closed doors right after a race. He would usually start partying, which could go well into the next day. Since it was Sunday, a lot of people would pack up to leave after the race, but most stayed over to Monday or well into the following week.

"Ready?"

She glanced over at Thorn. He was completely dressed, and the look he gave her let her know he liked her outfit but preferred her naked in bed with him. She smiled. Leaving the confines of the hotel room was a good idea. Chances were they would be going another couple of rounds tonight.

"I must say, Thorn, you're in a real good mood, tonight," Stone said grinning.

Thorn raised a brow as he glanced at his brothers, Stone, Chase and Storm. The four of them had left the party and stood outside smoking congratulatory cigars, compliments of one of his racing sponsors.

"Yeah, Thorn, it seems that four hours shut up behind closed doors with Tara did wonders for your disposition and mood," Chase added, grinning between puffs of his cigar.

"And I appreciate you helping me to win that bet, Thorn. I told these guys that although Tara was your challenge, you could overcome that little obstacle and would have her eating out of your hands and in your bed in no time," Storm added. "Yeah, victory today was rather nice for you in more ways than one, wasn't it Thorn?"

Tara had decided to come outside and round up the brothers to tell them their parents were on Dare's mobile phone and wanted to congratulate Thorn. She had stopped right before interrupting them, shocked at what she had overheard. There had been a bet between Thorn and his brothers that he would be able to get her in his bed? Today had meant nothing to him but winning a bet?

Backing up so they wouldn't see her, she felt tears of humiliation stinging her eyes. She felt just as humiliated now as she had three years ago when Derrick had embarrassed her in front of a church filled with people. And it hurt worse than before because of the magnitude of love she felt for Thorn. Her love for Derrick had been a young girl's love that had grown from an extended friendship between two families. But her love for Thorn was that of a woman, a woman who, it now seemed, had made a mistake, a big mistake for the second time in her life.

She quickly turned around and ran smack into Dare. He caught her by the arm to stop her from falling. He frowned when he saw the tears that filled her eyes. "Tara, what's wrong? Are you okay?"

She swiped away the tears that she couldn't stop. "No, I'm not okay, Dare, and I don't appreciate your brothers making a bet on me that way. And you can tell Thorn that I hope never to see him again." Without saying anything else she pulled away and went back inside.

After Storm's statement, Thorn's temper exploded and he looked at his brothers for the longest time without saying anything, fighting down the urge to walk across the space of the veranda that separated them and knock the hell out of each one of them.

"I think I need to set the record straight about something. My relationship with Tara had nothing to do with the bet the three of you made," he said through gritted teeth, trying to hold his anger in check and remember the four of them shared the same parents.

"She means more to me than a chance to score after two years." He sighed, not giving a royal damn what he was about to admit to his brothers. The way he felt, he would gladly shout it out to the world if he had to. "I love Tara. I love her with everything that's inside of me, and it's about time the three of you knew that."

Stone's shoulder was propped against the building and he wore a huge grin. "Oh, we know you love her, Thorn.

We've known it for a while. Getting you to realize that you loved her was the kicker. The only reason we said what we did a few minutes ago was to get you pissed off enough to admit what Tara means to you.''

''And it might be too late,'' Dare said, walking up to join the group. He wore an angry expression as he faced his brothers. ''Your little playacting may have cost Thorn Tara's love.''

Thorn frowned. ''What the hell are you talking about?''

Dare shook his head, knowing all hell was about to break lose and that somehow he would have to find a way to contain Thorn's fury. ''Mom and Dad called and Tara volunteered to come get you guys. Evidently she overheard the first part of the conversation. When I saw her she was crying so hard she couldn't see straight and bumped right into me when I came to find out what was taking all of you so long.''

Dare shook his head sadly. ''She gave me a message to give you. She told me to tell you that she doesn't want to see you again.''

Hearing enough, Thorn spun around, and, without giving his brothers another glance, he quickly went back into the building in search of Tara.

''She left, Thorn,'' Shelly Westmoreland said, frowning at her brother-in-law. ''She was crying and came back inside just long enough to get her purse. She left through that side door. Exactly what did you do to her?''

Thorn couldn't wait to give Shelly an answer. More than likely Tara had returned to the hotel and he planned to be right on her heels. He had a lot of explaining to do and he also intended to tell her just what she meant to him.

When Thorn got to the hotel he saw that Tara had not been there, and he started to worry. One of the members

of his work crew indicated he had given Tara a lift from
the victory party back to the hotel to get her rental car.
When hours passed and she still hadn't come, his worry
increased. Even when his brothers showed up to apologize
and discovered Tara hadn't returned, he could tell that it
made them feel worse, which, as far as he was concerned,
served them right.

He had finally gotten them to leave after Dare had placed
a call to the sheriff in Daytona, whom he knew personally.
After checking things out, the sheriff had informed them
that a vehicle fitting the description of the rental car that
Tara was driving had been spotted on the interstate heading
toward Bunnell.

Thorn paced the confines of the hotel room. He was angry with his brothers but angrier with himself. He should
have spilled his heart and soul to her when he'd had the
chance. Now she would assume that what she had overheard was true and would believe that he was another man
who had humiliated her.

He knew he had to let her know how much he loved her
and just how much she meant to him. Over the past two
years she had been many things to him: his challenge, his
sweetest temptation and his woman.

Now he had to convince her that he loved her and more
than anything he wanted her as his wife.

Twelve

Tara woke up early the next morning in her old bedroom. She glanced around. Her parents had pretty much kept things the same, and she was glad that when she'd left home two years ago she hadn't packed every stitch she owned, otherwise she would not have had a thing to wear. Luckily for her, her closets and dresser drawers were filled with both inner and outerwear that still fit her.

She knew her parents had been surprised to see her when she had unexpectedly shown up last night asking if she could stay for the next couple of days, just long enough to get a flight back to Atlanta. They hadn't asked her any questions but had welcomed her with open arms and told her she knew she could stay for as long as she liked. She had also contacted the rental car agency to let them know she intended to keep the vehicle a while longer.

She sighed deeply. Her parents had always been super and she appreciated them for everything they had ever done for her. Her brothers had returned to college and her baby sister had left that day for an out of town trip with the school's band for a week. In a way she was glad none of her siblings were there to see her go through heartbreak a second time.

Flipping onto her back she knew she had decisions to make. Maybe it was time for her to leave the Atlanta area. A friend of hers from med school was trying to get her to think about coming to Boston to work. Maybe relocating to Massachusetts was exactly the change she needed.

"I see that young man of yours won the big race yesterday in Daytona, Tara Lynn. It was in the newspapers this morning and the whole town has been talking about it. You must be proud of him."

Tara smiled over the dinner table at her father. As usual, he had closed his office at noon on Monday and had come home for an early dinner. As long as she could remember, her parents had been members of a bowling league and usually headed for the bowling lanes every Monday afternoon.

"Yes, I'm proud of him," she said stiffly. She knew her parents had figured out that Thorn had somehow played a part in her unexpected appearance on their doorstep last night. She sighed, deciding to tell them an abbreviated version of things, just enough for them to know her relationship with Thorn was over.

She was about to open her mouth to speak when the phone rang. Her father got up quickly to answer it in case it was a parent needing his help with a sick child. He still did house calls occasionally.

"Yes, sheriff, I'm fine, what about you?" Tara heard her father say. She frowned, wondering why the sheriff was calling her father. She then remembered the sheriff and his wife were part of her parents' bowling team. He was probably calling regarding that.

She noticed her father's gaze had moved to her and she raised a brow when moments later she heard him say, ''All right. I'll let her know.''

After he hung up the phone he rejoined her and her mother at the table. Her mother asked what the sheriff had wanted before Tara got the chance to do so. Frank Matthews leaned back in his chair with his gaze locked on his daughter while answering his wife's question. ''It seemed that Deke just issued a special permit.''

Her mother's brow rose. ''What sort of special permit?''

Before her father could respond, the sound of thunder suddenly filled the house. ''My God,'' Lynn Matthews said, getting up from the table. ''That sounds like thunder. I don't recall the weatherman saying anything about rain this evening.''

Frank Matthews shook his head. ''That's not thunder, Lynn,'' he said to his wife while keeping his gaze fixed on his daughter. ''Deke issued a special permit for a bunch of bikers to parade peacefully through the streets of Bunnell.''

Lynn Matthews's features reflected surprise. ''Bikers? What on earth for? Bunnell is such a small peaceful town; I can't imagine such a thing happening.''

A smile touched the corners of Frank Matthews's lips when he answered. ''It appears one of the bikers, the one leading the pack, who also happens to be the winner of yesterday's championship motorcycle race in Daytona, is headed for our house. It seems he's coming for our daughter.''

Tara blinked, not sure she had heard her father correctly. ''Thorn? He's coming here?''

Her father nodded. ''Yes. It seems he and his band of

followers are making their way round the corner as we speak.''

Tara frowned, wondering why Thorn and the other cyclists would be coming here and why her father thought he was coming for her. Before she could voice that question, the roar of cycles nearly shook the house.

She sighed deeply as she stood up from the table. The reason Thorn had come meant absolutely nothing to her. The bottom line was that she didn't want to see him. "Send him away, Daddy, please. I don't want to see him."

Frank gazed lovingly at his daughter. Her heart had been broken once and he didn't want to see it broken again, but he felt the least Tara should do was to listen to what the young man had to say. He told her as much.

"But there's nothing he can say to change things. I love him but he doesn't love me. It's as simple as that."

Frank sighed. If that was what his daughter believed then it wasn't as simple as she thought. According to the sheriff, Thorn Westmoreland was wearing his heart on his sleeve. Frank knew he had to be firm and make Tara face the fact that she might be wrong in her assumption that Thorn didn't love her.

"All right, Tara, if that's how you feel, but this is something you should handle. If you want him to go away, then it's you who should send him away. Tell him that you don't want to see him anymore. I won't do it for you."

Tara met her father's eyes and nodded. That was fine with her. She would just march outside and tell Thorn what she thought and how she felt. Evidently Dare hadn't delivered her message. "Very well, I'll tell him."

Marching out of the kitchen Tara passed through the living room and snatched open the front door. Stepping outside she stopped dead in her tracks. Motorcycle riders were everywhere. There wasn't just a bunch of them, there were hundreds, and they were still coming around the corner, causing more excitement in Bunnell than she could ever remember.

It seemed the entire town had come out to witness what was going on. And what made matters worse, Thorn and his group had gotten a police escort straight to her parents' home. Blue lights were flashing everywhere. She had never seen anything like it.

But what really caught her attention was the man who sat out in front of the pack, straddling the big bike that had come to a stop in front of her parents' home. She glanced around. In addition to Thorn, his four brothers were on bikes and two of them carried a huge banner extending between their bikes that said Thorn Loves Tara.

Realizing what the banner was proclaiming made tears appear in Tara's eyes. In a public display, Thorn was letting everyone in the entire town of Bunnell—his friends, biking partners, associates, his family, just about anyone who wanted to know—what she meant to him. She had been more than a bet to him.

She watched as Thorn got off the bike and slowly began walking toward her. She inhaled deeply as she watched him, clad in jeans, a T-shirt and biker boots and holding his helmet in his hand, come to a stop in front of her.

He met her gaze and reached out and gently wiped a tear from her eye. "You should know my brothers well enough by now to know they're full of it and you can't take them seriously the majority of the time, Tara. I didn't make a bet with them, but they did make a bet among themselves. They wagered that I wouldn't realize how much I loved you until it was almost too late."

He glanced behind her, saw her parents standing in the doorway and decided to lower his voice to a whisper so they wouldn't hear the next words he had to say. This part was personal and between him and Tara.

"And it was more than just sex between us, Tara. I love you and should have told you yesterday, but the physical loving we shared blew me away, and I didn't get around to telling you how I felt emotionally. But I'm telling you now that I love you with all my heart and with all my soul."

The tone of his voice then went higher as he said, "And I want to proclaim my love to you in front of everyone here. And I want them to see that I'm wearing my heart on my sleeve."

He turned slightly and showed her the sleeve of his T-shirt. There was a big heart on it with the words Thorn Loves Tara. He got down on one knee and took her hand into his. "I, Thorn Westmoreland, love you, Tara Lynn Matthews. And in front of everyone, I am pledging my love to you and promising to love you for the rest of my life. I promise to love you, honor you and protect you. And I'm asking you now, Tara, on bended knee, with my heart on my sleeve, in front of everyone, to marry me and become my wife and soul mate. Will you?"

Tears clouded Tara's eyes and the words she longed to say got caught in the thickness of her throat, but somehow she managed to get them out, words that would ultimately join her life with Thorn's. "Yes, Thorn, I'll marry you."

It seemed people everywhere began clapping, shouting and cheering. In the middle of the pack of cyclists, someone released a bunch of helium balloons that went soaring high into the sky. Each one had on it the words Thorn Loves Tara. Tara was touched at the extent Thorn had gone to in broadcasting his love for her.

Thorn got back to his feet and it seemed that Dare materialized at his side with a small white box which he handed to Thorn. Thorn opened up the box and took out a sparkling diamond ring. He reached for Tara's left hand and placed the huge diamond on the third finger, then brought her hand to his lips.

"Thorn's lady and soon to be Thorn's wife," he said softly, his eyes still meeting hers as he kissed her hand. He then pulled her into his arms and kissed her lips, ignoring the cheers and applause.

Tara kissed him back, until she heard her father clear his throat several times. She and Thorn finally broke apart and she turned and smiled at her parents, then said, "Mom, Dad, this is Thorn, the man I love."

Two days later, in a hotel room in West Palm Beach, Tara lay in Thorn's arms. She could hear the sound of the ocean, the relaxing resonance of waves hitting against sand. She closed her eyes as she remembered the intensity of the lovemaking she and Thorn had shared earlier. He hadn't been slow and gentle. This time he had been tender, yet he had taken her with a force that had overwhelmed her, pleasuring them both, riding her with the precision and expertise that was strictly his trademark, and thrusting deep then pulling out, repeating the process over and over again until he had her thrashing about as sensation after sensation tore into her.

He had whispered into her ear words of love, words of sex, promises to be delivered both in and out of the bedroom, and when they had reached a climax simultaneously, she knew that, physically as well as emotionally, she was a part of him and would always be a part of him.

"Tara?"

She glanced up. He was awake and was watching her. "Yes?"

"I love you."

She smiled. He had told her that over a million times since bringing her back here from her parents' home. "And I love you."

They had decided to marry over the Memorial Day weekend. Thorn had been open with displaying his affections for her in front of everyone, and it seemed the entire town had been there.

Her parents' bowling game had been cancelled, and some of the neighbors had set up grills and a huge barbecue followed, with all the steaks and spareribs a person could eat donated by Grahams' Supermarket in honor of their hometown girl marrying a celebrity.

Tara had been standing talking to Thorn when she'd turned and seen Danielle walking toward her. At that moment any bitterness she had felt for the woman who'd once been her best friend left her. She knew there was no way things could ever be the same between them, but Tara no longer felt the deep anger just thinking about what Danielle and Derrick had done.

She introduced Danielle to Thorn and told her the same thing she had told Derrick a few days earlier. She congratulated them on their upcoming child, wished them the best and told her that she hoped they would always be happy together.

Not wanting to think about Danielle and Derrick any longer, she brought her thoughts back to the present and thought of something else. "Thorn?"

"Yes, sweetheart?"

"I heard Chase say that you have another race in August. Do you plan to go celibate after our wedding until the race?"

Thorn met her gaze. "No, my celibate days are over. There's no way I can have you around me constantly and not want to make love to you."

"Aren't you worried about the impact that may have on winning the race?"

"No. I always thought racing and building my bikes were the most important things in my life and at a time they were. But now things are different. You are the most important thing in my life, Tara. You are my life. It doesn't matter to me if I never win another race because I have the ultimate prize, my greatest award, accolade and treasure right here in you."

"Oh, Thorn." She leaned up and her mouth met his. She kissed him like a woman in love as emotions swirled through her. She and Thorn would spend the rest of their lives together and would make many beautiful babies together.

Babies? They hadn't discussed babies. She pulled back, breaking off the kiss.

He lifted a brow. "What's wrong?"

"Do you want babies?" she asked, looking at him intently.

He smiled. "Yes, I want babies."

She returned his smile. "Good. How many?"

He chuckled. "As many as you want to give me." And deciding to go ahead and answer the next question he figured she'd be asking, he said, "And it doesn't matter if they are girls or boys. I will love and cherish any child we have together."

He leaned forward and brushed his lips across hers, then, deepening the kiss, became intent on giving her the greatest pleasure he could. His hands stroked her everywhere and he conveyed the heat of his hunger to her, needing to find solace in the warmth of her body again, knowing in his heart that he would always want her, need her and love her.

He broke off the kiss to climb onto her body, he straddled her and then he entered her warmth, going deep, slow and easy, feeling the muscles of her inner body clutch him, hold him and welcome him. When he looked down at her, he saw love shining in her eyes. Love that he returned.

Then, in one quick movement he began riding her, thrusting inside her, nearly pulling out and going back in again, holding her gaze as he did so, lifting her hips to receive him in this very soul-stirring way. He wanted her panting, groaning and screaming. He wanted to kiss her again until her mouth quaked, her body trembled, and every part of her brimmed over with passion—rich and explosive. He wanted to imprint this night in her mind forever.

This lovemaking was more vigorous than any before and together they moved in unison as he lowered his head, seeking her mouth and going after her tongue. And like everything else he wanted, she gave it to him. He openly displayed his hunger for her—his hunger and his love.

And then it happened. Rampant desire raced through him, caught fire and spread like a blaze to her. He continued pumping, thrusting as their bodies strained and flowed with a pounding rhythm toward a release that lingered a breath away. He felt her dig her fingers into his shoulders and broke off the kiss, threw his head back and sucked in a breath he felt could be his last at the exact moment her body clenched him for everything he had.

This time their joining felt like a spiritual connection, the climax that tore into them stronger, deeper and richer than any before. Before either could recover, she climaxed again and he immediately followed her lead, moving faster, riding her the way he had always wanted to, the way he had always dreamed of, straight through the waves and soaring for the stars.

"Thorn!"

He found strength to look down into her face.

His woman.

He met her gaze and he knew. Their life together would always be filled with love and passion, and he couldn't think of having it any other way.

Epilogue

Tara no longer hated weddings.

She inhaled deeply as she looked around the church. Memories assailed her as she remembered the last time she had worn a wedding dress here, and now today, in front of some of those same three hundred guests, she had married the man she loved, Thorn Westmoreland.

She, Thorn and the wedding party had hung back to take a multitude of pictures. Everyone else had left for the reception, which was to be held in the ballroom of a beautiful hotel on the beach.

Thorn had left her briefly to go in the back to talk to the minister about something, and she happened to notice the Westmoreland brothers as well as the Westmoreland cousins, who'd all been part of the wedding party, standing around talking. As she watched, she saw three of the Westmoreland brothers, Chase, Stone and Storm, exchange money.

She raised a brow wondering if they had made another wager about something. She smiled upon remembering how Stone, Chase and Storm had confessed to her the whole story, then had apologized for causing a rift between her and Thorn.

Adjusting her veil she decided to find out just what kind of a bet the brothers had made and whether the bet had once again involved her and Thorn.

Chase had just explained the bet that he, Stone and Storm had made to his cousins: Jared, Quade, Spencer, Ian, Durango and Reggie Westmoreland. He was grinning broadly, since he had won. "Hey, five hundred dollars isn't bad for a day's work. I told all of you that Thorn wouldn't be able to hold off on marrying Tara until June."

He looked at the money he'd just gotten from Stone and Storm. "And I appreciate you guys letting me take this off your hands. It will come in handy for that state-of-the-art pressure cooker I want to buy for the restaurant."

The next thing he knew, the money was snatched out of his hand. "What the hell!"

He spun around and came face to face with his new sister-in-law's glare. He backed up a step. "Oh, hi, Tara," he said innocently. "I thought you and Thorn were somewhere in the back talking to the minister."

Tara continued to glare and crossed her arms over her chest. "Thorn is the one who's talking to the minister. And am I right in assuming the three of you made yet another bet?"

Stone, Chase and Storm looked chagrined, but Stone came to their defense and said, "Yeah, but this bet was made before we promised we wouldn't be betting on you and Thorn again, so it doesn't count."

She nodded. "Well, this is a church and you shouldn't

be passing betting money around in here so I can only do one thing about it.''

Chase raised a panicky brow. "What?"

"Donate it to the church. My father is the Sunday school superintendent here and I'm sure this donation will be appreciated.'' She then smiled sweetly before walking off.

"Tara?"

She turned around and met Chase's brooding eyes. "Yes, Chase?"

He crossed his arms over his chest. "Only you can get away with doing something like that."

She smiled and nodded. "I know." She turned back around and began walking.

"Tara?"

She turned around again and met Storm's worried gaze. "Yes, Storm?"

"You aren't going to tell Thorn about the bet are you?"

Tara smiled. "No, Storm, I won't say a thing."

She turned back around and started to walk away.

"Tara?"

She slowly turned around for the third time, meeting Stone's amused expression. "Yes, Stone?"

His smile widened. "Welcome to the family."

Tara chuckled. The Westmoreland men were something else.

"Thanks, Stone."

She then turned around and ran smack into Corey Westmoreland, Thorn's uncle. A recently retired park ranger from Montana, he had made the trip back home three times in less than two years to attend his niece and his nephews' weddings.

Tara smiled. According to the Westmoreland brothers, their fifty-three-year-old uncle was a confirmed bachelor. That was too bad, Tara thought since he was such a good-looking man. What a waste. A part of her hoped there was a woman out there somewhere for Uncle Corey.

"My nephews aren't causing problems are they?" he asked, chuckling. Then he glanced across the room, sending his eleven nephews a scolding glare.

"Nothing I can't handle, but thanks for asking," she grinned, thinking what a nice smile he had and how much his smile reminded her of Thorn's.

"Good, and if I haven't told you already, I think you're just the woman Thorn needs. I know the two of you will always be happy together. If you ever want to get away and see some beautiful country, tell Thorn to bring you to my ranch in Montana for a visit."

"Thanks for the invitation. I'll make sure to do that."

At that moment Thorn and the minister came from the back. She immediately caught her husband's gaze and smiled. "Excuse me, Uncle Corey," she said, and began walking toward Thorn. When she reached him, he pulled her into his arms.

"Ready?" he asked, placing a kiss on her lips.

Tara knew that all the love she had for him was shining in her eyes. "Yes, I'm ready."

She would always be ready for him and made a silent promise to show him later tonight just how ready she was.

*   *   *   *   *

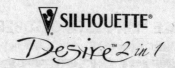

SILHOUETTE®

Desire™ 2 in 1

AVAILABLE FROM 15TH OCTOBER 2004

WITH PRIVATE EYES Eileen Wilks

Dynasties: The Barones

Rough-around-the-edges private eye Ethan Mallory couldn't tell society deb Claudia Barone that his prime suspect was her brother. Neither would Ethan hide his attraction to her—it was red-hot, and out of control.

PASSIONATELY EVER AFTER Metsy Hingle

Dynasties: The Barones

Steven Conti tracked his runaway lover down in the snow-covered Montana mountains. And instantly he saw the reason for her flight; Maria Barone was pregnant with his child!

IN BED WITH THE ENEMY Kathie DeNosky

The Country Club

When federal agents Cole Yardley and Elise Campbell were assigned to a gun-smuggling investigation, they broke all the rules and shared a night of passion. One night became many, but would solving the case end their relationship?

CHEROKEE BABY Sheri WhiteFeather

One look, one dance, one night of unforgettable passion with a sexy stranger. Julianne McKenzie hadn't been able to resist. And now she carried his baby! He gave them a home, but would he ever give them his name and his heart?

FULL THROTTLE Merline Lovelace

To Protect and Defend

Once burned by her love-'em-and-leave-'em ex, hurricane hunter Kate Hargrave was feeling cautious when she met hot-shot test pilot Dave Scott. So how was Dave going to convince her he was a one-woman man?

RULING PASSIONS Laura Wright

For once Crown Prince Alexander Thorne's honourable intentions were overruled by chemistry when he rescued a red-haired siren from the sea. Could her love transform the duty-bound prince into a man ruled by his passion?

So This Is Christmas

Sherryl Woods
Beverly Barton
Leanne Banks

Available from 15th October 2004

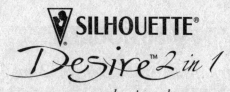

SILHOUETTE®
Desire™ 2 in 1

are proud to introduce

DYNASTIES:
THE BARONES

Meet the wealthy Barones—caught in a web of danger, deceit and…desire!

Twelve exciting stories in six 2-in-1 volumes:

0104/SH/LC78

SILHOUETTE®

Sensation™ and Desire™ 2-in-1
are proud to present the brand-new series by
bestselling author

MERLINE LOVELACE

TO PROTECT AND DEFEND

These heroes and heroines were trained
to put their lives on the line, but their
hearts were another matter…

A Question of Intent
Silhouette Sensation
September 2004

Full Throttle
Silhouette Desire 2-in-1
November 2004

The Right Stuff
Silhouette Sensation
December 2004

0904/SH/LC93

SILHOUETTE®
Desire 2 *in* 1

is proud to introduce

DYNASTIES:
THE DANFORTHS

Meet the Danforths—a family of prominence...
tested by scandal, sustained by passion!

Coming Soon!
Twelve thrilling stories in six 2-in-1 volumes:

MAGGIE SHAYNE

TWILIGHT HUNGER

His touch promises ecstasy. His kiss
offers immortality...

Published 17th September 2004

Jayne Ann Krentz

"one of the hottest writers in romance today" USA TODAY

Twist of Fate

Published 17th September 2004

When she was good,
she was very, very good.
And when she was bad, she was...

NAUGHTY MARIETTA

NAN RYAN

Published 17th September 2004

SILHOUETTE SPOTLIGHT

Two bestselling novels in one volume
by favourite authors, back by
popular demand!

A Passionate Pursuit

The Girl Next Door by Trisha Alexanda
Hesitant Husband by Jackie Merritt

Wilful, beautiful and marriage-
minded—these sexy sirens are
determined to capture the
men of their dreams…

Available from 15th October 2004

2 FREE

BOOKS AND A SURPRISE GIFT!

We would like to take this opportunity to thank you for reading this Silhouette® book by offering you the chance to take YWO more specially selected titles from the Desire™ series absolutely FREE! We're also making this offer to introduce you to the benefits of the Reader Service™—

- ★ FREE home delivery
- ★ FREE gifts and competitions
- ★ FREE monthly Newsletter
- ★ Exclusive Reader Service offers
- ★ Books available before they're in the shops

Accepting these FREE books and gift places you under no obligation to buy, you may cancel at any time, even after receiving your free shipment. Simply complete your details below and return the entire page to the address below. You don't even need a stamp!

YES! Please send me 2 free Desire books and a surprise gift. I understand that unless you hear from me, I will receive 3 superb new titles every month for just £4.99 each, postage and packing free. I am under no obligation to purchase any books and may cancel my subscription at any time. The free books and gift will be mine to keep in any case.

D4ZED

Ms/Mrs/Miss/Mr ....Initials ....

Surname .... BLOCK CAPITALS PLEASE

Address ....

....

....Postcode....................................

Send this whole page to:
UK: FREEPOST CN81, Croydon, CR9 3WZ